RISE GOLDEN
APOLLO

THE OLD WORLD SAGA BOOK TWO

RISE GOLDEN APOLLO

First edition published April 2021.
Second edition published March 2022.
Third edition published May 2023.
(This is a third edition novel)

Book cover art by warrendesign
Manuscript design by Joel Preston

ISBN 978-0-6457791-1-0 (Paperback)
ISBN 978-0-6457791-2-7 (Hardcover)
ISBN 978-0-6489690-9-9 (eBook)

To contact the author email: contact@joelprestonauthor.com
joelprestonauthor.com

RISE GOLDEN APOLLO

THE OLD WORLD SAGA BOOK TWO

JOEL PRESTON

Other Novels by This Author:

In the Shadow of Monstrous Things

In the Shadow of The Old World

Fall Silver Artemis

Novellas by This Author:

The Wendigo Incident: An Old World Saga Novelette

Earth's Mightiest Warrior: An Old World Saga Novella

Strange Lights in a Dark World: An Old World Saga Novella

This novel is dedicated to the memory of my friend Brad Hardy.
May we all aim to be the person he was.

FOREWORD

I met Joel back in 2018 when he arrived in my home town to begin a new chapter in his life. During the first year of our acquaintance with one another, I had begun writing scripts for a project I was interested in starting. I had the ambitious idea of producing a podcast that covered the entire history of Ancient Greece. Over the next 12 months, Joel and I would often converse on the topics I was writing about, as well as the processes of writing - technically and psychologically. In the end I started my show, Casting Through Ancient Greece, taking one step at a time allowing the power of consistency, care and compounding effort work its magic.

Joel had begun talking about his desire to write a book, which had always been a goal of his. We spoke in-depth about Greek history and especially Greek mythology, topics he found fascinating and where he would draw quite a bit of inspiration from. Eventually Joel would tell me, "I had shown him the way", and he was going to finally commit to writing his first book, where he would stop thinking about doing it and would just do the work. Joel would also begin applying the power of consistency, care and compounding effort. In 2020, Joel would release his first novel, In the Shadow of Monstrous Things.

Though, this was not the end. Joel spoke at length with me about the grander picture of his series and the lore that he wanted to build around it. The idea was to tie in other novels that would all have a connection to the same world. The next step was this book, "Rise Golden Apollo". The story and what he imagined would be even more ambitious than before, where not only would he call upon the entire pantheon of Greek gods, but the beings from Christian tradition.

Joel has now released the updated version of Golden Apollo to which he asked if I could provide him a few words on his journey and the book itself. I have gladly taken up this request, as I think we have both been on a similar journey over the past few years, although on somewhat different paths. I think we have a common appreciation for the commitment and effort we have both poured into our passions, and I feel extremely proud of how far Joel has come and what he has achieved in his writing. I think after reading, "Rise Golden Apollo" you to will see the imagination and devotion he has committed to these pages in presenting an exciting and fanciful journey.

MARK SELLECK

CASTING THROUGH ANCIENT GREECE

CONCERNING THE DISAPPEARANCE OF ZEUS

The following is a translation of a scroll unearthed in remarkably well-preserved condition. The below transcription has been provided in English by Dr Malcolm Selleck of the Australian National University. Dr M.S suggests, based on the letter's contents, that it was addressed to Emperor Trajan. It has been dated to approximately the year 105 AD.

- BEGIN TRANSCRIPT -

I write these words hoping they will reach you in time, as I know the Imperial fleet will be departing from Brundusium any day now. I bid you best fortune in the expedition against Dacia.

As we discussed prior to my departure, I have visited the famed Oracle of Delphi and listened to the words spoken by the anointed of Apollo. I lingered in the room and absorbed the vapours in the air. It is enough to make anyone light headed, yet not so dizzying as to make the jumbled words of the oracle more meaningful.

After an afternoon of listening to abstract ramblings, the oracle moved into a trance of worrying significance. Her eyes flashed gold and her voice became deep and monotonous. She spoke with concern of things to come, things I must now tell you while they are fresh in my mind!

The oracle spoke not of the Emperor of Rome, but of God-King Jupiter himself. He said mighty Jupiter, storm-bringer, is not long for this world! She warned that forces beyond even him are stirring in the darkness of the eternal night.

I will repeat her prophetic words here and now to the best of my memory. Please note, she used the common local vernacular 'Zeus' for Jupiter.

"Lo comes the fall of Cloud-Gatherer Zeus, who journeys forth into the abyss where even the primordial mothers and fathers dare not step. His punishment will be swift, for elder things and great old ones do not heed the authority of men or gods. In the dark, the crawling chaos turns his eyes towards the Storm God's vacant throne; a plaything for his malevolent schemes. Turn away! Turn away now! Do not meet his gaze! Cry as his family forget! They will search, but neither long nor hard enough to see the truth! All the lands must pray that Zeus turn from this path, lest all the gods be set on the road to ruin... Though the God of Prophecy sees far, Apollo will not know until it is too late. Drums, eternal drums beat in the night and in their melody comes the footsteps of another. A broken and sundered king walks from war towards a terrible destiny. Turn away now! Turn away now and do not meet his gaze..."

I have never experienced a prophetic uttering quite like this. The oracle had no memory of her words when she left the trance. She spoke of a distant far off fate. I will journey to the nearest temple to an Olympian and pray - pray a god is listening and will heed this message. Though I am sure war fills your mind, do not let this prophecy be forgotten. I am sure it can be interpreted for its proper meaning back in Rome.

I will let you know what my journey to the temple reveals.

Your servant, Julius Celsus II.

- END TRANSCRIPT -

THE BATTLE FOR THE UNDERWORLD

A Visual Guide

AN ILLUSTRATED GUIDE TO THE SIGNIFICANT CHARACTERS
AND CREATURES WHO DWELL IN THE UNDERWORLD.

APOLLO
OLYMPIAN
Greek God of Healing,
Medicine, Archery, Music
and the Arts, Poetry, Flocks
and Herds, Knowledge,
Oracles, Light and former
God of the Sun. He is a son
of Zeus.

DEMETER
OLYMPIAN
Greek God of Agriculture
and Grain, Sacred Law, the
Harvest and the Cycle of
Life and Death.

CHARON
MINOR GOD
The ferryman who carries
the souls of the newly
deceased across the River
Styx.

CERBERUS
GUARD DOG OF HADES
Son of the monsters Typhon and Echidna,
Cerberus waits of the shores of the River Styx as
a guard against those who do not belong in the
Underworld. Always loyal to Hades, he prevents
the dead from leaving.

HADES

PERSEPHONE

Hades is the God of the Dead and the God of Riches. He is eldest among his brothers, Zeus and Poseidon and helped in the war against the titans, which led the gods to ruling the cosmos.

Persephone is the daughter of Demeter and Zeus. One day, while picking flowers, Hades abducted Persephone and brought her down into the Underworld to be his wife. Because she ate six pomegranate seeds (the only food that grows in the Underworld), she was cursed to spend six months of the year down there. At the request of the gods, Persephone was allowed to return to the mortal world the other six months of the year, resulting in the seasons. Together they rule the Underworld, maintaining balance in all things.

HECATONCHEIRES
MONSTERS

The three Hecatoncheires are named Briareus, Cottus and Gyges. They are giants with one hundred arms and fifty heads. They serve as the guards of the prison of the titans in Tartarus.

THE FURIES
MINOR GODS

The three Furies are named Allecto, Tisiphone and Megaera. They are the Goddesses of Vengeance and punish crimes against the natural order.

DEMON
MONSTER

Ancient beings that have lived in the Underworld since time immemorial. Some gods theorise they are failed attempts at creating humans, while others believe they were lice on Tartarus' back.

MOROS
GOD

The Goddess of Fate and Doom. She is one of the oldest of the gods and is a daughter of the primordial night.

MORPHEUS
GOD

The God of Dreams who usually resides in his own realm, the Dreamscape. Though often he lingers in the Underworld, as death is like a dream...

HECATE
GOD

The Goddess of Magic and Witchcraft. Hecate takes the form of an old crone and is particularly adept in using runes. She taught magic to humans.

HYPNOS
GOD

The God of Sleep and father of Morpheus. Because of human's need for sleep, it is said Hypnos owns half their lives. He is the twin brother of Thanatos, the God of Death.

AION
GOD

The God of the Zodiac and a God of Time, Aion often speaks in riddles. He floats inside a ring with twelve segments and is far more concerned with the stars than with the world of mortals.

CER
GOD

The Goddess of a Violent Death. She is another daughter of Nyx and a sister of Moros. She can often be found on bloody battlefields and in the eyes of mad soldiers.

STYX
GOD

The goddess from which the river is named. All oaths sworn on the River Styx are unbreakable. Styx played an influential role in helping the gods defeat the titans.

HERMES
OLYMPIAN

The God of Speed, Thieves, Wit and Cunning, Athletes, Roads and Travellers, Hermes is the half-brother of Apollo.

THE FORCES OF HEAVEN

MICHAEL AND LUCIFER
ARCHANGELS

Of the seven archangels, Michael is known as the leader of all the armies of Heaven. He is a dragon-slayer and the voice who spoke to Moses on Mt Sinai. Lucifer, also known as 'the Morning Star' is the most beautiful of the archangels and lusts for power. He is also prideful. Their brothers are Gabriel, Uriel, Raphael, Selaphiel and Barachiel.

BELIAL
FALLEN ANGEL

A warrior of the Gladius Vaticanus, many hundreds of years in the dark of Tartarus twisted Belial into a demonic Hell creature. Evil occult groups around the world worship him.

ANGELS

The main soldiers in Heaven's army. The angels are humanoid spirits with two wings fueled by the power of human prayer. They fight with swords, lances, bows and all manner of weapons. The more humans that believe in them, the more powerful they become.

GLADIUS VATICANUS
ANGELS

The soldiers of the hill of prophecy. These angels are an elite fighting force under the direct command of Lucifer.

THE GREAT SERPENT OF HEAVEN
MONSTER

A red seven-headed dragon recorded in the Book of Revelations as an agent of the Apocalypse. It is a creature of pure destruction that cannot distinguish between foe or friend. Only Lucifer has the power to quell the rage of the beast. It is the ultimate weapon of Heaven and where its fire touches will forever be cursed to be a burning wasteland.

PROLOGUE

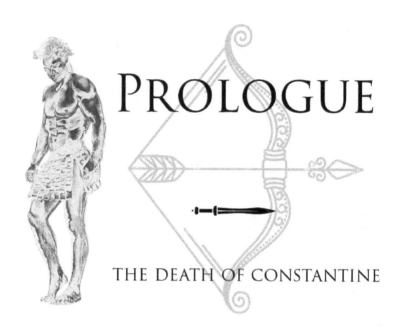

THE DEATH OF CONSTANTINE

Constantine appeared meek as he smothered himself in soft blankets. 'The Great' he was called; Constantine the Great, though that title wasn't fitting now. He was a withered husk of the man he used to be. He looked weary, the kind of weary that no amount of sleep could fix. The cold air chilled him to his bones, dimming the internal fire that had carried him through his momentous life. How had it come to this?

Somehow, Constantine knew he was dying. And of all places he'd been rendered too weak to travel it was in Nicomedia, not his beloved jewel of a city, Constantinople. He'd made it his mission to build a city that eclipsed even Mother Rome, and he'd succeeded. Now Constantine faced death so far away from his home.

None of this was as it should be.

Constantine coughed violently. There was a flurry of movement as a man dressed in elaborate brown robes approached.

"Eusebius," Constantine croaked.

"Imperator," Eusebius answered politely, though there was an air of impatience in his voice.

"Are they coming?" Constantine asked.

"Soon. The priests of Nicomedia assemble as we speak. Have you made your decision?"

Constantine frowned. He knew what he wanted to do, but did not know if it was the right thing.

Eusebius' relentless gaze pierced him. The man's receding hairline and long brown beard did nothing to dull his imposing presence. He was a man of conviction, and Constantine respected that.

"Out!" Constantine ordered, pointing towards the closed door.

A procession of guardsmen and servants alike shambled from his presence.

"Not you, Eusebius. I have matters to discuss with a man of God," Constantine stated.

Once the room was devoid of all others, Constantine spoke to the priest in a hushed voice.

"You know what choice I must make now, for I fear my time to depart this world swiftly approaches."

The glow from a series of lamps on the far wall illuminated

both men in a soft orange light as they cast long ominous shadows across the room.

"Your choice was made long ago, great Emperor," Eusebius murmured. "Leave the memory of Sol Invictus behind and embrace your legacy. God is with us, even now."

Constantine knew that Eusebius' words were true. God had guided him through treachery and turmoil his whole life. The angels of Heaven had always been with him, directing him down the righteous path. He, Constantine, had reunited the fractured Roman Empire. He had returned the stolen belongings of the persecuted and allowed greater freedom of belief than there ever had been. Christianity was his faith and he had served it to the best of his ability. Yet, there was something that worried him… the memory of the past haunted him as he lay on that bed.

"That moment, so long ago, concerns me Eusebius…" Constantine coughed.

The priest frowned and looked to be contemplating how best to respond. "Tell me again what you saw?" he said after a long pause.

"On the eve of battle, I looked into the sky and saw a cross of light bearing the inscription, 'with this sign, you shall win'… I carved it on the shield of every soldier and we saw victory and a unified Rome that day."

"A cross in the sky was most certainly a divine manifestation from Jesus of Nazareth. Our Lord ensured your victory, not some pagan god of the old world!"

Constantine glared at the priest, who quickly fell silent.

"I know the power of God too well. This was a blessing

from Sol Invictus, from Apollo… the Golden God saw my army through that battle. I know it. Long have I forsaken the gods of old, because it was right to do so, yet Apollo aided me when it was needed most."

"You are a Christian! Your life has been spent furthering the aims of the Church. It is hardly a secret, Imperator. Did Apollo slay your enemies for you? No. Did Apollo reunite your empire? No."

"Still, to turn my back entirely on the gods of old…"

"A difficult question, to be sure," a new voice spoke.

The room was bathed in light as the door swung open to reveal a procession of new figures entering. They were all men wearing bizarrely bright ceremonial robes. Their clothes seemed to shine with an unworldly gleam as they moved.

Rage flooded Constantine as he wondered why his guards hadn't stopped them. But there was something about these men that he knew, something he felt in his soul.

Constantine thought he could hear the faintest sound of music in the air, like a quiet hum on the breeze. The lead man had a pale angular face and long curly hair, on which sat a wreath of flowers. It had been a long time, but after a moment, the dying emperor recognised the leader's face.

"Selaphiel," he breathed. "Finally…"

"Lord Constantine," Selaphiel replied formally.

Eusebius bowed low and backed away from Constantine's bed.

"Who are the others?" Constantine asked.

"They are tasked with delivering you to your glorious new

home in the City of Heaven."

"I do not wish to depart the mortal world," Constantine stated desperately, life briefly filling his dull eyes.

"I know this, great Emperor. But to reap the rewards of what you have sewn means to pass from this world to the next," Selaphiel smiled.

"I was promised immortality by your kind," Constantine pleaded to the newcomer.

"And you will receive it. But to do so, you must first shake free the bonds of mortality that bind you. And before the golden thread of your life is cut short, you need to first fully commit yourself to God. You have known this moment was coming for a long time. Now that you stand at the precipice of destiny, do your feet dare move forward?"

Constantine gulped, then coughed.

Eusebius stepped from the shadows of the room and addressed Selaphiel warily, "My lord, begging your pardon, but with whom do I speak?"

Selaphiel turned and faced the priest. The air seemed to radiate with power as Selaphiel stood proud before Eusebius. Six enormous white feathered wings sprung from his back in a glorious display, causing Eusebius to fall backwards in shock.

"My Lord!" Eusebius grovelled, crawling forward to kiss the feet of the archangel.

"I reveal myself to you now, Eusebius of Nicomedia, as an agent of the Lord God. I am an archangel in his service and I have a very important task for you, one that will ripple through time, altering fates and destinies."

Constantine smiled as he observed the speechless Eusebius. To meet with an angel of Heaven was an impossible honour, let alone one of the seven archangels.

The divine visage of Selaphiel spurred something in Constantine. All doubt in his mind dissipated in the archangel's glow. He suddenly knew his purpose and would see it through.

"I am ready," he breathed.

Two of the others who'd accompanied Selaphiel rushed over to help the old man to his feet.

"Collect your instruments of baptism, priest. The time has come that Rome would unite with Heaven," Selaphiel ordered.

"I will assemble the priests of Nicomedia for confession. Imperator, you will have to lay your soul bare before us to be embraced by the loving arms of God."

Constantine nodded.

"Be hasty, Eusebius. Soon envoys of the old order will arrive here. Time is not our ally," Selaphiel commanded.

Eusebius looked temporarily confused as he observed the magnificence of the archangel. Fear and reverence were intermingled in his eyes, and yet, it was still clear that he wasn't willing to question the divine being's words.

Constantine again spoke directly to Selaphiel, painfully aware of the sound of bargaining in his own voice. "Let me linger in the mortal world and I will never again wear the purple robes of an emperor, only the white robes of the neophyte."

"Before all other things can be considered, first you must be baptised. We will prepare you now."

• • • • •

CONSTANTINE FELT THE DIRT between his toes as he was led towards the river. He was now adorned in a plain white robe with his guards helping him to walk, as he was dreadfully weak. The crisp air filled his nostrils and Constantine savoured every breath of it, as they could very well be his last on Earth.

The bank sloped gently into the water of a small river smothered by sparse trees. This was the place where Constantine would finally commit his soul to God, the true ruler of the world. The sins of his life would be washed clean and he would be pure before the divine.

The parade of priests, guardsmen and angels disguised as humans stopped before the river. Eusebius strode forward until he was waist-deep. He held what looked like a long wooden spoon with a deep bowl in his right hand and beckoned the emperor forward.

Selaphiel took Constantine under the arm. He gently guided the old man into the water.

Constantine could feel the current flowing around him. It was cold but bearable. The river ran as a torrent of change for the world. No longer would the mighty Roman Empire be bound to the multitudes of hedonistic pagan gods. Instead, there would only be one true path into the light. Of all Constantine's deeds, he figured this baptism could be the most important.

Selaphiel brought Constantine before Eusebius and released him.

Constantine swayed as he tried to maintain his balance while the archangel moved out of his vision.

"Do you renounce the false gods of your forebears, and on behalf of your empire, renounce all false idols?" Eusebius asked.

Constantine frowned. This wasn't a usual question asked during a baptism. Though, he figured things must be different for an emperor of Rome.

"I do," Constantine murmured.

"I baptise you in the name of the Father, the Son and of the Holy Spirit," Eusebius proclaimed, plunging his tool into the water.

Selaphiel assisted the old man to lean backwards.

Eusebius released the water he'd collected onto Constantine's head. It fell in a trickle from his skin into the river. Each small drop was like a pounding drum as it splashed into the water below. To Constantine, it sounded like the distant drums of war…

There was a sudden burst of expanding air, like an invisible shockwave was rippling out from Constantine. Goosebumps rose on his skin and his hair stood tall on his arms. He felt like he was being embraced by the power of the Lord.

Then, everything changed.

Selaphiel returned Constantine to his upright position and screamed, "Seize them!"

Constantine spun his head wildly.

The archangel was pointing into a nearby bank of trees, where two hooded figures could be seen moving.

Wings spread wide from the angels' backs as they took to the air, no longer hiding their true forms. At unfathomable speeds they flew into the forest, summoning ropes of golden light to bind the interlopers.

One of the hooded strangers appeared to be laughing, as if playing along with an elaborate ruse.

Selaphiel waved his right hand through the air, and every mortal present, except Constantine, fell into a trance.

"What's going on?" Constantine wheezed, but even Eusebius had slumped forward, his head dangling in front of him.

The two heavily cloaked figures were dragged into the clearing before the river, though they didn't seem to be offering any resistance.

Selaphiel flew towards them and pulled their hoods back, revealing two men that Constantine didn't know. One was a young man with bright blonde hair and sparkling blue eyes. The other had sullen features with sunken eyes and deathly white skin.

"Is this the sort of greeting you'd offer us, archangel," the blue-eyed man jested with Selaphiel.

The archangel clicked his fingers and the glowing rope around the strangers vanished.

"Apollo," he sighed. "And your companion?"

"I am Thanatos, the God of Death," the sullen man introduced himself, though he looked at Selaphiel warily.

"Apollo?" Constantine spluttered.

"Yes, Imperator," Apollo bowed. "Word has reached the high clouds of Olympus that your journey across the mortal plain nears its end. As has been customary with your predecessors, an Olympian has come to accompany you on your journey to the Fields of Elysium."

Constantine grimaced. Other than his vision decades ago

he'd never paid heed to the old gods. They were a relic of the past and didn't offer his empire a way forward. The old gods weren't interested in making a better world, like the one true God was.

"I am not dead yet," Constantine spat, feeling anger well up within him.

"The fates have assured me that the golden thread of your life is all but used up. But come now, Constantine, this is not a sombre occasion," Apollo answered his remark jovially.

"I expected you earlier," Selaphiel stated.

"I have been in Constantinople for many days now," Thanatos grumbled.

"Yes, dear Thanatos here had some trouble locating the good emperor," Apollo laughed. "Why are you here, Selaphiel?"

The archangel gave the god a quizzical look and then said, "How disconnected are you from the politics of modern Rome, Apollo?"

"Before his untimely disappearance, my father Zeus decreed an end to the god's direct involvement with the empire. Though sometimes, when it is needed, we still act," Apollo winked at Constantine.

"Sol Invictus… so it was Apollo," he thought. It didn't matter now, he'd chosen his path.

"Nevertheless," Apollo continued, "I have seen your brothers in their attempts to win the hearts and minds of the people. To what end I can only begin to guess."

"What has just happened here?" Thanatos interjected. The God of Death was gazing at the unconscious form of Eusebius beside the half-submerged Constantine.

"Something new," Selaphiel said quietly.

"There is something in the air," Thanatos continued. "Some unknown power gathers, I can feel it.."

"HHNNGGHH!" Constantine gripped his chest. His body was coursing with sudden intense pain. It was blinding. Selaphiel caught the emperor before he collapsed into the water.

"We will retire to the manor," Selaphiel informed his angels.

"I will take the emperor," Apollo stated, gliding over the river towards him.

"His time is short. I will begin preparations for his journey to the Underworld," Thanatos stated, apparently losing his interest in the odd scene before him.

Selaphiel said nothing, though this didn't seem to bother either of the gods.

"I want… the angels…" Constantine wheezed.

"I am the God Apollo. You would request the hands of lesser beings guide you?" Apollo questioned.

Constantine was struggling to breathe, though the pain was diminishing as quickly as it had appeared.

Unable to speak, Constantine was lifted from the water and flown back to his bed chamber.

• • • • •

BACK IN THE COMFORT of his bed, all Constantine could do was listen to the conversation of the divine beings around him. Everything was hazy and blurred, yet he held out hope that the angels would grant him the immortality he so desired. There was still time. He was still alive.

Thanatos had departed, grumbling something about, *"Needing to speak to the nymphs."*

The three angels in Selaphiel's entourage had left shortly afterwards, and none had returned. Apollo and the archangel spoke as if they knew each other, though there was a distinct air of unease about them. Constantine had known the same feeling many times in his political life. It felt like there was a scheme afoot.

"I am surprised, Selaphiel, that your brothers are not here. Where is fearsome Michael or dear old Lucifer, who thinks he is so beautiful?" Apollo asked the archangel, who was standing beside Constantine's bed.

"All of my brothers are preparing," Selaphiel replied simply.

"For what?" Apollo asked.

"You will know soon enough."

"Is that so?" Apollo rolled his eyes.

"My father wishes to know about yours, Apollo," Selaphiel said, in an abrupt change to the topic.

"He wishes to know about Zeus?"

"His disappearance, more accurately," Selaphiel added.

"We do not speak of such things," Apollo mumbled quickly.

"It is fascinating though, isn't it? Mighty Zeus, head of the Olympic pantheon at the height of his power, just vanishes from all knowledge."

"I see that rumour of this has reached the realm of Heaven."

"My father grows ever more curious as to what exactly could interfere with a being of such magnitude."

Apollo sighed and said, "I have nothing of value to share on this topic. We searched for a time, but he is gone. To even guess at what happened would be an exercise in foolishness."

"You mentioned rumours, Apollo. Perhaps you could clarify some that have reached me?"

Apollo gave the archangel an unconvinced nod, seemingly hesitant to pursue this line of conversation.

"I heard that a foreign giant visited Olympus."

"Olympus had many visitors from strange lands at that time. The giant of Jotunheim was no more peculiar than anything else, though Zeus seemed impressed enough to impart mighty gifts upon him."

"And word reached us that the last son of Zeus was very unhappy with his father."

"Do not play coy with me, Selaphiel," Apollo shook his head. "I know of who you speak and that Dominus has spent time in the company of your kind. The man is small, meek and of no consequence to us, no matter what oaths of vengeance he has sworn."

"He is your brother, Apollo," Selaphiel laughed in exasperation.

"My true brothers are gods. If I were to count all the mortal children of Zeus as my kin then the list would be beyond counting."

"Dominus, at least, is not strictly mortal. He has lived a life far longer than that of the average man."

"To have some legacy of the divine is not uncommon, be it strength, speed or life. It does not change what he is."

Selaphiel frowned and rubbed his bare chin. "There are many gods who have risen to prominence during the Roman Empire that are not part of your original order. Spirits who have ascended to true divinity. Would you deny them too? Would you discard the mighty Janus so easily? It seems like folly to do so."

Apollo just shrugged. It appeared to Constantine that the archangel's opinions meant very little to the god.

"And what of this so-called Sundered King?" Selaphiel asked finally. "Is he one of your order who is hiding in the dark and performing unusual magic?"

"I have never heard of such a being," Apollo answered.

"Hmmm," Selaphiel frowned. "A wildcard in all this then. He appears to be connected to dark primeval powers that are so abstract even God doesn't understand them."

"To call your father 'God' is a great insult. There are many gods. He should not try to claim this as his personal title. It is lucky that his arrogance has been permitted this long."

Selaphiel shook his head. "Soon my father will be greater than Zeus ever was. For my father to carry such a title is appropriate."

Apollo laughed in earnest.

"There has been a change. You have been blind to the ways things are going for a long time, Apollo. Even now it flows like the rising tide across Rome," Selaphiel grinned.

"I am the God of Knowledge and Prophecy, and I know not of what you speak. Don't be offended if I put little stock in your words."

Selaphiel shrugged.

"Selaphiel, please…"

Constantine's quiet voice cut through the casual conversation. He was reaching towards the archangel.

"Where is Thanatos?" Apollo looked to the door in alarm. "He needs to be here for the passing of Constantine!"

"Selaphiel, I don't want to die... I did as you asked..." Constantine groaned weakly.

"Rest well, Constantine. A new world wakes as you begin your slumber," the archangel placed his hand on Constantine's forehead.

Constantine watched as Apollo opened the only door to the room. The entire atmosphere changed in an instant.

Just behind Apollo, the dying emperor could see the God Thanatos bound in heavy chains, looking bloody and beaten. Ichor, the blood of the gods, was leaking from a myriad of wounds across his body and his black robe lay in tatters around him. The room itself was all but blasted apart. A spectacular, but silent battle must've taken place.

"Apollo," Thanatos began in a hoarse voice, "he has renounced us. All of Rome has renounced us and embraced the angels. The balance of power has already shifted. I have spoken to the nymphs who will be now alerting Olympus. Flee this place and get to the Underworld! Hades must know! The Palace of Dawn will send one of their steeds for you."

Thanatos gasped as if suddenly gagged by some invisible power.

From out of nowhere, Apollo manifested a magnificent golden sword and moved to cut Thanatos free of his bindings.

He was stopped by the appearance of the three angels who'd

followed Thanatos. They were no longer dressed in ornate ceremonial robes but instead had donned golden armour. They all held swords at the ready.

"You dare to think you can challenge me?" Apollo boasted.

"We will not see you reach the Underworld," Selaphiel whispered from beside Constantine.

Apollo turned from the menacing faces of the angels back to the archangel.

Selaphiel had summoned a weapon from thin air. He held a magnificent spear, of a craftsmanship Constantine had never seen, that was wreathed in a deadly translucent flame.

"Selaphiel, please. You are but minor spirits compared to a god. If I wished to, I could click my fingers and obliterate you all. Do not force such a fate upon yourselves."

"You have lived too long a life unchallenged Apollo. The world has changed. Allow me to illuminate this new truth for you."

Selaphiel lunged for Apollo, directing his spear at the god's chest. Apollo blocked the attack with his sword, a look of shock etched on his face. It was evident that the archangel was far stronger than he'd anticipated.

Selaphiel struck Apollo again, this time with a flurry of attacks, causing the god to have to dodge and weave into the other room, where he was quickly surrounded by the three other angels.

Apollo's eyes blazed with light as he shot a fireball at Selaphiel, who summoned a golden shield of energy around himself. The archangel responded in kind by shooting a jet of his own energy at Apollo, which sent him careening through the wall.

"What is this devilry?" Apollo cried.

"The future," Selaphiel grinned maliciously. The other angels laughed.

"Kill him," the archangel ordered.

The three subordinate angels spread their wings and flew at Apollo. The god braced and released a searing explosion of fire in an orb around himself, like a small star was being formed with Apollo inside.

When the fire cleared, Apollo was gone.

Through the charred and sizzling hole in the roof, Constantine could see a horse with a bright red mane carrying the god into the sky.

"Go on Apollo, go to your Underworld! Warn them that the doom of the old order is coming! Every domain of your realm will soon be ours!" Selaphiel called to the retreating figure.

A frustrated-looking Selaphiel returned to Constantine's bedside.

"Soon God's glory will encompass the world. Our war begins, but yours is ended, Emperor."

Constantine exhaled. Suddenly, the great games of cosmic beings meant very little to him. He'd done his part to build a better world, and now the angels would do theirs.

Everything went dark. Constantine the Great took his final breath, right as the war for the spiritual heart of the world began.

PART ONE

THE ARTEFACT

CHAPTER ONE

THE GOLDEN SWORD

- 2017 -
LEBANON

The wind whipped over the ocean as two sleek black zodiacs skipped across the waves towards the shore. Onboard were the members of the Australian 2nd Commando Regiment. They sat expressionless in the cold as their boat battled with the turbulent waters of the Lebanese coast. Hail plummeted from above, belting the soldiers with freezing precision.

Among them was a woman dressed in full military attire and goggles, though she was no soldier. She resisted the urge to shiver or show any weakness to the stone-faced commandos, despite being terribly cold.

Her name was Melissa Pythia, a first-year agent of the

Australian Security Intelligence Organisation. She was a rookie spy, and this was her mission.

The shoreline ahead was dark, save for a small chemical glow on the beach.

Not far inland was the town of Cheik Zennad. It seemed like a sleepy place, full of farmers and merchants. However, being so close to the Syrian border during the prolonged civil war meant that swathes of unsavoury characters had been noticed passing through.

The town itself, however, wasn't the destination of the commando team.

"No one is outside, the storm is keeping them in," a voice from the nearby HMAS Arunta called through the signaler's backpack. It was barely audible above the crashing waves and thundering storm.

The outline of the ANZAC class helicopter frigate was barely visible against the swirling storm clouds. Only the occasional flash of lightning revealed its presence.

Melissa wiped the salty sea-spray from her goggles as the boat bounced off another wave. She looked at the heavily armed men around her. Her bland life in Sydney felt like a distant dream right now.

Two months ago, local police had thwarted a terrorist plot in Melbourne, Australia.

Members of a Jihadist group, Almalayikat Alsabea, a Syrian splinter of ISIS, had been able to send their ardent followers into Australia. They had laid out a plan to perform a terror attack like the world had never seen, the specifics of which

Melissa didn't like to think about. While the public hailed the foiling of the terrorist operation as a great victory, to those in government it was too much of a close call.

ASIO was tasked with determining the source of the attack. Melissa was one of the agents told to sit at a desk and figure out who was responsible and where they had come from.

After her recent deployment to Afghanistan, this was a welcome relief. Melissa had been part of an experimental year-long training program in which she'd generally excelled. It had seen her almost immediately deployed to the Middle East for in-the-field intelligence work, though that deployment had come with life-threatening events and near misses. The idea of spending some time at desk in Australia was to be warmly embraced.

That feeling was short-lived, as through circumstances she couldn't explain, she kept having dreams about a particular brown panel van, only identifiable by a crudely drawn image of an angel on the top, driving through the ruins of a city.

Every night, this van would speed through her mind.

Then, one day, as she was casually monitoring satellite feeds, she saw it. The angel, with its pin-prick eyes and goofy smile, driving north from Tripoli.

She followed it as it drove to the Areda Border Point, then to Aleppo, then back into Lebanon.

Her co-workers put it down to dumb luck, but Melissa wasn't so sure.

Registration checks, followed by family checks, then a dive into social media revealed that Almalayikat Alsabea were operating out of a small compound in the north of Lebanon.

It didn't seem like a run-of-the-mill operation. ASIO determined there was intelligence to be gained. Something was off. As to what, the higher-ups weren't sure. It was more of an intuition that something important was being hidden at the beach-side facility than something tangible.

ASIO spoke to ASIS, the Australian Secret Intelligence Service, who tasked one of its spies to investigate.

That spy was Matthew Pyne.

Matthew Pyne was broad-shouldered beefy man living in Beirut posing as a gym owner. It was a role he was well-suited for, and he made his disappointment evident when he was reassigned and sent north.

Unfortunately, a foreigner poking around the surrounds of Cheik Zennad was immediately noticed and Matt disappeared off the radar completely. All communication went dark.

The Australian Government determined a covert rescue was in order. This also provided a chance to gain some physical intel on the facility.

As she'd discovered the compound, Melissa was the first choice to be deployed. The HMAS Arunta was already in the Mediterranean performing exercises with the Greek and US navies. She was quickly prepped for deployment, then sent to rendezvous with the ship, along with the 2nd Commando Regiment.

The Zodiac bounced off a tumbling wave and she felt her stomach do loops. Melissa was nervous, but she was ready.

Melissa felt a little sea-sick as the boat drew close to the shore. The small glow on the beach was from a Cyalume stick; a chemical light used to display a safe landing location. A soldier, already on the beach, had determined the best path at low tide.

Four of the men dropped from each zodiac into the ocean and began dragging the boats ashore.

The beach was lined with small shrubs and the commandos pulled the boats directly into them, caching the two Zodiacs under camouflage netting.

The operation consisted of ten people in total. The nine that had arrived on the Zodiacs and one who met them on land.

From onboard the HMAS Arunta, the drone operator radioed in, "Still quiet."

Melissa could feel the wind blowing even through her webbing and overalls. She privately admired the drone operator's skill being able to fly in this weather.

Just up the beach was their destination. Melissa could see dim lights through the upper windows of a building.

The compound was a collection of three structures.

The closest to them, on their right, was a small house. It had a flat roof and was routinely patrolled by armed men.

The second structure, to the left, was a large shed and in the centre was a two-story home with another flat roof. Based on the satellite feed, it appeared to have sniper's nests on top. It was in the larger structure that ASIO believed Matt was being held. It was also the building that several imams had been visiting in the last few weeks, conspicuously frequently. These weren't local preachers, but venerated religious scholars with infamous reputations in the Arab world.

During this storm, however, everyone was inside. Everything had been planned down to the minute.

Melissa watched the signaler setting up his small antenna on the beach. She could barely see anything. Mounted to the front of her helmet was a night vision apparatus. She flicked it down over her goggles and in the green hue she could at last see, though the splotches of rain were going to be a continuing annoyance.

One of the soldiers had already moved off from the group to provide over watch on the small cluster of buildings.

Once the signaler had set up his antenna, the voice of the drone operator came clearly through their earpieces.

"Site movement, building three."

"Roger," the squad commander, Corporal Goldring, affirmed. "Two hundred out, the beach is clear."

The soldiers broke into groups of five and four, moving as two units through the darkness up a small rise to the edge of the compound.

A flimsy chain-link fence circled the buildings.

The soldiers positioned themselves. One crouched and, with a pair of a bolt-cutters, hacked horizontally at the bottom of the fence. It only took a minute for it to be snipped away enough for the soldiers to roll it up from the bottom. They all slipped underneath and moved forward, Melissa in the middle of the procession.

The wind whistled and electric sparks exploded above as the commando team moved like shadows to the front face of the big silver shed.

They split up.

Team one began moving up the left side of the shed, while team two paused to watch the flat-roofed house. Melissa nervously followed the lead of the other team two members. She was second last in their ranks.

ASIO had equipped her with the same weapon as the others. A rifle unique to the Australian Army. The EF-88 AUS STYR's were armed with sleek black prototype silencers. Each individual's webbing contained pockets jammed with extra ammunition magazines and tools.

Goldring crouched at the head of team two.

"Anything?" he said into his microphone.

A member of team one replied instantly, "All clear north side, moving to building three."

"Wait," the voice of the drone operator chimed in.

Melissa tried desperately to wipe the heavy raindrops from her googles.

"Movement," the drone operator said, "building three."

A man, his identifying features barely visible in the dull lights from the two-story house, had stepped out. They heard a thud as he slammed the door shut behind him.

He moved into some low-lying shrubs by the door and unzipped his pants.

There were two muffled gunshots, then a thump as a body crashed into the ground.

Team two moved silently as they dragged the dead man out of sight.

They positioned themselves around building three.

"Move up," Goldring commanded.

Melissa's team darted forward, straight between the shed and the house on the right.

One of the soldiers jiggled the door handle.

"No go for door," he said. "Breacher!"

"Guess we are going loud," Melissa mumbled. Her heart was in her mouth and beating at a million miles an hour.

One of the soldiers pulled out his breaching kit.

He moved towards the door and placed small dabs of plastic explosive on both its hinges.

"Going noisy," Goldring said.

The soldier pressed a button on his detonator and a small explosion echoed out. The door collapsed forward.

The soldiers moved in.

The world slowed.

Melissa heard gunshots. Then, it was her turn to move.

She followed the soldier in front into a narrow hallway. There was a bright red rug on the floor. On the right, was an arched opening that led into a kitchen. Melissa saw two men with AK-47s lying dead on the ground, splayed out against the stone. On the counter-tops were wires and mechanical parts. It looked like they were in the right place.

There was shouting in Arabic upstairs, and the slamming of doors.

They moved forward. Team one split off through an opening to the left that led upstairs.

Goldring paused behind a flapping purple curtain at the end of the hallway. Melissa caught glances of an expansive living room just behind it.

26

As they moved into the living room the soldiers fanned out. Black flags with white writing lined the walls. At least half a dozen prayer mats were piled on the floor. To the back of the room were several large cabinets, all pushed out from the wall. Two soldiers moved toward the cabinets to check the space behind them.

One of the soldiers signalled towards a hatch in the floor. Before Goldring could acknowledge it, all hell broke loose.

From behind the cabinets three sets of hands holding rifles emerged, spraying bullets wildly.

Melissa dived behind a nearby couch and listened to the pops as the bullets ripped through it. She wasn't hit.

One of the commandos wasn't so lucky. He yelled in pain as he fell to the floor, blood gushing from wounds on his left shoulder and arm.

"COVERING!" Goldring shouted as he fired straight into the cabinet, the wood splintering as bullets impacted it.

The wounded man was quickly dragged back down the hallway by his fellow soldiers. Melissa popped her head up. She could see a heavily bearded man in a white robe crawling around the side of the cabinet. He raised his gun and pointed it directly at Goldring, who was completely exposed.

Melissa raised her STYR and looked down the sight.

She exhaled and squeezed the trigger.

The man fell back in a hail of gunfire.

From his webbing, Goldring grabbed a flashbang and threw it towards the far side of the room.

Melissa ducked back behind the couch and shielded her eyes.

A brilliant white light flared up. Then, the sound of furniture tipping as two men stumbled out from their hiding places and blindly fumbled their way around.

Melissa heard gunshots from behind her. Armed men had appeared from the other two buildings and were now battling the soldiers from outside.

Goldring didn't hesitate to attack the disoriented men. He ran forwards and hit the first man with the butt of his rifle, knocking him out cold.

The second man pulled a large knife from his belt and lunged. He couldn't see the Australian soldier, courtesy of Goldring's flashbang, but could hear him.

Goldring turned just in time to see the knife narrowly miss his stomach.

Melissa once again aimed and fired.

The man fell dead.

Melissa could hear further gunfire from outside now. It was louder and not being suppressed with a silencer. The commando providing over watch from the beach had to be firing at the emerging threats from the other buildings.

Goldring looked at Mel and murmured, "Thanks."

Mel nodded.

There were low thuds coming from above. The other team upstairs was encountering resistance.

Gunfire was echoing through the night air. All of this noise was bound to attract unwanted attention. They had to move.

Mel scanned the room. There weren't any computers or documents. But she felt funny, like a sixth sense was screaming to her that there was something here she needed to find.

Goldring did a quick sweep of the room. There were no other entries or exits, just the hatch in the floor.

It was closed with a small golden padlock.

"I can pick it," Mel informed Goldring as she walked over.

"No need," Goldring replied as he blasted it with rifle fire.

The padlock shattered.

Only the two of them were lift in the living room. As for the rest of team two; one man was injured, and the two who'd dragged him off were now defending the door. The other team could now be on the roof, potentially firing down from the sniper's nests.

Goldring looked at Mel, "I'll cover the entry; you'll have to go."

Melissa nodded. She took a deep breath and steeled her nerve.

Goldring prepped another flashbang, then ripped the hatch open and tossed it down.

It exploded in the darkness.

A second later, Mel slid down the ladder into the basement.

Her night vision was once again down over her goggles as she turned around with her rifle raised.

She looked left.

She looked right.

There was no one else down here, just piles upon piles of old cardboard boxes. She saw dusty folders full of papers spread about the floor. If this was all intel, they'd need a truck to get it out.

Melissa pushed forward into the darkness. There was a thin discernible path between the towering piles of information.

There was no light whatsoever. It was claustrophobic in the dark.

She walked forward cautiously, her rifle up and her finger resting just outside the trigger-guard.

She moved past the boxes and into a small brick room.

There, tied in the centre, was a white man-shaped blur. It was Matthew Pyne.

He was tied to a chair and his hands were bound. She heard a small snore ring out. Matthew was completely asleep.

Melissa slapped him in the face and he woke with a start.

"Who's there?" he demanded.

"Australian rescue team," Melissa said quickly, releasing her gun to its sling. She withdrew a knife and promptly cut Matt free.

"Ugh, I can't see a thing down here."

"I'll walk you out," Melissa said.

Even as the words left her mouth, they felt distant.

She began feeling faint, and her vision became blurry. Almost as if her eyes were clouding over.

Matt was saying something, but she couldn't hear him.

Instead, she heard the voice of children. She could see them too!

There was a young boy with bright blonde hair, and a girl with blue eyes, who looked to be his twin. They were laughing.

Then she saw a snake.

A colossal snake.

It was impossibly big.

The vision changed. The boy was now older, and he sported a silver bow and a golden sword. He was preparing to fight the snake.

Then, Melissa saw a woman, sitting in a temple that was possibly underground, with vents of steam rising around her. She had elaborate robes on. People were bowing before her, asking her for... something; prophecy and predictions. They wanted to know what was going to happen. Hundreds and hundreds of people...

The woman in the temple was raising her hands to her head. She pulled her hood back to reveal... Melissa. The ancient woman was herself?

A violent shaking pulled Melissa free from the images in her mind.

"What are you doing? Get us out of here!" Matt yelled.

"What was that?" Melissa muttered. She couldn't leave yet. There was something here she needed to find.

Acting on instinct, she raised her gun and fired it at the back wall of the room. She blasted the bricks apart.

A golden light was gleaming through the bullet holes.

She reloaded and continued firing.

Chunks of the wall plummeted to the ground below. Melissa rushed forward and pulled the damaged bricks out of the way.

"Are you insane?" Matt asked bluntly.

"Can't you see it?" Melissa said excitedly.

"See what?"

"The golden light!"

"What are you talking about, its pitch black in here!"

Melissa had flipped up her night vision. The light was illuminating the room. Behind the wall was a natural void in the rock. Sitting in that void, absolutely blazing with light, was the most magnificent weapon Melissa had ever seen.

It was a sword of pure gold. It was intricately detailed. Carved into the blade was the image of horses, with manes of fire. They were pulling a chariot through the clouds. The cross-guard was designed to look like two lyres springing out from the blade. On the grip, tiny images of people dancing besides swirling musical notes were expertly drawn. The pommel of the sword was the sun, with triangular, sloped points jutting out along its circumference to mimic flames.

There were other scattered objects in the small cave. But Melissa only had eyes for the sword. She tentatively reached out and gripped it.

Instantly, the scene changed.

Now, she saw a vision of herself. She looked older.

Ruins surrounded her as she carried the sword.

She saw herself raising the sword. As she lifted it higher, the ruins transformed into a black fiery pit where deformed bodies reached out in agony. Unknown creatures moved in the flames. Before her eyes, the fire spread across the world.

Now she was like an eagle, looking down as cities burned and people fled. The world was agony. It was pain. Screams filled the air. The planet was burning.

Golden light burst through the clouds from high above and began extinguishing the flames.

Then, everything went dark.

She was alone in the black.

A figure emerged. A man, only he wasn't a man. He had six

glorious wings splayed out behind him. Beside her, another man appeared. He was tall and muscular, with blonde hair and blue eyes. The new man took the sword and his entire body turned golden.

Then, Melissa was once again in the sky, watching the fire retreat and the world return to normal.

While the world below seemed peaceful, the clouds around her seem to twist and warp, taking on the shape of a fearsome black wolf.

Melissa gasped.

She was in the basement again; her right hand wrapped tightly around the handle of the golden sword. Only now it was no longer glowing.

Matthew was positively fuming. He squeezed hard as he gripped her shoulder in the dark.

Melissa composed herself. Seeing visions wasn't a good sign. But the mission wasn't over. She could figure out what that bizarre experience meant later.

She pulled the night vision apparatus back down.

"Hold on," she told Matt.

She marched back through the stacks of paper and towards the ladder. Goldring had clearly closed the hatch behind her, as no light was filtering down.

Melissa put Matt's hands on the ladder and commanded, "Up!"

Matt didn't need to be told twice.

He raced upwards until he slammed his head into the hatch and lifted it open through sheer force.

He cursed, and Melissa stifled a laugh.

She followed him, climbing one-handed, still gripping the sword.

When she clambered back up into the room, the first thing she noticed was that the gunfire had ceased.

Goldring walked up to the pair of them.

"The site is secure, for now. Evac is coming shortly."

Goldring nodded curtly at Matt, then paused as he looked at Melissa's new treasure.

"Nice sword," he said.

A commando yelled out from the entrance.

"Time to go," Goldring stated. "Top floor was a gold mine. Computers, documents, everything. Sorry agents, but we don't have time to let you two re-sweep the house."

Melissa looked at her prize and simply said, "Something tells me we got what we need."

The three of them moved out of the two-story building.

The whir of helicopter blades filled the air. As soon as they'd blown the door off, it had become a loud operation. The benefit was that they didn't have to take the Zodiacs back across the turbulent sea.

The ground was littered with the bodies of the compound's usual residents. Among them were women with AK-47s. Their niqabs flapped quietly in the wind.

Matt didn't look so bad, appearing like he'd been relatively well taken care of.

He shot a funny look at Melissa.

"What was that?"

"What?" Melissa responded.

"How'd you know that sword was behind the wall?"

"Female intuition."

"Jesus," Matt scoffed. "You know, when you are rescuing someone, generally the focus is the rescue, right?"

"I had a couple of focuses. Something odd has been going on here, maybe this sword is the key to it. You got rescued in the end, didn't you?"

Matt turned away.

Melissa couldn't take her eyes off the golden weapon. She could feel its warmth through her glove. She almost felt connected to it. And that vision. What did it mean? A world on fire...

Before long, the helicopter was zooming across the ocean with Melissa, Matthew and the wounded soldier on board.

Melissa was cold and wet, but alive. The pilots didn't allow her to hold the sword in flight, so it was locked away in a Pelican case on the floor. She couldn't stop fixating on the visions.

The ruins she'd seen, they looked so familiar. Maybe it was somewhere in Rome.

"All roads lead to Rome," she thought as the floodlights of the ship came into view ahead.

CHAPTER TWO

MELISSA PYTHIA

- SEPTEMBER 27 2019-
ROME - THE PANTHEON

Throngs of tourists made their way down the Via degli Orfani towards the mighty pillars of the Pantheon. Gelaterias sat on both sides of the busy road, proudly displaying dozens upon dozens of tantalising treats. Flavours from the bold to the exotic lured in tourists easily tempted during long days of endless walking.

It was late September in Rome and the sun bore down on the ancient city with surprisingly intensity.

Several people loudly exclaimed their displeasure as they wiped the sweat from their brows. Cries at the lingering doom of global warming were uttered almost as frequently as remarks about the history of the Pantheon.

Sitting just off the Via degli Orfani, in the shade of a large parasol at the front of an unremarkable coffee shop was an inconspicuous woman muttering to herself.

"Damn thing," Melissa whispered as she adjusted her earpiece.

She looked nothing like she had during her deployment to Lebanon in 2017. Gone was the rifle and military attire, instead now she appeared completely civilian.

Melissa was in her late twenties and traditionally beautiful by western standards, with soulful brown eyes and gleaming black hair. She wore a simple summer dress. It was white and strapless at the top, and flowed out into a skirt patterned with red flowers. On her head was a straw hat with oversized sunglasses in the shape of love hearts sitting on the brim. Even with her love-heart sunglasses, she didn't look remotely out of place. With tour groups of millennials all over the city, Rome was swimming in a sea of man-buns and brightly coloured clothes.

In front of her was an open laptop. She'd made sure to sit so the screen faced the brick wall of the coffee shop.

"Melissa, do you copy?" a man's voice spluttered through her earpiece. The connection was bad.

"Yes," she replied, barely moving her mouth.

"You don't have to act like a ventriloquist. Italians are always talking to themselves."

"Seems racist, but okay," Melissa shot back.

"The meeting is 1:30 pm. In ten minutes, pick up your laptop, and walk towards the Pantheon. You know what the man looks like?"

"Of course," Melissa responded coolly.

The heat was getting to her, making Melissa more irritable than she'd usually be. She carefully scanned the faces of the people walking by. None matched the image of the man on her laptop screen. Her target was in his late-forties with slicked-back grey hair and a manicured beard.

All Melissa had to do was bump into him and place a bug on his person. The bug was minuscule, and as soon as it was dropped into a pocket, it would attach itself to the fabric; hardly noticeable.

Melissa got up, closed her laptop, plopped it into her oversized brown handbag and began moving down the street.

The pillars of the Pantheon appeared before her.

The place was absolutely bustling. At least three different groups of Chinese tourists were taking pictures in front of the old structure. Trip leaders, in close proximity, grew progressively louder as they shouted their well-rehearsed facts over one another.

Melissa wasn't tall enough to see over the crowd, so she made her way towards the fountain. She looked at the carved fish heads spewing water down into the pool with mild disgust. Melissa didn't appreciate the art at all.

Carefully, she walked up the small steps to get a better view of the crowd.

She saw him.

Leaning casually against one of the front pillars of the bullet-ridden temple was her target flicking casually through his phone.

Melissa frowned. It would be hard to just bump into him as he was. It would be better if he was deeper amongst the crowd. Melissa sat on the edge of the fountain and continued to observe him, pondering her approach.

"He is at the front of the Pantheon," she said quietly.

"We have eyes on him, it looks like someone else is approaching."

"A very public meeting..." Melissa murmured.

"Smart, in a way, in a city like this. It is easy to hide in plain sight."

An elderly man was strolling towards the Pantheon. He was bald with round spectacles sitting crookedly on his nose.

"ID on this guy?" Melissa asked.

"Marcello Soncin. Antiques dealer. Patriarch of a local crime family."

Melissa found herself absent-mindedly grinding her teeth. She needed to plant the bug now. Every missed word spoken between these two could be critical to her mission.

"Mel..." the voice in her earpiece started.

"I know, I know," Melissa replied. She stood up and stepped down from the fountain into the crowd.

She squirmed her way through a family of American tourists who'd stopped to take pictures. A thin film of sweat transferred from their meaty arms onto her as she pushed by.

She continued to weave through the crowd, taking care not to enter anyone's photos, though it was an almost impossible task.

When she drew near the pillars of the Pantheon, she held her phone above her and pressed the video recording button. She looked just like any of the other dozens of people trying to be social media stars.

"Here I am at some old building... I don't know what it is,

but it looks pretty neat!" Melissa girlishly giggled.

She walked forward, looking at herself. In her left hand, she gripped the small black device between her fingers.

"Oh my god, look at all the bullet holes they are just insane – hey!"

Melissa walked straight into the man with the slicked-back hair. Marcello Soncin, the old man now standing beside him, gave her a frustrated look.

"Stupid girl," her target said in a thick Italian accent.

Before anyone had noticed anything, Melissa released the device in her fingers into the man's jacket pocket.

"Excuse me!" Melissa scowled.

"You walked right into me! Bastarda!"

Melissa pointed her phone in the man's face, "I have over one hundred thousand followers. Do you want them all to see what a jerk you are?"

The man waved his hand at her dismissively then turned to Marcello, "Ci sono trope persone stupide qui, andiamo."

Melissa had no idea what he said, but was certain stupid was in there.

The two men stormed off into the crowd, muttering obscenities to each other in Italian. Melissa instantly sensed that the two men weren't fond of each other. In fact, they seemed uneasy.

"Bugs working. Audio and location being tracked. Well done," the voice in the earpiece crackled.

"The social media generation has made our line of work too easy," Melissa grinned.

The device that she'd planted on the man looked like a small piece of black plastic. It was roughly the size of a micro-SD card, yet capable of tracking locations and transmitting audio within a couple of kilometres with amazing clarity. It was a spy's tool.

Melissa Pythia was on-duty as an Australian spy.

Despite her odd last name, Melissa, or Mel as her friends called her, was born and bred in Sydney. At 28 years old, working undercover in Rome, her life looked vastly different to how it had four years earlier.

It was at the tender age of 24 that she'd tentatively put in an application for ASIO. The recruitment process was top secret, with applicants not even being allowed to tell their families they were applying.

Melissa had always lived with a particular fear, though not a unique one. In Sydney, people often ridiculed themselves for having 'Sydneyitis'. It was a term used to describe residents of the bustling metropolis who had no desire to leave it and expand their horizons.

Easy excuses like family, or working some uninspired job, allowed people to bottle their dreams and never pursue them. Instead, they'd commit to buying an overpriced house and being in debt forever. Whatever opportunities presented themselves could always be dismissed with the excuse of a home loan.

It was just one of the many masks for fear that Melissa was deeply embedded in it at the age of 24.

As her mid-20s approached, Melissa found herself asking the question 'why' a lot. Her friends were all shallow and toxic. They played games with each other's emotions for no reason. Her job left her hating life.

It was her grandfather that had come to her rescue.

"Dearest Melissa," the eccentric Mr Pythia had started, "why are you still here?"

"I don't know Grandpa," Melissa had shrugged. "Mum and Dad are here; my friends are here; I have a life."

"My girl, you don't have a life. You have an existence. Where is the adventure? Where is the challenge?"

"I'm happy with this."

"When was the last time you were scared, properly scared?"

"I don't know, never, I guess. Who wants to be scared?"

"When you are looking down the barrel of that gun, and you have to make a choice that matters, that's when the fear makes you feel alive! It gives you purpose!"

"You're so silly," Melissa said as she placed her hands on top of her grandfather's.

"It is true. You have a destiny about you. I saw it the moment you were born. You are smart and beautiful. Don't rot here waiting for life to come to you. It will never come."

"Grandpa, I'm fine!" she'd said, slightly exasperated.

Mr Pythia had just frowned at her. He leaned his head on her shoulder.

"When I was your age, I never said no. Promise me, next time something comes along that will change your life, that you will take it. Don't even think about it. Just do it. Shake things up. Us old people know a thing or two about living you know?"

"I know grandpa," Melissa smiled lovingly.

The next day, Grandpa Pythia suffered an unexpected heart

attack and died.

It was not long afterwards that an acquaintance of Melissa's mentioned that ASIO were recruiting.

She committed without thinking, just as her grandfather had asked.

Not only had Melissa been accepted, but she'd also excelled. So much so that she was folded into an experimental twelve-month course that combined the elements of ASIO's intelligence training with the in-the-field knowledge of an ASIS (Australian Secret Intelligence Service) agent. She was effectively trained to work for both organisations, but fell under the umbrella of ASIO.

Months of interviews and tests transformed into further months of fighting, weapons training and scenarios. She'd wanted to quit so many times it was beyond counting, but when she felt weak, she thought of her grandfather and kept going.

Eventually, she stood proud among her graduating class as a spy for the Australian Government.

They'd wasted no time in dropping her in the deep end. Right away she was sent to Afghanistan to do intel work for an Australian Army unit training local police.

Intelligence had picked up on several rebel groups attempting to infiltrate the surrounding countryside and build support.

It was a politically sensitive issue that required a delicate response. Should the people begin supporting militia groups in the region, it would've undone years of hard work.

Through extraordinary circumstances, Melissa had found the rebels. And as her grandfather had said, she'd never felt more fear than when that gun was pointed in her face. But she'd never been more alive. She was sharper, thought more clearly, and she fought her way out. In doing so, she managed to uncover a terrorist network far more extensive than imagined being established in the area.

For three blisteringly hot days she'd wandered the Afghani desert before being found.

Her work had earned her a medal and a lot of attention. She was quickly given her pick of international jobs. Still, it was the subsequent job in Lebanon that had put her on the path to Rome. A case of hers, that had been cold for a long time, had suddenly gone hot. Her golden sword was calling her again.

"Mel, Mel, HELLO?" the voice in the earpiece shouted.

"Ugh," Melissa thought.

The voice on the other end belonged to Matthew Pyne, the same man she'd rescued in Lebanon.

"Returning to your location," Melissa informed him.

She walked into the crowd then back up the street. Not far from the coffee shop was a square courtyard called the Piazza Capranica.

The courtyard was lined on all sides by multi-story buildings in various shades of orange. Sitting on the black pavement were rows of red rent-a-bikes. A few cars were parked in front of the bikes, restricting the narrow road space. Behind the vehicles was a beat-up white van.

Melissa quickly opened the sliding door and jumped inside.

It was cramped and hot. Right beside the door was a portable air conditioning unit humming weakly. A few computer screens were set up that were linked to small wireless cameras in the area.

Two men occupied the vehicle.

One was their IT guy, Teva Henry. He had brown skin, short black hair and was incredibly lean. He was Tahitian. He wore thick black headphones and was intently focused on the notepad in front of him.

The other was Matt Pyne with his gelled-up brown hair and square jaw. Matt could have passed for an American college football star in his younger days. He had a huge upper body and strength to match. He'd spent his 20s lifting weights and dieting. But now, as he approached his mid-30s, Matt was finding it harder to hide the gut that was poking out. He'd always had this dream about being on a mission and having an action-hero moment. It had never come to pass, but he frequently voiced what he would've done in many situations, had he been there.

Matt did have a barely-hidden arrogance about him that Melissa found both annoying and endearing.

"You didn't stuff it up," Matt raised his eyebrows at her. "Audio is coming through loud and clear."

"You thought I would?" Melissa responded coldly.

"It's been known to happen," Matt smirked, turning towards one of the screens.

Mel dismissed his snide remark and asked, "Do we have a name for our target yet?"

Teva answered without pausing his rapid scribbling, "No. Marcello Soncin has only referred to him as 'sir'."

"What do we know about Marcello?"

"Only what was in the initial briefing. He is the head of a major crime family. He deals in stolen artworks and relics."

"Calling our target 'sir' can only mean he is some kind of public official, surely?" Melissa asked.

"Or that he has some connection to the Catholic Church," Matt added.

"Quiet!" Teva hissed, as he stopped writing and paused on the conversation being played through his headphones.

Melissa's eyes wandered from Teva to the tracking bug's receiver on a nearby seat. They then travelled to a locked case propped against the rear doors. She knew that contained Matt's disassembled sniper rifle, a weapon she hoped they wouldn't have to use.

Melissa sat and waited for Teva to report back the contents of the conversation.

"Yep, it is the sword," Teva affirmed after a couple of minutes.

"The right sword?" Matt asked.

"Yes," Teva replied, "golden, otherworldly, when you are in its presence you have prophetic dreams. It is definitely what we are searching for."

Melissa grinned. Finally, her prized item from Lebanon was re-discovered.

"Melissa," Teva turned to her, "they are going to it now. Follow them. Be careful, the conversation is very tense. Something isn't right."

"Their destination?" Melissa asked, suddenly full of adrenaline.

"Somewhere near the Basilica delle Guglie Gemelle. About 20 minutes from here on foot."

Melissa slipped off her shoes and pulled a pair of runners

from a nearby bag.

"Are they walking?" she asked.

"No, cars are getting them."

"Right, I'll meet you two there. With the traffic, it will be faster for me to go on foot."

She couldn't wait for the van to navigate the small streets and endless traffic. There was something about that sword that called to her, and this time she was going to find out what it was.

She hopped out the door and began jogging down the street. She knew the way.

With her big hat, love-heart glasses and flowing white dress, she looked slightly ridiculous as she pushed past people and dodged cars.

She turned onto a side-street that took her through a narrow alley. The doors on the bottom level of a multi-story apartment block were all old and splintered. It looked like the kind of place that invited trouble.

An unfamiliar voice called out to her as she passed.

"You only have a matter of hours, dear!"

Melissa turned and looked back down the alley.

An old woman had emerged from one of the ground-level apartments. She was hunched and seemed positively ancient. Her face looked like the caricature of a witch, with a long-pointed nose and bug-eyes that seemed too big for her skull, not to mention the wide mouth that was devoid of most of its teeth. Across her shoulders and back was a white shawl covered with strange markings.

"What?" Melissa called back to her.

Using a wooden cane, the woman hobbled forwards. Melissa looked at her wristwatch anxiously.

The old crone looked Melissa dead in the eyes. "It is not the past. It is happening right now, only 1682 years ago. You will see soon. It is your destiny to find him."

"Find who?" Mel asked, completely bewildered.

"The owner of the golden sword."

The old woman took the shawl from across her shoulders and held it before Melissa. The strange symbols stretching across it seemed to be growing clearer by the second.

"What is this?" Melissa asked, rubbing her eyes.

"There is something in your blood that speaks to the runes, girl. What is your name? I felt your presence as you passed."

"Maggie Steeleheart," Melissa answered. She offered her undercover name. The old woman didn't buy it for a second.

"Your real name?"

Melissa felt strangely compelled to answer. "Melissa Pythia."

"Pythia…" the old woman chuckled to herself.

"Yes, I know, it means some old Greek thing." People in Europe often commented on her odd family name.

"More than some old Greek thing. He will be confused when you find him. He will need the sword; you will need the sword. Only you can pull him from the fire. Only you will be able to see."

"Pull who? See what?" Melissa asked, frustrated.

"The golden god."

"Melissa, can you hear me, they are moving," Matthew Pyne's voice crackled through the earpiece.

Melissa turned to leave, but the woman grabbed her by the hand. She felt her skin burn.

"Ouch!" Melissa said. She looked at the back of her hand, one of the strange shapes from the shawl was burned onto it. Her skin was sizzling.

Matt's voice buzzed in again. Melissa didn't have time for this.

"I have to go," she said as she began running down the alleyway.

The old woman called after her, "It is happening now! The gates will open for the ferryman on the black river soon! You must get the sword! Fate and doom will be your eyes as history unfurls before you!"

Melissa turned a corner and the words faded from earshot.

"The ferryman on the black river? What?"

Melissa made a mental note. She'd need to follow up on how some random old woman knew about the golden relic she was in Rome to recover. The whole encounter had been very suspicious, yet it was like there was a small voice in Melissa's brain telling her to let it go.

The old woman wasn't her concern right now. She had a mission to complete.

CHAPTER THREE

A TETHER TO THE PAST

Melissa considered Rome to be a city of wonders, in no small part due to the abundance of ruins scattered throughout its heart. Ruins that she'd been eager to see for some time.

Prime real-estate was left off the market for the preservation of the thousands of years of history buried under its citizens' feet. The city that sat as the heart of one of humanity's greatest empires still had many secrets to be unearthed.

Left off the list of Rome's usual tourist sites was the Basilica of the Twin Spires. Namely, because it was not ancient or finished. Built during World War II, the basilica was designed to look old. It was built in the style of Rome's ruins, with typical double colonnades and a semi-circular apse.

What made it unique was the two tall spires that sat on either side of the main building. They were intended to be twin clock towers, but the work was never completed.

Allied bombs fell on the basilica during its construction in 1944, and it never recommenced. Now, just off from the bustling city centre, sat ruins that were rarely visited or acknowledged.

The Basilica of the Twin Spires, or the Basilica delle Guglie Gamelle as it was called locally, was nothing more than an eyesore. But for less-than-reputable folk who wished to conduct shady business dealings just out of the public eye, it was a god-send; save for one glaring weakness.

A great big bomb hole in the central structure was overlooked by the right tower. Should someone climb the tower, they had a front-row seat to watch whatever was going on inside the main structure.

This was rarely an issue, as neither tower had a door and the insides were hollow, save for a platform at the highest level. There was no way up.

ASIO was well aware that the Basilica delle Guglie Gamelle was used for criminal dealings.

Being so close to the heart of the city, it just made business that little bit easier for those who didn't want to travel to secret hiding places in the countryside.

Melissa and Matt had visited the site in the days prior and prepared it for ASIO use.

Melissa had climbed the tower up and down, placing almost invisible hand-holds all the way up. They looked like brown lumps of clay clinging to the tower's side.

A hole had been knocked into the upper level large enough for a person to crawl into.

To anyone who'd be bothered to notice, it just looked like natural wear-and-tear at the top of the tower. On the side that faced the basilica, a few select bricks had been removed to create a clear view down. It had been a labour-intensive day and fortunately for Melissa, it was going to pay off now.

Melissa looked like an oddly-dressed version of Spiderman as she quickly scaled the tower and crawled inside.

It was just in the nick of time too, as she heard the low rumblings of vehicles pulling up below. She'd just beat them. Thank god she hadn't given the bizarre old woman in the alley any further time.

Thanks to the tracking bug she'd planted, she could tap into the connection and hear every word of the meeting below, all through her phone. Admittedly, the technology wasn't super-reliable. Teva and Matt would have an easier time with the bug's receiver in the van.

Melissa looked down through the gaping hole in the basilica's roof and saw men already inside. Two bald muscular security guards waited with their hands behind their backs. In between them was a formidable black case.

The security guards didn't move an inch as Marcello Soncin strolled into the room.

He nodded curtly at the guards, then turned to face the man who'd accompanied him.

Melissa replaced the wireless earbuds in her ears and listened in to the conversation through her phone.

"Is that it?" the man with the slicked-back hair asked.

Marcello Soncin nodded.

"The price has been agreed," the man nodded. "Let me see it?"

Marcello coughed violently before speaking. "I have heard stories that this weapon gives funny dreams. This sword... it has a strange power. When you hold it, you can see things. Visions of the future."

"Allow me to hold it and see if these rumours are accurate," the man replied.

Melissa found it incredible odd that the two native Italian men were speaking in English.

The buyer walked towards the case. The two burly security guards each unlocked a clasp and opened the box.

Melissa gasped.

It was there.

The golden sword.

Marcello stepped to the side as the buyer leaned over and gripped its hilt. He tried to raise it up and slash it through the air a few times, but struggled with its weight.

The sword hummed briefly as it sliced through empty space.

"Fascinating..." the man muttered.

Mel watched the sword gleam as it moved.

Visions flashed through her mind again. She saw a river. She saw soldiers, flying through the air... Winged men in chariots and a monstrous guard dog attacking them...

Melissa slapped herself. She had to focus.

All of a sudden, the man dropped the sword and fell to his knees. He looked straight up at the ruined roof of the basilica.

After a moment, he stood back up, looking shaken.

He picked the sword up and quickly dropped it back into the case.

"Lock it up Marcello, have your men put it in the back of my car. I need to make a quick call."

"Can we tap his phone call?" Melissa asked, quickly swapping back to the earpiece that was connecting her to Matt and Teva.

"Impossible," Teva replied, his voice mingled with static.

The man with the slicked-back hair disappeared from Melissa's view as he exited the building.

Her vantage point allowed Melissa to see a boy of about ten emerge from the shadows and follow the buyer.

The buyer spoke in quick Italian. The bug picked it up clearly, but the conversation would need to be translated. Melissa watched as the small boy ran back in toward Marcello Soncin.

Marcello leaned down as the boy whispered into his ears.

Curiously, he then commanded his thugs to put the black case down.

"Melissa," the voice of Matt came through the earpiece.

"Go ahead," Melissa whispered.

"We are close to your location and noticing a lot of suspicious vehicles around here. Based on what data I can get; they seem to belong to the Soncin crime family. There are also others; black troop carriers with armed men. I think both sides in this deal have a contingency plan. Don't reveal yourself."

"Copy," Melissa affirmed.

Internally, she was considering her options. This golden sword had disappeared entirely in 2017. It was gone without a trace; no leads, nothing. It was of particular interest to several Australian Government departments. This may be her only chance to get a hold of it and she wasn't going to waste it.

The buyer walked back into the basilica, looking annoyed at the fact the relic wasn't in his car yet.

"My grandson, he listens," Marcello growled, stroking the boy's hair. "On the phone, you said the value of this sword is almost priceless. A real treasure. I fear, once again, we have been underpaid."

"Do not cross me," the buyer stated. "A deal has been made, see it through."

"I wish to change this deal," Marcello snapped.

Melissa knew things were about to spiral out of control.

Armed members of the Soncin family were springing from every crack and crevice of the unfinished church.

The Soncin's themselves were easily recognisable. They wore dark expensive suits. Other men, wearing jeans and polo shirts were also appearing. They were hired goons kept on the Soncin's payroll.

The men surrounded the buyer and pointed their weapons at him.

"This has escalated bizarrely quickly," Melissa whispered.

"You've got more incoming," Matt warned through the earpiece. "I think I know who they are. Gladius Vaticanus. A shadowy paramilitary group linked to the Church. I think these criminals have picked a bad day for a dodgy deal."

"Enzo," Marcello Soncin started as Melissa hastily changed over earbuds again, "did I not warn you that the next time you tried to manipulate me in terms of the price you pay in our dealings, that I would make an example of you?"

The buyer, apparently named Enzo, looked from side to side. "It appears as if you were always going to make an example of this transaction."

Marcello Soncin then asked a strange question, "What did you see when you held the sword?"

"I saw a great dragon with many heads burning the world to ash. What did you see, old man?"

"I never touched it. My sons saw extraordinary things. Things that will come to be. I do not need a prophetic sword to see the future. You have used us to do your dirty work for far too long, at too low a price. I foresaw that this time would be no different."

"You think you are a big fish in Rome, Marcello. But there is no bigger fish than the Catholic Church. We are sharks."

Gunshots rang out.

Somewhere, at the edge of the ruins, members of the Gladius Vaticanus had taken the goons of the Soncin crime family by surprise.

Melissa turned and looked out the hole on the other side of the tower.

Men in military apparel were moving in formation towards the basilica.

The soldiers were dressed in dark grey overalls, with black body armour fastened tightly to their chests. They had black helmets on with two built-in rings in front of the eyes.

Melissa quickly determined the rings must be some kind of augmented reality display. These guys were well equipped.

Because the crumbling Basilica of the Twin Spires was considered a dangerous ruin, the alleyways that entered into the area were blocked off with moveable fences. The only road access was impeded by a thin swinging gate locked with a chain and padlock, which the Soncins had the key.

The structure was on a flat expanse of land within a circle of other buildings that hid it from mostly from the publics' view, other than the twin towers that peaked up. Pieces of concrete and other debris from the bombings had been flung across the dead grass and lay scattered about the area. It was that maze of concrete chunks that the Gladius Vaticanus used to mask their approach.

Small gunfights began breaking out on all sides of the basilica. Melissa saw two men collapse at the base of her tower.

Melissa thought quickly. She ditched her comical sunglasses and hat, and pulled her dress off. She was wearing black leggings and a sporty crop top underneath it, which would have to do. She didn't want her billowing flowery dress inhibiting her.

She turned back towards the hole in the roof.

The man named Enzo had drawn an enormous pistol. It was a huge silver Desert Eagle. He started firing deafening shots.

Marcello's two bodyguards took cover behind some old pillars and periodically peered out to return fire. Marcello himself had already vanished from view.

"Melissa," Matthew's voice spoke into her ear, "we have to move the van. Police are arriving. They are blocking off the area;

they are on someone's side here, probably the Vatican's. Get out of there."

"The sword is sitting in a black case, unguarded. I can get it."

"Abort mission, Melissa," Matthew said sternly. "This is insane, we don't know what is going on. If you get caught, we are going to have a hell of time getting you out."

Melissa could hear the nearby wailing of police sirens.

Plumes of smoke were emerging across the battlefield. The pseudo-soldiers had smoke grenades.

Melissa was committed. Perhaps she was being stubborn or foolhardy, but destiny was drawing her to that sword.

She flung herself out of the tower and began crawling down, a little too recklessly. She almost slipped and fell several times.

Melissa reached the ground and backed herself against a chunk of debris. She was weaponless, but she had other advantages. She was short and quick.

A plume of grey smoke appeared just ahead of her. Through the corner of her eyes, she saw two of the soldiers hastily striding towards it. They were slightly hunched and their guns were up.

"Breathe," Melissa told herself.

She inhaled deeply, then moved.

She darted towards another pile of rubble.

Gunfire rang out and Melissa heard someone nearby moan and collapse.

She peaked her head out and saw a man in a Hawaiian shirt lying in a pool of his own blood.

His pistol was now lying in the grass beside him. Melissa reached for it.

She racked the gun once and a bullet flew out the top.

The entrance to the basilica was too hotly contested; there had to be another way in. As it was a wreck, she figured there'd surely be a hole to crawl through.

Melissa gritted her teeth and moved again. The side of the basilica was about ten metres away.

A spray of gunfire flew overhead, missing her by millimetres. She collapsed flat into the grass and paused.

More screams and shots echoed out.

She heard a gruff Italian voice just ahead. A man, with blood dripping from his forehead, approached her with his pistol raised. He was stumbling and looked dazed. Something must have hit him hard.

Melissa rolled to the side and pushed herself up.

The man started firing wildly at her. Bullets flew into the grass causing small explosions of dirt to erupt.

Melissa pointed her newly acquired pistol at him, but before she had the chance to fire, the man was blown off his feet by a powerful shotgun blast. One of the Gladius Vaticanus, running from the main battle, had shot him right in the back.

The dead Soncin slumped forward. The barrel of the soldier's shotgun still smoking as he looked at Melissa, confused.

Mel could see the faint holographic blue in front of his right eye from the AR glasses.

He pointed the shotgun at her and Melissa reacted quickly, firing two shots. They both connected with his bullet-proof vest. He wouldn't die, but Melissa knew he'd be seriously bruised.

From a nearby smoke cloud, two Soncins emerged, crashing-tackling the injured soldier.

Melissa ran for the side of the basilica and pressed herself against it.

She moved towards the back of the building, sticking close to the wall. The bulk of the fighting was toward the entrance.

Much to her annoyance, she couldn't find a single hole she could fit through to get inside.

She kept going, scanning the walls up and down.

Something caught her eye. A strange shape etched into the wall. It was similar to what was drawn on the weird old woman's shawl from the alley.

Melissa touched the carving.

The wall collapsed in a cloud of dust and a man-sized hole opened up to her.

"Success," Melissa thought.

With another surge of adrenaline, she ran into the building, weaving around the simple columns.

The entire basilica was basically just one big empty room, comprising only of rubble and pillars.

Before long, she saw the hole in the roof open wide above her. The central area was empty. All of the fighting had moved outside.

She closed her eyes. When she'd first encountered the golden sword in Lebanon, it was like it had called to her.

It was a long shot, but maybe she could feel it again…

"You, girl."

Melissa felt cold steel press against the back of her head.

"Don't shoot," Melissa bargained instinctively. "We can

talk about this."

She heard a click.

The man had pulled the trigger! But his magazine was empty.

Melissa spun on the spot and kicked the gun out of his hand. She then pointed her own weapon at him.

She looked at the fear in the sweaty man's eyes. He had one hand pressed to his stomach in an attempt to stop the blood from an unseen wound pouring out.

"Where is the sword?" Melissa hissed fiercely.

"Marcello took it," he said in accented English. His eyes were wide and his voice pleading.

"Where?"

"The sewers," he stammered.

Melissa launched a front kick at the criminal. It connected directly with his bullet wound. He screeched in pain and fell back.

Soldiers of the Gladius Vaticanus burst through the entry door. They targeted Melissa with their laser-pointed rifles and shouted in Italian.

Melissa moved quickly.

"Marcello can't have taken the sword," she thought. *"He is so old and frail he could barely lift it. His goons must have taken it."*

She thought back to the bald-headed security guards.

There was nowhere to go in the basilica. Melissa ducked for cover behind a half-built altar sitting in a dark corner of the room.

She could hear the quick stomps of the soldiers' boots as they ran for her.

"This is not your doom..."

Melissa swivelled her head wildly. Who'd said that?

Then she noticed, not more than a couple of metres ahead, that there was a large crack in the ground.

And she could also hear what sounded like sloshing. Someone was moving through water beneath them!

If Marcello's goons had escaped into the sewer system with the sword, then they must be right beneath her. The entrance had to be close, but with soldiers closing in, Melissa didn't have time to search for it.

Just as the two soldiers approached the ruined altar, Melissa sprang up and launched herself across it.

She flew between the two soldiers in a kind-of aerial cartwheel. They were taken completely unaware by this sudden display of unexpected acrobatics.

Melissa quickly plucked a grenade from one of the soldier's belts and pulled the pin. The two men dived for cover, half-expecting Melissa to blow herself up. Instead, she lobbed the grenade towards the crack in the ground.

It exploded with deafening force.

Mel ducked behind the ruined altar to avoid the wave of shrapnel.

Before the dust had a chance to settle, she was moving again.

The hole in the ground was now big enough for her to fit through and, without thinking, Melissa lowered herself down, supporting her entire bodyweight with her hands. Releasing her grip, she dropped into the sewer.

CHAPTER FOUR

A GOD OF DREAMS

- SEPTEMBER 27 -
ROME - THE SEWERS

Melissa wiped the sweat from her brow. It had been a lucky escape, aided by the soldier's poor reaction times. She grimaced as she processed her new circumstances. This wasn't some spectacular Roman or Etruscan sewer system. It was modern; it was a circular grey tube and it was gross. The dirty brown water rose to her shins as she sloshed forward.

Now the most pressing question she had was: did she go left or right?

A booming Italian voice answered it for her.

Laughter echoed down the tube from the right. The sound was almost jovial; as if the explosion from the grenade had caused no concern at all. They did sound quite far ahead already, so Melissa gritted her teeth and began the journey towards them.

She knew the goons wouldn't be moving fast, as they'd be carrying the black case with them. It was heavy and awkwardly shaped. They'd have to walk front-to-back in the narrow space to transport it successfully. And in that case was her prize—the golden sword of prophecy. The same sword that was stolen after she'd discovered it in the terrorist compound.

After her return from Lebanon in 2017, she'd recorded her experience with the sword; how she'd sensed it through the wall, the golden light and the visions. She didn't think anyone would ever read any of it, and if they did, they'd probably just put it down to some kind of trauma.

She was wrong, however. The first to make contact was a man named Brett Sayer, the head of an obscure government department Melissa had never heard of before. They were called the AST, or the Australian Supernatural Taskforce. They were a highly-classified, secretive group that responded to paranormal threats. Naturally, Melissa found this ridiculous. Still, her experience with the golden sword generated enough doubt that she signed on to do their two-week training course. She learned that how the AST worked was that when a response was needed, security-vetted personnel from the police, ASIO, ASIS and the military were called on for temporary secondments. Normally it was just intelligence gathering, witness interviews and paperwork. Still, in rare instances, they did have actual jobs to attend.

Before this deployment to Rome, Melissa had been working with the AST on a case in north-eastern Australia. A monster had appeared in Far North Queensland that Melissa had been helping to take down, until the call to go to Rome came in. It turned out what the taskforce did wasn't so farfetched and their interest in the golden sword was completely reasonable.

After her return from Lebanon and the initial contact from the AST, the next to enquire had been a professor of history, anthropology, languages and archaeology, Doctor Malcolm Selleck.

He was young for a professor, in his late thirties and extremely fit. He was also signed up to work for the AST, however, it had been ASIO that called him in to evaluate the sword.

Doctor Selleck had taken one look and then launched a barrage of questions at Melissa about where it was found and how it was hidden. He'd called it a 'historical marvel' and a work of such craftsmanship that it was almost alien. Melissa suspected the professor had a bit of an obsessive personality the way he gushed about it.

Doctor Selleck had taken the sword back to the Australian National Museum in Canberra for further study. Then, one fateful night, the sword was stolen from the vault. Security footage captured nothing. The guards saw nothing. It was as if the sword had simply vanished.

Melissa had warned against moving the priceless object from ASIO's secure headquarters. But to them, it was just some artefact.

Strangely, she'd had dreams that somebody would steal it. But obviously she didn't report them for fear of seeming crazy.

The expert thievery attracted a lot of attention from ASIO.

The response was less about the artefact and more about the organisation's wounded pride.

When at last, not more than a few weeks ago, word that a young man in a bar in Rome had been talking about prophetic visions, prophetic visions from a golden sword, the spy organisation reacted immediately.

Melissa got the call. She hopped on a plane from Cairns to Singapore, then straight from Singapore to Rome. Rendezvousing with ASIS's man on the ground, Matt Pyne, they were joined shortly after by Teva, and it hadn't taken long to deduce that the sword was in the possession of a local crime family being sold to a mysterious buyer.

Their goal was to retrieve it.

Through great effort, and some luck, they'd encountered a guy, who knew a guy, who knew another guy, who knew that a buy was set up with a suspected member of the Soncins. It would most likely take place somewhere hidden in the city and they'd also deduced that the buyer had to be an influential figure. Now, thanks to the appearance of the Gladius Vaticanus paramilitary force, Melissa was all but certain it was the Vatican.

Now, she was here, stomping through water that contained... well she didn't even want to think about what was floating around her.

Trying to move silently through the sewer was nigh on impossible, so she didn't bother. She moved as quickly as she could towards the echoing voices.

During her acrobatics across the ruined altar, she'd lost the gun she'd stolen. Weaponless and wearing nothing but work-out attire, the odds were not in Melissa's favour.

The voices ahead stopped.

Melissa froze.

She heard a splash. They must've lowered the case into the water.

Creeping forward, she rounded a small bend. Before her stood the broad back of a bald-headed guard. Melissa didn't know what to do now. She scanned around, seeing nothing but dirty water.

Apparently, the lead man needed to relieve himself. She had precious little time to make a move.

She heard the sound of a zipper go up and the talking recommenced.

Melissa moved forward, crouched, until she was directly behind the tail-end man. Carefully, she raised her right hand and pushed the little tab forward on his holster. It was a safety mechanism designed to stop an attacker just ripping a pistol out and using it against its owner. She did it so slowly there wasn't even a click. The man noticed nothing.

She then gripped the butt of the weapon and drew it from the holster entirely.

Melissa was armed again.

She stood up and flipped the gun around in her hand, then, with a mighty WHACK, slammed it into the back of the guard's head. He collapsed like a pile of bricks.

Upon hearing the sound, the other man turned and instantly drew his pistol.

Melissa threw herself backwards as three rounds came flying

at her. She fired a volley of shots at the man, two of which connected with his chest.

Melissa plunged into the shallow water as the man looked down at himself, then fell forward.

A guilty feeling rose in Melissa's chest. She didn't like killing, and this one seemed preventable. Still, it was part of her job.

She turned the man she'd knocked out over, so he didn't drown in the water.

Melissa shuddered as her wet hair flopped over her face.

The top of the black case was sitting just above the water level. It was still unlocked from earlier.

Melissa flung it open.

There it was again, over a year since it'd been stolen—the golden sword.

She gazed at its mesmerising gleam. What was it about this sword that spoke to her so much? It was almost as if it whispered to her. She reached down and touched it.

Instantly she withdrew her hand.

Visions swept across her mind. She saw a massive three-headed dog, ghosts of dead armoured men battling with flying winged soldiers and more importantly, she saw the sword in the hands of a golden man.

She closed her fingers around the grip and pulled the sword from the case.

A voice echoed in her mind, "*It is happening right now, only 1682 years ago…*"

She lost her mind to a strange fog.

The flashing images began again. Melissa saw some kind of

giant monster fighting a dragon. She saw a great black castle, unlike anything in the world, melting in a torrent of flame. A six-winged angel, a different one this time, was trapped in the dark and couldn't see. Slowly, fire was rising around him. The angel's face was distorting. His wings were becoming red. Twisting spiral horns grew from his head as his teeth extended to fangs. He turned and looked at Melissa, who was ripped suddenly from the vision.

Though, she wasn't standing in the sewer anymore. Instead, Melissa found herself in an empty land of purple twilight. She pinched herself to make sure she wasn't dreaming.

"What the hell is this?" Melissa asked the glittering expanse of nothingness around her.

A slender man with a long black pony-tail appeared before her, causing Melissa to cautiously step back. She could see odd movements in his pitch-black strands of hair. It looked like galaxies were swirling and comets with long icy tails were moving from strand to strand across his head. It was like this man was made of living art.

He looked at her curiously.

"A dreamer?" he asked in a sleepy voice.

"Ah, no," Melissa replied hesitantly.

"No, no, you are quite right," the man said, almost sounding bored. "This is something else. Perhaps a divine artefact? Not many of those left…"

"A golden sword," Melissa interjected.

"Oh yes, that makes sense, the God of Prophecy and Knowledge and all that. Do you know that prophecy is, in many ways, a dream? A dream of the future. It must, at last, be time... this is very exciting."

"Time for...?"

The man with the cosmic hair looked at Melissa with a piercing gaze.

"You must be an oracle," he concluded.

"What?"

"I suppose they call them prophets these days."

"You are saying a lot, but not saying much," Melissa commented indignantly.

"Well, this golden sword you've found. It is an object that belongs to a god. A god whose story you will learn soon. A god who has been missing for a long, long time... I can sense the tides of fate moving around you, even now..."

The strange man waved his hand and summoned a glittering purple cloud, which he promptly sat down on.

"Let me explain, in brief. A divine artefact will always have some kind of effect on humans around it. But for us to have this conversation, you must, in some way, be directly linked to it. Delphi would make sense."

Melissa shook her head. She looked at the swirling galaxies in the man's hair and figured she must be hallucinating. She had to be... but then, something he'd said made sense.

"The sword... it has kind of... called to me," Melissa stammered.

"I imagine you sometimes have prophetic dreams. More frequent and with greater clarity in the presence of that artefact?"

"Yes..." Melissa nodded.

"You must claim the sword and take it to where he will emerge. Let your dreams guide you."

The intelligence officer brain in Melissa was working overtime trying to interpret all this cryptic speak. It didn't help that the cloudy plain she was standing on was dulling her senses.

"What is your name?" Melissa asked.

"Morpheus," the man answered with a smile.

"What are you?"

"A god."

"What, like THE god?"

"There is no 'the god'. I'm afraid we are out of time. Heed my words, as only you have the sight required to see the Golden God. Take the sword and free him from the fire. Oh, and I hope your head doesn't hurt too much."

Melissa felt a sharp pain in the back of her skull and a warm trickle of blood started running down her neck.

As Melissa fell, she felt the arms of a soldier embrace her. He picked her up and slung her over his shoulder.

A second blurry soldier fished for the sword in the water and picked it up. He then pointed his pistol at the unconscious security guard floating on his back and fired.

Everything went black.

• • • • •

MELISSA GROANED AS SHE opened her eyes. The first thing she noticed was the coarse feeling of the rope binding her hands together. She then felt the hardwood of the chair to which she was tied.

Next, she noticed the breeze. She was outdoors.

Warm air flowed across her face. She could see that her hair was ratty and tangled, and stinking from the sewer water. Her clothes were still slightly moist. It must have been a while. She blinked several times in quick succession.

She recognised where she was, and for a moment, couldn't believe it.

Melissa was seated under the viewing platform on the lowest level of the Colosseum.

To her left and her right, not far ahead, she saw the huge rusted steel beams that held up the platform.

Every day, tourists in their thousands wandered about above her, gazing in awe at the wondrous structure around them. Directly in front of Mel were two rows of ruins sitting on patches of dirt and green grass. The ancient constructions had moss growing all over them.

She knew she was looking at the once subterranean tunnels of the hypogeum.

Now crumbling, long ago they'd housed giant cages for fearsome beasts and chambers for warriors ready to embrace death in battle.

She could see the sides of the Colosseum stretching up, illuminated in lights from outside. The towering walls lined with archways baffled the imagination. A person could get lost in the sheer history and scale of the place. But Melissa wasn't here to sight-see. She was a prisoner, and her senses were coming back to her.

"Really, this is a stupid place to put me, isn't it? There are people everywhere outside!" she called loudly, throwing caution to the wind.

Almost immediately, a pair of gloved hands stuffed a wad of material into her mouth and then wrapped the same stuff around her face.

She'd been gagged.

Melissa tried to speak, but all she could do was make muffled noises. She could hear footsteps approaching from behind. A man stepped gracefully in front of her. It was Enzo, the buyer.

"You bumped into me at the Pantheon," he said in his heavy Italian accent. "I do not forget a face."

Melissa struggled at her bindings.

More footsteps approached.

Two soldiers emerged from the shadows around her. She could see the blue of their augmented reality glasses.

"Facial recognition technology built right into the helmets. Good, no?" Enzo grinned smugly. "I'd ask you who you are and who you work for, but I'd just be wasting time. Now that we have seen your face, we will find you."

He motioned to one of his soldiers, who approached until he was uncomfortably close. He clenched his fist and punched her square in the face. The force was so strong that Melissa's chair was knocked backwards. She felt her nose break and blood stream down her jaw.

An unseen soldier behind Melissa righted her chair.

Melissa felt woozy. Tears welled up in her eyes. The pain was immense.

Enzo continued as if the vicious attack had never happened. "I assumed you were one of the Soncins. You look the part. But no, you are a government agent, aren't you?"

Melissa could see information whizzing across the holographic display over the soldier's right eye. He hit a button on the side of his helmet, and Enzo's phone pinged.

"Ah, let us see…" Enzo said as he scrolled through his phone. "Maggie Steeleheart, teacher, Australian. Unlikely."

Warm blood was beginning to drip from Melissa's chin.

"Thank god you aren't a Soncin. We will treat you a bit nicer than that criminal scum."

The second soldier walked over. He released his rifle to its sling, then with a thundering CRACK, threw a roundhouse punch into Melissa's jaw. She almost felt it dislocate. It was all she could do to stop from blacking out.

"Take off her gag," Enzo ordered.

The gag was pulled from her face and thrown onto the ground. It was now soaked in blood.

"Talk!" Enzo commanded.

"I need the golden sword to free the Golden God…." she muttered. She was delirious. Melissa looked up and saw a blue-shirted security guard walking through the ruins with a flashlight. He paused and looked at the group under the viewing platform, then simply kept on moving.

Enzo took great pleasure in watching the hope fade from Melissa's eyes.

"Do you know who we are?"

"Gladius Vaticanus. Italian sell swords," Melissa spat, clarity returning to her.

A fire flared to life in Enzo's eyes.

"We are not Italian! We ARE ROMAN!"

Melissa shrugged. She'd managed to slip a thumb free of her bindings. She had skinny wrists while the rope was thick and heavy. Small movements were quickly loosening it. She just had to make sure the soldier behind didn't see.

"You work for the Vatican. I know about your little group," Melissa stated, shooting Enzo a stare so cold it could freeze water.

"We are what remains of the Praetorian Guard. Only there are no more emperors. We serve the Pope. The divine voice of God on Earth, who sits in the heart of Rome."

"Funny. You make it sound grand. The truth is you are just well-funded mercenaries who are at the whip and call of your masters in the clergy. All you do is maintain the balance of power between mafia families in Rome. You are nothing!" Melissa spat blood at Enzo's feet.

Enzo's eyes bulged and nostrils flared. This was not a man who was used to being insulted. He raised his hand to slap Melissa's already battered face, but stopped himself.

"I get carried away sometimes," he chuckled.

He then drew his big silver Desert Eagle and pointed it at Melissa's head.

A gunshot boomed through the quiet Colosseum.

CHAPTER FIVE

GLADIUS VATICANUS

I
t wasn't the powerful boom from Enzo's handgun that rang through the Colosseum. It was quieter. The hiss of the silenced sniper was followed by Enzo's groan as the bullet ripped through his chest. He held his hands over the wound in disbelief, then collapsed to the ground.

The soldiers fumbled their guns, taking cover as they scanned the auditorium for the shooter. The man who'd been positioned behind Melissa ran forward and grabbed Enzo under the arms. Before he could drag him a step, another shot zoomed out. It pierced the soldier's body armour and he collapsed next to his boss.

Pressed up against one of the rusted steel beams, the soldier who'd punched Melissa spotted the sniper. He flung himself around and crouched, only to be hit with unexpected gunfire from behind.

Melissa had wriggled free of her bindings.

She picked up the rifle from the deceased man and turned it on the other two soldiers. They collapsed into crimson pools of blood.

Melissa saw the flash of a muzzle above. Hidden in the upper rung of the ancient spectator seats, kneeling behind the old Roman brickwork, was Matthew Pyne with his sniper.

The three soldiers who'd been guarding Melissa were the only ones privileged enough to watch Enzo's display, but Melissa knew there were others nearby. The local police were potentially on the side of the Gladius Vaticanus too.

They had to get away from here.

Melissa looked around. Her head was spinning. She gingerly touched her nose. The instant burst of pain confirmed what she already knew; it was broken.

She studied the rifle in her hands. It was equipped with a holographic sight and silencer. It looked brand new and was of a make and model she didn't recognise.

Melissa scanned the area. It occurred to her that whatever path had been used to drag her beneath the viewing platform was almost certainly guarded.

Her best chance of escape was out through one of the tourist entrances. It was unlikely they'd have armed men stationed in plain sight of the public. She walked toward the nearest platform support beam. Slinging the rifle across her back, she began to climb.

At the same time, Matt was rushing towards the viewing platform. He'd packed his sniper into its case and was carrying it as he clambered down the ruins.

Melissa felt jagged pieces of rusted metal cut her hands as she scaled upwards. Matt quickly appeared above her, leaning down to watch her climb. He held out a hand for her, and she took it gratefully.

It had been a hell of a day so far. Matt pulled her over the railing into the viewing area. The hypogeum stretched out below her, though she could hardly appreciate the beauty and the history right now.

"Why would they bring me here?" she asked Matt.

"The Gladius Vaticanus think they are ancient Roman soldiers. They do all of their dirty work at historical sites."

"How do you know that?"

"Me and Teva gathered what intel we could while we searched for you. Luckily the tracking bug was still on the buyer."

"This seems like a lot of effort for an ancient artefact," Melissa said quietly.

"Yeah, something else is going on here, I think. Or, that golden sword is more important than we realise. Come on, it won't be long before someone checks on them down there. I think they wanted some private time with you."

"Where are we going?" Melissa asked.

"Out of Rome," Matt answered. "Too many deaths. We need to distance ourselves from this."

"We need to get the sword," Melissa interjected abruptly.

"You are in no state-"

"We NEED to get the sword. Something is happening. I can't explain it."

Matt looked at her, confused.

Melissa didn't say anything further. She touched the back of her hand. It was still tingling from where the funny old woman had burned that symbol into it. Only now, there wasn't a mark to be seen. And there was no way she was going to tell her colleagues about speaking to the self-proclaimed god named Morpheus.

"Teva," Matt spoke into his earpiece, "do you have a location on the sword."

"It's in a nearby vehicle. I believe they're waiting for the buyer; he must be hand delivering it," Teva replied. Melissa had lost her earpiece, but could just make out Teva's voice through Matt's.

"Where?"

"There is a bus stop on the Piazza del Colosseo, to your right. Three vehicles are waiting there."

Mel looked around alarmed. "There was a security guard!"

"He's been subdued," Matt grinned.

Teva's voice re-entered the conversation, "Armed men are leaving the cars. You need to move. Take the main tourist exit, up by the spectator seats."

They didn't need to be told twice.

"If you didn't look so bad, we could blend in as tourists on a night-time stroll," Matt stated in a poor attempt at humour.

Melissa scowled.

Before long, the pair found themselves behind a thin black fence that usually funnelled lines of tourists into the attraction.

The entry gate was locked, and the Colosseum's surroundings were virtually devoid of people.

Melissa wondered just how long she'd been out for. It had to be quite late at night.

Fortunately, the main gate was locked with a simple padlock, and Matt had lock picking equipment on him. It only took him a moment to swing the gate open and re-lock it behind them.

Before the pair stretched a paved courtyard with sparse trees and silver light poles equipped with speakers.

To her left, not far away, Melissa saw the Arch of Constantine. It was lit up with bright lights.

Melissa knew of Constantine. He was the first Roman Emperor to convert to Christianity. That seemed important right now, though Melissa couldn't figure out why she felt that it was.

On the other side of the courtyard, blocked by another fence, was a tall ruined wall. It was in that direction that tourists found the Foro Romano, or the Roman Forum. Another piece of life from a bygone age. Again, for some unexplainable reason, it felt like an important place to be.

"If we go right and follow the circumference of the Colosseum, the cars should be there."

"And then what?" Melissa asked impatiently. "We can't exactly just walk up and ask for the sword."

Matt paused to ponder this.

"Move!" Melissa commanded, as she grabbed Matt by the shirt and dragged him into the shadows of scaffolding to their right.

Two soldiers came walking up.

It seemed the Gladius Vaticanus were bold enough to stride around in public with weapons this late at night.

As they approached, Melissa heard them loudly conversing in English. Apparently, the events in the Colosseum had so far gone unnoticed.

"... said to give him at least thirty minutes in there."

"What is this artefact anyway?"

"Some kind of sword. The boss is delivering it in person to the cardinal."

"What about Marcello Soncin?"

"No word, he escaped somehow..."

The voices trailed off as the two men continued walking around the perimeter.

"We can't let that sword get into the Vatican vaults. We will never see it again!" Melissa said, feeling panicked.

"I honestly don't know why you care so much," Matt shrugged.

"You didn't just get punched in the face for this," Melissa snapped back.

"What are we going to do? Hijack their car?"

"Guys, they've found the bodies. Whatever you're going to do, you have to do it now. The car with the sword is pulling away," Teva's voice flickered through Matt's earpiece.

Without thinking, Melissa bolted for the bus stop by the busy main road. Matt followed, his sniper case swinging wildly in his free hand.

Two of the three large black troop carriers were pulling out onto the road.

Melissa quickly deduced that the last was waiting for the soldiers still patrolling the Colosseum.

"Teva, get the van here now!" Matt commanded. While he wasn't totally onboard with Melissa's fixation on the mission, she appreciated his reliability right now.

Almost immediately, the dilapidated white van came zooming up to the bus stop.

Its arrival didn't go unnoticed.

Two men, one being the driver, jumped out of the remaining troop carrier and opened fire.

The front windshield exploded as bullets tore through the van's metal shell.

Melissa raised her stolen gun (the third for the day) and fired.

The two Gladius members ceased attacking them and took cover on the other side of their vehicle. Melissa kept firing in short sharp bursts as she ran for the van.

Teva was at the wheel. He'd barely even slowed down as he swung past the troop carrier. The side door was already open for them.

Melissa and Matt dived simultaneously and landed on top of one another inside the van as it zoomed off.

A second volley of bullets blasted through the back, puncturing Teva's computer equipment. The entire set-up sparked violently and died.

The van picked up speed.

Matt stumbled to his feet and slammed the sliding door closed.

Melissa scrambled into the front passenger seat next to Teva.

They were less than twenty metres away from the closest troop carrier, but it was weaving through the traffic fast. Up ahead, Melissa saw they were fast approaching the Piazza Venezia.

Rome's famous government building stood proud, with its vast Italian flags fluttering in the breeze.

She didn't want a prolonged car chase. She raised her rifle and fired. The back tyre of the troop carrier exploded. It swerved, completely out of control, and crashed into a bystander's car on the side of the road.

Teva skillfully avoided the crumpled smoking wrecks of the two cars and pushed on towards the remaining troop carrier. They passed the Altar of the Fatherland.

Melissa fired again.

Another successful hit.

The troop carrier careened off the road and hit a display of small conical plants on the roadside.

Teva grimaced. Melissa knew what he was thinking. This had now become a major international incident.

She kicked the door open and jumped out.

"Swing back around! I'll get the sword!"

Teva didn't need to be told twice.

He hit the gas, and the van sped off to find a good place to turn around.

Rifle raised; Melissa walked towards the crumpled Gladius Vaticanus vehicle.

One of the troop carrier's occupants fell from the left passenger door as Melissa wrenched the back door of the car open.

The black Pelican case was in there. She opened it, and the golden sword revealed itself once more.

"No time for visions," she said as she lifted it. The weapon was heavy and cumbersome. She couldn't hold the rifle at the same time.

Bullets whizzed over her head.

She was being shot at from down the road! Bullets were also flying towards Teva's white van. He wasn't going to be able to get her now.

Melissa dropped the rifle and ran away from the main road.

Into the ruins.

Into the very heart of ancient Rome.

Somehow, she knew where to go. She could feel the sword guiding her.

CHAPTER SIX

AN ORACLE OF DELPHI

Melissa paused to take a breath. Not too far away, Italian police sirens were blaring. What a day this had been. If it hadn't been so dark, Melissa assumed she would've looked quite the sight perched on a pile of ancient bricks in the ruins of the Roman Forum.

In the reflection of a small discarded mirror she'd found, Melissa saw that black bags had appeared under both her eyes. Her nose and upper lip were coated in blood. It was beginning to dry and crack, with small portions crumbling away. Her nose was askew and very broken. She couldn't breathe through it at all.

Her hair was clumped and matted, and her clothes reeked of the sewer.

Melissa Pythia was a mess.

Essentially, ASIO's entire operating procedure had been thrown out the window. The amount of paperwork this would generate would be tremendous. Fortunately, when she wasn't fighting criminals, Melissa was very good at managing paperwork.

She rested the golden blade across her thighs. It was humming with energy and seemed to be glowing faintly. The weapon was extraordinarily heavy, and had Mel not been so chock full of adrenaline she would've struggled to carry it.

That man, Morpheus, who called himself a god, had said there was a task to achieve that only she could manage.

While doubtful thoughts bounced around her head, somehow, she knew that she was being driven towards something.

Some unknown force was compelling her onwards.

The Gladius Vaticanus were desperate to deliver this weapon to the Vatican. There had to be a reason why, beyond just treasure hunting. They were willing to kill to do it.

For lack of a better word, Melissa was feeling an impending sense of doom.

Teva and Matt would be long gone by now. She was sure headquarters would be in touch with a long 'PLEASE EXPLAIN' e-mail shortly. She chuckled as she realised the absurdity of thinking about e-mails right now.

She had no phone, no weapon (other than the sword), and no plan.

Melissa looked around.

She knew where she was. The ruins were very recognisable. She was in the once beating heart of the Roman Empire, the

Foro Romano.

Due to the sheer magnitude of unearthed ruins, there were plenty of places to hide.

The sword had led her here, and now it seemed to be telling her to wait. Some distant event was about to reach its conclusion, and she needed to be here when it did.

"Hell is a terrifying place," a croaky voice said.

Mel jumped up in fright, taken entirely by surprise by the old woman who was approaching through the darkness.

"These tired old legs... takes me a long time to get anywhere these days. So, I don't go anywhere that isn't worth going."

"You again?" Melissa said. She instinctively touched the back of her hand. She felt a rise where there hadn't been one before. The funny symbol that was burned into her skin had reappeared. She'd almost forgotten that had happened. The old woman gently lowered herself down next to Melissa.

"Witches rune, that is," she said, pointing at the shape in Melissa's skin.

"So, you are a witch?" Melissa asked.

"You seem surprisingly willing to believe in witches," the old woman laughed.

"I've seen some monsters in my time."

"As have I, my dear."

Melissa looked at the glowing shapes on her shawl.

"What does it mean? This symbol you've put on the back of my hand?"

"Simple little thing. When you are around divine power, it will appear. Gives you an indication as to who you are truly dealing with."

"Right..." Melissa replied. This was all so silly.

The old woman gazed at the sword. "Haven't seen this for a long time. Thought it was lost. Well, you can forgive me, the place where it was hasn't been accessible for hundreds and hundreds of years."

"Lebanon?" Melissa asked.

"No deary, the Underworld. The lands of the dead. Sometime in the fourteenth century all the passages were closed. Used to be secret paths all over the place to the Underworld, but no more. Totally inaccessible. That is why the sword brought you here."

"You may need to go back a step," Melissa muttered quietly.

"I think, perhaps, when you know what you are, it will make more sense."

The woman stood as quickly as her old joints allowed and began drawing in the dirt with her long brown walking stick.

Whether she was still foggy from the punch, or just too exhausted, Melissa didn't know. She just sat there looking at the sword.

A swathe of red dots appeared on Melissa's chest. They were followed by torchlight.

From behind the rubble, Gladius Vaticanus soldiers were appearing. They flicked on the torches at the end of their advanced rifles.

Melissa put her hands up, resigned to defeat. There was no getting out of this one.

"Damn it," the old woman muttered, looking around. She continued scribbling in the dirt.

"Don't move," a masked Italian voice shouted.

"Gladius Vaticanus," Melissa whispered through the side of her mouth.

"Devil worshippers," the old woman replied. "Soldiers of the hill of the prophecy. I know their kind."

Melissa stood up, letting the sword fall from her lap to the ground.

For a long moment, nothing happened.

A helmet-less man in the back was staring at the old woman curiously. He pushed through the ring of soldiers with a hungry look on his face.

"Surely not!" he shouted, sounding astonished. "I thought you were all gone!"

Melissa noticed that something was off about this mercenary. His eyes were brown with vibrant and sporadic tinges of red running through his irises. Long purple veins stretched across his face and down his neck.

"Belial," the old woman bowed courteously.

The man, apparently named Belial, snapped his fingers, and all of his soldiers slumped forward. It was like they'd all been overcome with the same sudden trance.

"Who are you?" Belial asked with wide grin. His eyes were brimming with delight. He looked like a hyena that had just cornered helpless prey.

"A memory of a bygone age," the old woman smiled. She kept her eyes on him as she continued to draw in the dirt with her walking stick.

"This raises so many questions. Why are you here? Now? With THAT sword?"

He walked closer.

"I am warning you," the old lady said fiercely, her pleasant demeanor vanishing.

"Oh, go on, do it! Do something. Show your true self, goddess," Belial sneered. He stressed the last word, letting it linger in the air. "Let the angels in their legions come for you."

"I suspect you want that as little as I do."

"Given current circumstances, we have a tentative working relationship," Belial snarled. He scanned the drawings in the dirt. "Witches runes? A Goddess of Witchcraft perhaps? Or... magic! No wonder you've been able to hide for so long. Right under the nose of the Church."

Belial snapped his fingers, and all of his soldiers woke up.

The soldiers were utterly unfazed; as if nothing had happened. They moved in closer.

Melissa gulped. There were too many guns pointed at her this time.

The old woman turned to Melissa.

"I have been hiding for too long. Fighting the good fight from the shadows. Teaching generations my craft. Perhaps it is time... I think it is Apollo's turn."

Across the woman's arms, orange symbols began glowing. They were like a spiderweb of interconnected characters.

"Learn who you are. He will need you to find himself. He is a God of Knowledge and Prophecy, but he won't have access to any of that when you find him. You are linked to his true power. Use it to restore him. Turn the tide."

The old woman tapped one of the scratches on the ground

with her walking stick.

A blinding white light began filling the spiral shaped etching. It spread towards Melissa's feet. She shielded her eyes as the light snaked around her body.

A sudden rush of wind engulfed her, blowing her hair straight up.

Belial looked enraged as he leapt forward.

Through the light, Melissa could just see the hunched old woman take a daring step forward.

Only she wasn't hunched any more. From behind, she looked young, healthy and beautiful.

Glowing symbols were floating around her. The Gladius Vaticanus opened fire, but all their bullets dropped uselessly to the ground.

With a wave of her hand, she sent the entire ring of soldiers flying away, except for Belial...

Then, there was darkness.

• • • • •

MELISSA WOKE UP on soft green grass. A salty sea-breeze filled the air. The warm sun above bathed her in light. She was no longer in Rome.

Floating before her eyes was another of the foreign runic symbols that the old lady had been so obsessed with drawing.

Melissa reached for it and found she was able to delicately hold it in her palm.

"What is this?" she said quietly.

"A gift," the rune spoke back, in a nasally high-pitched tone.

Out of sheer fright, Melissa released it back into the air as she jumped backwards.

The rune floated in front of her eyes for a minute, then flew straight for her face.

Melissa had no time to dodge it. It collided with her, and she heard a snap.

Her broken nose had fixed itself.

"Consider this a kindness as it took a lot to send you here. I apologise for not being able to fix the black eyes."

"That's fine," Melissa responded gratefully. "Where am I exactly?"

"Your home," the rune answered, sounding as if she'd asked a stupid question.

"Once again, I find myself needing more explanation," Melissa said dryly. She inhaled deeply through her nostrils. It felt good to be able to breathe fully again.

"This is Delphi, in Greece. The home of the Pythian priestesses. They are oracles of the God Apollo."

"What do you mean by god?" Melissa asked. "That Morpheus guy with the weird cosmic hair said he was a god."

"A god is a being above a human that has a specific domain in the world in which they rule. Or in the case of Apollo, many specific domains. He is very powerful."

"So, what was Morpheus the god of?"

"The God of Dreams. His father, Hypnos, was the God of Sleep."

"Sleep and dreams have a god?"

"Do you not find them important?"

"Well... I guess they are."

"Gods fill voids in the universe. They draw power from their role. True gods are always powerful, but their power may increase in times of great faith and devotion. All gods have the power to alter the world, but some have powers beyond fathoming. The very universe bends to their will."

"Right," Melissa murmured, scanning the grassland around her. She could see white buildings in the distance.

"What does this have to do with me?"

"You are deeply connected to Apollo, which is why you were drawn to Rome at this time."

"But I'm not in Rome right now, am I?" Melissa asked, feeling immediately stupid. Of course she wasn't in Rome.

"Well, you are, and you aren't. I have pulled you into a memory. A memory found in your blood. You have been removed temporarily from the physical world, but when this memory fades, you will return."

"That old woman did this?" Melissa asked, struggling to comprehend what the disembodied voice was saying.

"The old woman was the Goddess Hecate, who has influenced the world in more ways than you might suspect. Witchcraft is a powerful tool. It allows mortals to access abilities beyond their kind."

"Well, what happened to this Hecate? Why isn't she here?"

"A long story of divine war needs to be told to answer that question. A story you will soon see. I fear Hecate sacrificed herself to save you. Very few gods remain from the old world.

They have been hunted for a long time. They live as mortals, only using their powers sparingly, as to not attract attention."

"Okay," Melissa said. She understood what the voice was saying, but it felt like a lot of information for her to comprehend. "Who hunts gods? Is it people?"

"Angels hunt gods."

"And what are you then?" she asked.

"A small imprint of Hecate's mind, sent to guide you. To help you understand what you must do. Walk down the path."

Melissa saw a road of white paved bricks heading up a sloping hill in the near distance.

She looked up, and saw two eagles flying towards each other from east and west.

"That is another memory, not from your blood, but from this place. Because you are who you are, you can see more than most."

Melissa reached the start of the path. She turned back. From her vantage point, she could see the ocean. She noticed a large number of ships were docked just off-shore. They weren't modern. Several smaller transports, filled with men, were rowing towards the beach.

"What year is it?" Melissa asked as she began the journey upwards.

"394 AD. Welcome to the fall of Delphi."

Clumps of trees lined the path, broken by clearings which seated elaborate shrines.

"These are treasuries constructed by the Greek city-states. Even after the rise of the Roman Empire, many still come here and pay tribute as their ancestors did."

They continued to walk past the treasuries. Gold, jewellery and fine art lay scattered about the path.

"I'm amazed people don't steal this," Melissa marvelled.

"This is a sacred place," the voice told her.

The path continued higher. The trees became less dense, and a view of rolling hills greeted Melissa on both sides.

After what felt like a hike, she reached the edge of a large terrace supported by a wall of oddly shaped bricks.

A vast amphitheatre sat to the left of the terrace and just ahead was a magnificent temple. A strange boulder sat at the temple's front. The rock was smooth and cone-shaped, and the ground had been delicately manicured around it.

"The Omphalos stone. The naval of the world," the guiding voice informed Melissa.

Melissa approached and ran her hand down its smooth side.

"That was inside a titan, you know?"

Melissa withdrew her hand. She didn't know what that meant, but generally, if something has come out of something else, you don't want to touch it.

Behind the stone, the entrance to the temple was breathtaking. The front was lined with white pillars that stretched wide at the base and tapered at the top. The temple had a triangular roof, and carved into its face were images of the Olympian gods. Atop the roof was a golden statue. It had to be at least be fifteen feet tall. It was of a young man, with a green laurel wreath across his head.

People were scattered about the temple's entrance. They had manicured beards and wore elaborate finery. Their fingers and necks were graced with the presence of silver and exotic gems.

No one acknowledged Melissa as she walked by. They didn't even give her a second glance. She felt like a ghost.

The tall doors to the building were open, so Melissa walked in.

She gasped in amazement at what greeted her. Inside the long, rectangular room, behind the support pillars that lined its sides, was an enormous stone carving of a serpent. Fangs bared; its head reared up against the back wall. Melissa noticed that just under the giant serpent's head was another incredibly detailed, jewel-encrusted door.

In the middle of the room, facing the stone snake, was the statue of a young man with his bow drawn. The bow was a glistening silver, and on his waist sat an elaborate golden sword.

"The sword!" Melissa exclaimed, pointing at it.

"Just a replica," the voice chimed in.

They walked past the tall fire pits burning inside the room towards the door. Some kind of incense was burning in the pits. Just walking through the temple filled Melissa with a dizzying euphoria.

The bejewelled door was closed.

Melissa raised her hand to open it, and it slipped straight through the solid material.

"This is a memory," the disembodied voice of the guide said. "Move as you see fit."

With a deep breath, Melissa stepped straight through the closed door.

On the other side was a room that looked like it had been cut straight into the rock face.

Two men, who were obviously priests of some description, stood beside a volcanic vent. The end of the vent was shrouded by a red curtain.

Melissa could see the steam and vapours rising through cracks in the ground. They wafted throughout the room, but floated most prominently as a cloud around the red curtain. It was enough to make a person nauseous.

Melissa walked towards the curtain. She was beaten there by one of the priests.

He pulled it aside to reveal a hooded woman. Her head was bowed and she looked to be deep in prayer. The priest said something to her in what Melissa assumed was ancient Greek. The woman slowly lifted her head and pulled the hood back.

Melissa gasped.

She was looking at herself.

The woman didn't look like an ancestor of hers or some long lost relative. It was her in every way. She was even the same age.

"What is this?" Melissa demanded.

"Hmm?" Mel's other self said, looking directly at her. The doppelganger's pupils were dilated, making her look distant and distracted.

"Who are you?" Melissa demanded from her twin.

"I am the Pythia. The priestess of Apollo. With his powers of prophecy, I see that which will be... I am the Oracle of Delphi," the doppelganger murmured.

"Pythia..." Melissa said slowly, "My last name is Pythia."

"You are here at my end, and I am here at your beginning,"

the oracle said in Melissa's voice. "I am pleased to see you. I thought I was the last. Apollo's power has slowly bled from the world. It is all but gone now..."

The two priests were looking at each other confused. It was customary for the Pythia to ramble, but to them, Melissa assumed that this time it looked like she was talking directly to someone they couldn't see.

"Be prepared for what comes next," the oracle said solemnly before bowing her head again.

The clanging of swords and shouts came from outside. The two priests rushed out of the room to see what the commotion was.

"What comes next?" Melissa asked.

"Fire and death," the oracle replied, as an armed man burst into the room.

He was a Roman soldier.

He looked at the parted curtain revealing the Oracle of Delphi. He hesitated, then launched a javelin right at her.

With a spout of blood, the javelin impaled the oracle against the stone vents. She fell limp, instantly dead.

"NO!" Melissa screamed. She reached out and touched her hand to that of the oracle's. Her skin was already cold, despite the warmth of the room. The oracle began to disintegrate into orange light.

Small glowing specs swirled around the room. They became a whirlwind around Melissa, sinking into her.

Somehow, Melissa knew what was happening.

The voice of the rune rang out, "The power of the Oracle of

Delphi will return to the world when its source does! You are bound to him. Find him! Use the sword! NOW, REINCARNATE!"

She began to see images of her parents. Of her childhood. Of her life in Sydney. But it was the final image that terrified her.

Fire and death.

CHAPTER SEVEN

FATE AND DOOM

- SEPTEMBER 27 -
ROME - FORO ROMANO

Melissa fell to her knees. She'd just witnessed an ancient version of herself be impaled by a javelin, then dissolve into light, followed by flashes of her own childhood. She clenched the grass in a tight grip.

That voice had said reincarnate. That could only mean one thing; that woman had been her. She'd died but then been born again in the modern era. Why now though? Was her destiny really entwined with this mysterious golden sword?

She struggled to wrap her mind around the concept. It was so ludicrous, yet, it was happening.

She could feel a small line of ants begin running over the back of her hand.

The runic symbol was still there, burned to her skin. The fact she could see it meant divine power was present. That's what Hecate had told her.

She stood up.

She was back in the ruins of the Roman Forum.

The green trees and sea-breeze of ancient Delphi were gone. That island was a place she'd never been before, yet it had felt so familiar.

And the sword was still there too! Just lying on the ground, where she'd dropped it.

The soldiers of the Gladius Vaticanus had disappeared, along with the old woman and the creepy man named Belial.

Melissa brushed her stinking matted hair out of her face and picked up the golden weapon.

Sparks of intuition exploded in her brain in a firestorm of purpose.

She suddenly knew what she had to find.

The tourist path through the Foro Romano wound beside towering pillars and partial buildings that still stood, even after thousands of years.

There was an object she needed to locate among the ruins — a ram's head with a five-pointed star carved into its temple.

Melissa felt a bit like she was losing her mind, but knew the hand of destiny was pushing her ever onwards.

She broke into a run. Looking comical with the golden sword dragging at her side, she scanned every piece of rubble for signs that it had once been a statue.

She painstakingly searched the ruins of the Temple of Caesar in the dark and then tried the Temple of Vesta next.

Nothing.

Melissa was frustrated. She wanted to scream. She knew she was in the right place, but where exactly did she need to be?

It was still and quiet in the Roman ruins.

Too still.

Too quiet.

After the car crashes and very public gunfire, the place should have been swarming with police. They should be searching the ruins right now. Yet, there was no one other than Melissa.

She was anxious, something wasn't right. Strangely, the magic she could handle. The stillness of the ruins, well that was another matter entirely.

The road wasn't far away. There were no traffic sounds, but it was probably very late by now. Melissa realised that she had no idea what time it was.

Then, she saw him.

A man was creeping about the ruins, not far from her. Melissa could see clearly by his silhouette that he was holding a pistol.

Melissa backed herself against an old Roman wall.

She held her breath and listened.

He was muttering to someone. It sounded Italian.

There could only be one group sneaking around the ruins now, the Soncin crime family.

Clearly, the Gladius Vaticanus had no qualms with being armed in public, but they seemed to have vanished. She doubted that if they were still here that they'd be bothered with sneaking around.

She gulped, the old woman may have got rid of the Gladius Vaticanus, but the crime family was still on the hunt for their treasure.

That's probably why the police weren't looking around. They must've been bribed by the Soncins.

She peeked her head around to glance at the spot she'd seen the man.

He was gone, but there was something else there. Carved into the side of a crumbling pillar was a symbol that was out of place.

It was a witch's rune.

A clue!

Melissa rushed towards it without thinking.

From out of the darkness, a man with a pencil-thin moustache and gelled black hair crash-tackled her. She dropped the sword.

"Found it!" he shouted.

Melissa launched a swift right hook into his face.

The man just absorbed the blow and continued to pin Melissa down.

Another man ran out of the darkness and heaved up the golden prize.

"No," Melissa thought, *"I'm so close, I can feel it."*

"Hey! You!" Melissa shouted.

The man on top of her looked down.

Melissa head-butted his face with all the force she could muster. This time, it was her turn to break someone's nose. The man fell back, both hands clasped to his face.

Melissa rolled onto her shoulders and then leapt to her feet.

The second man clumsily swung the sword at her.

Melissa pivoted to the left and aimed a powerful knee strike at the man's groin.

It connected with immediate and devastating effect.

He doubled over in pain.

Melissa pulled his shirt over his head, then, gripping his collar, thrust him into a nearby wall.

Seizing her moment, Melissa grabbed the sword.

She turned around to see a small revolver pointed at her. The man with the smashed nose fired right as Melissa swung the weapon up with all her might. The bullet pinged off the blade.

Melissa reached down and grabbed a chunk of ancient stone beside her. Roughly the size of a fist, she lobbed it at the Soncin's head.

It connected with his already broken nose in a sickening crunch. He fell back and wailed in agony.

Sword in hand, Melissa bolted for the witch's rune.

Melissa pressed her hand to it. The earth gave way beneath her and she collapsed into a dark subterranean room.

The golden sword began glowing with a brilliant light that bounced off the marble walls.

Small patches of grass and weeds had forced their way through the ancient brickwork of the roof.

The place was mostly empty, save for a pedestal in the middle.

It looked as if long ago the room had been adorned with magnificent paintings and statues, but they'd been completely destroyed. Small pieces lying about the floor provided the only clues to the majesty this place once held.

As Melissa walked towards the central pedestal, she noticed that the entire floor was in fact a mosaic. The image was so large that she couldn't fully see what it was depicting. From her vantage point at least, she saw men in togas fleeing from tsunamis of flame.

She reached the ram's head.

Now, all she could do was wait. The Soncins hadn't seen her fall into the dark room and were presumably still looking for her up above.

"Oracle of Delphi, was does that even mean?" Melissa sighed, speaking to the gloom around her.

Even with her recent experience with talking runes, she didn't expect a new voice to answer her question.

"It means you have a destiny intertwined with an ancient deity," a womanly voice stated.

Melissa turned swiftly, looking for the speaker. There was no one to be seen.

"I think I'm about up to my limit with gods and magic for now…" Melissa grumbled.

"Then you have an unpleasant night ahead. I can feel it, in the twisting river of fate, that Apollo is awake. Even now, he moves towards this place, unaware of the grave danger he is in. You will help him."

"Who are you?" Melissa demanded.

"My name is Moros. We will meet very soon. For you to understand the path you now walk, you must first know the events the brought you here."

"What events? What are you talking about?"

"Your eyes can see what no other humans can. Embrace fate and embrace your destiny. See now the ancient past so it may guide you into the future!"

Melissa felt a strange energy wash over her. Her vision faded as she felt unfamiliar thoughts emerge in her head. This wasn't a vision. She was stepping out of her own brain and into the mind of another.

Her eyes turned gold, and Melissa was lost in another being's memory of the ancient past. The key to her future was held in the tale of a great cataclysm she was about to witness first hand. She decided not to fight it and let this new story consume her.

PART TWO

THE BATTLE FOR THE UNDERWORLD

CHAPTER EIGHT

A KNOCK AT THE GATE

- 337 AD -
THE UNDERWORLD

A mysterious figure sat alone in a dark room. Her mind was clouded by a fog so blinding and choking she could barely perceive her own thoughts. Words like rain flooded her mind. Feelings, manifesting as the tides of fate flowing in the cosmic sea, washed over her.

"Something monumental is about to happen," she thought.

The air was thick with the taste of doom. The world was no longer turning in its proper order. A great upheaval was coming, being brought by something dreadful that was right now stirring in a far-off land. Yet, she didn't know what was coming and by all rights, she should.

"Moros," a voice called from the dark.

"Yes," the woman answered.

Moros was her name. She was the Goddess of Fate and Doom. Born of the primordial night and the sister of darkness, Moros was ancient beyond the gods and the titans. Many feared her as a bad omen, though this was not just. With her flowing brown hair and storm-cloud eyes, Moros watched as destinies changed and played out across time. Fate was her domain and she changed it as she saw fit. When moments for greatness came, she elevated the heroic and punished the cowardly. Or, at least, that is how it was usually was.

Her ability to know the future and all its possible branches had dimmed recently. She could feel the flickers of destiny all around her, but couldn't turn them into a great fire of knowledge. She was impeded and diminished.

"Moros," the ethereal voice called again.

"Speak and bring clarity to the chaos that infests my mind," Moros murmured.

"Go to the council chamber of Hades, but do not fight what is to come. Time will be damaged soon, and as fate clings to time as a necessary parasite, you will be at great risk. Apollo is the key. Keep him safe. If the Golden God falls, so shall you."

Moros understood. She knew who the disembodied speaker was. It was herself, her power of fate manifesting in a way that she could understand it. As the personification of fate and doom, sometimes the concepts themselves spoke to her, though they were never very precise.

Moros rose to her feet. The Underworld was her destination, and it would be a long journey over forests and fields to get there.

She knew time was short.

● ● ● ● ●

THE BLACK WATERS OF THE River Styx lapped gently against the bank as a silent shape drifted by. The short expanse of rich volcanic soil that lined both sides of the water quickly turned into large cavernous walls of looming grey rock that rose high into the dark ceiling above. Only a weak hint of sunlight reached down the long winding tunnel that dived deep into the earth.

On his long wooden barge, the ferryman paddled quietly. His eyes betrayed a darkening storm of troubled thoughts. Whispers had reached his ears — very worrisome whispers.

Little did the ferryman know that an unexpected guest was now travelling on his barge, though he could not see her. Moros did not yet want to make her presence known in the Underworld, so sat perfectly invisible on a long wooden seat. She could feel the ferryman's concerns in her mind.

The spirits of the departed, that lined the banks by which the ferryman travelled, spoke of a changing world. There hadn't been any souls by the river today, which was odd. And there was something strange about the sky.

"Truly dark times," the ferryman muttered.

He plunged his oar deep into the water with barely a splash.

Creatures flitted about in the darkness above, watching him curiously. His boat glided towards a great gate that stretched across the width of the cavern. Sensing his approach, the old metal doors swung wide to grant the ferryman entry.

A light appeared in the corner of the Moros' eye. She turned to see a great ball of fire roaring towards the barge. It ignited the entire cavern in a brilliant light. At an immense speed, the fireball blasted past them and through the open gates. A deafening series of barks echoed across the walls from not far ahead. The fireball had woken the guard dog.

The ferryman gulped. If the old sun god was here, perhaps the rumours he'd heard were true? Maybe the Emperor of Rome was dead.

Moros was surprised to hear such thoughts coming from the ferryman. She should be the first to know of the death of an emperor, yet hadn't felt his doom at all. This was troublesome indeed.

Moros observed the ferryman curiously as he wiped the sweat from his brow. His pale skin hung loosely from his bones. He was wretchedly skinny, with a long white beard that fell to his navel.

"Do not open again," the ferryman commanded to the gates after he passed through.

The gates shut and with a metallic clink, locked themselves.

The river widened before them, stretching out into the gloom.

To her left Moros saw six glowing red eyes, each the size of a dinner plate, open and watch them pass. The figure of an enormous beast sat cloaked in darkness on the far bank. The lamp that dangled off the front of his boat was not bright enough to illuminate the monster.

The beast that guarded the gate rose to its feet and snarled. The ferryman nodded curtly at the monster.

"I'm afraid I don't have time for games, Cerberus…"

The great black dog slumped back down and whimpered.

The barge was moving swiftly along the river now, guided by an invisible current. The sound of rushing water filled Moros' ears. In the total darkness of the cave, his boat tipped forward over the edge of a large waterfall. The barge fell for several seconds before it gracefully landed in the churning pool of water at the bottom. The world was no longer dark.

Before them was a stone dock that jutted out into the water. Fixed to the ceiling of the cavern, high above, was a large bronze orb that emitted a dazzling light.

The dead called it 'the Light of the Underworld'. It was devised by Helios, the new sun god, and crafted by Hephaestus, the God of the Forge. The orb was fixed high above a mighty black castle and acted as a light source for the lands of the dead.

The castle was a wonder unto itself. At first glance, the titanic building looked to have been pieced together from gigantic shards of shattered black glass. The central spire pointed upwards like a pyramid towards the orb. Several towers and balconies, all equally black and shining, sprung out from the central structure. Every addition to the building ended in sharp black points and every inch of it gleamed in the false light.

The docks, however, were of a simpler design. Stone passageways, made in the early days of the titans, ran forward for hundreds of metres before they reach the lower levels of the castle. A circular courtyard that held a singular enormous elm tree sat before the grand doors of the structure. Moros knew that as spirits walked past the tree, they were stripped of the false dreams they'd clung to in life. It was across this courtyard that the ferryman usually led the spirits of the dead.

Moros also knew that a being such as the ferryman would never enter the castle, as he was not there to be judged.

Footsteps echoed down the dock as a figure rushed towards the barge.

"Charon!" a panicked voice called.

Moros saw a portly man in a white robe running towards the ferryman, Charon.

"Rhadamanthus," Charon bowed. "What brings you to my docks?"

Rhadamanthus was one of three judges of the Underworld and had been doing his duty here for thousands of years. It was rare to see him removed from the castle.

"What news have you heard along the banks of the five rivers?" Rhadamanthus puffed.

"Rumours of the passing of Emperor Constantine have reached me," Charon, the ferryman, croaked back. "What we have feared... has it come to pass?"

"Thanatos has not returned," Rhadamanthus said, looking distinctly worried.

Thanatos was the God of the Dead and an old friend of Moros.

"Was he there? For Constantine's passing?"

"Yes, he promised he'd send word immediately... there has been nothing..."

"Where is Hades?"

Rhadamanthus began pacing back and forth, "He is with Apollo, he arrived shortly before you did. I told you that some growing power is interfering with the Underworld!"

Moros began moving away from the two. She suspected, as they did, what was happening. Rumours that the Emperor of Rome had been consorting with angels had been circulating for years, though she had always dismissed them as nothing of consequence. Could the Goddess of Fate and Doom have been wrong?

"I'm worried, Charon," Rhadamanthus stated plainly. "We've underestimated this upstart religion for too long. It isn't like other faiths. They don't know their place; they don't abide by the natural order. They are expansionist and aggressive."

"A death bed conversion doesn't change anything," Charon sighed, stroking his long beard.

"It changes everything! That simple declaration will sweep across Rome like wildfire! Already the balance may have shifted."

Charon opened his mouth to reply but was stopped by an eerie sound.

A horn was being blown. The sound was deep and booming, rising in the middle and falling at the end. It echoed off the walls and sat in the air.

Then, there was a thundering crash. The sound of an explosion completely silenced the waterfall. The horn blasted out again, and the barking of Cerberus could be heard in the distance.

Rhadamanthus looked at Charon, "They are here."

Moros had lingered too long on the dock. With great haste she moved towards the Castle of Hades to convene with the gods of the Underworld.

· · · · ·

THE FACES OF THE DEITIES of the Underworld were all glued to a blue fire in the centre of the council chamber when Moros arrived. The flames showed images of the different corners of Hades' realm as they flickered.

Moros shed her perfect invisibility and greeted the gods.

Hades, the ruler of the Underworld, looked mildly surprised to see her. "First Apollo and now you, Moros," Hades murmured.

"Fate has guided me to this place, though I admit current events have taken me unaware. What is happening here?" Moros asked.

Hades was hesitant to answer quickly.

"War," Apollo answered in Hades' place.

"Perhaps a little dramatic a term," Hades sighed.

"They are stronger than you realise," Apollo argued.

The Goddess of the Underworld, Persephone, looked to her husband, Hades, then to Apollo.

"Apollo, please, no matter what following they have, or what strength they have mustered through faith and prayer, they are nothing compared to us."

"I barely escaped Nicomedia, the Archangel Selaphiel almost stopped me," Apollo grimaced.

A couple of the gods scoffed as they leaned back in their chairs.

Some of the lesser-known gods didn't care much for Apollo. He'd been immensely popular in the days of the Greeks, and during the rise of the Roman Empire, his allure hadn't dimmed. Even now, people still prayed to him and offered sacrifices in his name. Moros knew all too well that jealousy ran rampant amongst the gods. Apollo always adopted a youthful appearance. He had wavy blonde hair and bronzed skin that contrasted with his blazing blue eyes. Sometimes, when he appeared before mortals, he turned himself gold all over, something which had long ago earned him the nickname 'Golden Apollo'.

Despite his youthful looks, Apollo was nonetheless a god who'd lived a long life, fought many battles and seen much suffering. It was clear that the events that were transpiring now concerned him greatly.

Apollo again turned his attention towards Hades. "Hades, they want the Underworld, all of it."

Hades had been diplomatically dealing with foreign gods for thousands of years. The Olympic pantheon had held dominion of the Underworld since the early days of the world. As other gods staked their claims to different parts of the planet, they'd all met with Hades to negotiate control over their own territories within the realm of the dead. Hades acted as a glorified land-lord to the heavens and hells of religions from every corner of the world. Now, these upstarts from the Middle East were attempting to seize control of the whole thing. They were knocking on his door, and he was considering how to answer.

Hades turned and addressed the room. "We have diminished."

The gods and goddesses all fixed their attention to him.

"As we were meant to, it is the right of every god to fade when they feel their time has come. We haven't been active amongst the humans for a long time. Even if the sudden rumours that Rome has abandoned us are true, it hardly makes a difference. Humanity is fickle, their faith changes on a whim and we must accept that."

"The angels don't see it that way," Apollo interjected. "They want faith, they want worship; and not just in their own regions, but everywhere. They draw unimaginable power from it! The Roman Empire is just a small stepping stone to their bigger plans."

"Unnatural scum," a glowing figure at the side of the room spat out.

The speaker was Hypnos, the God of Sleep. He was a usual resident of the Underworld and Moros wasn't shocked to see him here now.

"Please, Hypnos," Hades sighed. "There is very little that separates them from us."

"We were born," Hypnos stated, rising to his feet as his golden cloak gleamed in the light, "the natural union of gods and titans and primordials. For some of us, the universe itself willed us into being! They were built, that god of theirs created them, not to fill natural voids in the universe as we do, but to serve him! They are abominations! Constructs of some rogue!"

"Hades, we must send a message," Apollo stated, cutting off the disgruntled Hypnos.

"I agree," Hades responded.

Apollo looked shocked.

Moros observed Hades much as she'd done with Charon earlier. Hades appeared as a middle-aged man, with pale skin and an unkempt brown beard. His body looked strong, but his eyes looked tired.

Hades turned towards the blue fire in the middle of the circle of chairs.

"Show me the gates."

The fire rose from its pit, and in its twisting flames, the gates to the Underworld were clearly shown. They were bending and buckling under some immense force. Through the gaps in the bars, at the head of a mighty host, were two six-winged figures.

"Michael and Lucifer," Apollo growled, pointing at the fire. "Archangels, gods in their own right, according to some."

Moros frowned. A new religion had come to make war on the old order, and she hadn't felt it at all. This was a troubling revelation.

"Apollo may be right," Moros spoke up. "They have kept their intentions hidden from the very concept of doom itself. This attack should've been known to me, which makes me fear their unknown power."

Hades looked from the vision of the gates to the group. Moros followed his eyes as they fell on his beloved wife, Persephone. They moved to the other divine beings in the room. Hecate, the Goddess of Magic was there. Then was Hypnos, the God of Sleep and his son Morpheus, the God of Dreams. Next to Morpheus was an empty chair, usually occupied by Thanatos, the God of Death. A few more empty chairs separated Morpheus from Cer, the Goddess of Violent Death. Beside Cer sat the three Furies, who were born from the blood of the great Titan Ouranos. Their role, as it had been for an eternity, was to torment those who committed heinous crimes against their blood relatives. Torment from the Furies was a fate worse than death.

Perhaps the oddest being in the room was Aion. He stood by himself, in the middle of a bronze hoop. The hoop was made up of twelve sections, each one representing part of the zodiac. Aion didn't walk; the ring floated vertically, and he floated upright inside it. While every other god present wore clothing, Aion was perpetually naked, and always seemed to be pre-occupied with the stars. Even when indoors. He just stood staring at the ceiling, mumbling to himself. Her intuition told her that there was something very important about Aion right now, though she couldn't determine what it was.

Two Olympians made up the final residents of the room. Apollo, the former God of the Sun and current God of Music, Healing, Knowledge, Archery, Oracles and who knows what else. Apollo was the only one among them not to have had his name changed by the Romans. The other Olympian among them was Demeter, Hades' mother-in-law. She was the God of the Harvest, and as powerful as Hades or Apollo. The seasons themselves bowed to her whims.

Hades addressed Demeter, who was standing alone against a painted pillar.

"Demeter, can you speak with any of the gods on Olympus?"

"No," Demeter frowned, "it seems we are cut-off.

Demeter was absent-mindedly twirling her right hand through the air. With every rotation, snowflakes fell from her palm to the ground. Then, after a moment, the snowflakes turned into brightly coloured flowers, which lazily floated downwards towards the immaculate floor.

"Forget the Olympians!" Hypnos yelled angrily. "A simple wave of your hand will destroy that host of angels, Hades."

Cer, the Goddess of Violent Death, now spoke. She directed her glowing red eyes at Hades.

"Styx slumbers," she said simply. "Wake the river and watch it drown them all."

Cer smiled a wide, unnerving smile. All the beauty drained from her face and was replaced with a look of madness. Moros didn't much like the goddess as she was quick to anger and disgustingly brutal, but she was right.

The River Styx was named after the Goddess Styx, who in years past aided the gods in their time of need. All oaths sworn before the River Styx were unbreakable.

"You don't have to wake me," a raspy voice called from the shadows of the room. "They did that already with that infernal banging. Someone wants to break down your gate, Hades, did you know?"

A soaked-looking woman stepped into the firelight. She was cloaked in an ethereal mist and her skin was a translucent blue. Water fell from her lengthy black hair in a steady stream, but evaporated when it hit the floor.

"Styx," Hades smiled.

"About five hundred winged men, with golden belts and golden helmets wait outside your gates. They look like Eros, in a way. What are they?"

"Angels of Jerusalem," Apollo answered in place of his uncle. "They have come to claim the Underworld."

"Claim the Underworld?" Styx asked. "That doesn't even make sense. Lord Hades, would you permit me to silence them?"

"If you wouldn't mind, Styx," Hades said.

The drowned-looking goddess nodded, then fell into a puddle on the floor.

Apollo looked alarmed, "Uncle, you don't understand, they wouldn't be here if they didn't think they could win! The angels aren't weak, Michael especially -"

Apollo paused, as through the dancing flames, he saw the river spring to life.

• • • • •

THE HOST OF ANGELS hovered in position behind the silver gate that blocked the way forward. At the front of the party, four angels were directing a large swinging battering ram. It was carved in the image of an actual ram and moved on invisible hinges. With every hit, the gate buckled further.

The angels all looked like mortal men, except for the two vast wings that jutted from their upper backs. They had armoured gauntlets, boots and helmets and carried lances and swords. Further back, angelic archers floated in position. At the rear were rows of chariots, pulled by winged horses. One of the chariots contained a mighty horn.

At the head of the army, two individuals stood different from the rest. They had an imposing presence and radiated authority. Six long feathered wings sprang from their backs. They were coated from head to toe in elaborate white armour. The one on the right had a cape of red and blue. The other sported a long cloak of silver. They were the commanders of the legion of Heaven; the archangels.

The angels exchanged nervous glances. They did not know what waited beyond the gates.

None of them noticed as the black water beneath them began swirling.

Silently, the waters of the River Styx reached up and dragged an oblivious soldier down into their depths.

Long arms of liquid burst up in spouts and began knocking the formations of angels across the cavernous walls.

At the front of the pack, the archangelic brothers, Michael and Lucifer, looked back in alarm as the cries of their soldiers filled the air. Individual tendrils of water became like black blades slicing through their ranks.

Lucifer gave his brother a cunning smile, "It begins."

Several of the angels dived towards the water with their white lances stretched before them. Great waves rose from the river and swatted them away. Others sliced at the tentacles of water, duelling with them as if they were an armed foe.

"Do you see her, brother?" Michael asked Lucifer, lowering the visor of his golden helmet. It was fashioned in the image of a roaring lion.

"Yes," Lucifer said simply, holding out his right hand. A silver trident manifested in it. "She is the river."

"The gate is almost broken," Michael said, gazing as the ram smashed itself into the crippled structure again. "How do you feel?"

Lucifer flexed his free arm. "I feel powerful; I feel there has been a change in the air. A change great enough to topple Olympus itself."

"Olympus will fall, brother. The Underworld is our calling."

Lucifer smiled his cocky smile, then plummeted from the air into the water below.

The river ceased its attack immediately, and the arms of water dived back down into the depths.

After a minute the still waters parted as a figure burst upwards. Lucifer rose and spread his six white wings wide. He was wreathed in green flame, and his eyes blazed with white light. Power emanated from his every pore. He looked like victory made flesh.

In his left hand, carried by the crown of her hair, was the Goddess Styx. She hung limp in his grasp, blue mist falling from her skin. Lucifer held her before him and spoke to the congregation of angels.

"A new power dawns in this world!"

He was met with a boisterous cheer.

Michael floated over, and from an ornate sheath on his waist, drew his sword. It was long and silver, with a golden handle inscribed with numerous intricate images. The sword distorted the air around it and hummed with every small movement.

With a swift slash, Styx's head left her body.

Lucifer held the dripping wet head high and shouted, "HEAVEN RISES!"

He was met by thunderous cheer and the blowing of the great horn.

He closed his eyes and channelled his power into the dead goddess. The fire that lined his body flowed down his arm and into the decapitated head. There was still power in the remains of Styx, power he could exploit.

Lucifer opened his eyes.

He tossed Styx's head at the gate.

It exploded in a deafening blast of blue light and showering black rain.

The gate to the Underworld disintegrated in the explosion. The angels raised their shields as chunks of divine metal flew into their regiments. The entire cavern shook. Michael held his sword high and charged forward. Heaven's host followed him.

● ● ● ● ●

HADES TURNED FROM THE FIRE to his wife, "Dearest Persephone, please go to Tartarus and fetch the Hecatoncheires."

Persephone rose from her chair, winked at her husband, and then disappeared into thin air.

"The rest of you, go and greet our guests."

Moros was uneasy. The gods were certainly confident in their abilities, but in her heart, she knew that devastation was coming.

She watched as Apollo flew from the room in a flash of fire. She would follow him and keep him safe, as fate had willed her to do. That was her purpose now. Her fate was tied to his and for better or worse, she'd see the Golden God through this battle.

CHAPTER NINE

THE SOLDIERS OF HADES

- 337 AD -
THE UNDERWORLD

The angelic chariots raced into the gloom of the cavern. They gleamed bright with Heaven's light. The darkness above the river dissipated as the first three vehicles of war sped through the wreckage of the gate, travelling in close formation. One angel held the reigns of the winged horses while the other readied his lance.

The foot-soldiers, gliding behind the chariots, paused when they heard the first screams of horror.

An enormous figure emerged from the bank at the far side of the river and leapt towards the vanguard. It was impossibly huge, at least the size of a multi-story building, and covered in black fur. The great three-headed dog caught the first chariots in its jaws. They splintered in Cerberus' crushing bite. Both chariot and operators alike were broken and consumed by the mighty guard dog of the Underworld.

Moros had donned her guise of perfect invisibility and followed Apollo towards the gate. She watched beside him as the angels began their assault.

The second wave of chariots raced towards Cerberus and began circling around his three heads. Cerberus spun in frustration, trying to catch the gliding carts in his mouths. The angels reached for their golden bows. They had no physical quivers. Instead, when the archers pulled the draw-string back, arrows made of blinding light appeared. A volley of the light arrows flew from the bows and pierced Cerberus' skin. Each hit enraged the dog more as he twisted in the shallow water. The arrows forced Cerberus back against the sides of the cavern.

"Aim for his eyes!" an angel called as he readied another arrow of light.

The chariots lined themselves up in front of Cerberus, who was now pinned against the wall.

Three archers readied their bows and fired. Arrows flew into one of the glowing red eyes of the dog and blood burst from the socket. Cerberus buckled and whimpered in pain.

The lead charioteer lowered his bow and picked up his long white lance. He held it like a javelin. In his hands, the lance became wrapped in the same blinding light that formed the arrows and tripled in length.

"Good-bye, monster," the angel smirked.

He launched the lance at Cerberus, but it never hit the dog.

A ball of fire intercepted the lance and sent it hurtling towards the river. The fireball turned itself around and flew towards the chariots, which scattered in its wake. It stopped moving, and the flames parted to reveal a man sitting on the back of a flaming horse.

Apollo had entered the fray.

He was quickly met by Lucifer, who pushed through the surrounding angels to greet Apollo.

"Apollo," Lucifer bowed, not hiding his look of disdain.

"Lucy," Apollo said in kind.

A volley of arrows flew towards Apollo. Apollo simply waved his hand and the arrows vanished.

"Hades won't like that you broke down his gate and hurt his pet," Apollo warned.

"Soon Hades won't have such trivial concerns."

"It is a shame you didn't write ahead. We could've prepared your room in Tartarus."

Lucifer motioned to his warriors. Several angels drew their swords and launched themselves towards Apollo.

Apollo drew his golden sword and quickly engaged the angels. With a quick flurry of strikes, he disarmed his attackers. Their swords fell into the river below.

Lucifer raised his hand and mumbled, "Enough of this."

The archangel flicked his wrist, and the fallen swords flew from the river back towards their owners.

"Nice trick," Apollo joked, calmly patting the neck of his horse.

"It isn't a trick," Lucifer responded coolly. "It is a tiny ember of my power. One that this day will be ignited into a great flame."

Apollo laughed and boasted, "I am a god of Greece. I am a god of the Roman Empire. What can you possibly hope to do here?"

"You were a god of the Roman Empire," Lucifer responded with a dark smile.

Lucifer thrust his left arm forward, and a jet of green fire shot towards Apollo. Apollo tried to wave it away as he did with the arrows, but he didn't expect the raw strength behind the attack.

Moros reacted quickly, cloaking Apollo in a protective barrier of her own energy. The fire hit him square in the chest and sent him careening off his horse into the river. His horse, with its mane of red fire, bellowed and galloped away.

Since her death, the River Styx had became tumultuous and unstable. Moros couldn't follow Apollo into the torrent. She'd have to find him when he emerged. At least she knew he wasn't dead.

Lucifer laughed as he watched Apollo fall, but it was cut short when a recovered Cerberus bounded towards him. He'd momentarily forgotten about the three-headed monster. The great black dog caught the archangel in its jaws and shook him violently as the nearby angels rushed to Lucifer's aid.

• • • • •

MOROS FLEW TO THE BOTTOM of the waterfall, where the fight had begun in earnest. Behind the castle was a city that resembled an ancient version of Athens. It served as a temporary home to recently departed spirits and a launching point to the four different realms of the Underworld.

The spirits who dwelled there had taken up arms against the horde of angels, and skirmishes between the ghostly soldiers and the winged host from Heaven were breaking out all over the white stone streets. The dead were equipped with the shades of the weapons they'd died holding, and they functioned equally well in death as they had in life.

The angels were significantly more powerful than the ghosts of the dead, yet found themselves struggling with the sheer skill of the soldiers who'd spent their lives fighting. The spirits of the dead also had a significant advantage in the nearby presence of Hypnos, the God of Sleep.

Hypnos sat atop a tall white pillar in the centre of the city and meditated. Energy radiated out from him. It took the shape of an expanding sphere that was slowly encompassing the city. As the sphere reached the angels, they were overcome with an inescapable tiredness. They collapsed to the ground and were hacked to pieces by their spectral combatants.

This was where the other archangel had come.

Michael, sensing the edge of the invisible sphere of sleep approaching, flew up to greet it. He held his hands in front of him. He could feel Hypnos' energy as an expanding wave.

Concentrating his power, Michael solidified the wall of sleep. He then drew his sword and plunged it deep into the barrier of frozen energy. The expanding wave shattered like glass. It was easy for Moros to see that Michael's power had reached the level of a gods.

A host of angels, seizing their moment, flew toward Hypnos. Hypnos smiled a foolish smile.

Moros knew he should flee for his life, but Hypnos thought these angels were nothing to him, like he was being attacked by nymphs or spirits. The God of Sleep was not awake to the truth of his situation. Hypnos stood tall on the white pillar, his golden robe billowing around him, and pressed his palms out towards the approaching angels. The lead angel screamed as he began disintegrating. The angel paused in mid-air and clawed at his face. He felt every painful moment as his body turned to dust.

Hypnos frowned. He looked to be concentrating harder, but the angels kept on coming, seemingly resistant to him.

Then, a white lance impaled Hypnos. Moros rushed forward but in vain.

"Rest well, sleep god," Michael said as he withdrew the lance.

Moros felt the doom of Hypnos in her bones. She knew what would come and retreated. Hypnos burned with an unspeakable rage as the ichor leaked from his body. His look of anger was quickly replaced with a serenely calm grin; before Hypnos exploded.

A shockwave blasted out, crumbling the pillar. A wave of white mist washed across the city and settled at ground level. Ghost and angel alike fell instantly comatose when they touched the mist. The combatants on both sides either took to the air or clambered up buildings to escape the noxious substance.

As the angels soared upwards to escape the toxic fog, three figures dropped down to meet them. The flapping of large wings filled the air as the Furies descended upon the host of Heaven.

The three sisters, Alecto, Megaera and Tisiphone, swooped down from above. They screeched as their great black bat wings wrapped around their targets. The highest angels were caught first. When the wings opened up, nothing but severed body parts remained, quickly plunging into the mist below.

The angels had no blood, but their design was based on humans. Rough chunks of flesh and shimmering silver bone whistled as they crashed into the ground. Using their deadly claws, the Furies ripped the angels apart. It was so sudden that the warriors of God didn't have time to scream.

Michael observed the swooping black creatures with a look of disgust. The Furies were older than the gods and beings of pure malevolence. They would be a difficult foe for the angels.

One of the sisters flew towards Michael; her long black claws outstretched. She looked like an old woman, with a long nose and wispy strands of thinning white hair. The skin of her face and neck was a sickly pale green. The rest of her naked body, along with her enormous wings, was as black as night. Her figure was hunched and contorted, and across her torso, dozens of snakes slithered and writhed.

"Spear!" Michael commanded.

A nearby angel threw a spear toward Michael, which he gracefully caught.

Michael lobbed the weapon straight at the approaching Fury. She instantly transformed, becoming a turbulent swarm of insects. The mass of stinging bugs engulfed Michael. He swatted in vain as the bugs ripped through his skin and bit into his eyes.

"Enough!" Michael screamed. A wall of fire manifested

around him, driving the bugs back.

The swarm transformed again. The bugs became rumbling storm clouds that pelted a torrent of rain at the archangel. The storm consumed him, blocking his vision and violently thrashing him back and forth in an orb of wind. Michael slashed through the air with his humming sword, to no avail.

A volley of light arrows pierced the storm on all sides, causing it to retreat from Michael. Angels had surrounded the Fury, firing wave after wave of arrows into her. The storm shrunk, and with a crash of thunder, reformed into the old crone. She shrieked in frustration and pain as the weapons of light forced her back.

Michael composed himself. He scanned left to right. Hearing their sister's cry, the other two Furies were descending on him. He raised his sword high and prepared to meet them.

• • • • •

MOROS TURNED HER MIND from the Furies to Apollo.

Where would he have washed up?

She moved towards the dock on the River Acheron. Unlike the pier before Hades' castle, which lacked opulence, this one was designed to impress. Grand temples to the twelve Olympians lined its forefront. The dock housed three magnificent ships, which ferried souls of the dead to their final destinations.

The most sinister-looking vessel, made of black iron with no sails, dived straight down into Tartarus, the home of the damned. It took nine days to reach the grim depths of Tartarus, descending through water, rock and fire. Only the souls of the terrible had to make this journey.

The largest of the ships on the dock travelled from the Acheron to the River Lethe, then to the Asphodel Meadows, where most humans ended up. Here, the spirits would drink from the river when they arrived, forgetting their lives and their identities. Souls in their hundreds of thousands wandered the meadows aimlessly, in blissful ignorance, until their energy faded.

People who lived extraordinary lives took the final vessel, a magnificent warship with gleaming white sails. It travelled to the Elysium Fields, the home of the heroic. The ship sailed by towering cliffs of red rock and thundering waterfalls until it reached endless fields of ever-green.

An extraordinary deal was reached long ago that allowed Odin, the chieftain of the Norse pantheon of gods, to place a gateway to his halls of Valhalla in the Elysium Fields. The Norse gods generally operated within their own planes of existence. Still, Odin was so inspired by Elysium and impressed with the heroes who dwelled there, that he'd allowed a replica of the halls to appear in the Greek Underworld. It linked directly to the Nordic realm of Asgard. This union of gods allowed the mightiest warriors in history to train and battle to their heart's content; if they chose such a pastime.

If Apollo had gone anywhere, he would've gone there in search of warriors. Moros was sure of it. She focused her energy and within a moment she was in the Elysium Fields, far from the battle proper.

As expected, Apollo now stood on the soft green grass before the Valhalla gateway, soaking wet and filled with rage. Being a

Greek god in his family's Underworld, he had a certain freedom of movement across its various realms; the same as Moros. The gods could simply think of a destination in the Underworld and arrive there.

Apollo spoke into the air, "Achilles, Odysseus, Jason, Perseus, Theseus, Spartacus, Caesar."

Seven pale shades emerged before the god. They were all dressed in the armour of their eras, equipped with the weapons they'd used in life. Julius Caesar was present in the full garb of a Roman general. The rebel Spartacus was dressed in a simple brown tunic, holding swords in both hands. Around the legendary hero Jason's shoulders was a spectral representation of the Golden Fleece, and Achilles held his fabled shield to his torso. Theseus, the founder of Athens, wore nothing at all, except a helmet with a tall red crest springing from it. In his hand was a simple club. Next to him, Odysseus held a bow at the ready, with his long brown beard falling over his blue robe. The seven ghostly men bowed before Apollo. It was clear that the god was assembling his own army.

"Lord Apollo," Caesar murmured.

Apollo beckoned the men to rise.

"You know, Julius, the Romans view you as a god in your own right, you don't need to bow."

"What people believe and what is the truth are often very different things. How goes my empire?"

"Your empire may be the doom of us all," Apollo said darkly.

"Are you proposing games of some sort?" Achilles asked the god.

"No, quite the opposite," Apollo grimaced. "The seven of you are the first warriors that sprang to mind. I need you to rally the soldiers in the Elysium Fields. The Underworld faces a new peril. An enemy army has broken through the gate. I need heroes to fight with me."

Theseus stepped forward, swinging his club back and forth, "Who are we fighting? Who could pose a threat to the Underworld?"

"The creations of a foreign of a god. He seems to be making a power play and has sent his legions to claim the Underworld as his own."

"So, they are monsters?" Theseus asked, grinning.

"No, they look like humans. Angels, they are called. Winged men. They are powerful, yet they have not experienced true war. The freshly deceased Roman soldiers in the City of Hades are giving them some trouble. I intend to give them some more."

"What would you have us do?" the shade of Jason, leader of the Argonauts, asked.

"Rally the legions here, prepare to fight, I will enter Valhalla and ask the warriors there if they'd like a new war."

This time, the rebel Spartacus stepped forward.

"You cannot, Apollo. The door is barred. Asgard is under siege."

Apollo looked at the mighty door before him. Moros reached towards it with her mind. Flashes of battle passed across her vision. Angels were on the other side.

"They attack Asgard too?" Apollo asked quietly.

"I spend a good deal of time with our Viking brothers,"

Spartacus informed him, shooting a distrusting glance at Caesar. "Too many Romans here. Not long ago, one of their gods barred the door and severed the link to Asgard. I fear what has befallen us has befallen them too."

"We don't need them!" Achilles said abruptly.

"No, I don't think so," Apollo considered. "We have the greatest soldiers in history here, as well as some of the greatest mythical heroes of all time."

Internally, Moros' mind was trying to process this startling new information. Had the angels launched an attack across the world? Is that why only two of the seven archangels were leading their charge here?

Odysseus walked toward the god, "Lord Apollo, we are still trapped in the shades of our mortal bodies. How do we fight winged men when we cannot fly?"

Apollo pondered this for a second before answering, "You know my brother Hermes? With his winged hat and winged sandals?"

The shades nodded.

Apollo snapped his fingers, and winged sandals wrapped themselves around the feet of the seven men.

"As you are dead, it doesn't take much for me to give the entire populace of the Elysium fields the power to fly."

Julius Caesar looked positively delighted as he soared up into the air. Theseus, then Jason, launched themselves up.

"Even with these marvellous sandals, it will take some time to fly to the City of Hades," Perseus said.

The others stood on the ground, their eyes fixed to the spot beside Apollo, where a swirling purple mist had appeared. Within the smoke, there were blinking lights and swirling galaxies. Blue comets with long icy tails flew past as the fog grew wider. Out of the mist, the form of a new god appeared. It was Morpheus, the God of Dreams.

"My father has fallen," Morpheus stated.

Morpheus waved his right arm through the air. Suddenly, above the fields of green grass, rows of ghostly boats emerged.

"These will be faster than the wind," Morpheus informed the heroes.

"How can you make these vessels move through the Underworld so quickly?" Apollo asked.

"Death is like a dream," Morpheus informed him, rubbing his bare foot against the soft grass, "There is much I can do in places where people rest for eternity…"

Apollo rose into the air. "Call the dead legions. You will be my generals. We fly to war."

The seven legendary figures faded before him.

"Will you join us in war, Morpheus?"

"I think not Apollo," Morpheus said, "I am the God of Dreams. This looks to be a nightmare. I will aid you from the shadows. When the time comes, look to your dreams for guidance."

Apollo seemed to have expected this answer. Morpheus was often cryptic in his responses. It came with his domain.

"Good luck," Morpheus called, as Apollo ascended.

Apollo smiled. Michael and Lucifer didn't know what was coming for them.

He held his magnificent sword high and marvelled at it. There was no finer weapon to smite an archangel.

When Apollo was out of earshot, Morpheus spoke again. "Will you not fight, Moros?"

"Clever as always, Morpheus. My invisibility defeats even the most attuned divine perception, yet you know I am here."

"As you see all things in fate, I see all things in dreams," Morpheus yawned.

"I do not see this fate," Moros muttered quietly. "The only thing I know is that Apollo has a significant role to play yet. As do you. This battle will not be your end."

"I will aid you where I can," Morpheus offered.

"My power is being blocked by an outside force. I cannot see a clear path forward. When the time is right, I will call on you."

Morpheus nodded. "Apollo will be safe in the company of his army. There is something strange about the archangels. It seems they have a goal beyond just conquest and I would have you discover it. Right now, Lucifer and his elite soldiers move on the Castle of Hades. They will meet fierce resistance from the Queen of the Underworld, when she returns from her current task. Go to the castle and see Lucifer's true purpose here revealed."

With a turn and a swish, Moros teleported away from the green field, her destination Hades' imposing castle.

CHAPTER TEN

A VIOLENT DEATH

- 337 AD -
THE CASTLE OF HADES

First to storm the jagged black castle was a force of twelve heavily-armoured angels. Their hands and forearms were guarded by golden gauntlets and their breastplates depicted a towering triangular city surrounded by cloud. The eyes of the angels were hidden behind their carved faceplates, each designed in the style of a different animal.

These angels were the elite. They'd named themselves the Gladius Vaticanus - *the sword of the hill of prophecy.*

As Lucifer battled Cerberus above, the lead angel, whose helmet was designed to replicate a bull, sent his squadron down the waterfall and towards the castle. When he passed the elm tree in the courtyard, he gently ran his armoured fingers down its trunk. The magical tree was set ablaze, becoming a raging inferno surrounded by stone.

Moros scowled. This was an act of great disrespect.

The Gladius Vaticanus moved towards the colossal black door of the castle and paused.

A shining lamb swirled into being before them and gazed curiously at the heavily armed soldiers. It tilted its head from side to side, a shimmering mist gently falling from it with every movement.

The bull-masked angel, silhouetted against the blazing tree in the courtyard, pointed at the door of the castle. The little lamb turned to face it and grew in size, quickly became a horned ram. It then transfigured further, expanded outwards and changing shape entirely. It morphed into a swinging battering ram, the same that had smashed down the gate. Of its own accord, the heavy centre bar that was fronted with the ram's face, swung back on translucent ropes, then pelted towards the castle door.

It only took one strike. The door shattered on impact, falling into pieces of black glass. The chief angel snapped his fingers and the battering ram disappeared in a swirl of silver fog.

The angels charged into the castle, with Moros following close behind.

The entry chamber wasn't black like the external walls. It was white inside, with every wall covered with gigantic mosaics depicting stories from Greek myth. Banners displaying the symbols of Athens, Sparta and Rome, among a hundred other city-states and cultures fell from the ceiling. Two enormous staircases, with alternating white and red steps, twisted up the sides of the room and out of view, leading further into the towering structure.

In the very centre of the chamber was a collection of flowering plants and small trees. This garden was a gift from the Olympian Goddess Demeter to her daughter, Persephone, so that she knew what season the world above was experiencing.

Behind the garden was another spectacular door, decorated with silver carvings. This door opened to the chamber of judgement, where the mighty figures of Rhadamanthus, Minos and Aeacus had seats. Every departed soul in the Mediterranean region came to this place. Their acts in life determined their placement in death.

This was a place of significant importance and the gods were going to defend it. Standing amongst the circle of ornately arranged shrubs and flowers of the garden was a lone figure. It was a woman with a bowed head. Her long brown hair cascaded forward, hiding her face. She wore an elegant maroon dress, tied at the waist with a lavish purple belt. Moros had seen her last in the council chambers. She was Cer, the Goddess of a Violent Death.

Cer didn't move as the angels encircled her.

The twelve golden figures hovered cautiously around the circumference of the garden. They looked toward the bull-masked angel for guidance.

Impatience got the better of their leader. In a lightning-quick movement, he aimed his spiked mace at Cer's head.

She looked up.

For that short second, the angel was stunned by her beauty.

Her skin was like porcelain and her face; it was as if she was hand-sculpted by the finest artist in the world. But her eyes were unnerving. They were a vivid red and filled with madness.

As the mace came crashing down, her face changed. The woman's mouth widened grotesquely, revealing rows of sharp pointed teeth. She became deathly pale, and black shadows emerged around her eyes. Her hair sprung to life. Like the tentacles of an octopus, it darted up and wrapped itself around the mace, halting it in mid-air. The chief angel struggled to rip his weapon free from the mess of moving strands that entangled it.

"Do you know who I am?" the woman whispered, her misshapen mouth opening and closing abnormally wide.

The chief angel grunted as he tried to free his weapon.

"They call me the Goddess of a Violent Death."

Cer thrust her right hand forward, her fingers pointed outwards. When they connected with the faceplate of the angel's helmet, the metal sizzled and bubbled. The bull-faced design deformed in the heat. She pushed her hand into the metal, and through the front of the angel's skull. He didn't have time to scream as his face exploded inwards.

The eleven other angels moved into the garden; weapons drawn. Cer disappeared in a flash of black smoke, only to appear on the far wall, clinging to it like a monstrous spider.

The angels turned, and those with bows fired arrows of light in her direction. With another puff of smoke, she vanished.

She appeared behind one of the angels and kicked out the back of his knee. The force was so explosive that his leg severed at the joint. His heavy golden greaves and sabatons clanged on the floor. Cer gripped the angel by the shoulders, and with a forceful pull, tore both his arm off. Cer smiled a terrifying smile before she vanished again.

The soldiers of the Gladius Vaticanus had an array of weapons on their belts. Some held long pikes and halberds at the ready and spun on the spot cautiously.

Cer's bare feet appeared on the shoulder plates of an angel wearing a warthog faceplate.

"Look out!" one of the warriors called.

Cer jumped up, moving her feet to the head of the angel. With a quick twist of her legs, she snapped his neck, and he crashed to the floor. His fall echoed up and down the entrance chamber.

Cer laughed and shouted, "His death was too kind; I am not living up to my name!"

The angels swarmed towards her, but she vanished again.

For several long moments, she didn't reappear.

One angel, gripping a long halberd with both hands and wearing the carved face of an impala spoke out, "Focus, she is a God of Death surrounded by death, you can feel her in the air."

"You are right, I can —"

The soldier who had just started speaking stopped and made a rasping, retching sound. His body shook violently.

His armour began to sizzle. Then he cried out.

"Ariton, what is it?" the impala-faced angel asked quickly.

"Belial... I... I..."

A long, feminine arm burst from Ariton's right side. Then, another arm emerged from beneath his left shoulder. The new limbs began feeling up the angel's torso. They followed the lines of the breastplate until they found its centre, then the two searching hands plunged inwards and ripped out two chunks of angelic flesh and armour plating. From the hole they'd dug in the centre of the angel's chest, Cer's face emerged, grinning horrifically.

The angel twitched and writhed in the air as Cer began digging herself out of her host. She pulled him apart from the inside, piece by piece, all the while laughing.

Then she stopped.

One of the angels had swung his halberd into his comrade's back. The heavenly blade sliced through the armour and straight into the goddess. The momentary shock was all it took for the angels to gain the advantage they needed. At once, a barrage of light arrows flew into her exposed face. They pierced both of her eyes.

Cer roared in anger, her hair waving wildly through the air as it ripped the angel's body apart. In her blind rage, the goddess exploded her host, evaporating him in a powerful shockwave.

She reached out with her hair, moving it as if it were a limb, wrapping it around the necks of the two closest angels. With two swift strikes, the hair was cut and the intended victims released. They collapsed out of the air and hit the ground hard, choking and gasping.

Another volley of arrows flew into Cer and she fell back into the garden.

The impala-faced angel, Belial, raised his long pike, ready to impale her.

"Halt!" a voice called from the doorway.

Belial looked back to see who'd commanded him.

He was here.

Lucifer, looking slightly dishevelled, was hovering in the open doorway. His armour featured puncture marks where the guard dog had caught him in its jaws.

Lucifer glided up to Belial and looked at the blind form of Cer on the ground. Ichor leaked from wounds across her body.

"Leave her with me," Lucifer ordered quietly. "Continue upwards. Take the castle."

The impala-faced angel nodded and gestured to his surviving soldiers to form up.

Lucifer summoned ropes of light to bind Cer into place. Cer screamed as she twitched against her bindings.

Lucifer turned to the surviving soldiers. "Remember your mission here, leave no stone of this castle unturned."

Belial, having assumed command of the troops, began issuing orders. "Astaroth, Asmodee, Oriens, Amaymon, take the eastern stair. Leviathan and I will lead the rest through the western passages."

Screeches began carrying down from high above them. The tell-tale noises of waiting creatures higher up echoed through the entry chamber.

"Demons of the Underworld," Lucifer informed his soldiers. "I saw them crawling along the outer-walls. Pay them no heed! Go!"

The eight remaining angels in Lucifer's advance force split up and moved off.

Lucifer landed in front of Cer.

"You are a small fish in all of this, lovely goddess," Lucifer murmured. "I'm sure when history remembers the Olympian gods, you'll get a footnote somewhere."

Moros wanted to help, but knew it was not her place to do so. Cer's fate was sealed, and Moros needed to know what the archangel was going to do with the goddess.

Lucifer held out his right hand, and with a flash of light, a curious object emerged in it. It was entirely bronze, with a long tube that jutted out of a circular grip. Half a sphere emerged from the metal where the two ends of the grip met. The pipe ended with a sharp point.

Without a word, Lucifer thrust the pointed end of the object into Cer's temple. A blinding light filled the entrance chamber.

Moros watched on sadly. She knew what was happening now. The archangels had crafted devices that could steal the power of a god. It made sense, considering their natures. Moros didn't have time to fully process the implications of this development now.

Moros closed her eyes in sorrow. When she opened them, a bunch of bizarre symbols were floating in front of her. They were witches' runes. They were omens of Hecate, the Goddess of Magic. Moros reached out and pointed at one of the floating characters. A voice that only she could hear whispered out.

"A great doom is upon us. When the time is right, come to the hidden cave."

Hecate often spoke in riddles. Much like Morpheus, the God of Dreams, Hecate, the Goddess of Magic, had a significant role to play in coming events.

CHAPTER ELEVEN

BATTLE FOR THE UNDERWORLD

- 337 AD -
THE CITY OF HADES

Moros left the shimmering black tower behind and flew over the City of Hades. She now saw that the departed Roman soldiers, who had been valiantly holding their ground in the city, were beginning to falter. They stood back-to-back on the tops of the buildings, avoiding the deadly mist of Hypnos, the now dead God of Sleep, below.

The flying angels had the distinct advantage of being able to swoop down with their long spears, pikes and halberds, and attack the shades from out of their reach. The weapons of Heaven outmatched the pale ghostly shields of the soldiers. Although, those who had died with bows and quivers full of arrows found some success in attacking the angels from afar.

The versatility of the Roman army had also equipped some of the departed with rope and nets, which they used to lasso and pull down the flying soldiers. The angels had grown wise to this quickly and simply began pelting the soldiers with their own arrows from high above. The remaining chariots quickly disposed of soldiers who were caught off guard.

After a struggle with the three Furies, it seemed that Michael had found himself unable to beat the demonic sisters with pure strength. Cunningness had become his weapon of choice. Using his quick speed and angelic power he'd managed to lure the monsters towards Hypnos' mist and plunge them into it. The three sisters were now trapped in a deathly sleep, somewhere on the ground.

Moros could see that Michael was frustrated. The Furies had presented a significant challenge to him, even with his boosted power. It would be unwise if he wasn't concerned about powerful gods like Hades, who strangely hadn't emerged yet. The archangel was surely also considering the fact that the angels of Heaven had struggled in facing the departed shades in battle. Could the experience of a human in life really leave them so well equipped to fight a superior being, even in death? Moros knew the infinite potential of humans and their great courage, but the angels didn't. They were young and their experience was limited to small geographic areas.

Even so, the battlefield was falling under the angels' control. Doom swirled around the archangel as an aura of death and destruction. Moros flew close to Michael and, using her magic, pierced his mind.

His thoughts were on three of his brothers, who were right now leading a grand assault on Olympus. The legions he'd brought to the Underworld were nothing compared to the golden army advancing on the home of the Greek gods. The angels were trying to reshape the world in one swift, all-encompassing assault.

Michael was a born and bred warrior. He'd trained his whole life. The archangel was powerful, quick, agile and skilled with every weapon. Sometimes, he even took the guise of a young human man and enlisted in the armies of empires. Michael had fought skirmishes in Mesopotamia; stood shoulder to shoulder with the tribesmen in Europe; and battled alongside the Roman army through generations of conquest. He'd even lived the life of a sword master in exotic Japan. The discipline of those eastern warriors had taught Michael that there was a lot to respect about the inner-strength of humans.

Michael relished being amongst them. He was careful never to reveal his divinity. He never used the great power within him. Michael fought with human strength. Sometimes he was slow, and he suffered mortal injuries. Of course, Michael couldn't die, but in his mortal form he felt the extreme pain of injury in war. Every type of conflict the humans offered, he partook in, and the humans provided so much of it.

Now, his glorious moment, the conquering of Olympus, had been taken from him. Michael had envisioned himself standing on the ruins of Zeus' palace, holding one of the god's fabled lightning bolts high.

His father's will ensured that moment wouldn't come to pass.

Instead, Uriel, Gabriel and Raphael commanded Heaven's

legions in the sky. He and Lucifer had been tasked with the Underworld, a lesser battle.

Their other two brothers led a third surprise attack on the Norse gods. It was a minor force, designed to serve as a distraction. The last thing Heaven needed was Odin sending his warriors to aid the Greeks. It was unlikely, but stranger things had happened.

Moros left his mind as Michael looked toward the shining castle. Crawling deformed creatures were climbing its sides and disappearing into the building. From their height, they looked like pale ants swarming across it. They were demons of the Underworld. Moros knew they'd offer Lucifer and his Gladius Vaticanus little trouble.

The battle almost won; the angels began forming back into their ranks. Several still swooped and jabbed at the remaining shades, almost playfully.

Michael looked toward the dock.

"Burn the temples!" he commanded.

From their belts, the angels drew thick torches that ignited as soon as they were raised. They descended toward the twelve temples, screaming chants of victory.

Something caught Moros' eye. Just beyond the dock, high above the still water, a green shade had emerged. Its long shape was reflected on the dark river below.

Then, beside the first shape, dozens more appeared. The green figures were gliding forward. Michael squinted, they seemed to be ghostly transports of some kind.

Even the angels, who'd begun manifesting large pots of

bubbling bronze ooze at the bases of the temples, paused in their destructive fervour.

"FORM UP!" Michael yelled. The angels rose and readied their weapons.

Boats in their hundreds appeared over the river. Horns blasted and battle cries from civilisations beyond counting rang out.

Seven shades appeared, hovering in the air in front of the boats. Apollo's seven champions stood firm, dressed in the battle attire they'd worn in life. They were heroes of myth, from bygone ages. Their legends preceded them, even to the angels of Heaven.

The rhythmic beating of drums began. Noble soldiers who'd fought in armies that were civilisations apart synchronised as the chorus echoed out.

The slow *THUD, THUD, THUD* was awe-inspiring.

Next to the seven champions, other dead heroes began emerging. Atalanta, the mythical huntress with her bow, stood beside them. The centaur Chiron appeared, and beside him emerged Alexander the Great. Bellerophon, Aneas, Leonidas, Hannibal Barca and hundreds of others appeared.

Moros grinned. All the great heroes of the Greek and Roman worlds were here.

"So, this is how these great figures of humanity choose their final end…" Michael whispered.

A crash sounded behind him. Michael quickly spun in the air to see the massive form of Cerberus leaping across the angled surface of Hades' castle and onto the rooftops of the city. The dog was bloody and bleeding, but very much alive. His four huge paws sat on four separate buildings. Sitting on Cerberus's neck, was Apollo. He stood up, and his skin became solid gold. His hair froze in place as his body took on this shining new form. Even his clothes transformed into gold. Cerberus shrank from his giant form to the size of a horse, becoming a far nimbler mount for Apollo. The guard dog was too large a target for the angels, so Apollo was ensuring Cerberus could stay in the fight as long as possible.

Apollo lifted his golden sword high and pointed towards Michael.

"The end begins," Moros thought.

The army of the Underworld charged. Soldiers in their thousands, each equipped with winged sandals, flew towards the angels. The legion of Heaven similarly blasted towards the ghosts. Their weapons clanged as they violently clashed together.

Cerberus' three jaws quivered. His eyes were menacing. The great dog jumped into the air, lunging for the nearest angel.

Apollo, his golden body encased in fire, flew off Cerberus.

Michael went straight up and Apollo followed, with Moros close behind.

Apollo thrust his sword towards the archangel. Michael parried with a sharp turn. Moros noticed that Michael's shimmering blade was cloaked in a translucent white fire. It was an incredible piece of weaponry containing a dreadful power.

Michael struck at Apollo with a flurry of swift strikes. Apollo blocked them all then flipped backwards in the air. He quickly sheathed his sword and drew his bow, firing a silver arrow right at Michael's face. Michael bent backwards, narrowly avoiding the sharp arrowhead. Apollo readied another arrow, still flying backwards, and fired another shot.

This time, with his free hand, Michael caught the arrow in mid-air, and with a sharp turn, flung it back towards the former sun god.

Apollo rolled to the side.

Seizing his moment, Michael lunged, pointing his sword at Apollo's chest. Apollo dropped his bow and using his divine energy, he held Michael's strike at bay through pure force of will.

Instead of trying to force his attack, Michael withdrew his sword and backed away.

Apollo righted himself, re-drawing his own sword. The two divine warriors launched themselves back at each other, throwing strikes faster than a human eye could see. Electricity began crackling through the air around them.

A chariot came racing past Apollo. Its two operators fired arrows of light at the god, however, they disintegrated when they hit Apollo's aura of fire.

The beating of wings filled the air as the Greek hero Bellephron came soaring past on the back of a winged horse, loudly jesting with the heroes Caesar and Spartacus as he forced the chariot away.

Savage and wild, a legion of primitive Gauls flew between Moros and Apollo and fearlessly dived into the angels' ranks.

Caesar rallied all the nearby Roman troops to him and began issuing orders. The Romans respect for him was eternal, and they obeyed without objection.

The angels were beginning to falter. They were hugely outmatched by the army of the glorious dead. The ancient Greek and Roman heroes fought well enough to combat any of the angels, and a group of well-coordinated soldiers easily defeated angels who were caught off guard.

In the chaos, Moros was further separated from Michael and Apollo. Feeling uneasy, she attempted to navigate the battle towards them, but found herself forced closer and closer to ground level, where the smaller Cerberus was devouring everything that came near him.

Hovering above Cerberus were the legendary Amazon warrior women. They shot a rain of arrows into the advancing angels' ranks.

One of the angels paused as he raised his shield to avoid an arrow hurling towards him. Moros noticed, at the same time as the angel, that Cerberus was beside one of the bubbling pots at the base of a riverside temple. The angel grabbed his torch, which instantly ignited, and tossed it towards the pot. The torch swirled through the air and landed in the ooze.

Moros quickly reacted, returning Cerberus to his original giant size in the second before it happened.

The entire building exploded.

Dust and rubble flew everywhere, crashing into ghost and angel alike. The explosion ignited the pots besides the adjoining temples, and within a moment the entire dock became a fireball. The temples of the Olympians were torn apart.

The shockwave threw Cerberus off his feet and into the river, although it was too shallow to submerge the guard dog. Cerberus lay on his side, like a furry black island, one head underwater and the other two whimpering meekly.

Seizing their moment, a group of angels dived, seeking to

thrust their spears into the beast's brains. They were beaten to the dog by another mythological figure, Queen Hippolyta of the Amazons. She stood proud between the angels and their prey, becoming their target instead. The warrior women of Greek myth attempted to fly to their most famous queen, but the enemy was faster.

Hippolyta readied her bow and start firing ghostly arrows at the angels. Her long black hair flowed behind her as she loosed one large arrow. It pierced straight through an angel's armour and sent him careening into the water. She loosed another. And another, but the angels kept coming.

Just as their lances were about to impale the queen, their wings went rigid. Frost appeared on their faces. Frozen in place, they tumbled out of the sky. In front of Hippolyta, a new shining figure rose.

Moros breathed a sigh of relief. It was about time that one of the most powerful of the gods arrived.

Demeter, Goddess of the Seasons, had joined the fight.

Her long curly hair flowed from beneath the wreath made of corn on her head. Beside her, floating of its own accord, was a long bronze staff, taller than the goddess, with a small flame on top. Clasped firmly in her left hand was a sheath of wheat.

The sudden arrival of the goddess sparked attention from the angels, especially Michael.

Apollo was already presenting a match for him, and Demeter was another Olympian. She was worshipped before even Zeus was. Agriculture was a fundamental aspect of human life, and it was said that Demeter herself had first shown early humans how to sew corn. Her influence was immense. Michael would want to take her out of this fight quickly.

Demeter rose into the middle of the chaos. Her eyes went white.

"Winter," she shouted, her voice booming off the walls.

A freezing gale whipped up. Gushing torrents of wind began careening across the battlefield. Angels who were caught in the streams instantly froze and fell, their bodies shattering on impact with the ground.

The angelic soldiers concentrated their power and manifested golden shields of energy around themselves as protection.

Moros knew that this would take a heavy toll on their ability to fight, as the concentration required to maintain that aura of energy was taxing.

Seeing the angels protecting themselves, Demeter tried a new approach.

"Spring."

On the distant walls of the vast cavern, small sprouts of greenery pushed their way through the rock. In seconds, the shoots stretched into vines, which whipped towards the battlefield. They began wrapping around the angels, choking them and flinging them into the walls, or down into the mist.

The commanders of the angelic squadrons quickly identified the enormous threat that Demeter posed. They rallied what soldiers they could and charged toward her.

"Autumn."

An orange mist formed around Demeter. The angels burst through it, only to pause. They looked down at their hands. Lines were forming as their flawless skin began to wrinkle. They felt their faces sagging.

Signs of old age were appearing. They hunched over. It was like she'd cursed them with humanity. Angels didn't age or wither. But now they were all becoming old men. Skin started falling from their bones, and quickly they faded to dust.

"You may know me as the Goddess of the Harvest, but I am also the Goddess of the Cycle of Life and Death. It is time for you to become acquainted with that cycle."

Michael yelled out in frustration. He managed to put three angels between himself and Apollo. They were skilled enough to block Apollo's attempts to manoeuvre around them.

Michael flew towards one of the commanders, Moros zooming towards them both.

"I cannot fight both Demeter and Apollo!" Michael shouted in anguish.

The commander turned to him, after slicing through the middle of an attacking shade. "At least that three-headed dog has been dealt with, I think it is time we called in a monster of our own."

Moros wondered what monsters Heaven had at its disposal.

Michael turned towards Cerberus in the water. His dismay was evident as he noticed a lone figure on a small canoe paddling towards the giant dog. It was the ferryman, Charon.

Charon placed his hands on the massive side of the beast and began whispering some spell.

The eyes of Cerberus once again burst open.

Michael looked at his commander, exasperated. "Have you

received word from our secondary force?"

"Yes, my Lord."

The angel held out his palm, and from it, a small ball of light emerged. The ball quickly became a scroll that read, *"The other entrances have fallen."*

The commander looked back at Michael and stated, "Camael has Lucifer's pet with him."

"My brother will be upset if we summon the Serpent of Heaven without him."

"Lucifer seems otherwise engaged trying to take the castle."

Cerberus was once again rising to his feet. His entire left side was charred and burned.

One of his heads flopped, lifeless. The other two looked fierce.

"Enough with this blasted dog!" the commander spat, looking frustrated as Cerberus once again bounded into battle.

"I will ask Camael to summon it," Michael grimaced. "That dog only has three heads, let's see how they deal with seven."

The commander smiled.

The ground shook violently as the water of the River Acheron swirled. Moros could sense something rising through the rock at supersonic speed toward the battlefield. Another goddess was coming, bringing three powerful allies. Persephone, Queen of the Underworld, had been sent to collect the guards to the prison of the titans — the Hecatoncheires. The battle was about to become a lot more difficult for the forces of Heaven.

CHAPTER TWELVE

GIANTS AND DRAGONS

- 337 AD -
TAENARUM

Moros felt an unpleasant twinge as her mind departed the battlefield and swamped her with images of a nearby town in the mortal world. It seemed that reinforcements for the angels were swiftly approaching through the gate to the Underworld at Taenarum.

She knew the mortal residents of Taenarum had forever lived with a poorly kept secret. When visitors came to the town, they never failed to notice that all the vases and pottery (the number of which was beyond counting) contained images from the same pair of myths.

In little stores across the bustling marketplace were images of Heracles dragging Cerberus from the Underworld. The demi-god and the monstrous dog could be seen everywhere.

Still popular, but not as prevalent, were images of Orpheus attempting to bring his departed wife up to the world of the living.

Most travellers found these vases a curiosity at best. They were more interested in the town's lavish purple dye and green marble slabs. Taenarum was close enough to the sea that the salty breeze sweeping through was an ever-present, pleasant phenomenon.

Also a phenomenon was the gaping cavern on the hillside, not far from the town. Ancient Spartans had built several temples around the black opening, yet no individuals ever ventured within its depths. People only ever spoke of it in whispers.

Roman dignitaries, on the occasion that they visited the town, often inquired about the cavern. Once they heard the myths, they usually marvelled at the curiosity, but left it be.

The residents of Taenarum found it bizarre that on this particular summer's night, legions of oddly dressed men were marching through the town towards the cavern.

They looked kind-of Roman. They were dressed like Romans, only they were wearing heavy greaves, gauntlets, and sabatons of elaborate gold. On their backs and across their belts was an array of weapons. Swords, bows, knives and torches, along with pikes and halberds were strapped across them.

Many had golden open-faced helmets, although the lesser ranks didn't have any kind of head protection at all.

At the head of each company were two heavily defended soldiers, equipped from head to toe in suits of armour. They had helmets with tall silver crests, making them look particularly fierce.

The sound of the clunking boots on the ground was enough to wake the entire populace of Taenarum. In their thousands, the shining soldiers marched through the town, into the countryside, and then down into the darkness.

The cavern had long been rumoured to be an entrance to the Underworld. Years ago, Heracles, or Hercules as the Romans called him, had dragged Cerberus out through that very opening as a part of his labours. The great musician Orpheus, second perhaps only to Apollo in skill (though some said greater), had led his departed wife to that very opening.

As soon as the legion of Heaven passed through the cave's mouth, their hidden wings spread wide and they began soaring down the tunnel.

At the head of the column of angels was the commander, Camael. He was venerated among his own kind for his strength and courage. He was distinguished from the rest by the red and blue robe that flowed behind him as he soared. Fixed to the left side of his belt was a silver rectangle, with a simple red dragon carved into its face.

Michael had mentioned Camael earlier. He had something to do with this unknown monster the forces of Heaven could summon.

In her mind's eye, Moros watched as Camael, followed by his legions, emerged from a hole in the rock face high above the River Styx. Immediately, the angels swarmed into the cavern and passed through the wreckage of the gate. They cast an ominous shadow as they flew below the Light of the Underworld and over

Hades' castle.

For the first time since the battle started, Moros made herself visible. She called out to the forces of the Underworld, "Reform your ranks! A new force emerges from the river!"

The ghosts of the departed blew horns and quickly fell into hastily designated formations to meet the new threat.

The angels, currently engrossed in the raging battle, rejoiced at the arrival of their comrades and rallied.

A fireball sent Apollo's attackers hurtling out of the sky. With a rush of air, he teleported himself next to Demeter.

The Goddess of the Harvest was now shooting long coils of fire around the battlefield. It was the burning power of summer that often scorched the land. Her shield of autumn fog had no effect on Apollo. The pair watched the new cloud of angels descend into battle.

Moros then joined them, appearing beside two Olympians with a pop.

"There are thousands of them," Demeter whispered. Concern was etched on her face.

"The heroic dead have been more than a match so far," Apollo said confidently.

"Because they outnumber them five to one," Demeter said.

"What say you, Moros? What does fate have waiting for us?" Apollo asked her.

"It is cloudy and unclear. I can only see small pieces right now, not the whole. The power of the angels is unexpected in its scope and complexity."

Apollo frowned. "If the Goddess of Fate does not know,

then this battle's outcome is not yet determined. We will send these wretched angels into the abyss!"

"Despite their valiant efforts, I fear the army of the dead's longevity in this fight," Demeter murmured.

"Do not be concerned; in my experience, humans always rise to the challenge in unexpected ways. Do not forget that Hades and Persephone are yet to join us," Apollo grinned.

"Of course, Apollo. My daughter should be arriving shortly."

As if Demeter's words were prophecy, a loud rumbling echoed out from the river.

The rumbling grew until it was a roar, before an enormous pillar of rock burst forth by the ruined dock. Molten lava dripped in globs and sizzled as it hit the water.

Standing on the pillar was Persephone, the Goddess of the Underworld.

She wasn't alone.

The goddess was barely noticeable in the shadow of the three giants behind her. The Hecatoncheires had arrived.

The sudden appearance of the monsters paused the battle completely. Even Michael froze, floating with his mouth agape at the sight of the ancient Greek monsters.

The Hecatoncheires were three beings that were as tall as mountainsides. Persephone was but a dot in front of the lead giant's big toe. Their size wasn't their defining characteristic however.

Splayed out from each of their shoulders and backs, like the feathers of a peacock, were one hundred arms of varying shapes and sizes. Their two primary arms, in the position where arms usually sat, were the dominant appendages, vast and muscular.

Even more bizarre were the giant's fifty heads. From each of their bare upper chests, a mass of heads, like the top of a stalk of broccoli, exploded out, giving them a bulbous look. The heads were all bald, with large wild eyes, and like the arms, came in an array of shapes and sizes.

These were creatures from the early days of Greek myth; they had assisted the gods in their war against the titans. For an eternity, they'd sat as the formidable guards of the deepest darkest prison of Tartarus.

The three giants observed the swarm of small feathered beings invading the Underworld.

"Dear Persephone," one of the heads from the lead giant, named Briareus, began, "you would bring us up here to swat insects?"

"Yes, Briareus," Persephone said. "You, Gyges and Cottus are to end this little skirmish as quickly as possible. I am going to the castle. I have a particular punishment in mind for the leaders of this attack."

With a smile and spin, Persephone disappeared. Moros made note that she should quickly return to the castle as well, as fate told her that Persephone's coming actions were of great importance.

The three Hecatonchieres thundered forward. The entire cavern quaked with their footsteps. They pulverised the rubble of the temples beneath them and with one swipe, Briareus knocked dozens of angels out of the air. Running around their legs, even Cerberus at his true size looked like a miniature dog.

Angels fired volleys of arrows at the monsters, so many that they became a blinding stream of light.

The Hecatoncheires used their many arms as a shield and pushed forward against the rivers of piercing light. Once the rain of arrows had ceased, the giants were left bleeding from a thousand wounds.

The sheer number of angels that had to form up to fire the cloud of arrows allowed the army of the dead to regroup and mount a counter-attack.

Michael glided over to Camael. Moros donned her invisibility and joined them, torn between hearing their plans and following Persephone.

"You brought it with you?" Michael's eyes were fixed to the red dragon on Camael's belt.

"Of course, Lord Michael."

"The time to unleash it is now."

Camael plucked the metallic plate from his belt and handed it to the archangel.

He looked uneasy, and Michael noticed.

"You object to summoning the Serpent of Heaven?"

"No… Lord Michael. It is just that the Serpent of Heaven is an agent of chaos, meant only for destruction. I fear that if we summon it now, it will turn the Underworld into a fiery pit. It cannot be stopped; it will burn until there is nothing left unburnt."

Michael considered this.

He watched as a group of angels dodged the swinging hands of Briareus, only to be caught in the leaping jaws of Cerberus. His attention then turned to Demeter, whose simultaneous torrents of ice and fire were obliterating angels as they entered the battle.

"So be it," Michael sighed. He pressed down firmly on the

metal plate and snapped it in half.

With a sound like exploding thunder, an enormous rip in the air formed above Michael. It looked like a jagged lightning bolt in the sky.

Several terrifying screeches carried through the tear in the fabric of reality.

At once, Moros knew something terrible had happened. Fear and dread filled her very being. Whatever this thing was, it was wrong.

A gigantic snake-like head tentatively poked through the tear. Its serpentine eyes peered at the mass of soldiers battling below it. Its forked tongue flicked out. The serpent's scales were blood red, and it had a row of deep purple spines emerging from between its eyes and travelling down its long slender neck. Two bright red horns sat on either side of its head. It hissed and slipped back into the tear.

On the ground, Cerberus went wild, leaping and barking, his attention solely focused on the hole in the sky.

The rest of the army barely paid any attention; the fighting had intensified.

Demeter and Apollo felt the change in the air. The brief elation they'd felt from the arrival of the Hecatoncheires was instantly replaced with unease. Whatever that snake-head was, it was radiating divine power.

Apollo held his arms up and focused his energy on the rip in the sky. Moros teleported beside him and did the same. It was a simple portal, if much larger than most. They could definitely seal it up if they concentrated their power.

It didn't work. Whatever was on the other side was infinitely more powerful than the two gods combined. A huge red body fell through the rip and collapsed onto the ground.

Seven red snake-heads on long slender necks sprouted out from a thick scaly body. Jagged purple spines ran down the length of the beast, and great bat-like wings unfurled from the ridges on its back.

Plumes of heat radiated out from the creature. Its yellow stomach sat against the ground, between four clawed feet. The beast was vast, only slightly shorter in height than the mountainous Hecatoncheires, but much longer. Its tail whipped and thrashed, collapsing buildings throughout the City of Hades.

The torrents of icy wind from Demeter simply dissipated against its reptilian skin. Its heads snapped at the battling angels and ghosts in the air around it. Several of the heads seemed to be fighting with each other. Torrential jets of flame shot out as they writhed back and forth.

Camael was already issuing orders to his generals, telling formations of angels to stay well clear of the dragon.

Cerberus bounded forward and latched his enormous jaws onto the twitching tail of the beast. Three of the monstrous heads of the dragon immediately turned backwards and blasted columns of fire at the dog. Cerberus yelped and ran toward the river, his fur set ablaze.

The Hecatoncheires ran at the dragon, mounting a three-pronged attack. Demeter paused her assault on the angelic forces and generated icy barriers of wind around the three giants.

The angels seized their moment to attack Demeter, but

Apollo and Moros stood as her faithful guard, quickly subduing the waves of attackers that advanced.

While Apollo had long ago given up his position as the God of the Sun to Helios, its solar fire still burned in him. When the mass of attackers became too much for bow and sword, Apollo began blinding them with the light of the sun. Rays of sun-fire shot from his golden body.

Moros, meanwhile, called on the black energy of doom in the form of lightning to strike down her foes.

Both of the god's magical attacks paled in comparison to the blasts from the Serpent of Heaven. Its heads swung wildly, firing infernos of flame in all directions. The air of the Underworld began to sizzle in the heat. Demeter's strangling spring vines began to wilt on the walls.

The giant Cottus attempted to wrap his arms around all seven waving heads of the dragon at once. They squealed and shrieked as dozens upon dozens of arms gripped the thin necks of the dragon. Each hand tried to point the heads upwards, so that the devastating tornados of fire blasted towards the roof.

The other two Hecatoncheires tried to aide Cottus, running up and wrapping more arms around the struggling necks. The three giants pulled together, in a vain attempt to rip the necks out of their sockets.

Angels flew down around the giants' legs. They were careful to avoid Hypnos' mist and began firing arrows at the giants' legs. A trickle soon became a waterfall of blood as Gyges collapsed. Two of the heads he was holding slipped free from his grip and began shooting a torrent of fire at him.

Gyges was engulfed in flame. Demeter focused as best she could to shield him, but was interrupted by Michael swooping in. Gyges screamed as his flesh melted in the fire. In seconds he became dust.

Cottus attempted to regain control of the free heads, but the fire forced him back. The jets of flame sent both he and Briareus stumbling away.

The Serpent of Heaven spread its leathery wings and took off, slowly rising into the air. With all seven heads free, it blasted devastating fire towards the giants.

Apollo teleported himself in front of the monster and managed to redirect the flames, though it visibly drained him to do so. He drew his golden sword and flew towards the slithering necks, a speck in front of the dragon.

"This creature is very similar to the hydra," Apollo yelled to Moros, "so I will take a similar approach."

The god's aim was to cut each head off with his golden sword, then burn the stump, just in case it regrew or regenerated. He was tiny as he flew into the mass of weaving necks. As she had earlier, Moros used her magic to shield him.

Seeing Apollo's charge, the mythological heroes Theseus and Perseus flew in to join him. Both had experience hunting monsters in their day, though none this large.

On the ground, Briareus and Cottus began hurling chunks of stone and earth towards the flying dragon.

Demeter found herself fully engaged in her battle with Michael. All the support she'd been offering the army of ghosts was gone. The archangel was proving a match for her.

Though, it was painfully apparent that Michael was once again having difficulty confronting this other Olympian. He was also distracted as the Serpent of Heaven was burning ghost and angel alike. Moros deduced that the dragon had no side in this fight and seemed intent on total destruction. She'd heard Michael state that Lucifer was the only being in Heaven that had a rapport with the beast.

It was clear that the angels needed Lucifer in the fight now. He was still in the castle, presumably making his way towards Persephone.

Moros reluctantly decided to abandon Apollo and go to Persephone. Fate told her that what happened next would have consequences that would ripple through time. She needed to know the destiny of Lucifer.

CHAPTER THIRTEEN

THE FALL OF LUCIFER

- 337 AD -
THE CASTLE OF HADES

The air was alive with electricity. Chaos reigned supreme over the City of Hades. The ground rumbled and shook violently, vibrating Hades' castle. Its gleaming black walls reflected fire and death.

Buildings crumbled in the wake of the giants, their rubble disappearing into the toxic fog that still smothered the ground. Fire from the great Serpent of Heaven flew wildly across the cavern. Winged angels and flying heroes from myth clashed together. This was not just a battle for a place; it was a battle for the very soul of the world.

Lucifer's advance team, the Gladius Vaticanus, had scaled high into Hades' palace, stealing treasures and slaying hordes of demons as they ascended.

The demons of the Underworld were not creations of Hades; they'd been there since time immemorial. The crawling monstrous creatures lived in all sections of the Underworld, even the ones rented out to other pantheons of gods. They took on vastly different shapes and appearances, coming across as tall fearsome monsters in some places, and as wretched broken humans in others.

The nature of the creatures had been mused upon by the Moros, with no clear conclusions drawn. They showed intelligence, seemingly at random, and at the very least could be made to reliably guard the castle.

The Gladius Vaticanus had no trouble dispatching wave after wave of the monsters as they poured into rooms through secret tunnels and passages in the outer walls.

Moros found the Archangel Lucifer in the upper levels of the castle. He'd battled his way through dark corridors and winding staircases and left his team of heavily armoured soldiers behind as they cleared each room. Orders had been given for Lucifer's team to recover as many divine relics as they could get their hands on.

Using his weapons, including his green fire, Lucifer smote his foes with righteous fury.

It was clear that he'd almost been overwhelmed by the horde of demons on more than one occasion, as his face now carried the scars to show it. His robes were ripped and fell loosely from his shoulder, exposing his bare chest. His elaborate white armour had been tossed away. He looked every bit the hero he was worshipped as. Moros had heard Lucifer be called 'the glorious morning star' by his mortal followers, and it seemed appropriate as he single-handedly fought on, towards the peak of the castle.

After dispatching a demon at the top of a narrow flight of stairs, Lucifer came face-to-face with an ornate black door. Several carved figures jutted from its surface. They moved like they were made from liquid streams of silver.

Moros floated invisible just behind Lucifer as he stood mesmerized, watching the dancing figures move about the door front.

"Enter, archangel," a voice from behind the door called. It was soft and sweet, like music. Moros knew this to be the voice of the Queen of the Underworld, Persephone.

The entire door melted before Lucifer, leaving an open archway that led into a magnificent room.

A four-poster bed, with ruby red covers, sat furthest from the door. White silk curtains were drawn, hiding the speaker from Lucifer's sight. He could see the silhouette of a woman.

The floor was made of grey stone cuttings, fit together with impossible precision. The room was circular, and four lamps emitting blue fire sat opposite each other on the wall. One chest of drawers had a curious object sitting on top of it. Lucifer's eyes quickly snapped to the unassuming jar. It was brown and straightforward, with rows of carvings running up its face. It was an object of immense power, and Moros knew the archangel was cataloguing it in his mind.

Lucifer's attention was drawn from the jar towards the bed as the white curtains parted, revealing the Goddess Persephone.

"The wife of Hades," Lucifer uttered in mild surprise. "And

here I thought it would be your husband that would greet me as I claimed his castle."

Like all the Greek pantheon, Persephone was beautiful. She sat with her long slender legs dangling off the bed, eyeing the bare-chested Lucifer up and down.

The goddess had a simple turquoise dress draped over her that shimmered as she moved. Two long, immaculate portions of hair fell forward and framed the sides of her face. Her hair was plaited at the front and fell into tangled waves at the back. A simple wreath of white daisies and green stems sat across the top of her head, forming a delicate crown. Her wrists featured jewellery made from vegetation spliced with gold; a combination of nature and man-made elegance. She looked at Lucifer with her silver eyes and smiled seductively.

Lucifer seemed taken aback by the appearance of the goddess. Moros knew that to him Persephone looked divine, like a creature from a higher world. Certainly, from an older world than his.

He walked toward the bed.

Moros wondered exactly what the goddess had planned. Clearly seduction was involved, which was fitting as it was a weapon the gods had used throughout history.

With a puff of smoke, a black goblet appeared in Persephone's right hand. She reached inside and picked up a pomegranate seed, which she slowly placed in her mouth.

Moros had to stop herself from audibly gasping. Persephone's plan was genius.

Lucifer stopped just short of the bed and leaned against one of the posts. "I was told the Underworld only offered monsters and death. Perhaps it provides some delights too?"

Persephone smiled and twirled her hair.

"Many delights and many terrors," Persephone said, looking up at the archangel.

"The terrors I can handle," Lucifer said, lowering his hand and brushing it against the side of Persephone's face. Persephone blushed.

"You seem confident of yourself," Persephone said, pushing Lucifer's hand away.

"My name is Lucifer, Archangel of the Kingdom of Heaven. The morning star."

"And I am Persephone, Queen of the Underworld. A goddess."

"Goddesses and angels… we aren't so different, you know?" Lucifer murmured softly.

"Oh, is that so? You think you compare to a true goddess, one who has ruled this domain for thousands of years?"

"Thousands of years is a long time; things become stagnant. Heaven brings change. Perhaps you should consider embracing this change. There could be a place for one as beautiful as you in our new world order."

"Golden armour and a silver tongue," Persephone stated as she reached for another pomegranate seed.

Lucifer confidently reached down and plucked the pomegranate seed from her fingers. He didn't give it a second thought as he placed it in his mouth. The archangel gazed down at the silver-eyed goddess, who was watching him curiously.

She stood up. Her long, shimmering dress flowed loosely

around her. It was almost see-through. She was only as tall as Lucifer's shoulders, and when standing her face came to be only inches from his chest. She raised a finger and ran it down the crease between his muscular pectorals.

"You are wonderfully crafted creatures…" Persephone said. "What are you?"

"The same as you," Lucifer replied simply. "To the humans, a god."

"But you don't call yourselves gods."

Lucifer shrugged, "My father is the only true god among us. He is the truth and the light."

"Those of us here, whose kingdom you have invaded, were born gods. We were born, whether through more human means… or through the universe bringing us into being independent of any external control. How were you born? How did you achieve your divinity?" Persephone leaned up and whispered in Lucifer's ear, "Tell me what made your splendour?"

Persephone was so close that her goblet pushed into Lucifer's stomach. He reached down and grabbed a handful of pomegranate seeds.

"My brothers and I were crafted in your image, the image of the gods. And the image of the humans, to be both of your betters. To be the new gods. My father designed us, and with his power brought us into being. Certainly, creating new gods through the pleasures of the divine flesh, to fill empty niches in the universe, has a certain appeal," Lucifer winked as he stroked Persephone's hair. "But we are better. The flaws of gods and humans remain within us, admittedly, but we were made to bring this world into a glorious new age. And now we are."

Lucifer thrust the palm full of seeds into his mouth. Moros knew the sensation of the fruit of the Underworld, with the closeness of Persephone, would be intoxicating to Lucifer. Lust was always a weakness of both gods and mankind. It was a symptom of the virus that is life. Even the mighty Lucifer wasn't above this sin.

Lucifer reached for the right strap of Persephone's dress and gently lowered it down her shoulder. Persephone turned away and blushed.

"You wish to replace my husband?"

"In more than one way," Lucifer said.

"Why do you want to own the Underworld?"

Lucifer pulled back slightly. For a moment, he looked annoyed at the question. He reached into the goblet and took two more pomegranate seeds.

"You, and your kind, the gods of the Romans, Egyptians, Aztecs and Vikings, all of you. Your power doesn't diminish without humans. You have guided them, played with them and done whatever you've wanted with them. If humanity were to disappear tomorrow, you could still shape the world as you see fit. Your ability to control your godly domains wouldn't change. Their prayer and sacrifice and worship boost your power, but you don't need it to be strong." Lucifer paused, briefly lost in thought. "We need it, all of it."

"Why?"

"I can't reveal our plan."

"Perhaps I can entice you?"

Persephone drew two more pomegranate seeds from the goblet and placed them in Lucifer's mouth.

Lucifer reached for the other strap of Persephone's dress. He pointed a finger, and from it a blade of light emerged. He cut the strap in half. Persephone's shimmering dress fell to the floor. The naked body of the goddess was so close to Lucifer.

Persephone thrust the goblet into Lucifer's hand. She slowly reached up and grasped a piece of his tattered robe. She gripped it firmly, and then, displaying her impossible strength, flipped the angel over herself and onto the bed. Lucifer landed on his back, his six mighty wings instantly retracting. The naked figure of Persephone turned around. Lucifer absent-mindedly reached into the goblet and ate another pomegranate seed.

"Do you know how I came to be the Queen of the Underworld?" Persephone asked.

"Because you are divine beauty manifest..." Lucifer gushed.

"More than that," Persephone stated coldly, her tone changing quickly. "Hades, on his chariot, burst through the earth and kidnapped me."

Lucifer ate another of the seeds, barely comprehending what the goddess was saying as he stared at her.

"When my mother found out, she persuaded Zeus to send Hermes to demand my release. Hades tricked me into having to stay in the Underworld. Do you know how he did that?"

Lucifer shrugged as he rolled his finger along the inside of the goblet, looking for the final pomegranate seed. Without even looking down, he found it and promptly placed it in his mouth.

Persephone smiled wickedly. She snapped her fingers, and

her dress sprang up and wrapped itself around her body.

Lucifer's eyes widened in alarm. He tried to sit upright, but some invisible force was holding him down.

"He had me eat six pomegranate seeds. I was young and naïve. I didn't know that only one food grew in the Underworld. The pomegranate."

Rage shot through Lucifer's body. He tried to open his mouth to speak, but he was being gagged by Persephone's power. The goddess had sprung her trap.

Moros could feel Lucifer struggling against Persephone's magic. His power was immense, but she was the Queen of the Underworld. She was no minor deity and this was not the place to challenge her might.

"On that day, I ate six pomegranate seeds, Lucifer. I was condemned to spend six months of every year here in the Underworld."

These words sunk like a stone in Lucifer's stomach.

Persephone continued, "You just ate twelve pomegranate seeds. As a divine being, no matter how perfect you think you are, you are condemned to this place! Twelve months of every year, you must be in the Underworld. Kill us all, burn it all down, it no longer matters for you, you'll have to live in the fire you have made, forever!"

Persephone's laughter rang through the chamber. Moros felt the waves of destiny wash over Lucifer.

Persephone picked up Lucifer's trident from the ground. She casually twirled it around herself, then thrust it towards Lucifer's head.

As the three points flew towards him, Lucifer exploded with

anger. Green fire burst out from him in all directions. Persephone's grip released as she leapt back to avoid the shooting flames.

Lucifer sat upright and roared out in rage. In that second, the room became the epicentre of a devastating explosion. A supernova of green fire rolled outwards from Lucifer at the speed of sound.

The entire area instantaneously disintegrated. Again, Moros reacted quickly enough to shield Persephone from the explosion as she teleported out of the room. The fireball burst from the side of the castle and out into the battle. Angels and soldiers alike fled the expanding flames.

There, in the gaping hole where the side of the castle used to be, floated Lucifer, his six wings spread wide. Something was noticeably different about him. The curse was already taking hold. His wings had turned red, the same red as the pomegranate seeds. His eyes also were a haunting red, eerily similar to Cer's.

Moros looked to Michael, who was gazing at his brother. The other archangel didn't have time to process Lucifer's change, however, as a beam of ice shot towards him from Demeter.

The hole in the castle reached down to the lower levels, where the heavily armoured, beast-masked angels had been searching. They flew up to their commander.

"Lord Lucifer, what happened?" Belial asked.

Lucifer looked at him coldly but didn't speak.

The Gladius Vaticanus floated around their commander. Lucifer looked down.

Persephone was standing directly below him, on the roof of a small white building, surrounded in mist.

Her face was burnt. Her silver eyes stared straight up, taunting the archangel.

Lucifer dived towards her at immense speed. A ring of flame burst out from him, then vanished as he descended. His soldiers followed him down, diving in formation behind Lucifer.

Persephone watched them come.

Demeter, who was locked in battle with Michael, desperately tried to break free from the archangel.

She screamed and reached out in vain when she realised there was no way she could get to her daughter in time. There was nothing Moros could do. She knew that Persephone had made a choice that couldn't be undone. The Queen of the Underworld was going to do away with Lucifer permanently.

Persephone had felt Lucifer's real strength the moment he generated the fireball. Her plan had worked, the archangel was now imprisoned in the Underworld, unable to ever leave. This was intended to be punishment for his hubris when the legions of Heaven failed in their battle.

But he was so powerful that she knew he had to be removed from this fight. He was far more powerful than she could have ever expected. Trapped in the Underworld wasn't good enough. Lucifer had to be buried deep.

Persephone whispered to the ground.

"Tartarus, hear me…"

Upon hearing these words, Moros quickly teleported as far away as she could.

Persephone wasn't speaking to the deepest realm of the Underworld, she was speaking to the primordial deity Tartarus himself. He was an ancient being, older than any god or titan, who slumbered within the darkest depths of the Underworld. The great prison that held the titans and the eternally punished was named after him.

The earth groaned. The sound stopped the fighting. Then, the city of Hades exploded upwards.

Enormous jaws, made of rock, burst forth from the ground. Each tooth was the size of a building and made even the giant Hecatoncheires look tiny in comparison. Persephone stood directly in the middle of it all.

Lucifer and his angels couldn't stop their descent in time. The earthen jaws reached high above them and clamped shut, sealing Lucifer and his angels in complete darkness.

Persephone was powerless in the presence of Tartarus. This had been her choice. Only Hades and she, due to their status in the Underworld, could call on Tartarus. Even then, they'd never dared to do it. Other than the fact they'd never had a reason, to wake a slumbering primordial always incurred a significant penalty. Persephone knew that she wouldn't be able to teleport away. She only had one choice. The choice all gods have a holy right to; to give up her position and fade from the world.

In that moment, Moros knew where Persephone's mind would go. She thought about her husband, Hades, the man who so long ago had abducted her as she picked flowers in a meadow. She loved that man, despite his flaws. She'd had a wonderful life. The temples honouring her and the festivals in her name would last for a long time to come. Persephone smiled and accepted her fate. She became dust in the darkness.

Lucifer, on the other hand, didn't accept this new fate quietly. The rock walls were ignited with his fire as he slammed his fists against them. He mustered all the force he could in an attempt to break out, but the stone didn't budge. His soldiers poked at the walls with their swords and pikes, but every weapon shattered on impact.

The colossal jaws receded into the earth as quickly as they'd appeared, leaving a ruined city in their wake. The ground had been so upheaved that the cloud of mist from the God of Sleep, Hypnos, was finally dispersed.

Michael looked on in horror as his brother, and a team of their best fighters were swallowed by the very ground itself.

Demeter stopped attacking him, caught in a fit of uncontrollable sobs.

"What was that?" Michael asked, raising his sword threateningly.

"The very bones of the Underworld," Demeter cried, now detached to everything around her.

"Persephone…" an agonized whisper carried out across the walls.

Michael twisted his head to find the source of the voice.

Standing on the dock, wrapped in a black cloak with his head bowed, was Hades. He'd at last arrived to join the war. The true battle for supremacy of death was about to begin.

CHAPTER FOURTEEN

FIRE AND DEATH

Plumes of black smoke billowed around Hades. He lowered a silver helmet over his head. In its face were three narrow vertical openings lined with red. It featured a tall crest made from pointed black feathers.

Moros immediately recognised the piece of armour as the Helm of Darkness. It was crafted in the time before history by the cyclops with her help, as a weapon Hades could use against the titans. It granted the wearer perfect invisibility; not just from sight, but from sense as well. It replicated Moros' power exactly. Generally, when a god turned invisible, they were lost to human eyes, but generally other higher beings could still see them. The Helm of Darkness vanished its wearer entirely from everything in the world.

The helmet sat comfortably on Hades' head. He had a reputation for rarely leaving the Underworld. It was an image he maintained through the use of the helmet.

The mighty god often slipped it on when he wished to escape his tiresome duties and walk amongst the green trees and under the blue sky of the mortal world. In the spring, when Persephone would leave the Underworld to be among the blooming flowers, Hades would use the helmet to join her.

Hades stroked at Cerberus' fur. His poor dog was burned and bleeding. He looked over his city. It was all but destroyed.

The buildings that remained were being trampled by the Hecatoncheires or dismantled in the fire from the Serpent of Heaven.

His castle had an enormous hole in the side from Lucifer's explosion.

Hades had never seen his kingdom in ruins before.

"Moros," Hades stated.

She appeared beside him and the King of the Underworld gripped her hand. "Know my journey. Fate is malleable to your whims as you are to its. To bring order to the world, you must see the path downwards. I would have you hear the words that the prisoned monster Ouranos spoke to me."

Again, Moros mind was cast far away. She now looked behind Hades' eyes as he left the council chamber at the beginning of the attack.

Only he knew the secret paths to the deepest prisons. The structure that held the titans was vast and fortified, but if an invader searched hard enough, they could find it. The Hecatoncheires dwelled down there. Hades travelled with his wife and Demeter to the titans' prison. Once they'd fetched the fifty-headed giants, he buried the chamber with rock. As an added protection, he used his divine power to ward the path, so that it would always disappear to those who searched for it.

He bade farewell to his wife before descending further into Tartarus.

His journey down took him through earth, water and lava. The prison of his father, Cronus, was unguarded, except by unbreakable curses. It was so deep that Hades suspected it could never be found. Cronus was locked in a prison deep inside the inner layers of the planet. It had no door, and no path led to it. In the eventuality that someone dug deep enough, the chamber was cursed to move so that it could never be accidentally pierced.

Hades suspected that despite his father's body being eternally trapped, his mind could still wander the world. Zeus had often sworn that he saw Cronus appear as a distant shadow on his wedding day. Hades warded Cronus' chamber too and willed into the dirt that he never be found.

Then, Hades had dived further towards the roots of the world. None but himself, Cronus and ancient primordials had ever come this deep. No god had ever imagined that Tartarus stretched this far down. He fell through molten rock into a cavern. The entire world burned at unimaginable temperatures. Only one place, called the 'Cavern of the Sky', was still cool.

It wasn't quite pitch black as a blue glow illuminated the area. Balls of light floated through the air and chattered with each other. They were wisps of an ancient breed. Spirits that lived at the core of the world. The cavern was vast and massive stalactites hung from the roof. Running across the ground, directly through the middle of the chamber was a foreboding black chasm. Somewhere, either chained inside the abyss or buried beneath it, was Hades' grandfather, Ouranos.

Hades was careful not to touch the ground or any of the stone in the Cavern of the Sky. It was all toxic. Ouranos' hatred spewed as poison out from him, infecting the rock and bleeding up towards the mortal world. The Cavern of the Sky was lethal to the touch.

"Hades," a voice boomed out from the depths.

"Ouranos," Hades replied hesitantly. He was hoping his presence hadn't been noticed.

"It has been an age since I was visited by you…"

"An age too short," Hades replied.

"It is fitting that we should speak at the end of all things."

"This isn't the end of anything. We will expel their forces from the Underworld."

"You would not be checking your prisons if you truly believed that to be the case."

"How do you know about the attack from the angels of Heaven?"

"Once I was the God of the Sky, and no matter how far into the earth I am chained, I still hold my domain."

"But you cannot do anything, you are completely bound for all eternity in your prison."

"Free me and I will erase them from existence…"

Hades almost laughed. "Even I doubt I have enough power to free you. I am here to do the opposite, to ensure your prison remains hidden forever."

Ouranos' booming voice echoed out again, "The cycle continues, Hades. For them as it did for us. Sons will betray fathers; brothers will fight brothers. Our family's time has come, but the story is the same no matter the gods who reign. You would be wise to release me, rather than to face what will come when the perversion of Heaven is noticed…"

A thought came to Hades as he floated there among the whispering wisps.

"Tell me, this god of the angels, is he a primordial being? He seems to have appeared in some remote corner of the world, actively seeking to spread his influence. It isn't the usual behaviour of your kind."

"You do not listen, grandchild. Do not fear the father, fear the son. Mark my words, the time will come when the father will flee this world forever. A thousand eyes will turn on him from the abyss…"

The ground rumbled as Ouranos issued his warning.

Hades finally asked the questioned he'd longed to for hundreds of years. "I want to know what happened to my brother. He requested that I allow him to speak with you, not so long ago, though he made me swear not to ask about the contents of your conversation. Then, he vanished. What happened to my brother. What happened to Zeus?"

"Zeus came to me with questions about the monsters of the ancient world. I warned him to turn from his path lest he invite destruction to his realm. There are things that watch from the dark and ancient rules that mustn't be broken…"

"You will give me no clear answer then?" Hades sighed.

"Free me and I will tell you of the early days and how to fight what is coming from the stars…"

The King of the Underworld didn't have time to play his grandfather's games. He had a war to fight.

Hades felt the protections around the Cavern of the Sky with his mind. It all seemed secure. The power that held Ouranos was much older than him, he doubted there was anything he could do to hide the prison further. He didn't want to be lured into a prolonged conversation with his grandfather about long-forgotten myths and forbidden ancient knowledge.

Without another word, Hades blasted upwards, out of his grandfather's cell. This deep in Tartarus, even he couldn't teleport at will. He had to make the long journey back up to the battle.

· · · · ·

CAMAEL ISSUED ORDERS TO RAIN unending arrows on the spot Moros and Hades were standing. A blinding volley flew through the air from all directions.

Hades simply waved his hand and dissipated every single one of the thousands of arrows. He then disappeared as he lowered the Helm of Darkness. Moros did the same, cloaking herself with invisibility.

Hades flew up and observed the ruined city with Moros beside him. The ground was littered with deceased angels who'd previously been hidden in the fog. With another wave of his hand, he brought them back to life, but it wasn't life proper, he reanimated their bodies. The rising resurrected angels stumbled to their feet and swayed on the spot. Their eyes lacked pupils or irises. They were white and empty.

The angel zombies that didn't have damaged wings took to the air. The grace with which they'd moved in life was lost entirely. Hundreds of them flew up and lunged for their former allies.

"What is this horror?" Camael asked.

"This is the power of the God of the Underworld," a nearby angel replied.

A screech drew Moros' attention.

The tiny figures of Apollo, Perseus and Theseus were expertly weaving through the necks of the Serpent of Heaven and slicing at the central one. The waving heads were tangling themselves up, trying to snap at the three.

Apollo had assumed that his golden sword would be able to cut through the gargantuan necks like butter. But the red scales proved to be resistant to his weaponry. He had to dodge the jaws and attempt to hit the same spot over and over. It was taking minutes for the smallest abrasion to appear. Whatever this dragon was, it was designed to be incredibly difficult to kill. Moros again moved towards the Golden God, in order to shield him from the dragon's fire.

Apollo noticed a group of resurrected angels slowly floating towards him with their dead eyes.

The Serpent of Heaven also noticed, and its seven heads

began firing seven different infernos towards the places where all of the dead were rising. The ground was set further ablaze.

Everything in the path of the fire was incinerated.

The two surviving Hecatoncheires ran for the water of the River Acheron, even though it was only deep enough to submerge their feet.

The great fire blazed below the battle in the air. One by one, the shades of the heroic dead were falling. The thousands of angels that had arrived through Taenerum were overwhelming the heroes and warriors from history.

Spartacus fell to half a dozen lances piercing his legs and sides. His shade vanished from existence besides that of Caesar, who'd commanded a shield wall to be formed to defend from the flames of the serpent. Caesar and his soldiers simply evaporated when the fire was spewed towards them.

A cloud of angels, including a fresh legion of chariots, poked at the legs of the Hectoncheires. It was like the bites of hundreds of stinging ants that finally toppled Briareus and Gyges. The giants had been keeping the Serpent of Heaven located in one spot by lobbing hefty chunks of the city at it. Free from the barrage of thrown boulders from the one-hundred-armed monsters, the Serpent of Heaven began flying back and forth along the length of the battle. Apollo couldn't match its speed. The dragon cast a long shadow over the inferno it had created.

It had no side in this fight.

It just burned everything.

The heat started boiling the river. Demeter and Michael's battle broke apart as they fled the shooting flames. Some of the heroes, like Jason, tried to rally the dead to him. But the fire consumed all.

The angels began to flee the battlefield. They flew over the castle and back towards the River Styx. Camael tried to issue commands, but pandemonium was breaking loose.

Hades had been invisibly flying across the battlefield, slaughtering angels and resurrecting them on the spot as his own soldiers. But his plan to win through numbers was turned to ash by the Serpent of Heaven.

Moros saw Cerberus collapsed in the shallows of the River Acheron. The dog's eyes were bleeding, and it had horrific burns across its body. It could barely stand. Moros felt the life quickly leaving the guard dog.

When the Serpent of Heaven landed on the side of Hades' castle, like a grotesque red lizard on a large black rock, she saw Hades remove his helmet beside his loyal pet.

Cerberus was struggling to get up. His two active heads were still snarling at the serpent and the fleeing angels. Even as his body was failing, Cerberus was still trying to perform his duty.

"Cerberus, my old friend and loyal guard," Hades murmured, running his hand down one of the dog's massive ears. "You have completed your task; it is time to rest."

Cerberus' eyes turned toward his master. The dog couldn't see him but could hear his voice and knew he was there. Cerberus whimpered softly.

Hades raised his hand and a ghostly lyre appeared in front of his pet. The small spectral instrument began playing a lullaby composed by Orpheus. Cerberus' eyes closed as the music lulled him to sleep. He looked content.

Hades pressed his right palm against Cerberus' side and the huge body of the dog faded to dust. All that remained was a small statuette of the beast, which Hades picked up.

A tear rolled down the god's cheek. Moros felt his pain. Persephone, Cerberus... what more could this day take from him?

The Serpent of Heaven set to work melting Hades' castle. The towering pyramid of sharp spires was turned into molten black goo beneath the flapping wings of the monster.

Apollo had given up attempting to fight the dragon and had joined Demeter in combatting Michael. Somehow, the archangel was taking on both of them.

Michael was focused. He moved instinctually. With his arms, he blocked Apollo's strikes, and with his inner senses, he guarded against Demeter's magic. Lightning sparked and whipped around the three divine figures.

The staff that floated at Demeter's side was shooting flames at Michael while she summoned icy gales from her hands.

Michael flew straight up and Apollo followed. Demeter floated in place, concentrating her power. Michael skimmed the top of the water as he dodged pointed cones of ice that rained down from Demeter. He quickly led Apollo further down the river.

"Don't try to flee!" Apollo yelled.

"I'm not trying to flee from you," Michael said indignantly.

Apollo turned around and looked in horror as long fangs bore down on Demeter.

"Demeter!" Apollo yelled.

Demeter stopped summoning shards of ice and spun around. Before her were the open jaws of the dragon.

The giant head clamped its mouth closed around her. Only it didn't close fully. Demeter had quickly wrapped herself in a sturdy ball of ice.

Apollo frantically tried to return to her, but Michael gripped him by the ankle and held him back.

Michael pulled himself forward and thrust his sword straight through Apollo's chest.

The Golden God gasped in shock and pain.

Horror fell across Moros. Apollo had to live this fight! This was not his time to die.

Apollo dropped his golden blade into the steaming river below, where it splashed and disappeared into the depths.

Even through the foggy ball of ice, Demeter could see an orange glow emerge in the back of the serpent's throat.

"No," she gasped.

Moros concentrated hard and released a wave of her most powerful magic. Time froze. This was incredibly draining for her to do and wouldn't last long. Only herself and Demeter were unaffected.

Again, fate churned like a whirlpool around Moros, guiding her speech. "A choice is to be made," she said to Demeter.

Demeter looked behind her and saw Apollo floating in mid-air, with Michael's shimmering sword piercing cleanly through him. She looked to Moros for guidance.

"You can survive the fire. But it will cripple you. You know this, Demeter," Moros stated calmly, though her voice was full of regret.

In her heart, Demeter knew that despite the insane power of the holy fire in the dragon's stomach, with her might concentrated, it wouldn't kill her. But it would get close.

Moros spoke the words that appeared in her heart, "Apollo is seconds from death. Only you can heal that wound, Demeter. This is your chance to decide."

Demeter knew what Moros was implying. She'd be a ruin in the face of the dragon's fire, probably easy pickings for Michael.

"Is this my fate, Moros? After my long service to this world?"

"In this moment, your fate is your own hands. I know Apollo has a part to play in events to come, though what it is I cannot tell you. There is much unknown about the future. Decide quickly, for my magic fades with each passing second."

Moros knew that Demeter was thinking about Persephone. The loss of her daughter was a heavy burden.

She made her decision.

Demeter reached out, and around Apollo's wound, small plants began winding. It was a plant of her own creation that she called the Spirit of Spring. It would prevent his death.

The goddess turned and looked back at the orange glow. She gave Moros a small smile as time resumed.

Michael drew his sword from Apollo's chest. Apollo began falling, but Michael used his power to hold the Golden God in place, just above the water. He floated down and again raised his sword high.

"A battle well fought," Michael stated formally.

Hades was caught between the two Olympians. He cursed himself for being distracted with sentimentality for his dog.

Apollo was closer to him.

Hades teleported behind Michael and shot a powerful wave of energy into the archangel's back. Michael was sent hurtling towards the far wall.

Hades, not wanting to be burdened by the statuette of Cerberus, forced it into Apollo's body. It sunk into him with a blast of light, a gift the god could use at a later time.

A tsunami of fire burst forth from the serpent's mouth. Demeter could sense the sheer power behind the torrent. This creature was a divine weapon of ultimate destruction—something for the end times of the world. There was nothing she could do as her power left her and flew into Apollo's wound.

In an instant, the goddess who'd been guiding hunter-gatherers as they mastered agriculture and presiding over the harvests since civilisation began, was obliterated in flame.

Hades felt the death of his sister within him. Rage filled the newly created hole. He took off the Helm of Darkness and placed it firmly on Apollo's head.

"Moros, take him."

She appeared before Apollo and began dragging him away from danger.

Hades, meanwhile, flew toward the Serpent of Heaven. He was beyond a simple Olympian's power, and the Underworld was his.

Hades reached out and coils of black smoke wrapped around the Serpent of Heaven's body. Its heads twisted, confused.

Hades thrust his arms down, flinging the monster into the ground with surprising force. He rolled his arms to the side and the dragon was thrown against the far wall.

Using his mind, Hades bent the very fabric of the Underworld to his will. The looming grey rock that made up the cavern cracked, and huge boulders came tumbling down onto the Serpent of Heaven. The sound of the monster's massive bones breaking echoed through the flaming ruins. Hades wrapped smoke around the now loose boulders and began forcing them together. The dragon squealed as it was crushed on all sides.

Then, the rocks fell, and the dragon was released.

Hades looked down to see the gleaming end of a silver sword, wreathed in translucent flame, poking through his chest. There was no pain, but his body felt strange. Ichor leaked from him.

Michael floated around Hades and stopped in front of him. He looked at his sword and admired its craftsmanship.

Moros knew again that there was nothing she could do. The time of the great gods of old was over.

"The Michael Sword, they call this. It was crafted by a relative of yours, Hephaestus. We have him in chains in the Citadel of Heaven; have had for some time. He made weapons for my brothers and me... unwillingly, I should add. Lucifer got a trident, I'm assuming that is buried in Tartarus now."

Moros could feel Hades body dying. The entire Underworld was shuddering.

Michael sheathed his sword. In his hand, a bizarre object appeared. It looked like a bronze tube with a circular grip. It was the same device Lucifer had used on Cer.

"Seven weapons for seven archangels. Each designed by a god to kill gods. This little thing, on the other hand, was designed by my father."

Michael thrust the pointed end into Hades' temple. Light billowed out where the device made contact.

The light shocked the Serpent of Heaven into moving again. It spread its wings wide and soared down the river, blasting fire as it went. Soon it would reach the Asphodel Meadows and the Elysium Fields, where all would become ash in its wake.

When the light dissipated, the God of the Underworld was no more. Michael vanished the peculiar device he'd used and looked around.

The angels that hadn't fled the battle were looking around cautiously.

Everything was still.

They'd won.

But what was the prize? Rubble and flame.

Moros now had to ensure that the angels didn't find the gravely injured Apollo.

"Call back those who fled!" Michael commanded. "Fan out, Apollo is still here! Bring him to me!"

Camael floated towards Michael, still in earshot of Moros. "Well done, Lord Michael, the Underworld is ours. What do we do now?"

Michael turned to him and simply stated, "Find Lucifer. Find my brother."

CHAPTER FIFTEEN

A WOUND IN TIME

Moros dragged Apollo through the air toward the far wall of the cavern. Demeter's magic had saved him, but only barely. Thin green stalks with small white flowers had sealed up the injury.

Apollo was perfectly invisible with the Helm of Darkness on his head, and Moros' own powers of invisibility meant she couldn't be seen by the angels. They glided undetected, only pausing when Moros reached the far wall of the cavern.

She ran her hand along the wall. A crude marking had been carved into the rock. Moros murmured something, then flew straight into the rock face. They passed through the stone and emerged in a small circular cave. The rock face was a simple illusion created by Hecate, the Goddess of Magic.

Moros lowered Apollo to the ground.

The cave was dimly lit, revealing that Hecate had carved runes across almost the entirety of the space. Even the dirt Apollo was lying on had hastily drawn symbols all across it.

Hecate got up and plucked the Helm of Darkness from Apollo's head. "We will need this more than him."

She placed the Helm on the cavern's far wall then returned and observed Apollo's wound closely.

"How is he?" Hecate asked.

"Alive, thanks to Demeter," Moros responded.

Aion, the God of Time, who was floating off to the side in his zodiac ring, spoke out, "How are you, dear Moros?"

"Troubled," the goddess replied.

"How goes the doom?" Aion asked.

Moros thought about the question, then hesitantly said, "They have won. I worry about us. The angels will seal every exit. I doubt there is much we can do to escape without detection. We can hide, but eventually they will find us. I don't think we can fight our way out. There is no aid arriving from Olympus, the thrones in the clouds burn along with the Underworld."

Hecate stopped carving symbols into the walls and looked up. "There will be a time to fight. Use your powers Moros and tell us what you feel from Apollo."

Moros knelt over the Olympian and placed her hand on his head.

"I'm sorry, Apollo."

Black energy burst from Moros' hand, completely enveloping

the Golden God.

Apollo slumped unconscious on the dirt.

Moros stood back up. "Apollo's energy is distant. I feel him far away, far from this doom. It's as if he is involved in a distant event. But he is lying right here. I can't explain it, but I feel the fates of all of us in this cave are tied to Apollo."

"You are feeling time as distance," Aion explained to her. "What we are about to do, when we do it, will damage the world. We are feeling the effects of an event that hasn't happened yet."

"What do you mean?"

"Non-linear paths exist. A road that leads from this place, that ends at this place."

Moros didn't understand. Hecate and Aion had been absent for the entire battle, so clearly they had some kind of plan established to get all of them out there. Apollo's injury was potentially going to create an unexpected problem, however.

"Apollo is too weak to fight. Demeter's magic has kept him alive, but it has not cured him. Michael's blade has been designed to obliterate gods beyond hope of recovery," Hecate explained. "I can wake Apollo up, but to heal him, we need time. We also need to remove him from the far-reaching arms of Heaven."

With her finger, she drew a shape in the air. The symbol began glowing green, then dropped into Apollo.

He woke with a start.

Apollo stumbled to his feet and looked at the three gods around him. He felt his chest, where Michael's heavenly sword had cut him. The god looked odd, like he was sapped of his strength; almost as if he was a shade of his former self.

"You barely cling to life," Hecate said.

Aion floated slightly closer to Apollo and observed him curiously.

"Why are you here? Hiding and not fighting?" Apollo demanded.

Aion poked at the air, as if he was attempting to solve a complex mathematical problem with his finger. Hecate once again began drawing elaborate runes on the ground.

"Demeter is gone, Persephone is gone, and even now Hades… but the day is not lost. We can fight on! Your magic Hecate, they will not be prepared," Apollo pleaded.

Hecate paused her etching and looked at Apollo with her big purple eyes.

"Fight on we shall, Apollo."

"Yes, Apollo. We will fight… well you will, I suspect," Aion interjected. His cloudy, cosmic eyes locked onto the god.

Apollo looked completely exasperated. "Then let's go!"

"Not now," Aion said simply, as if he didn't have a care in the world.

"What?"

"At the turning of the tide," Hecate said, furiously scratching symbols into the rock.

"Please do not speak to me in riddles, Hecate."

"Olympus has fallen, Apollo."

"Impossible," Apollo muttered, shaking his head.

"They are not like us," Hecate stated, once again crouching into the dirt and scribbling away. "The decree of Emperor Constantine is like a ripple that becomes a crashing wave, drowning the world. The angels have been designed as conduits for the power of human belief. Phenomenal power was thrown upon them the moment Constantine declared his conversion to Christianity."

"Human belief empowers us all, to some degree," Apollo retorted.

"Not like this," Hecate explained. "It seems just the act of a human believing in Christianity or Judaism or any of the variations generates untold power within them. Power enough to destroy us, something that a mere century ago seemed impossible."

"It is all very troubling," Aion muttered.

Apollo suddenly doubled over in pain.

"How do you know all this?" Apollo asked through sharp breaths.

"While you were fighting, I was looking. As was Aion. Witchcraft and time can provide a lot of information. The force that made the angels and the archangels, this god of Jerusalem, has been playing a long game. What the game's purpose is, I don't know. You will need to find out. If this all works."

The runes scrawled across the ground began glowing red and purple. Hecate stood up and started walking the circumference of the cavern muttering.

Aion's ring turned horizontally and began floating around his waist. He dropped to the floor.

Moros was stunned, she'd never seen Aion touching the ground before. Aion's zodiac ring rose above his head and floated toward Apollo. It lowered itself around Apollo and began rapidly spinning.

"Explain this!" Apollo commanded. He felt a swirling mass

of energy gathering around him.

"The battle for the Underworld is lost," Hecate said calmly. "Hades final act was to seal the prisons of the titans, of Cronus and Ouranos for all eternity. They are hidden beyond what searching eyes can find. No matter how deep they delve into the dark of Tartarus, they will never find those monsters."

"And Zeus," Moros thought. *"One of Hades last acts was to try and find out what happened to the missing God-King Zeus."*

"They are taking divine energy from the gods they defeat. Both Cer and Hades felt this new fate. You are too weak, Apollo, and we can't assist them further by handing you over," Moros added.

The wind became a gale around Apollo as the ring spun faster and faster. The runes, carved into the walls and etched in the dirt, were beginning to jump up and float as symbols of light in the air.

"What is this magic, Hecate?" Apollo shouted.

"An experiment. This is Aion's power. Your body needs to heal. I hope the runes keep this cave hidden long enough for that to happen."

"How long until I am healed?"

"I don't know."

Moros read the runes on the ground and now fully understood what Hecate's plan to save Apollo was. He was a burden on them, so her and Aion were going to remove him out of time entirely until he was healed. Somehow, the pair had known at the start of the battle that they'd need to prepare this magic... but how?

"Avenge your family, Apollo, avenge us. Seek the truth. In my heart I know your place in this story does not end now," Moros said sorrowfully.

"I see it in the stars," Aion added.

The Golden God was becoming a blur.

"Do not linger in the Underworld, take the secret paths, hopefully they will still be open to you!" Hecate called over the wind.

"I will follow him, for as long as I can as he journeys away from reality," Moros told Hecate and Aion. She closed her eyes and sent her mind into Apollo, so that she could see as he did.

"It will not last long," Hecate said.

Moros, now in the mind of Apollo, could barely hear Hecate's voice, and could no longer see her. The world had become blinding flashes of light. Sparks of green, purple and blue danced around him. He felt disconnected from his godly domains.

Reality shattered like glass around Apollo. He was surrounded by stars and spinning galaxies.

He could see something was moving in the centre of it all, far from his vision. Apollo focused on it, it looked like a black storm cloud, twisting with red lightning. He felt like he knew what the cosmic storm was, but couldn't quite place it. He heard beating drums and piping flutes in the dark.

Then, he woke to a world of fire.

Moros gasped and fell backwards. Apollo was gone. His journey was now his own to complete.

Hecate contemplated the Helm of Darkness while Aion muttered to himself.

"What does fate tell you that we do now, Moros?" Hecate

asked without looking up.

"We escape the Underworld," Moros said with an air of finality. "Dark days are ahead of us. Heaven won't stop here or with Olympus and Asgard. They will scour the world for gods in their quest for total domination. Long centuries of hiding await us."

"Aion and I have prepared our escape. The magic is hidden in the runes around us. Come Moros," Hecate smiled.

"It is funny, but even now I feel Apollo's power bleeding from the world like a slow drip. It will take decades to diminish fully. There will come a time when we will feel his power slowly trickle back into the cosmos. That will be our time to act," Moros affirmed. She looked from Hecate to Aion, then moved in close to study the runes further.

This was not the end of the gods.

PART THREE

A GOD AND HIS PROPHET

CHAPTER SIXTEEN

APOLLO LIVES

- 2019 -
HELL

The heat hit apollo like a sledgehammer. The cave was hot. Moros, Hecate and Aion were nowhere to be seen. The runes scratched into the wall were damaged and faded, appearing like they'd been there a long time.

Apollo looked at his chest. The wound from Michael was wholly gone. Also, at some point, his golden form had receded. He looked human again.

Apollo attempted to rise from the ground into the air, but he could not fly. He tried to teleport himself to the other end of the cave, but that also didn't work. Having no freedom of movement meant the Underworld was well and truly removed from the Olympian's control.

But there was something more. He felt diminished. How long had it been?

Apollo walked to the entry wall and attempted to touch it. His hand slid through the illusion of rock. Apollo then peeked his head out.

What he saw stunned and horrified him.

The cavern that had held the City of Hades, the castle, the waterfall and the rivers was now completely transformed.

There was no water to be seen, only sizzling red rocks. The entire area looked like a sunbaked desert. Amongst the boulders, Apollo could make out pieces of rubble that looked like chunks of an ancient building mostly buried in sand. The place was deserted.

The cavern had a sky to it — an artificial red sky bustling with gigantic storm clouds. The entire Underworld must have been completely terraformed in his absence.

He walked back into the cave. To his surprise, on the back wall, sat the Helm of Darkness. Apollo picked it up, and from the helmet a symbol appeared in the air. The character quickly became a message.

"At great risk, I have instructed this helmet be left for you, as it is your only means of escape. Do not try the old paths. Hell is sealed. Follow your sword. If it looks like this helmet will fall into the hands of the enemy, touch the rune."

The message looked like it came from Hecate. He also saw that another rune had been carved right into the helmet's temple. He avoided touching it.

Apollo put the helmet on his head and walked back to the

entrance. He peered down at the ground below. Normally he would just jump, but in the back of his mind was concern. He didn't know what had happened to him.

If Apollo had lost his divinity, then jumping would lead to a human's death. With a sigh, he lowered himself out of the entrance and began climbing down the cliff face.

It was a long climb down.

When he reached the bottom, he scanned left and right, though no direction provided a clear path to follow. It was just fire and sand as far as the eye could see.

A creature scuttled passed Apollo on all fours.

A demon.

It had long jagged teeth and no eyes. It jumped from rock to rock, periodically stopping to sniff. It looked disgusting, like an elongated deformed baby.

The Helm of Darkness kept him hidden. Apollo instinctively reached for the grip of his golden sword, but it was gone. He remembered that it had dropped into the River Acheron when Michael had stabbed him. Where the river was now, he had no idea, as the entire landscape had shifted.

Apollo decided his best course of action was to follow the demon. Perhaps it was going somewhere.

Apollo tailed the monster for hours as it ran up steaming hillsides and through dark lava-filled crevices. He struggled to keep up as he was sapped entirely of his divine strength and speed. Michael's sword was undoubtedly a devastating weapon.

He wondered about his family. His twin sister Artemis wouldn't have been on Olympus during the attack from Heaven.

His half-brother, Hermes, may have also been absent, as he frequently was. Would they have returned to help their kin, or fled from the angels? Apollo honestly didn't know.

The demon was scuttling further and further away. He saw it descend over a crest in the near distance and disappear.

At one point, whether by the haze of the heat or a simple illusion, Apollo thought he saw a long wooden home on the other side of an unpassable chasm. Since he couldn't get to it, he chose to ignore it.

He'd been going uphill for the better part of an hour and assumed it was another rocky cliff-face he was approaching.

Apollo sat beside a large boulder to rest. He was dreadfully tired and before he knew it, he was nodding off.

"Ah, Apollo, good," a voice broke through the fog of dreams.

Apollo looked from side to side. He was surrounded by purple glittery clouds and blinking multi-coloured lights.

"The Dreamscape? Morpheus?" he asked, recognising where he was.

In a swirl of mist, Morpheus appeared before Apollo.

"Humanity doesn't suit you, Apollo," Morpheus chuckled.

"What do you mean?"

"That wound inflicted upon you was designed to kill a god, with no chance of survival. It took almost all of Demeter's power to save you. So much so that it seems she couldn't save herself. You lived, but as a shell of your former self."

"Are you saying that I am human now?" Apollo asked, his look of dismay profoundly etched across his face.

"Perhaps you retain some of your godly capabilities, I am

not sure. When you return to the world, you will have to find a conduit to your old power. I suspect that you can be restored to your glory quite easily, though I don't know. This is all new for us."

"Where am I, Morpheus? Is this still the Underworld?"

"Yes, and it is fortunate that your depleted body needs sleep, as we would not be able to speak otherwise. The domain of dreams crosses all barriers."

"What happened here? It is a scorched ruin."

"The Serpent of Heaven burned and continued burning. The Archangel Lucifer was trapped for a long time by Tartarus. He was the only one who could control the dragon, apparently. By the time the angels removed the monster, the rivers had boiled. The grass and trees were gone. The Underworld was a fiery pit."

"How long have I been gone?"

"About 1700 years."

Apollo stood in shocked silence. 1700 years? Why had it been so long?

"The world is a different place now, Apollo," Morpheus continued. "It was sensed that you would re-emerge soon though. It was predicted that there would be about thirty or forty years leeway, give or take."

"Explain," Apollo commanded.

"I will be brief, as even in the Dreamscape, I can be found if I use my power too long. The angels are always watching... they have a way to detect us. What Aion and Hecate did was give you the chance to heal. They basically forced you out of the world, and when your body was ready, Hecate's runes drew you back in.

What felt like moments for you was 1682 years."

Apollo was struggling to comprehend this. The fall of the Underworld, the battle he'd just been fighting, was an age ago.

"To force a god out of reality takes quite a bit of power, it damaged the world quite substantially. The whole thing left a wound in time, like a tear in the fabric of reality, that bled out in surprising ways."

"How did you know I was coming back now?"

"The re-emergence of the last Pythian priestess. She was killed when your power faded from the world. It took a while to dissipate due to the nature of the wound in time. And again, it seems she has reincarnated, about thirty years too early, due to the nature of the aforementioned damage."

"The Pythian priestesses were granted the power of prophecy through me," Apollo started. "This means that she is a conduit to my power! Through her, I can restore my godhood!"

"Perhaps. Events are in motion — events to do with the archangels. I think the timing of your return is not just due to healing. Let your oracle guide you. She is waiting for you at the end of the sealed Roman portal to Hell; the Emperor's Portal."

"How do I get there, Morpheus?"

"Not far from you is the fortress that marks the entrance to the First Circle of Hell. In that fortress, you will find a building that looks like the Roman Forum. At its centre is a pedestal, marked with the image of a ram's head emblazoned with a five-pointed star."

"How do I open it?"

"Hell is entirely sealed off. Only an object of great power

can lessen the defences around that old gateway. Weaken the seal by destroying the Helm of Darkness on the pedestal. It will shatter the magic that holds the portal closed. Only then will your oracle be able to see you. She has your sword. If everything works, she will be able to use it to pull you out of Hell and into the human world."

"The portal will close behind me?"

"In theory, yes. Though I fear such an act may crack the barrier between dimensions beyond repair. Still, that is a problem for another time. You will only have moments. When you take off the Helm of Darkness, they will all be able to see you. Be quick and good luck."

Apollo woke with a start.

Immediately, he was on his feet and rushing toward the cliff-face.

Below him, not far away, was a circular-walled fortress with a spiralling tower in the middle. It was enormous.

Somewhere down there was his way out of the fire and back into the fight.

• • • • •

SAFE IN HIS CLOAK of perfect invisibility, Apollo approached of the fortress. The journey down the cliff-face hadn't been easy, but once he saw the fates of those around him, the physical strain he'd undergone quickly departed the god's mind.

Before him, hundreds of people, linked together with heavy chains, were being whipped by a procession of demons as they marched. They all wore tattered rags and groaned under the weight of the iron. They were hauling a heavy cart through the walls.

The demons were of a different make to what Apollo was used to seeing. The one Apollo had followed had been like an animal. These slave-drivers were armoured and carrying weapons. They almost looked like ogres with hideous bat wings protruding from their backs. Their faces were all missing something, whether it be half a jaw, an eye, or the side of their skull.

None noticed Apollo as he stepped through the towering gates into what looked to be a market place.

Apollo was taken aback. The demons of the Underworld had formed a society of some kind.

The place was swarming with them. They came in all shapes and sizes, and all looked positively monstrous.

It made sense, after all. If the angels had claimed the other underworlds, where different gods had cultivated various demons, and merged them all together, there would be a diverse array of them.

Still, seeing the horned and tusked creatures peddling wares to each other was a surreal sight.

Apollo was beyond curious as to what they could be selling. That question was quickly answered when he snuck close the nearest stall. Raw hunks of meat with shards of broken bone were piled in baskets and swarming with flies. Beside the meat where swathes of simply crafted weapons. Considering the animal-nature of the demons of ancient Greece, this was still impressive.

He bent his head upwards and looked at the twisting tower that stretched into the sky.

It was a foreboding structure that dominated the land around it. Apollo could see small, roughly cut windows along its exterior. He imagined that from up there, he could see the location of the hellish Roman Forum with ease.

A large muscular demon thundered past with a formidable silver axe in its hands.

Apollo knew that the magic of the Helm of Darkness was infallible. However, he was still hesitant about trapping himself somewhere surrounded by these monsters.

If he genuinely was mortal now, then some of these demons would have no trouble ripping him in half — a most unpleasant ending for such a well-known god.

From the cliff-face, he'd seen that the fortress was circular. It backed onto an enormous wall that stretched across the horizon.

Apollo figured that behind the wall was the 'First Circle of Hell', whatever that was. Nonetheless, if he followed the inner circumference of the fortress, he'd encounter the Roman replica eventually.

He set off further into the hellish depths. He'd been to Rome many times, so he was familiar with the architecture when he found it.

The Roman Forum stood proud before him. The white of the buildings clashed with the red stormy sky above. The entire structure was in a state of disrepair. While it wasn't a crumbling ruin, it was clearly unused.

He knew that there would most likely be a dedicated room

within he had to find. Somewhere specific where the power to move between dimensions could be gathered and controlled.

The animalistic demons from the waste-land scurried about the walls and through the shadows. It was the only place in the border-town he'd seen them inside the walls. Apollo figured that they could be the reason this place was abandoned.

Their presence made Apollo nervous. He had to destroy the Helm of Darkness to weaken the barrier enough to escape. Without the helm, they'd find him.

A thought then occurred to Apollo; how was he supposed to destroy the helm?

He was mortal, and the helmet was crafted by the cyclops for Hades. It wasn't something one could so easily dispose of.

"First, I'll find the room," he thought.

It wasn't hard. Within minutes, Apollo discovered a door behind the main open floor area. It led to a ceremonial room with a pedestal directly in the centre. On the pedestal was a sculpted ram's head with a five-pointed star carved into its temple.

Cautiously, Apollo removed the Helm of Darkness.

Screeches began echoing through the ruins.

The demons knew he was there.

They could sense the intruder. He placed the helmet on the ram's head. It balanced precariously on the stone horns.

Apollo was at a total loss as to what to do next.

The first demon crawled through the door. Its long slimy tongue licked its sabre-like teeth and across its face. The creature had no eyes. Its head consisted only of an oversized mouth and sickly grey skin.

It leapt towards Apollo.

Without his divine powers, Apollo couldn't summon his silver bow. He had to fight this monster the way an unarmed man would.

Apollo side-stepped the flying jump. He thrust his forearm around the demon's neck and placed it into a stranglehold. Its elongated limbs flailed and kicked in front of it.

The screeching demon's neck was too thick for Apollo to choke. He released it with a shove to its back, though the monster didn't go far.

It turned on its three-toed feet back towards Apollo and let out a high-pitched roar, which was quickly answered from further down the Hell Forum. It only took seconds for three more demons to crawl into the room. They snapped their long teeth at each other playfully.

Apollo gulped. This was no way for a god such as himself to die.

He thought back to the hidden cave. What had that message said?

Before he could finish his thought, the demons attacked. They crawled across the walls to either side of him and jumped. Apollo rolled as the two monsters crashed into each other – landing below the snapping jaws of a third demon.

Reacting quickly, Apollo slid his fingers between the gaps in the demon's teeth and held its mouth open. Big globs of saliva spewed across his face.

Another demon swatted its companion out of the way and went for Apollo's neck.

Apollo pushed himself to his feet, narrowly missing the swiping claws.

Through the corner of his eye, Apollo saw the faded witch's rune carved into the temple of the Helm of Darkness.

That was it. Hecate had prepared for this; in case the angels got their hands on the helmet. It was a magically-infused self-destruct button.

Apollo had no time for delay. One bite and he was done.

He jumped for the helmet as the long arms of the demons reached out behind him.

His finger touched the rune, and the Helm of Darkness exploded.

CHAPTER SEVENTEEN

APOLLO RETURNS

- SEPTEMBER 27 -
ROME - FORO ROMANO

Voices echoed in from above, waking Melissa from her trance. Her head burned like she was being assaulted by a terrible migraine. She'd just seen an entire fantastical battle through the eyes of a goddess. She desperately wanted to sit and contemplate what she'd just seen, but there was no time now. More Soncins were here, and they'd deduced where Melissa had gone. She was trapped.

With a thud, two new men landed in the same underground room as Melissa.

They both held torches in one hand, crossed over the top of a gun in the other.

Melissa stood firm by the pedestal; the heavy golden sword

raised in front of her as if daring them to come closer.

In the torchlight, with her spectacular black eyes and mangled hair, she looked like more of a witch than Hecate had.

"Give us the sword, now!" the lead man commanded. He was muscular with a big beer gut.

"Take it from me," Melissa snarled, her voice dripping with venom.

The two men Melissa had managed to defeat earlier now jumped through the hole as well. One still held his nose while the other walked awkwardly.

The four men closed in on her. They all holstered their guns and cracked their knuckles menacingly. They were looking to make this painful.

Melissa was all but happy to return to favour.

Melissa ducked and weaved beneath the strikes of the men around her. She attempted to parry their blows with the sword, but it was far too heavy for her to use effectively.

A punch caught her in the shoulder, knocking her to the floor.

Her eyes turned gold.

She saw a blonde-haired blue-eyed man dodging attacks from four monstrous creatures. She saw him dive for some ancient helmet and watched it crack and shatter in a wave of unfathomable energy.

The four Soncin men paused as they felt invisible power radiate through the room.

The sword in Melissa's hand shone brighter than she'd ever seen it.

Melissa got up and kicked one man in the chest. He barreled

over, taking another of the Soncins down with him.

She ducked beneath a wildly thrown punch and delivered a powerful upper-cut to another man's chin.

She could see their movements before they happened!

The last man standing was the one with the broken nose.

She ran towards him and jumped. Using her momentum, she slammed the butt of the sword down on his face.

He collapsed in a heap.

She turned towards the pedestal.

She could see him! The stranger she was meant to rescue! It was like he was here… but also some place else.

She had to act.

Melissa plunged the sword into the five-pointed star on the ram's head, then thrust it directly upwards. It carved smoothly through the stone and then through the open air. She was slicing through reality as if it was a freshly-baked cake.

A rip in the fabric of space and time manifested in front of her, electricity sparking around its glowing edges.

Melissa reached inside the portal.

Someone gripped her hand.

Melissa heaved and pulled a man across dimensions.

Already, the rip in space was sealing itself. But too slowly. The monsters on the other side moved nimbly and followed him through.

With a sound like booming thunder, the tear in the world collapsed in on itself.

"Give me the sword!" Apollo commanded to Melissa.

Melissa didn't think twice.

The demon's screeching echoed through the underground chamber and out into the Roman Forum. They felt the ground cautiously and tasted the air. This place was new and unfamiliar.

The Soncins, staggering to their feet, pointed their torches right at the monsters.

They didn't need to speak.

All four drew their guns and opened fire. The noise and flashes from the muzzles spurred the demons into action.

The four demons attacked each man one by one.

In the middle of it all, stood Melissa, the Australian spy in Rome, and Apollo, the ancient Greek Sun God, back-to-back.

Destiny had brought them together at last.

CHAPTER EIGHTEEN

A BOND ACROSS TIME

Melissa watched a Soncin man gaze up in horror as one of the gangly faceless creatures pounced on him. In his panic, he dropped his torch. The dull yellow light of his inexpensive flashlight revealed the monster's finer details. Its most worrisome feature was the row of razor-sharp teeth that jutted out from its jaws, each spaced an inch apart and as long as a finger.

The creature looked rotten, with its exposed ribcage and grey skin. A thin layer of mucus was dripping from its extremities. It leaked in sickening globules onto the man's face.

Its jaw quivered, then its mouth opened wide.

The Soncin gangster said a quiet prayer as he waited for the teeth to slice into his jugular.

A horrifying screech bellowed out as a shining golden blade cut cleanly through the monster's torso. The blade withdrew, and the creature collapsed.

The Soncin scrambled to his feet and looked at the man holding the golden sword with visible confusion.

Apollo was wearing a short ancient toga and had sandals on his feet. He was lean and muscular, with wavy blonde hair and brilliant blue eyes, and seemed to be wielding the sword with expertise. He looked like a marble statue of a Greek god had come to life.

A demon leapt, and the Soncin raised his pistol. He fired two deafening rounds. The creature paused as the bullets passed through it with a sickening squelching sound.

"What is that weapon?" the blonde-haired man shouted as he stabbed the collapsed demon through the head.

The Soncin ignored the question and picked up his torch, spinning the light wildly across the room. He saw one of his family members lying dead, now just a bloody pile of limbs and gunk. Next to the body was a demon with chunks of flesh dangling from its jaw.

Melissa saw what was about to happen before it did.

The demon leapt at the Soncin.

Melissa ran towards him and started firing rounds directly into the back of the demon's skull.

The impact of the bullets did little more than stun the creature, despite passing straight through its blank face.

It spun its head 180 degrees towards Melissa.

"Sword!" she shouted.

Melissa had deduced quickly that bullets couldn't kill these things. Much like how a werewolf requires silver bullets (something she'd learned recently), these monsters weren't of the natural world. They needed a supernatural weapon to defeat them.

Apollo tossed the golden sword towards Melissa. She caught it by the handle and almost fell over, only just avoiding dropping it.

She slammed it down into the demons back with an ungainly swing.

The demon squealed as the sword cut cleanly through its skin.

Instead of providing the thank you that Melissa was expecting, the Soncin instead lunged for the golden weapon.

Melissa kicked him hard in the chest.

He tumbled into a wrestling match between Apollo and his current foe, another of the hellspawn.

Apollo held out his hand and Melissa thrust the sword into it. In a quick motion, he cut horizontally through the demon's gaping mouth, causing the top half of its head to slide off the bottom.

The final monster launched a surprise attack from behind.

Melissa crouched and slid behind Apollo.

She rolled onto her shoulders and kicked upwards with both her legs.

Using its own momentum against it, the demon was sent hurtling upwards. It was just high enough for Apollo to impale it through the stomach with an upwards thrust.

Apollo stood with the sword high as the demon went limp above him.

Its slimy, disproportionately long arms and legs dangled in front of the god.

The two surviving Soncins scrambled to their feet and clambered out of the hole in the earth.

Apollo lowered his weapon and the demon slid to the ground with a squelch.

Melissa kicked at the slimy corpse and asked, "What is this thing?"

"Demon. Quite a problematic thing when mortal… Thankfully you had my sword. Never gave them much thought before, to be honest," the stranger said, almost jovially.

"Your sword?" Melissa asked.

"Yes," Apollo stated, his eyes piercing her. "My sword. Do you not see the decorative musical notes, lyres and the sun? Who else would it belong to?"

"The Australian Government, for one," Melissa retorted.

"I don't know what that is, but I can assure you, this is mine. If it had belonged to anyone else, there wouldn't have been a connection to cut me from the Underworld."

"So, you are this Golden God everyone has been talking about?"

"My name is Apollo," he laughed.

Melissa found him strange to look at, like there was something unworldly about him.

"Melissa," she replied, holding out her hand formally.

Apollo just looked at it.

"You are the Pythian priestess, are you not?"

He took Melissa's hand and held it firmly, "You are a direct connection to my divinity. See it restored!"

Melissa pulled her hand free.

"I'm an operative of ASIO. Not a Pythian priestess."

Apollo looked disappointed, as if he'd been hoping something miraculous would happen.

"I have my oracle and I have my sword. Both manifestations of my power, yet in their presence, I remain mortal," he muttered.

"Look, Apollo, I know something weird is going on here. We need to figure it out later, okay? It isn't safe."

Apollo barely paid her any heed.

It was then that Melissa noticed something odd. "You're a god, right? I've heard of you, I think everyone has, but Hecate burned a mark on my hand that appears when divine power is around. It isn't there, so you mustn't be divine…"

Melissa held out her hand and Apollo touched it gently.

"Hecate, you say?"

"She was here, not long ago."

Apollo moved for the hole in the earth.

"We must find her! Come, Oracle!"

"I don't like any part of that," Melissa muttered, before following Apollo out of the portal room.

After clambering out of the hole, Apollo froze in total bewilderment.

"What has happened to Rome?" he demanded.

"Ah, it fell a long time ago. The Empire, I mean. Rome itself is huge, the capital of Italy," Melissa gasped as she hauled herself out of the hole and onto her feet.

"1682 years…" Apollo murmured.

He turned to Melissa, "We need to try again."

"Try what?"

"You are an oracle of mine. The prophets of Delphi were gifted the sight to see coming events through my domain of prophecy. That power is alive and well in you."

"Your domain of prophecy… what? Look, we need to go now!"

"Sit down with me."

Apollo promptly sat down on the grass.

Melissa was anxious. She'd learned basic character traits in her spy training and knew that this man wasn't going to willingly follow her directions. She resigned herself to trying whatever he had planned. After the madness that had been this day, perhaps it was the most appropriate course of action. She sat cross-legged in front of him.

"Whatever you're doing, you need to be quick," Melissa urged.

Apollo closed his eyes.

"When do you see visions?" he asked.

"Randomly," Melissa answered. "It happens a lot around the sword, especially when I hold it."

"Take my hand and concentrate."

Melissa gripped Apollo's hand.

His skin was soft and smooth.

"Free your mind of our current circumstance. Search for the inner light, your inner power. The Oracles of Delphi can see forward, backwards and across time. They can see into the minds of others and vast distances across space. Your vision can even humble the divine before you. You are powerful beyond what you could ever know or suspect."

Melissa breathed deep and tried to let go of her unconscious thoughts. It was almost impossible. She was worried about the surviving Soncins and the disappeared Gladius Vaticanus. These two sources of potential surprise attack had to be accounted for.

"Touch the sword," Apollo commanded.

Melissa placed a finger on the golden blade.

Instantly, images blurred across her mind. She saw a castle in the snow. Her mind moved down long soviet-style tunnels into a glittery lab, where a cannister of a glowing golden liquid sat. That was quickly juxtaposed against an image of rolling orange sand dunes with an open entry way diving into the ground.

The vision changed to a wiry brown-haired man scribbling complex mathematical problems on a blackboard. The blackboard morphed into a black hole that Melissa's mind fell through. It was going backwards through time. She saw a primitive tribe of hunter-gatherers laughing amongst each other. Their leader was a bare-chested long-haired man with a square jaw and a distinctive scar across his eye. Then, that man was standing on a mountain top, confronted by a giant glowing eagle. The sky grew dark and she saw the clouds take the form of a monstrous black wolf, that swallowed both the moon and the sun...

Melissa shook her head, none of what she was seeing was relevant. She focused. There was something Apollo needed her help with. Something to do with the sword... but what did she need to find. She felt a spark, like a burst of electricity in her brain, then began speaking aloud. She couldn't control the words she was saying.

"The God of Storms punishes he who brings the fire down the mountain. The bearer of the greatest gift was chained but we were unchained. The fire unseals the lost spark."

Melissa jumped to her feet, white-faced and gasping. What had just happened?

Apparently, tears had started rolling down her cheek. She wiped them away, along with the looser pieces of dried blood still around her nose.

She looked at Apollo who was still locked in some kind of trance. Across his arms and upper chest, it looked like patches of his skin were turning golden, but the gold was receding as quickly as it appeared.

Apollo opened his eyes. They didn't have pupils or irises any more, there was just blinding blue light emitting from them. The ground around them trembled. The mark on the back of Melissa's hand bubbled up, but then faded almost as quickly.

The harsh light disappeared and Apollo slumped forward.

"Are you okay?" Melissa asked cautiously, grabbing Apollo under the arm.

"No," Apollo spat with anger. "I connected with you. I connected with myself, albeit briefly. I could feel my true form. Michael's sword must be a cursed blade! Designed to kill a god, but should that fail, it creates some kind of seal. This is power beyond what they should have been capable of creating!"

Apollo got to his feet.

He looked at the world around him and nodded.

"It was enough, that brief moment of connection with you. I am the God of Knowledge, and it was knowledge I gained. I saw the world turning for the last 1700 years. I know its history now, at least some of it. Knowledge on how to restore my divinity still eludes me."

"What do you mean, restore your divinity?" Melissa asked. "What happened to you?"

"Are you familiar with the Archangel Michael?"

"Yes. I looked through the eyes of a different god and saw the battle. I saw what happened to you," Melissa informed him. "But even without that, Michael is known across the world as an angel of Christianity."

"So that religion survived," Apollo murmured, looking lost in thought.

"Survived is the wrong word," Melissa responded. "Christianity is one of the biggest religions in the world. Along with Islam and Judaism, they have billions of followers."

"Billions?" Apollo responded. "All worshipping the same god; the same angels?"

"Yeah, they call their god different names, but it's all the same stories with different tweaks and updates."

"Incredible," Apollo said, "the worship from billions… it's unbelievable."

"Didn't your knowledge burst teach you this?" Melissa asked sceptically.

"Apparently not, it was only minor. Matters of the gods must have been missed, I assume along with a lot of other things."

Melissa opened her mouth to continue the conversation but was interrupted. A man had emerged from the darkness next to the pair.

He looked disoriented. His hair was wild and appeared singed in places.

"Ah-huh!" the man yelled.

Melissa recognised him. It was the man who'd been with the Gladius Vaticanus. The one named Belial who'd challenged Hecate. It couldn't be the same Belial from the battle for the Underworld, could it?

Neither he nor Apollo seemed to know each other. Melissa assumed that to Belial, Apollo just looked like a mortal man.

Belial was bruised and dishevelled. Blood seeped from wounds across his head and neck. His black body armour was hanging from him in tatters and there were prominent rips in the undershirt beneath.

Belial's eyes weren't fixed on Melissa or Apollo, but the golden sword.

"You, girl," Belial growled, pointing a finger right at Melissa, "that old woman who approached you and spoke to you, did you know her?"

"No," Melissa answered honestly.

Apollo clenched his fists.

"Give me the sword, now!" Belial commanded. The thick veins on his face were pulsating with anger.

"Who is this person?" Apollo whispered.

"Some higher-up of the Gladius Vaticanus, I assume," Melissa whispered back. Apollo's ears pricked up at that name.

"The same warriors of Heaven called the Gladius Vaticanus?" Apollo whispered urgently.

"What, no —" she started, before being cut off by Belial.

"Stop muttering to yourselves!" Belial screamed, sounding deranged.

Dull thuds appeared as more boots landed on the ground nearby. Disoriented Gladius Vaticanus soldiers seemed to be dropping from the sky.

Once they stumbled to their feet, they moved shakily towards Belial.

Some of the soldiers still had rifles. Others were holding twisted plastic wrecks, the remains of what had once been advanced weapons. The guns that were still operational were promptly raised and pointed at Melissa and Apollo.

The symbol of divinity on Mel's hand had risen due to Belial's presence. This man had to be same angel who'd stormed Lucifer's castle wearing the impala-faced helmet.

"It looks like that old woman gave you a hard time," Melissa stated boldly as the soldiers inched forward.

Her act of defiance was undercut by what Apollo did next.

Apollo threw his golden sword at Belial's feet.

It appeared that the Golden God was giving up.

That couldn't be it, Melissa thought. He must've figured that wherever they were taking the sword could be a good place for answers. There was a silver lining in surrendering. That, and Apollo might need more time to adjust to this new world.

Two of the soldiers approached and pushed both Melissa and Apollo against a nearby wall. They placed zip-tie handcuffs around their wrists.

Belial picked up the sword. Melissa noticed that he kept glancing upwards, looking at the sky nervously.

Melissa couldn't see anything, save for a few blinking stars above.

"What is it, sir?" one of the soldiers asked.

Belial responded, "Angels. They were here. They took the goddess away."

The look of disgust on his face was unmistakable.

Melissa and Apollo were escorted from the ruins into a waiting troop carrier. None of the soldiers asked their names, or any other questions at all. They seemed quite shaken.

The Via dei Fori Imperiali was devoid of traffic. Back towards the Colosseum and up ahead at the Piazza Venezia, there were the tell-tale flashing red and blue lights from police vehicles. The area had been cordoned off.

Melissa noticed that just across the road from the parked Gladius Vaticanus troop carriers was the Forum of Augustus. Its old brown and orange brickwork was lit up in the glow of multiple spotlights.

Melissa could have sworn she saw a small gleam from something metallic that shifted in the darkness by the building's ruined stairs. It had to be Matt! She was sure of it.

For the tiniest moment, the light had caught Matthew Pyne and his sniper rifle as he watched Melissa and the stranger get marched away.

She knew he wouldn't dare make a move now, it was too risky. He'd stick to the shadows.

Melissa felt a gloved hand roughly push her into the back of the car. Apollo followed shortly after.

With a splutter, then a roar, the troop carrier rumbled to life.

It took off in a procession of vehicles. Melissa shuffled on the uncomfortable seat and fidgeted. The inside of the car was dirty and smelt musky.

"We need that sword back," Melissa said, breaking the silence between the god and herself.

"You said something, back there, a prophetic uttering of some kind. Do you recall it?" Apollo asked.

Strangely, Melissa could remember it word for word.

She repeated it. *"The God of Storms punishes he who brings the fire down the mountain. The bearer of the greatest gift was chained but we were unchained. The fire unseals the lost spark."*

"The fire unseals the lost spark," Apollo frowned. Apparently, those words meant something to him.

"What does it mean?" Melissa asked.

"I think we need to find a treasure beyond measure… beyond comprehension. One that has been rumoured to exist in the world since man spread from Africa. Where would you find such a thing?"

Melissa looked out the window and watched the dark waters of the Tiber River flow by. She was dreadfully tired and not thinking clearly anymore.

They turned right and began travelling the wrong way across a one-way bridge.

Before them was a tunnel, with two sloped roads that ran up either side of it.

"Where we are being taken supposedly holds the greatest treasures in the world," Melissa said at last.

"Where are we going?" Apollo asked.

"Vatican City," Melissa informed him. "The Greek God Apollo is now a prisoner of the Catholic Church."

As those words left her mouth, a hatch to the front of the car opened, and a small canister was tossed into the rear. Gas started spewing violently from it.

Within moments, both prisoners were out cold.

CHAPTER NINETEEN

THE CARDINAL

Melissa woke to an obnoxious rattling. She found herself lying on a single bed behind iron bars. Something wasn't right. The Vatican didn't have a prison, at least as far as she knew. Where was she?

She watched a colourful member of the Swiss Guard unlock her cell door. Melissa had always thought the Pontifical Swiss Guard looked ridiculous and seeing this one fumbling with a ream of silver keys confirmed this. His head was adorned with a black Basque-style beret that sat above the pronounced white high-collar of his yellow and blue tunic. His red sleeves had pieces of yellow and blue cloth attached from the shoulder to the hands. A brown leather belt with a buckle emblazoned with the letters GSP sat on his waist, along with a ceremonial short sword with an s-shaped handguard.

Looking at the man, Melissa concluded that she was definitely in the Vatican.

"You are come with me," the guard said in bad English as he swung the door open.

Melissa could smell herself. She stank. She hoped this boy was taking her to a bath.

The walls of the prison were devoid of character and lit with bright fluorescent lights. It looked like there were only four cells, and Apollo wasn't in any of the others.

She was directed up a short flight of stairs, which ended with another metal door. It was unlocked from the outside, and Melissa was escorted into some kind of reception room. An office clerk sat at a nearby desk and typed away rapidly, while three other members of the Swiss Guard stood around twiddling their thumbs.

Melissa was directed to sit on a long maroon couch in the middle of the room.

She wondered how long it had been. It must've been after midnight when they'd been gassed in the car.

Light shone in through the windows. It appeared to be late morning. Through the reception room window, Melissa could see the circular brick base of a tower.

"That is Vatican bank," the nervous guard stammered, following her gaze.

"Where am I?" Melissa asked.

"Uh, the Barracks of the Swiss Guard," he answered, being

careful not to make eye contact.

"Why am I here?"

The door to the room opened and a slender figure entered the room.

"An excellent question," a new man smiled.

Melissa eyed this arrival up and down. He was clearly a member of the Catholic Church. A cardinal, in fact.

He approached Melissa.

"Vasilije Markovic," he offered.

"Maggie Steeleheart," Melissa replied.

Melissa eyed the golden pectoral cross sitting on his chest. He wore the signature dress of the cardinals with a scarlet mozzetta (a shoulder-length cape) draped across his upper-half and a square ridged Biretta hat. The white laces of his rochet sat on top of his long red silk dress. Although Melissa figured it'd be quite rude to call it that, especially since she knew the dress was called a cassock.

While he was smiling, his eyes betrayed an internal coldness. He was either in his late fifties or early sixties and spoke with a distinct Eastern European accent.

Melissa distrusted him immediately.

"Yes, a school teacher from Australia. Fascinating. I assume that fool in the toga was some drunken friend of yours?" Markovic asked.

"Quite the presumption," Melissa replied.

Markovic raised an eyebrow. "Hmm?"

"That he is my friend and not my lover," Melissa continued coolly.

The cardinal glared at her, then composed himself. Melissa deduced her for the kind of man who didn't approve of women having casual relationships, it was often an easy presumption with the old-school hardcore religious types. She could have some fun with this man, but more importantly, use his prejudice to throw him off guard.

"Have you ever seen the Vatican?" he asked casually.

"No," Melissa answered honestly. "It was part of my itinerary; before I was captured by soldiers and thrown into prison. I need to talk to my embassy."

"A simple misunderstanding, I assure you. I hope you will consent to join me in a stroll through the Vatican's gardens."

"What do you want from me?"

"Just to hear how a young Australian girl got her hands on a sword that belongs to the Church."

Melissa could see that Markovic was scanning her face intently, searching for hints of a lie. She was better than him.

"I'm not sure I should tell you anything."

"Come now, after we speak you will be free to go."

Markovic instructed the Swiss Guard to take Melissa to the Fountain of the Sacrament and wait for him there.

Before he left, he issued one more command.

"Let her have a shower and provide her with some new clothes."

Her ears perked up at this. If she was going to swim with the sharks of the Vatican, at least she could get into the water clean.

· · · · ·

241

THE FOUNTAIN OF THE SACRAMENT wasn't the spectacular site Melissa thought it would be. Two towers rose above her, like something you'd see on the side of a castle. Between them was a fountain comprised of several levels against a wall of rock. Moss and algae clung to the surfaces around the calm water.

Melissa sat on the edge of the fountain alone. The guards had simply dropped her off and driven away.

She tried to come up with an escape plan, but she didn't know the layout or defences of Vatican City nearly well enough.

She'd been given a pair of jeans, that actually fit quite well, and a simple black top. She'd washed all the blood off her face. Unfortunately, she couldn't do anything about the prominent black bags under her eyes. Still, Melissa felt refreshed.

"My dear," Markovic yawned, "you look much better, and the smell is gone."

Melissa scowled.

The pair began slowly walking down a path lined with tall trees. The beautiful buildings of the Vatican loomed around them.

"My team brought you here because they thought you were a thief and a criminal," Markovic feigned apology in voice. "I do not think so, I think you were in the wrong place at the wrong time."

"I'm not a thief!" Melissa pouted, feigning that she was offended at the very accusation.

"Criminals were snooping around the Foro Romano last

night, so you will have to excuse the presumption."

"Those soldiers seem like the criminals..." Melissa muttered.

"They are not soldiers," Markovic said quickly. "Just servants of the Lord, like we all are. Others were there too; I am quite surprised you did not see them."

"Where is my friend?"

"Probably sobering up somewhere."

Melissa found it incredibly odd that the cardinal was so downright dismissive of Apollo's presence last night.

"Will I see him again?"

"Of course, very soon. We wouldn't want to interrupt your holiday to wonderful Rome."

Melissa's mind was racing. This cardinal was trying to act casual, but she knew he was fishing for information. Had they searched the Roman Forum and found the bodies of the demons? Surely not, they just wanted the sword. But someone would stumble upon that hole in the ground sooner or later.

"So tell me, Maggie, how did you come to be in possession of the golden sword?"

Melissa and Cardinal Markovic stopped in front of the turquoise waters of the Eagle Fountain.

"It was in the Roman Forum, and I picked it up."

"I grow weary of this game. I think honesty will take us a lot further."

"What do you mean?"

"Look around you," Markovic said.

Melissa glanced at the throngs of tourists walking the gardens. Then, she noticed the men in black suits. Armed men. There was a contingency plan should Melissa try to escape.

"The Gladius Vaticanus answer to me. I know you were found in the sewer with the sword and I know you are, most likely, responsible for the death of Enzo Gelliuchi. So, tell me, who are you really?"

Melissa didn't answer.

"Where is the sword?" she asked instead.

"I'm afraid that you do not get to ask the questions here. We will find out who you are soon enough."

"I'd like to know more about you, Cardinal. You have a paramilitary death squad working under you right here in Rome. You are making deals for artefacts with criminals. Doesn't seem very holy now, does it?"

"These are trying times," Markovic sighed. "People no longer believe. The faith is diminishing. And what is left when the faith is gone?"

"What?"

"Monsters."

"I think most modern people would argue that the monsters are within the faith, not outside of it," Melissa said dryly.

"How wrong they'd be," Markovic replied, looking genuinely troubled.

"This is one of those, 'for the greater good' things, isn't it?" Melissa asked.

"The impetuousness of youth," Markovic responded. "I get the strong impression you aren't going to tell me your intentions here. I'm afraid I will have to leave you with someone slightly more persuasive."

Cardinal Markovic turned his back to Melissa and strolled away as if he didn't have a care in the world.

None of the men in suits moved forward.

"Perhaps they are letting me go?" Melissa briefly allowed herself to foolishly think. It definitely didn't feel that way.

Something caught her eye. She looked into the water of the Eagle Fountain.

The top of someone's head had burst through it.

A man, soaking wet, was rising from the water's surface, without generating so much as a ripple.

He had a terrifying smile.

It was Belial. Within a moment he was floating above the centre of the fountain.

Melissa looked around. It didn't appear that any of the tourists could see him. They were going about their days as if the dripping sinister-looking man in black overalls wasn't there.

"There is something special about you, isn't there?" he sneered at Melissa. "You see that which is unseen. Let us talk."

He landed right next to Melissa and leaned in close, "Don't speak to me. No one can see me, you don't want to look mad in the Vatican."

"Actually," Melissa stated boldly, "if there is any place in the world you can talk to yourself and not look bizarre, it is the Vatican."

A few tourists shot questioning glances at her.

The men in suits, finally, began moving toward Melissa.

"Let's go somewhere private to chat," Belial said, licking his lips.

CHAPTER TWENTY

MOROS

Apollo woke with a start. He was in some kind of holding cell with several others. First to attract his attention was a partially clothed man with a considerable beer-belly, violently burping and struggling to maintain consciousness.

"A follower of Dionysus," Apollo thought.

A couple of hipster French tourists were loudly complaining to an unenthused guardsman through the bars.

Blocking out the man's gaseous releases and the tourist's cries of despair, Apollo picked up on another conversation not far away.

A woman, her voice eerily familiar, was speaking.

"Yes, he was picked up last night. Based on how he was

dressed, it is assumed he is a drunk frat boy who clambered into the ruins on a bet. He just got caught up in everything that was going on."

Apollo looked down at his clothes. He was still wearing his godly garb. Though when he lost his divinity, his clothes seemed to have lost their shimmer.

He looked at the attire of the others in his cell. He did look very out of place. Still, he thought it bizarre that they would be so dismissive of him. It was a bit of a stretch that a random man would show up at the exact moment they recovered the artefact they were searching for.

Apollo pushed the conspiracy theories out of his mind and stood up.

He pulled on one of the bars to the cell. It was firmly embedded in the ground. He missed his divine strength.

Footsteps approached.

A man and a woman came into view.

Despite her voice, Apollo didn't recognise the woman at all. The man was a local policeman, but she wasn't. She was dressed as something else.

The lady had shoulder-length brown hair, wrapped in a neat bun, and was wearing a crisp white blouse and black boots. Resting on her nose were thin black glasses. She had long red fingernails and her lips were coated in shining red lipstick. Her rich black eyelashes flickered as she blinked.

"You," the policeman pointed at Apollo, "come here!"

Apollo walked to the side of his prison and faced them through the iron bars. The woman eyed him curiously. Her grey storm-cloud eyes twinkled. Apollo felt a distinct sense of foreboding as he faced her.

"What is your name?" the policeman asked sternly.

"Apollo, God of the Music, Knowledge and Prophecy," he responded plainly.

"Ha-ha, very funny," the policeman grumbled.

"My nephew has always had a warped sense of humour," the woman smiled. "I told you, there was a themed event at the University of Rome, you know how kids are, they get drunk and climb all over the ruins…"

Whoever this woman was, she seemed to be on Apollo's side. She was creating an alibi for him.

The woman placed her hand on the policeman's shoulder and ran it down his arm.

He huffed and looked down at her. "Well, as far as I can see, this is a case of wrong place, wrong time. He doesn't have clearance to be in the Vatican, so make sure he is out of here right away."

She nodded.

He pulled a jangling set of keys from his pocket and unlocked the holding cell door. The policemen gestured for Apollo to walk out, which he did.

"Get him some new clothes from the lost and found too," the policeman muttered as he swung the door closed.

Before long, Apollo found himself wearing jeans and a loose-fitting v-neck t-shirt.

The woman told him to leave his Roman-style robes and sandals in the lost and found box, which he begrudgingly did.

She had a car waiting outside the office of the Gendarmerie Corps of the Vatican City State.

As they hopped inside the immaculately clean vehicle, Apollo, at last, asked the question that had been burning in his mind.

"Who are you?"

The woman pulled her spectacles down over her nose and gazed at him, "You don't recognise me, Apollo?"

"No... but you seem familiar."

"It has been 1682 years since I last saw you, but I imagine only days for you."

Apollo peered into the depths of her eyes. In them, he saw something, something that was hard to describe. It was like the shadow of a lingering doom.

"Moros?" Apollo asked.

She smiled. "It is good to see you again, Apollo. It has been such a long time."

"You're still alive? The angels never found you?" Apollo asked excitedly.

Moros, the Greek Goddess of Doom, stretched her seat-belt across her.

"Hiding in plain sight," she said as she started up the car. "I've been trying to keep track of the old gods, the ones that are still around. The Vatican was the best place to do it. I've been the librarian of their secret archive for the last century."

"How have they not noticed?"

"I let this body grow old, and I retire. I then apply and win the open job application," Moros smirked.

"The angels don't sense your magic?" Apollo asked.

"There is always some low level of magic occurring at the Vatican. The Pope communes with angels. There is a scarred-faced man here usually, who undergoes a horrific transformation on the full moon. I believe he has been sent to Australia, of all places, recently. Tiny things I can get away with, and where we are headed now, I can get away with much more. Plus, the angels can only seem to detect magic that creates a physical change in the world, or so I have deduced. Though, I wouldn't readily test that theory."

"Where are we headed?"

"The Vatican Secret Archive, that is where they have taken your sword."

"I thought the sword would be the key to returning my godhood," Apollo started. "But even with that and my prophet, I am still mortal."

"Yes, I felt it in the air when you re-emerged. Your return to the world is connected with a coming doom. I feel it in my bones. I also heard your prophet utter a prophecy as to how you can restore yourself. It carried like a song on the wind to my ears."

"Do you remember the words?"

"The God of Storms punishes he who brings the fire down the mountain. The bearer of the greatest gift was chained but we were unchained. The fire unseals the lost spark."

"Do you know what it means?" Apollo asked.

"I suspect, as I'm sure you do, that we need to find the lost Temple to Prometheus," Moros replied.

"Such a place cannot be easily found, Zeus never located it."

"It wasn't built in his domain. Even as powerful a being as Zeus was, he rarely interfered in the regions of other gods. If that original flame that Prometheus brought to humanity is still inside his temple, I believe it will restore you."

As the car pulled up, Moros turned to Apollo.

"Your prophet can find the temple. I believe I know where the key is. It's with your sword, buried beneath the Vatican Secret Archive."

Apollo grinned. It seemed everything was coming together quickly.

"Where is my prophet?"

"In the Vatican somewhere. But let us focus on one task at a time."

Moros had pulled up directly in front of a large fountain. Apollo saw they were in an expansive car park teeming with vehicles. The drive from the police station had only been a couple of minutes.

"I'm sorry that you won't get to see the art tour of the Vatican Library, Apollo, I assure you it is quite spectacular."

"Would it not be better for us to blend in with all the humans?" Apollo suggested as he felt the heat from the sun blaze down onto his shoulders.

The Goddess of Doom ignored his suggestion; she already had a way in.

Moros dangled a Vatican security ID before Apollo.

"The actual Vatican Archive is like a fortress. Luckily, I have a key."

Moros led Apollo across the car park to a metal security door in a far wall.

It was covered in signs reading 'NO ACCESS'.

Moros swiped in.

Apollo followed.

They could hear the chatter of hundreds of tourists through the wall.

They came to another swipe door, and behind it, a stairwell going down.

"This access is used by the cardinals when they don't want others to know they are visiting the archive. I am the only staff member of the Vatican with a card that can get in this way."

"Where does this path lead?" Apollo asked.

"To a small reception room, where secret access requests are granted by me. Usually, only three people per day are allowed access into the archive. When the rules need to be broken, or if something is delivered in secret, they come through here."

They entered the reception room. Spectacular paintings lined every wall.

Apollo spun in a circle and marvelled at the images of angels and men around him, though some of them were faded and damaged.

Moros noticed him looking and explained, "Because the public doesn't see this place, it is not as well maintained."

Breaking up two images depicting events in the life of Jesus of Nazareth was a pair of bland metal sliding doors.

Apollo walked towards them as Moros fumbled behind the desk, looking for something.

He paused as he looked into the face of Jesus.

"Who is this man?" Apollo asked.

"A demi-god," Moros answered. "Their god is not so dissimilar from us, as it turns out."

"And where do these doors lead?"

"Down into the vaults below the archive. I do not have access. However, there is another door to which I do. A fortunate IT glitch that I may have willed into happening. We have to travel through the archive. It is a long walk."

Apollo turned his head towards the glass door behind the reception desk. Through it were long rows of book shelves that stretched as far as the eye could see.

At last, Moros retrieved her hidden key from beneath a stack of papers. Apollo found it odd to see such a revered goddess doing such trivial human things.

A question occurred to him.

"Moros, why didn't any of the humans find it conspicuous that I was there with the golden sword. In my mind it seems more suspicious than the reaction I received."

"I felt Hecate use her power last night, and at that moment, I used some of mine. To make it simple, I distorted your presence in the world. It is a slight alteration to the human's perception. When Hecate unleashed against whatever foe that found her, she would have attracted the attention of Heaven completely. It was a calculated risk, one of many more to come. I gambled on them being too absorbed by Hecate to notice me distorting the world.

"Now, people will hardly notice you. The spell will be broken if you give the humans reason to see you properly. It will have already worked on the camera operators of the Vatican. Sure, they will have seen you with me, entering secure doors, but they won't have registered it."

Moros pressed her funny-looking key into a small hole in the wall.

The glass door opened. There was a hiss as stale air was released.

"Quickly now," Moros commanded as she stepped into the archive.

Apollo followed her into the depths of the spiritual heart of the world.

CHAPTER TWENTY-ONE

THE VATICAN VAULT

Apollo moved with haste down the long rows of shelves. Catalogues of books, marked with Latin words and Roman numerals, sat in perfectly matching sets on either side of him as he advanced down the endless corridor.

The library was hauntingly silent.

Apollo's brief connection to his godly domain of knowledge had allowed him to get an understanding of the modern world. He privately wished that he was his true divine self, so all of these secrets around him could be absorbed.

"You regret your current mortality. I see it in your eyes," Moros commented as she strode along behind him.

Apollo looked back, still amazed at her appearance. This was the Goddess of Doom, an ancient entity of unimaginable power, and here she was dressed in black boots, black slacks, a white blouse and her hair all done up neatly in a bun.

The Goddess of Doom was conforming to a company's dress standards. What had happened to the world?

"Is the key to the Temple of Prometheus in these books?" Apollo asked.

"No," Moros responded. "Many secrets are kept here, but with the right permissions anyone can search these. We have to go deeper."

"The Gladius Vaticanus, Lucifer's soldiers, do they come down here?"

"No, only the Pope and the highest-ranking members of the clergy are allowed access. The Church is powerful beyond measure, and through their conquests, they have obtained countless treasures. The secrets of the vault are well kept."

"So, the fire of Prometheus is here, below us?" Apollo said excitedly. He could practically taste his godhood.

"No. Did you not listen before? The fire is in the lost temple. However, I have long suspected the key to said temple is down here," Moros frowned.

They continued along the dimly lit rows of shelves which seemed to stretch on forever.

"We have to go right to the end? Can't you just move us there?" Apollo asked, as he felt an ache in his mortal legs.

"Too dangerous, any display of divine power will summon the angels. We aren't deep enough yet for them not to notice any such actions."

"Isn't this place swarming with angels anyway? This is the heart of their religion! Why can't they sense you now?"

"The Vatican is a construction of men; its meanings and symbols are all constructed by humans. Their holy book is filled with lies. The angels don't care. They accept the phenomenal power generated from this place, but they have no active part in it. The Pope, the head of this church, communes with the Archangel Michael on occasion. It seems only Michael, of the seven archangels, actually cares about what's going on down here."

"Where are the angels on Earth then?"

"Jerusalem, I believe. There is a portal to the realm of Heaven there."

"How do you know this?"

"It's in these records around us. The portal to the Underworld was in Rome, the portal to the upper world in Jerusalem. It was created for the temple of King Solomon. Both were sealed in the fourteenth century, but recently the Jerusalem gate was reopened."

"Why?" Apollo asked.

"An excellent question," Moros responded.

The pair continued on. They passed by wide glass cases that contained ancient stone tablets and preserved scrolls.

Apollo asked the question that had been biting at him, "I want to know the fate of the gods. What became of Artemis?"

"I'm afraid I don't know. The Battle for the Underworld heralded a new era. The angels grew stronger and stronger. The world entered a dark age for humanity but a glorious era for the angels. Their human followers spread across the planet while the old gods were systematically hunted and exterminated. Some fought back. Shiva holds an uneasy truce with the Archangel Michael. The realm of Nirvana never fell.

"In South America, the massacre was felt strongest. I don't believe any of the gods of the Aztecs or Mayans remain hidden in the world. They fought, and they lost. I felt their doom."

"Why did this happen, though? Religions rise and they fall. Some gods linger, and some choose to fade. Why did they need to conquer the world?"

"War comes naturally to both gods and man alike," Moros answered wistfully.

Apollo didn't like this answer. He wanted there to be more to the story. There had to be more to it.

"We are here," Moros said abruptly.

The shelves turned on a ninety-degree angle. Right at the joint in the wall was the entrance to an elevator. It had shining silver doors and a nine-digit keypad on its side.

"A code?" Apollo said. "Such simple security."

"For now," Moros muttered. "The deeper we get, the more difficult access becomes. Fortunately, we have divine magic at our disposal."

"You said you couldn't use any of your divine power."

"Up here, no," Moros explained. "When we are closer to the power within the vault, using a few tricks to open the doors will be sufficiently undetectable."

Apollo was very intrigued by this statement. What power awaited in this vault?

Moros punched in a code, and the doors split apart.

The two gods stepped inside the cold metal box.

There were no panels inside. With a small squeak, the doors slid shut and the elevator began rapidly descending.

"VAULT ONE," a feminine voice rang out.

The elevator didn't stop.

"You input a code for the level you want," Moros answered the unasked question.

They zoomed down further.

"How many vaults do they have down here?" Apollo asked.

"I don't know as the secrecy is absolute. No one gossips to the librarian about it. All I know is that when a certain relic, bearing the aura of a titan was brought in, it was taken to Vault Twelve. I didn't even need to see it to recognise it, I felt it."

"So, this is largely a guessing game we are playing?" Apollo asked.

"Yes and no," Moros shrugged. "How many relics of the titans are there in the world, do you imagine? My guess would be none. The Titanomachy was an ancient event before even your time. Before the current type of humans were even around."

Apollo knew of the event she referred to. The Titanomachy was a war led by Zeus against Cronus. The original Olympians fought the titans and won. The titans were similar to the gods, but older, and for lack of a better term, less human. Some of the titans had allied with Zeus, one of which was Prometheus. The very same being who'd brought the divine flame to humanity, and was greatly punished for it. It was that flame that seemed to be the key to restoring Apollo.

"VAULT TWELVE" the speaker called. The doors opened.

Apollo and Moros stepped into a sterile corridor. Doors with small glass viewing windows lined the walls.

Apollo peeked inside the nearest one. There were arrays of scientific equipment inside, from test-tubes brimming with multi-coloured liquids to expensive elaborate machines, whose purposes Apollo could only guess at.

The corridor was long and at the end was a heavy sealed bulk-head door.

"Let us hope this goes unnoticed," Moros said.

She transformed.

At once, the beautiful librarian became a dignified old cardinal.

Moros, now an older man draped in Catholic attire, stepped towards a blue scanner on the wall.

It scanned her eyeball.

"Speak," a little voice rang out from the contraption.

"Cardinal Vasilije Markovic," she said in an authoritative voice.

"Please confirm the passphrase," the computer said.

Moros looked at Apollo confused, then wrapped one of her fingers in a glowing light. She reached out and touched the display. It crackled and died.

Moros transformed again.

She took on the form from when Apollo had last seen her, only a few days ago in the secret cave. The Goddess of Doom in her full majesty stood before him.

"We are committed now," she said quietly.

She placed one hand against the massive steel door and blasted it away. The door, and a good part of the wall, crashed into the room behind.

No alarms sounded, but Apollo knew Moros was using her magic to suppress them.

"I think that may have been noticed," Apollo laughed.

"Then let us be quick," Moros responded.

Loose wires were shooting sparks through the space where the door had been. Apollo and Moros carefully stepped over some jagged chunks of metal and into a circular room.

Across the room's circumference were small arches cut into the wall. Some were empty, but others contained cloudy glass barriers with objects suspended behind.

Apollo noticed that one of the arches held another hallway, that led into a different circular room.

There were eight display areas in total, in this room at least.

Beside each display was another scanner. Obviously, a further security check had to be performed to lower the glass wall to gain access to the object inside.

Apollo turned to Moros, "Do you sense it again? The titan relic? I have lost all inner sight; I feel nothing in this room."

Moros scanned the room.

"Yes, I think so," she said. "The glass on the walls isn't of this world. It is angelic; it suppresses the power of what lies within."

Apollo walked towards the display directly to his right. Through the glass, he made out the rough image of a rectangular hammer with a short handle.

The next arch along was empty.

The third again contained cloudy glass, with what looked like a long wooden stick attached to the wall behind it.

Moros went left to inspect the arches on the other side of the room. After a moment, they met at the passage to the next area.

The goddess saw that laser tripwires were running across the length of the pass.

She disabled them with a wave of her hand and they moved through.

The next room contained more objects behind foggy barriers.

"Enough of this," Moros said disgruntled. She walked towards one of the scanners.

"Can you not destroy the glass as you did the door?" Apollo asked.

"Probably, but it would take considerable time and effort," Moros responded, her voice changing as she morphed into another old man.

This time, he was adorned with a conical white hat and white robes.

She placed her eye against the scanner.

A small blue laser moved up and down across her iris. There was a clicking sound, then all of the glass doors began sliding downwards.

"I thought he might have special access," Moros said plainly.

"Who are you?" Apollo asked.

"The voice of God on Earth," she smiled.

Apollo wasn't sure what that meant, but he was impressed that the last 1700 years had lightened Moros up a bit.

Moros, still in the guise of the Pope, gasped in excitement.

"Let us bring your prophet to us. She has as much a role to play in this as you do."

She reached into a nearby archway and pulled out a sparkling pointed crystal. It had golden glowing Latin letters carved into its sides.

"Do you remember Janus?" Moros asked Apollo.

"Yes, he was a demi-god, I believe. Or was he a spirit? Two heads, one looking forward and one looking back. I remember the Romans classed him as a god among us."

"Because of these," Moros said, tossing the crystal to Apollo.

"What is it?"

"A Janus Crystal. The Romans called him the God of Doorways. More specifically, the God of Portals. You dismiss him too easily. He apotheosised like many others did."

Apollo twirled the crystal in his hand, "Can a mortal use this?"

"That is who they were designed for. We gods rarely have trouble with travel. Focus on your prophet and throw it against the wall."

Apollo did as instructed.

The crystal shattered, and the air of the room began sucking into a single point. Then, with a flash of lightning, a tear opened up. Blue sparks twisted around the opening in space. Through it, Apollo saw Melissa, and, more alarmingly, Belial.

He reached through the breach in space and grabbed Melissa by the back of the shirt. Apollo flung her towards him and she fell on top of him with a thud.

The look of rage on Belial's face was unmistakable as the portal quickly sealed up.

Melissa scrambled to her feet, only to find herself face to face with the Pope in an unfamiliar room.

"Well, they know where we are now," Moros sighed.

"What is going on?" Melissa asked, panicked, as she turned to Apollo.

"To the next room!" Apollo ordered. "We need to find a relic of the Titan Prometheus."

Melissa just stared at him in confusion as she got to her feet.

The three of them rushed through another archway into the third circular room. All of the angel-glass had lowered here too.

Apollo scanned the room.

He noticed that something to the left had caught Melissa's eye.

Sitting on a rotten lectern was a black book. It was bound in leather with metal clasps, and looked positively ancient. On its face was a black skull, barely distinguishable, save for its raised and bubbled texture. The skull looked like it had been crudely melted onto the front. It certainly wasn't human either. It had long tentacles that reached down from the upper jaw and snaked out randomly across the cover. Apollo felt a rush in his chest just looking at the book.

Melissa reached out for it, but Moros slapped her hand away.

"Stay away from Alhazred's writing," Moros warned.

Apollo noticed a notepad and pen on the ground in the arch. Someone had been studying this book recently. The words 'the power of Zeus' were plainly visible among the notes.

Moros rushed to the right of the room, and Apollo turned his attention to the object she was now carrying.

It was a stone torch.

There was a shallow bowl at the top that sat on a long-segmented cone.

Three rectangular slabs, each evenly spaced apart, jutted down from the bowl and connected with its handle mid-way down. It was a dazzling white and had five gold rings running up its length from the bottom.

"That doesn't look very ancient," Melissa said sceptically.

"I'd say it's roughly 75000 years old," Moros estimated, barely concealing a smirk. Humans saw time in such a small way.

"It looks brand new," Melissa moved in closer.

"That's because it came from Olympus," Apollo marvelled. "It reminds me of home…"

"And you need this torch? Why?" Melissa asked.

"This, dear human, is an object that was used by a titan for the most wonderful act in history," Moros began.

"Think about it," Apollo started. "Gods can generate light and heat of their own accord easily. Why would a simple decorative torch, in a palace on Olympus, ever need to be taken down to the mortal world? Because it was for a gift. A gift of divine fire. The gift that made humans the way they are."

"So, the gods gave us fire?" Melissa said.

"No, no, no," Apollo said quickly, "you achieved that quite well on your own."

"Have you ever heard of the human evolutionary phenomenon called the cognitive revolution?" Moros asked Melissa.

It was only then that Apollo noticed Melissa's look of distrust as she spoke to Moros. Melissa hadn't seen the goddess transform and could very well think she was talking to the actual Pope.

"No…"

A *bang* rang through the room. Someone else was headed to Vault Twelve.

The three of them rushed out of the third room, back through the passages, towards the initial entryway.

This time, the cloudy glass was down in the first circular room, and Apollo could see each archway's contents clearly. To his right, he saw his golden sword. Moros must've walked straight past it earlier.

He felt his fingers wrap around its grip and lifted it joyously into the air. Apollo was reunited with his weapon again.

Nearest to Melissa was a long brown stick suspended on a wall. She grabbed and held it in front of her.

Curiously, in her grip, the stick became smooth. The wood turned into scales, and the staff became a twisting red and black serpent. The snake slipped through her hands and fell to the ground. It turned and reared up with its fangs bared.

Melissa leapt back.

"What the hell…" she breathed.

"I've stopped the elevator," Moros said. "Crumpled it, though at best it will only delay them."

"It will be Belial coming for us. Is he an angel?" Melissa asked, not removing her eyes from the snake.

"He is no angel, at least not anymore. The priests don't want him in the Vatican. That gossip I am sure of," Moros responded. "If actual angels were coming, they'd be here by now."

The snake slithered toward Melissa. She pressed herself back into an arch. It curled, like a coiled spring, and launched itself at her. She reached out a hand to catch it, but as her skin made contact, the snake became a wooden staff again.

"Were there more of those Janus Crystals?" Apollo asked.

"Yes, one more, but I'm afraid to use it. If it's used again, others further away than the Vatican may sense it. It's impossible to know for sure," Moros answered.

"Can you teleport us out?"

"Not without calling down Heaven's host and revealing that Apollo has returned to the world."

Apollo saw Melissa gazing at the staff through the corner of his eye.

"Melissa," he said, "you have divine vision. You may be a prophet, but you can still see events of the past. That staff may not be of my design, but use your power and understand it."

Melissa closed her eyes and held the relic tight.

"I see a man standing proud with the staff before him. He is knee-deep in water. Towering waves are rearing up on both sides of him, creating a dry path through the middle of a vast sea. Huddled masses are praying as they move between the walls of water."

Melissa snapped back to reality. "I know that story... everyone does. Is this the staff of the Prophet Moses?"

"We are in the right place for such an object to be," Moros said.

"Who is coming? The soldiers of the Gladius Vaticanus?" Apollo asked, readying his sword.

"No, they would never be allowed down here," Moros

answered. "Their bosses on the other hand… I sense three foes — ones who can enter undetected. The Vatican isn't aware the vault has breached. Melissa is right, it has to be Belial and two of his kind."

"What is he?" Apollo asked.

"One of the original fallen angels. Swallowed by Tartarus in the great battle. A Knight of Hell."

"Wait," Melissa asked, "why would a being called a 'Knight of Hell' be working for the Vatican?"

"Lucifer and the other six archangels have been at odds for a long time. A tentative alliance has recently formed between them. It seems the factions of Heaven and Hell have found common purpose, though whatever Belial's goal is, I can assure you it isn't the same as the Vatican's."

Melissa, Moros and Apollo looked down the corridor as the doors to the empty elevator shaft were peeled open. The metal bent and screeched as a pair of fingers pushed through and split the doors apart.

With a crash, they were ripped clean from the wall and went tumbling down the shaft into the depths below.

A figure jumped through the open doorway, followed by two others.

The three men looked at Melissa's party.

Belial was at their head. He grinned his demonic grin.

"Your holiness," he said to Moros, still disguised as the Pope. "It seems there is a god of the old world in our midst. Let us find out which one."

CHAPTER TWENTY-TWO

THE KNIGHTS OF HELL

Saliva flowed down Belial's jaw. He looked deranged as he twisted his head from side to side. The deep maroon veins that crisscrossed his face were pulsing.

The other two men looked slightly less maniacal. One was dressed in a tailored grey suit, with a long fringe that flopped in front of his face. He resembled an emo business man. The other wore the dress of a cardinal and looked older, though his eyes were no less menacing.

"Cardinal Silas," Moros, in the croaky voice of the Pope, greeted the cardinal first.

"Your Holiness," the man named Silas bowed low.

"What is your real name?" Moros demanded.

"Asmodee."

"This is really an honour for you three," Belial said casually as walked towards Melissa, the fake Pope and Apollo. The entry scanners sparked and exploded while the fluorescent lights flickered on and off in his presence. "The Knights of Hell are a big deal in occult circles. There are cults honouring us individually all over the world. To have three in one place, at one time - it hasn't happened in an age."

"Then why are the three of you here?" Moros demanded.

The suited man spoke up, "We have a goal to accomplish."

"Last night, a goddess revealed herself. A goddess of magic. She'd been operating in plain sight through the use of runic symbols. She'd pass her magic into the rune, and it'd activate, independently of her. Very, very clever. No wonder the angels never found her. Well, not until last night," Belial added.

"Hecate…" Melissa whispered; gripping Moses' staff tight.

"What happened to her?" Apollo demanded.

"You should bow when you speak to me, mortal!" Belial spat at the ground.

Melissa still couldn't believe that everyone in the Vatican was so dismissive of Apollo.

The three knights were drawing close to the first circular room.

"Lord Lucifer's new plans are somewhat similar to the Vatican's. He needs the blood of Zeus, and the old gods are his only way of getting it," the suited knight said.

"Oriens is correct," Belial continued from his companion. "The Vatican is looking for a direct connection to a great power, long absent from the world. Lord Lucifer has his own plans for that power. How lucky for us that we have found yet another goddess."

Melissa was curious who the goddess was. She was the only female in the room, alongside Apollo and someone who was clearly impersonating the Pope.

Belial stepped onto the damaged bulk-head door and paused to look at his reflection in the metal.

"The Goddess Persephone tricked Lucifer, bound him to the Underworld forever. We were just caught up in it. Hundreds and hundreds of years we waited. In the dark, and in the fire, waiting for Primordial Tartarus to release us. Lucifer sent five of us into the world. The rest of the Gladius Vaticanus remain in Hell, operating from afar."

While Belial rambled on, Apollo quickly whispered to the Pope-impersonator, "They are angels, their power should be well beyond ours. We must flee."

A voice then spoke directly into both Apollo and Melissa's minds, *"No. They are different. When Tartarus claimed them, he severed their connection to Heaven. Their power remains the same as the day they attacked the Underworld."*

"No boost from the spread of their religion," Apollo replied. *"Maybe we have a chance here with Moros."*

"Moros!" Melissa thought. The Pope was actually the Goddess of Fate and Doom in disguise. The very same goddess whose eyes had shown her the battle that took place so many years ago.

During the Battle for the Underworld, Lucifer had been as powerful as an Olympian, perhaps stronger. But the angels of the Gladius Vaticanus weren't as strong as Lucifer had been. If their power had truly been severed, then the Goddess Moros had a fighting chance against these Knights of Hell. The risk was, that if Moros revealed too much of her power, it could summon actual angels directly to them.

"Do you want to see what it did to us?" Belial asked, still staring down at his reflection. "Those centuries trapped in the dark of Tartarus?"

The Knight of Hell hunched forward, and his overalls split open. Two black bat-like wings unfurled and spread across the width of the room.

Two spiral horns burst from the sides of his head. His hair caught fire and faded away as his skin turned red. His eyes became deathly yellow circles, and his fingers grew into long talons.

A forked tongue flicked out between his pointed teeth. The thick veins that ran across his face spread down his blood-red body.

The other two Knights of Hell didn't transform. They just looked on, amused, as Belial underwent his horrific change. His clothes fell from him in tatters as his legs bent backwards and became that of a goat's. A tail sprung out from behind him. It hissed as it took on the form of a bright green serpent with deadly fangs.

Melissa felt fear flow through her. She'd seen artworks and ancient pictures of demons before, but Belial was truly a monster.

Apollo held his sword fast in the face of the beast. Moros didn't look concerned at all.

She turned to Apollo, "Go back and get the other Janus Crystal. Melissa and I can handle this."

Melissa looked at Moros, aghast. "Me?"

"That staff in your hands, I sense impossible power radiating from it. Use it."

The Knights of Hell, clearly listening, looked to Melissa and her wooden stick.

Moros raised her hand, and a powerful shockwave rippled through the room.

Belial was sent flying back down the corridor, his wings scraping the walls.

Asmodee and Oriens lunged forward.

Apollo was already moving, back towards the third room where Moros had left the crystal.

As soon as the two knights made their move, Melissa felt the atmosphere change. The room got hotter as electricity twisted in the air.

A whip made of fire manifested itself in Asmodee's hand. Tongues of lightning shot out from it as the knight cracked it above him.

They went for Moros. Melissa watched in amazement as the hunched old figure of the Pope side-stepped the suited demon named Oriens, and sent a spinning kick right into the side of his face.

Asmodee whipped at Moros. She ran to the side of the room with both of her old withered hands clasped firmly behind her back. In a gravity-defying motion, she ran straight up the wall. If Melissa hadn't felt the danger the two fallen angels presented, she would have laughed at how comical it was.

She stood on the roof upside down, like a bat, and looked at the two knights below her.

Asmodee once again launched his fiery whip at her, but Moros simply pursed her lips and blew it out with a phenomenal jet of wind.

Asmodee's face contorted with rage.

The horned demonic figure of Belial flew back into the room at supersonic speed. Seeing his two fellow knights fighting Moros, he turned his attention to Melissa.

He gestured towards her with his gnarled red fingers, and Melissa began sliding across the floor towards him.

She leant back, but it was like she was caught in an invisible harness. Panicked, she pointed her wooden staff at Belial.

Melissa couldn't remember much of the story of Moses, save for some of the plagues that had assaulted Egypt.

"LOCUSTS!" she screamed.

A loud buzzing filled the air. Crawling straight out of the walls were insects. Hundreds of them. They began swarming through the room.

Oriens inhaled deeply, then breathed out a tornado of flame in an attempt to melt them. But Moros dropped from the ceiling and placed her hand over his mouth, causing Oriens' cheeks to expand and fire burst through his skin.

The locusts swarmed around Belial, latching on to his wings.

He sent out a shockwave and the bugs dispersed. But to his annoyance, they were instantly replaced with dozens more.

The air of the room was quickly growing thick with locusts.

"Enough of this!" Asmodee screamed. He clapped his hands together, and a small black hole appeared in front of him. Instantly, the swarm started to be sucked into the spinning singularity.

"Neat trick," Moros admitted, as out of nowhere she scooped up the black hole and swung her body around the knight. With a twist and a move like a slam dunk, she forced it into his open mouth.

The entire roomful of locusts began funnelling into the mouth of Asmodee.

Belial reached out for Melissa again, but the staff seemed to be protecting her from his magic. Belial opened his jaws wide and spewed fire at Melissa, though the fire dissipated in front of her.

"Try fire and ice!" Melissa yelled, tapping the staff on the ground.

Hail began pelting down from the ceiling, and plumes of her own fire burst from the floor. All of it was aimed at the three demons.

Belial shielded himself beneath his wings. Oriens, now with two significant holes in his cheeks, redirected the fire from the floor towards Moros.

The Goddess of Doom, still in the form of the Pope, was moving swiftly around the room, dodging attacks.

Melissa felt like she was beginning to connect with the ancient staff.

What had the burning bush said to Moses? She was sure it was something about performing God's wonders.

A daring thought occurred to her. What if God had given the staff to Moses as a representation of his power on Earth? The way Apollo talked, the angels were insanely powerful because of Islam, Judaism, Christianity and all of the other branches of that religion. That would mean the god of the angels would have power beyond comprehension. If the staff was still a direct link to that power, then she should be able to do almost anything with it.

"One more plague," Melissa thought.

The chunks of hail were growing larger and slamming into the Knights of Hell with extreme force.

Melissa tapped the ground again.

A thick, fat, slimy frog jumped onto her head.

Looking around, Melissa could see frogs emerging all over the room, quickly covering every inch of space. They were hopping around, jumping all over the Knights of Hell. Though, they didn't really seem to be doing anything other than causing mild annoyance to the knights.

As the last of the locust swarm was sucked into the black hole inside Asmodee's mouth and he was freed. Anger burned in his eyes. His cardinal's robes were singed and torn from the hail and fire.

Melissa found herself thinking that surely the Knights of Hell had more in them than this.

She watched as Moros hit Belial in the back of the head with the heavy torch from Olympus. She was barely using any of her power.

Melissa realised something. The fallen angels were probably holding back too. They also didn't want to attract the heavenly angels with any significant displays of force.

Oriens wrapped his arms around himself and hunched forward. He then dramatically released, flinging his arms wide.

From his suit, dozens of knives emerged, flying out in all directions.

Moros raised her hand and a barrier formed around her. The knives that approached her turned into sand.

Melissa wasn't so lucky. A knife bounced off the roof and came down across her right cheek, leaving a large gash.

She cried out in pain and dropped the staff.

The Staff of Moses again became a snake.

It slithered away. As it wound around the flames shooting from the ground, Melissa noticed that its fangs were bathed in brilliant white light.

Asmodee was struck first by the serpent. He had just re-summoned his whip and was striking at Moros.

The serpent plunged its fangs in his leg, and the fallen angel turned to stone.

Oriens was next. He was only a few feet from Asmodee. He too was frozen in place, becoming a grotesque grey statue.

Belial saw what had happened to his fellow knights and leapt into the air. He flew towards the elevator shaft.

Moros stopped him. At last, she took on her female form. The visage of the Pope melted away, and the Goddess of Doom became the stunningly beautiful vision she'd been in the Battle of the Underworld.

Moros wrapped the demonic Belial in a sphere of black energy and held him in place.

She brought the sphere back into the room and placed it squarely between Oriens and Asmodee.

The serpent slithered under it.

"How dare you think you can challenge a god," Moros stated, her eyes blazing with power.

Belial was kicking at the sides of his prison with his hoofed feet.

"What do we do?" Melissa asked, brushing a fat frog off her arm.

"Command the serpent," Moros instructed.

Moros looked at the snake that was formerly the Staff of Moses.

"Uh, seal them away," she said lamely.

The snake reared up, then dived headfirst into the floor.

A portal, similar to the one summoned by Apollo earlier, opened up.

Through it, Melissa could see endless sand dunes.

"Forty years wandering the desert…" she said to herself.

The two stone statues fell through first and crashed into the orange sand below. Moros lowered Belial down after them.

He screamed out to her, "I will have my revenge!"

As soon as the imprisoning ball of energy was through, the portal closed.

Melissa and Moros stood there, in a room full of hopping frogs.

The Staff of Moses lay still on the floor.

"We should take this with us, right?" Melissa asked, picking it up.

"No," Moros replied. "Down here, we can use such power because we are surrounded by layers of ancient powerful items. If we were to take that up to the surface and use it, the angels would immediately detect us."

Melissa was sorely disappointed. The Staff of Moses seemed

like the ultimate weapon, and she felt she'd only seen the very tip of its potential.

"Where is Apollo?" Moros asked.

Melissa was looking the goddess up and down. She loved the white ancient Greek-style dress she was wearing. It was simple, yet stunningly elegant. It was an amazing change from the hunched figure of the old man she'd just been.

Moros headed through the arch in the direction Apollo had gone.

Regretfully, Melissa placed the Staff of Moses back in its arch before following Moros. She privately hoped that one day she'd get to try it out again.

Apollo stood in the third room, staring into an archway. Inside was a three-tiered shelf, with each level having two of the exact same items on it. The odd-looking objects were bronze, with a long tube that jutted out of a circular grip. Half a sphere emerged from the metal where the two ends of the grip met. The end of the tube featured a deadly point, which looked like it was designed to be jabbed into someone.

He turned as he heard the footsteps of Melissa and Moros.

"Quite the battle you missed, Apollo," Moros said cheerfully.

The joy in her voice died when she saw the items that had so enraptured the Golden God.

"What is it?" Melissa asked, walking up to the pair.

"I'm not sure," Apollo said. "Moros?"

"Seven heavenly siphons for seven archangels," Moros said softly.

"There are only six," Melissa stated very matter-of-factly,

quickly counting them again.

"The seventh has never left the Underworld," Moros explained. "I saw it used on Cer by Lucifer."

"So, one was used on Hades…" Apollo said.

"By Michael, yes. I saw it happen as I was dragging you away."

"What do they do?"

"They were a back-up plan for the archangels, as best as I have been able to uncover. You know that the angels are fueled by prayer. With no faith from humanity, the archangels would be nothing but minor spirits; nothing compared to a true god."

"So they steal divine power. Did Michael absorb the power of Hades?"

"No," Moros answered. "The devices steal a god's natural divine essence. A true god doesn't need to be worshipped to be powerful. This simply transferred that ability to the archangels from the gods they defeated. So now, the archangels will never fall below the level of power they had when they used this device."

Apollo seemed to understand while Melissa didn't at all. Gods, angels, demons, Knights of Hell; this had been a long couple of days…

"The archangels can grow infinitely more powerful, but if every human forgot them tomorrow, they'd still have at least a base level of godly power thanks to these devices," Apollo muttered.

"Correct," Moros nodded.

"This is what they slaughtered Cer and Hades for?" Apollo spat, getting angry. "Something that wasn't rightfully theirs?"

"They intend to be the rulers of this world for all time, it seems," Moros grimaced, patting Apollo on the shoulder.

Melissa suddenly interjected, "But they won't be."

Apollo looked at her.

"People aren't religious anymore. Faith in all of the Palestinian religions is dropping rapidly. People don't like religion; they don't want to believe. It's been a corrupt and broken system for millennia."

"The turning of the tide," Moros chuckled. "Hecate knew all along. Before she ripped you from time, she said you'd come back at the turn of the tide. She never took the invasion of the Underworld well, you know?"

"Where is Hecate?" Apollo said.

"I assume in Heaven somewhere, as a prisoner. I don't think she's gone," Moros replied.

"Can we rescue her?"

"Difficult, and without your divinity, impossible."

"Very well, let us restore my godhood. Mortality wearies me."

"How do we do that?" Melissa asked.

"You gave us the answer already," Apollo said, smiling at her.

"I did?"

"The God of Storms punishes he who brings the fire down the mountain. The bearer of the greatest gift was chained but we were unchained. The fire unseals the lost spark."

"A prophecy," Moros said. "Good thing the Oracle of Delphi was reborn into the world."

"What does it mean though?" Melissa asked, exasperated.

"We have to go to the place where humanity stored the greatest gift they ever received from the gods."

"Which is?"

"The divine flame. The gift Prometheus brought down the mountain. I'd heard rumours there was a secret temple to Prometheus hidden in the mortal world."

"Well, what clues do we have to its whereabouts?"

Apollo answered, "Probably somewhere underground. I never saw it in my journeys across the sky as the Sun God. And if Zeus had been able to see it, he would have obliterated it. Perhaps it may have some kind of symbol that represents Prometheus. Like an eagle pecking at the stomach of a man chained to a mountainside."

Melissa's eyes went wide.

"I know where it is! I've been there before!"

Apollo twirled the Janus Crystal in his hand.

"What is our destination, prophet?"

"Afghanistan," Melissa said. "The secret temple to Prometheus is in Afghanistan."

CHAPTER
TWENTY-THREE

AFGHANISTAN

The first thing Melissa had noticed about Afghanistan was the cold. For some reason, she'd always imagined the war-torn country to be hot. She looked at the patches of snow blanketing the hillsides as her helicopter flew into the Uruzgan province.

Over 1500 Australian personnel had, at one time, been based there, but a mass withdrawal of troops in 2014 had left only a handful in the area.

A minor contingent of the Australian Army had committed to a further three years for the purpose of training local law enforcement as the region stabilised. However, much to the disappointment of the western world, the intended democratic reform had not come about.

After an almost decade long commitment by foreign forces, in early 2017, the Taliban was once again in control of the province, this time gaining more territory than they'd had before. Despite the ever-present danger, in the pockets of the region that remained free, the Australians endeavoured to honour their commitment to the local people.

In late 2016, ears on the ground had picked up murmurs of an increasingly radical element in Uruzgan. It wasn't the Taliban though, it was something else.

The idea of sending troops back into the region would have been political suicide for whoever suggested it. So ASIO and ASIS were tasked with sending in spies to assess the situation, although, since the last of the Australians were due to withdraw in July, it wasn't deemed an urgent issue.

Fortunately, just graduated were a batch of agents trained in the first-ever joint year-long program between Australia's two premier intelligence agencies. It was the perfect place to test the nerves and abilities of these new elite-level secret operators. Melissa was one of the guinea pigs chosen to head to the Middle East.

It was in Uruzgan that she first met Teva, her future partner in Rome. He was two years her senior in ASIO, but still very much a rookie operative. He'd been working in signals, specifically in encrypted communications. His calm but enthusiastic demeanour meant Melissa liked him immediately.

The Australian Army had been living in a compound outside of the city of Tarin Kot. It was in a farming valley beneath a small desolate mountain.

Foreigners weren't an odd sight in Tarin Kot, as the city was a hub for groups smuggling opium through the Uruzgan province.

In the Taliban controlled city, Melissa found herself frequently dressed in full Islamic apparel. Nothing was visible except her eyes. Because she had to be in the presence of a man, she was teamed with Teva. With his Tahitian heritage, he could pass for Middle Eastern, even if it was somewhat unconvincing.

Melissa and Teva spent long days in the city. They went to cafes and coffee shops, and wandered through local markets. They were listening; listening for talk of a new radical group called Almalayikat Alsabea.

This new threat was rumoured to be quickly developing a global presence since emerging in Syria. The Australian Government was interested in monitoring their activities.

What was unique about this new group, and quite unique among branches of Islam, was that Almalayikat Alsabea were heavily focused on the worship of their four archangels.

Black flags with white Arabic writing proudly displayed the names of Jibrael, Mickael, Israfil and Azrael in their secret facilities.

The more disturbing factor in this new religion's sudden popularity was its emphasis on blood sacrifice, particularly in the name of Azrael.

On the morning of February 9, in Tarin Kot, Melissa and Teva witnessed first-hand the brutality of the angel worshipers.

In the town square, a man in a simple gown and turban was forcibly kneeled onto a spray-painted five-pointed star.

Melissa wasn't sure of his crime, and had to suppress the urge to rush into the crowd and pull him away.

The mob in the town square was riled up. They were shouting and screaming in Arabic.

"What are they saying?" Melissa whispered to Teva.

Teva's face was strained, trying to pick up the words.

"Ah, just that is he a heathen and all the usual stuff," Teva muttered. He kept his head low. Neither wanted to draw any unnecessary attention to themselves.

Melissa tugged on his long brown robes urgently, "You can give me more than that, surely?"

"Hold on," Teva said, gripping Mel's hand.

A group of bearded thugs pushed past the pair.

"I don't know," he continued. "It sounds like some kind of business deal gone wrong."

A truck came rumbling down the street. Its rear tray was loaded with armed men. It slowed as it passed the jostling crowd.

"Taliban," Teva whispered.

Teva and Mel had been able to determine that the Taliban and the Almalayikat didn't get along. They seemed to keep a wary distance from one another. The truck sped up and continued down the street, with several of the soldiers peering back to get a final look at the crowd.

A man emerged from a nearby building holding a weapon. The crowd stopped shouting. In his left hand was a sickle, rust clinging to the surface of the blade.

The kneeling man whimpered softly.

Melissa pushed forward through the crowd. She wanted

a better view. A lot of the men gave her hateful stares as she squeezed between them.

Teva apologised in Arabic behind her.

Melissa assumed the man with the sickle was an imam.

He walked behind the cowering prisoner and wrenched his head back. He tightly gripped the whimpering man's long curly hair.

The imam placed the curve of his blade against the man's neck.

Without a word, he slashed through muscle and vein alike.

Blood splattered the dusty pavement.

The man was almost decapitated, only a thin stretch of skin still held his head to his neck.

The imam just held him there, and let the blood gush from his neck onto the ground.

The crowd cheered.

A churning wave of sickness and anger filled Melissa's stomach. Such cruelty... such malice...

She'd never imagined the world was like this. She'd heard it in her training of course, but to see it was another thing entirely.

A small brown-haired girl burst through the crowd. She was weeping and calling to the dead man in her local tongue. The girl was obviously the victim's daughter.

The imam saw the girl running forward and walked up to greet her. He raised one of his sandal bound feet and kicked her square in the face.

The girl careened back and landed hard on the asphalt.

Anger flashed up in Melissa's mind. She was blinded by

horror and rage.

She didn't think.

She just acted.

She burst through the crowd, her purple burqa billowing behind her.

Melissa threw a devastating punch right at the imam's face.

He collapsed, and Melissa jumped on top of him. Her small fists connected with his head over and over in a volley of blows.

Men from the crowd rushed over and grabbed her by the arms.

She was pulled off the imam and dragged back a few feet.

The imam got up. He was shaking with rage. Someone handed him a gun and he pointed it right at Melissa's face.

He spat out something derogatory in Arabic and put his finger to the trigger.

Someone from behind ripped off Mel's burqa.

The imam paused and lowered his gun.

A murmur ran through the crowd at the revelation that this was a western woman.

Then, something very hard hit Melissa in the back of the head, and her world went black.

• • • • •

A SPOTLIGHT, shining directly into Melissa's eyes, woke her up. The back of her head pulsed with excruciating pain.

She felt the plastic of the cable tie that was binding her hands together.

Fear and anxiety swam through her mind as nervous sweat fell in beads from her temple.

She wasn't wearing the burqa anymore. Someone had changed her clothes. She was dressed in khaki overalls. The thought of some terrorist undressing her filled her with even more dread.

Shadows were moving behind the blinding spotlight. Melissa saw thick wires snaking across the ground just ahead.

A man walked up and placed an eighties style news camera in front of her.

"Hey, where am I?" Melissa shouted.

The people in the room ignored her and kept working.

Melissa looked around.

She was in a cave.

Light bulbs had been drilled into the rock and were connected with grey wires fastened to the ceiling.

She felt the loose gravel shift under her feet.

Behind the spotlight, she saw the tunnel extend off into the distance.

She figured she must be in one of the extensive cave networks of the Uruzgan province.

Almost every military organisation in the world knew that Afghan-based terrorist groups used their knowledge of the cave systems to operate undetected.

She saw the black flags attached to the wall. She recognised the Arabic. They weren't Taliban. These were the same angel worshippers from Tarin Kot.

She felt the throbbing in her head come in waves. How long had she been out for?

Rushing into the crowd was reckless and foolish, she'd lost control, and now she might pay for that mistake with her life.

"Hey!" she called out again.

This time, a man walked toward her.

"Wakey, wakey," the man said in a thick Arabic accent.

"Where am I?" Melissa demanded.

"The last place you will ever be."

The man spat on her face. Melissa felt the warm ball of saliva roll down her cheek and drop onto her overalls.

He walked over to a nearby bench and picked up a sickle, the same that had been used in the town square. The man rolled it in his hand as if he were inspecting the quality of the blade.

Adrenaline rushed through Melissa again.

It seemed like they were going to kill her on TV. She only finished recruit training a couple of months ago, and now she was going to be remembered as a victim of radicalism.

She looked around hopelessly. There was nothing she could do, except pray for a miracle.

A red light appeared on the top of the video camera. It looked like they'd got it working.

A hooded person, draped entirely in black, walked over to the man who'd spat on Mel.

He took the sickle, then moved over to Melissa. He stood quietly beside her.

Shouts rang out in Arabic.

Another man, with a backwards American baseball cap on, moved behind the camera and pushed a button.

The small red light turned green.

The hooded person began to speak rapidly in Arabic, taking deliberate pauses to emphasise his points.

Melissa wished Teva was there, so she could at least understand what point he was trying to make before he slit her throat.

The man moved behind Melissa. She was aware of every one of his soft steps. To her, they were like the footsteps of fate.

The cold curve of the blade was pressed up against her neck. Piercing her skin, she felt a small trickle of blood run down her throat.

Melissa breathed in deeply and closed her eyes. At least she'd tried to live the exciting life she'd promised her grandfather.

Then, Melissa heard it.

At first, it was just a low rumble.

After a second, a colossal explosion boomed through the cave network.

It was so violent that the man behind her was shaken off his feet. The sickle fell into Melissa's lap.

The sound of gunfire was ringing through the air. There was so much Melissa thought an army must have invaded. An army here to save her! But that wasn't right. It was blasting out in all directions, ripping holes in the rock.

Then, she understood what must have happened.

Not far away, the extremists must've had a weapons cache. Something would have happened to set the entire arsenal off. She assumed rockets, and possibly even recovered missiles, all exploded, igniting all of the surrounding ammunition.

All of the men behind the filming apparatus were scrambling

in the chaos.

Melissa realised that only her hands were bound behind her back. She stood up, and the sickle fell to the floor.

She quickly knelt down and fumbled for its handle.

She got it! At just the right angle too, with the curve of the blade facing her.

Melissa pressed the blade against her cable tie bindings, and within a moment, she was free. She shook her wrists. The skin was red where it had been held.

The hooded man was also pushing himself up.

Without thinking, Melissa plunged the blade into his stomach.

She fell back in horror at what she had just done. She'd acted on impulse, again, and now a man was spluttering and dying in front of her. Admittedly, not a very good man, but still…

She got to her feet. Debating morality in war was not an option right now. Gunfire was still ringing out further down the tunnel system. It looked like there was only one way to go, towards the source of the explosion.

On the same bench that had held the sickle was a revolver. She checked its bullet count. She had six shots she could use to get herself out of there. Each one had to be worthwhile.

Melissa decided that she'd follow the wiring on the ceiling through the tunnel. She ran forward, her tired and depleted muscles screaming at her with every step. A lot of the bulbs were damaged or flickering and Melissa had to work to not trip over loose rocks in the poor light.

The gunfire stopped. The ammunition cache had burnt itself out.

A symphony of shouting men filled the tunnels of the cave system.

Melissa came to a fork. One rocky pass stretched off left, and another right. There was a yellow warning sign in between them. Unfortunately, the red lettering on the sign was in Arabic.

"Fat lot of good that is," Melissa muttered to herself.

She smelt the air. The smell of gunpowder was so strong that she couldn't tell which path it had come from.

Melissa gambled on the left tunnel.

She immediately began moving downhill and didn't like that at all. She had to remind herself that she had no idea of the layout of this underground network, and down could be equally as good as up.

The smell was getting stronger. Smoke lingered in the air. Boulders strewn across the ground forced Mel to conclude that she'd reached the site of the explosion. It looked like the cavern had been ripped apart. Metal shards and fragments of missiles sporadically littered the ground in front of her.

Two men were already in the cavern. They were speaking in hushed tones.

Melissa noticed that they both had flashlights in hand and were staring at the back wall.

She crept forward, holding the revolver at the ready in her right hand. She paused when she saw what the men were so fascinated with.

The rock face had been blown away to reveal a completely smooth silver wall. It was utterly alien to the rest of the tunnel system.

Melissa inched forward for a better view.

The explosion had exposed what was obviously an ancient door. Carved into its face was an exquisite image of impossible detail.

It showed a man chained by his arms to the side of a cliff. Agony was etched onto his face. Three distinct images were present next to him. To the far right of the door was the sculpted image of a mighty eagle soaring through the sky. Further to the left, the eagle was presented again, only this time its wings were forward as if it were about to land. Then, right beside the chained person was the third image of the eagle. It was hovering close to him, with a chunk of flesh hanging in its mouth. By its shape, Melissa guessed the chunk of flesh was intended to be the man's liver.

The door expertly showed the story of a man who was strung up to a cliff being eaten alive by an eagle, in astonishing detail.

The two men's flashlights moved away from the door to a smooth piece of metal that was jutting out from the wall-face. It was a clasp. Melissa assumed it was an ancient torch holder. These terrorists had accidentally unearthed some archaeological wonder. And, with what Melissa had learned over the last year about fundamentalists, they would most likely set about destroying it right away.

Melissa moved again, and her foot struck a piece of metal on the ground. It clanged into a nearby boulder.

Both men turned and looked at her.

Melissa pointed her revolver and fired two deafening shots.

The men collapsed.

"Four bullets left," Melissa thought, as she broke into a run. She left the chamber and its ancient door behind as she followed a new path upwards.

She came to another crossroads. Fortunately, this time, she could see daylight at the end of one of the tunnels.

She ran for it, but not before passing a colossal chamber to the left. There were hundreds of people inside praying. Apparently, they were all oblivious to the recent explosion, or they'd chosen to ignore it. These numbers were far greater than the Australian Government had predicted. She needed to get out and report this right away.

Also, inside the chamber, she noticed another statue. It was of a man, with six wings, holding a sword high above him. It was about twenty feet tall, and unlike the door earlier, was not ancient. It looked hastily made, almost like it was simple paper-mache over mesh wiring.

Melissa spared a second to note how odd this was, as in Islam they never depicted images of the gods and prophets they worshipped.

She panicked when she heard voices spring up not far behind her. Her two gunshots would've attracted a lot of attention.

She burst through an opening into the fresh air of the outside world. The ground crunched beneath her as she stepped out onto a patch of snow.

There were two vehicles to her right - a flat-bed truck and a rusted old motorcycle. It was painted sickly green and its tyres that were almost certainly too thin.

Open countryside stretched out around her. She was backed

onto a solitary mountain and there wasn't a guard to be seen. This facility was so well hidden that an entry and exit set-up wasn't needed.

Melissa threw a leg over the motorcycle and kicked it into gear. Through extremely good luck (and poor planning by the terrorists) the keys were waiting in the ignition for her.

With a cough, the motorcycle slowly came to life.

She hit the throttle, and with a guttural roar, Melissa was off into the countryside. She'd escaped.

• • • • •

IT TOOK THREE DAYS for Melissa Pythia to be rescued. Exhausted and dehydrated, she was thankful to be alive.

The stress of the ordeal had left her a little foggy as to the details. Still, she was able to pass on valuable information regarding the numbers and set-up of the Almalayikat Alsabea in the Uruzgan province.

She even received a medal from the Australian Government.

What she never passed on, was the alien silver wall she saw in that cave. In truth, she never thought about it again.

Not until Apollo described the symbols of Prometheus they were looking for.

CHAPTER
TWENTY-FOUR

ESCAPE THE VAULT

A pollo was impressed. This Oracle of Delphi was vastly different from the others that had come before her. Perhaps it was because she'd lived a life independent of her destiny; a life independent of the god whose power had brought her into the world.

It was in the eighth century BC that Apollo had whispered into the ears of the priests of Delos to travel to Delphi. It had been an ancient place of worship to Apollo's great grandmother, the primordial deity known as Gaia.

The hierarchy of the gods featured three distinct ranks of entities. Well, four, if one included the original being known only as Chaos.

From Chaos, sometime around the birth of the universe, the primordials had sprung into being. Much like the gods, they ruled their own domains. For example, the mother of Moros was Nyx. The Greeks called Nyx the Goddess of Night. But, being a primordial being, Nyx wasn't a god in the traditional sense. She didn't interact with humans. To her, all mortal life was indistinguishable from bacteria. Even to the gods, primordials were cold and distant.

Tartarus, the primordial who'd swallowed Lucifer, was said to be the very Underworld itself. As if that dimension was built around his metaphysical bones.

The primordials had similar qualities to gods and humans. They fought, loved and made friends, but all on a scale that was hard for even Apollo to comprehend. On the occasion that a god had to speak with a primordial, trying to extract a clear answer from them was like pulling teeth.

To humans, primordials were more akin to concepts rather than anything tangible to be worshipped.

A temple to a primordial on Earth was pointless, as such a being had no need for worship. This was why Apollo had decided to turn the temple on Delphi into one he could use.

From the primordials sprung the titans.

The titans weren't as vague in definition as the primordials. Some gods believed that the spectrum of feelings and emotions that would later emerge in humans entered reality with the birth of the titans. They could be cold, cunning and ruthless. From the Greek titans came the Greek gods, lesser beings who managed to win a war against their creators. The gods were similar to humans in attitude and temperament. They felt rage, jealousy, lust, and most importantly, they craved power.

For the longest time, humans weren't involved in their scheming and treachery. It wasn't until they began building cities and cultivating fields that the gods learned what immense value the little people had.

They learned that worship and sacrifice in the name of a god, or a pantheon of gods, slightly empowered those being worshipped. The gods then learned that power flowed upwards through their hierarchies, eventually reaching the head of the pantheon, as a greatly magnified force.

In the early days of civilisation, the gods bred with, and fought alongside the humans of their regions. They shared triumphs and sorrows. In Greece, Zeus had always warned that a time would come when the god's role in history would end. He said the world would become the domain of the humans alone. When that time came, a god could choose to fade. They could forever blend with the concept they embodied, losing all consciousness and departing the physical world.

Then came the day that Zeus himself had disappeared. Some argued that his time was up, and he chose to fade, though Apollo knew this to be wrong. What happened to Zeus was still a great mystery. It was like he'd been ripped from reality by some unknown force.

Apollo doubted his father's prediction that a time for all gods to cease would come. He was the God of Prophecy after all. As far as he'd always seen, divine beings always played a role in humanity's expanse across the world, and this would eventually be the case across the cosmos.

Apollo had usually been benevolent to humans. His Oracles of Delphi played a pivotal role in the wars and conquests of ancient Greece. He gave his prophets sight not only to see the current future, but also other potential alternative outcomes. Through their words, great kings and queens would determine the course of history.

The power of the oracles had faded when he left the world. But now it was back.

"Oracle," Apollo began.

Melissa looked at him and raised an eyebrow.

"Afghanistan, tell us what you know?"

"One, Apollo," Melissa started, "my name is Melissa. No matter what you think I am, my primary objective here is to recover that golden sword. If you have to come with it, that is fine, but I'll be turning you over to the Australian Government as well."

"You'd speak to a god like that?" Apollo huffed, looking down at Melissa with his sparkling blue eyes.

For a second, Melissa paused to admire how stunningly handsome the god was, then closed her fist and jabbed Apollo in the ribs.

Apollo reared back in surprise and pain.

"You seem pretty human to me," Melissa winked.

Apollo let out a reluctant laugh. This girl had an attitude that he hadn't seen in a long time.

Moros watched the pair of them, looking completely exasperated.

"Time is of the essence," Moros urged. "My power is preventing an assortment of alarms activating. That fight with the Knights of Hell was already risky enough. We need to make a plan."

"How long can you hold the security system at bay?" Melissa asked.

"As soon as we rise toward the Vatican, the angels will be able to sense me using my power. I'd say once we are back in the Secret Archive, I will have to release the alarms."

"That's no good," Melissa frowned. "The Secret Archive is like a fortress; we can be locked in there too easily."

"I agree," Moros stated. She glanced at the Janus Crystal in Apollo's hand.

Apollo also looked at the crystal.

"Can this take us to Afghanistan?"

"No," Moros answered. "They are short-range only. I doubt that could get us out of Vatican City."

"Flying out of Rome to Afghanistan is nigh on impossible," Melissa added. "Is there something in here that could amplify the crystal's power?"

Moros pondered this suggestion.

"Is there a temple to Janus that remains in Rome? If we were to escape from here, then a place dedicated to the God of Doorways would boost the power of his artefact," Apollo stated.

"Is this Janus guy big enough to have a temple? I've never heard of him..." Melissa asked quietly.

"You have heard of him," Moros stated plainly. "The month of January is named after him. And, there was once a temple to

Janus in Rome. In the Roman Forum to be exact. I believe it is the location at which you emerged last night."

"Was Janus in league with the angels?" Apollo asked suddenly.

"Look at how you dismissed him earlier, Apollo. It makes sense. He was venerated by the Romans, yet the Olympic pantheon didn't count him as one of their own. I've often wondered if the device that summoned the seven-headed dragon into the Battle of the Underworld was designed by Janus."

"Can someone explain who Janus is exactly?" Melissa said, sounding frustrated.

Just as those words left her mouth, the battered elevator appeared at the end of the corridor.

Apparently, Moros had un-crumpled it.

"Janus was a spirit who became a god through a process known as apotheosis. Usually, that term is reserved for humans achieving divinity. Still, it can be used more broadly," Moros answered, as the three of them moved toward the elevator.

That appeared to be good enough for Melissa. She shrugged.

"So, we are going to get into the Secret Archive, and the alarms will go off. Then, we have to get out of the archive, out of the Vatican, back to the Foro Romano, find where Janus' temple used to stand, and attempt to use the crystal to get straight to Afghanistan?" Melissa summarised.

"Sounds right," Apollo said.

Moros nodded.

The elevator stopped, and the doors to the Secret Archive slid open. Moros released her power and the long rows of shelves became filled with an ominous red light as a series of alarms started wailing all around them.

"Run," Moros ordered as she transformed back into the librarian.

Apollo swung left, and the other two followed.

They could hear the metallic creak of heavy doors lowering in the distance. The secret archive was sealing itself off.

"Damn," Moros muttered, "we will never make it."

"What's happening?" Apollo asked through rapid breaths.

"The library is surrounded by thick metal walls. Once they are closed, nothing can cut through them."

Apollo held his sword firm at his side.

"Nothing mortal, I'll bet."

They picked up speed. Minutes flew by as they heard massive steel slabs slam against the floor all around them.

The archive had become a tomb.

Apollo reached the wall of metal that had lowered in front of the secret entry door. Without hesitating, he plunged his golden sword straight into it. The metal screamed and sparked as Apollo heaved. Using all of his might, thrust the blade downwards.

Further minutes passed as Apollo cut a rectangular hole into the metal. Sweat poured from his brow.

With a final grunt, Apollo levered the sword and forced a chunk of the wall out, which clanged against the floor.

The glass door to the secret reception room was now visible.

Apollo paused to take a breath, and Melissa stepped up. Through the rectangular hole, Melissa aimed a powerful karate kick at the glass. It didn't budge.

She frowned, then asked for Apollo's sword. She lifted it with two hands, and then with an awkward throw, lobbed it at the door.

The glass shattered on impact, and further alarms started blaring.

The secret archive was now a deafening cacophony of noise.

Melissa climbed through the hole, across the glass and into the reception room.

Moros and Apollo followed.

"Why are the Swiss Guard not here?" Melissa shouted over the noise.

Moros didn't reply. She'd taken the lead out of the room and up the stairs.

Apollo took one last look at the exquisite paintings that plastered the walls, then followed.

Without encountering any resistance, they made it up the stairs and to the security door. The car park was just on the other side.

"What will greet us?" Apollo asked as Moros raised her access card to the scanner.

"Probably an army of police, Swiss Guardsmen and the Gladius Vaticanus," Moros answered.

Melissa stood behind the two gods, ready for whatever new challenge was about to face the trio.

The door swung open.

CHAPTER
TWENTY-FIVE

ESCAPE THE VATICAN

"GOT THEM!" Teva exclaimed excitedly through Matt's earpiece.

Matt knew that right now Teva was in front of a small laptop and that his screen would be buzzing with the camera feeds from the entire Vatican.

"She's with two others who don't look Vatican. They are moving towards the parking area," Teva informed him.

Ordinarily, security forces would be waiting on the outside, but Matthew and Teva had planned a distraction for them.

Posing as visitors, the pair of agents had entered the Vatican. As they wandered the well-worn tourist paths, they'd discreetly placed small devices called 'boomers' throughout the city-state.

All the boomers did, when activated, was play the sound of rattling gunfire, and they did so very convincingly.

The Australian agent's primary concern was freeing Melissa from the Gladius Vaticanus, and then getting them all the hell out of Italy. This mission had become a disaster. The three of them could be due for a substantial disciplinary hearing when they returned to home soil. The earlier they got back and explained what had happened, the better the outcome would be.

The plan was simple. Teva would remotely set off the boomers, causing an immediate action response from the Swiss Guard and Vatican Police.

Matt would then, using security passes he'd swiped, enter the same building Melissa had, subdue her guards and rescue her. It sounded too simple to be effective, but generally those were the most successful plans.

Teva had talked Matt into waiting for a few hours to see if Melissa was picked up on a security camera. The Tahitian had argued that a more precise location was needed for an extraction.

Matthew had been trying to understand the giant fractured sphere, the Sfera con Sfera, outside the Vatican Museum when the call came in at last.

"Activate the boomers," Matt ordered.

The sound of gunfire rang out across the Vatican. Tourists screamed in alarm as the frazzled-looking Swiss Guard directed people towards shelter.

Matt was on the move. Over one shoulder hung his bright blue duffel bag. Inside it, beneath a layer of x-ray proof padding, was an advanced black grappling hook laying on top of some explosive devices.

A Vatican policeman saw Matt moving away from the exits and ran towards him. He spoke in hurried Italian, attempting to point Matthew in the right direction.

"Sorry, mate," Matt grimaced as he clobbered the poor cop in the face. One punch and the man was out.

Matt followed Teva's directions to the car park, where a startled looking Melissa appeared in front of him.

She gave a relieved smile when she saw him.

"Boomers?" she yelled, as another volley of gunfire blasted through the air.

"You know it!" Matt yelled back. "Who are these two?"

"The God of Knowledge and the Goddess of Doom," Melissa replied.

"Right," Matt shrugged. He'd come to expect weirdness when working with Mel.

"They are coming with us!"

"Then let's go!"

Matt's entourage of three raced across the gardens. Tourists were still everywhere. Several had their phones out, trying to capture video of the invisible shooters while anxious looking guardsmen were making an effort to hurry them on. The Gladius Vaticanus were moving swiftly through the crowds with their guns up, looking for the source of the noise.

Matt, Melissa, Apollo and Moros raced past hedges and across the grass to the massive outer wall of the Vatican. Matt directed them into a small bank of trees where the group would be shielded from prying eyes.

He threw his bag to the ground and hastily pulled out the grappling hook.

He aimed for the top of the barrier wall and fired.

The nozzle, with its four prongs, shot upwards. It latched onto a tree atop the wall, deliberately planted to shield distant buildings from view.

He handed the device to Melissa.

She gripped it firmly and hit the retract button. At a jogging pace, she let the grappling hook drag her up the wall.

Within a moment, she was on top of it.

She tossed the device back down. It was purpose-built to be robust could take the fall without breaking.

Melissa was quickly joined by the other three as they whizzed upwards. The two strangers Melissa had brought looked amused as they scaled the wall.

Matt surveyed the streaming traffic on the Viale Vaticano below. The wall was much higher than expected.

"How do we get down?" Apollo asked Matt.

Matt eyed the stranger warily. He had assumed the other side of the wall would be climbable. How very wrong he was. Matt was also struggling with waves of internal disappointment, as he thought this was the moment he'd get to do something cool like an action hero would in a movie.

Matt saw a familiar white van, riddled with bullet holes, zooming down the road towards them. It had to be Teva.

The van pulled to a stop at the base of the wall.

"Well?" Apollo asked.

Matt was fumbling through his bag, looking for something.

"Gotcha!" he said, shooting a mistrusting look at Apollo.

In his hand was a plastic bag full of hand-holds. The exact same ones Melissa had used to climb the tower at the Basilica of the Twin Spires.

Matt opened the bag, then placed it in his mouth. He held on with his teeth as he swung his body off the wall.

He placed the first hand-hold onto the wall. It stuck.

He then placed the second one lower and began methodically moving down.

Police sirens could now be heard in the distance.

Matt picked up the pace, and a minute later, he was at the bottom.

Several cars stopped to watch the odd display. The other three scaled down the wall as quickly as they could. To on-lookers it must've appeared as if they'd just performed a daring daylight robbery of the Vatican.

They all piled into the van and Teva hit the gas.

"Where are we going?" he called from the front seat.

"Back to the Roman Forum!" Melissa ordered.

"This can't be good," Matt muttered as the van sped off, back into Rome.

CHAPTER
TWENTY-SIX

A GOD WITH TWO FACES

It was a strange group of people that were squashed in the back of the rickety old spy van as it rocketed down the Roman road. First, there was the librarian. Despite climbing down the walls of the Vatican, she didn't have a hair out of place or a single wrinkle in her clothes. She looked down at her polished red fingernails absent-mindedly as the van twisted around a corner. Beneath her, rolling on the floor, was the torch from Olympus. The apparent key to the hidden Temple of Prometheus.

Next was the tall muscular stranger with blonde-hair and blue eyes. In one hand, he was twirling an opaque crystal lathered with glowing letters. In the other, he held the otherworldly golden sword.

Then, flat on the floor sat Matthew Pyne, the big-armed ASIS agent. He had flicked open the clasps on a black case and begun quietly assembling a sniper rifle. He hadn't stopped sweating since his quick manoeuvre down the wall.

Melissa was the last person hunched in the back of the vehicle. She had a vicious cut running across her right cheek from where the blade summoned by the Knight of Hell had sliced her skin. Two prominent black eyes, residue from the night before, also decorated her face. She hadn't forgotten where she'd been viscously struck in the jaw either. It hurt a lot and was visibly bruised.

After some arguing, Teva had reluctantly accepted the fact that they were, for some reason, heading back to the ruins of the Roman Forum. The very place that Melissa had just been captured.

"I have two questions. One: who are they? And two: why are we going back to the Roman ruins?" Teva asked, not bothering to mask his annoyance.

Moros looked at Teva curiously, then went back to staring at her fingernails. It was like she could see something moving in the deep colour that was oblivious to everyone else.

Melissa answered as best she could, trying not to sound insane. Matt and Teva were ordinary people after all; they never had prophetic visions or spoke with gods.

"Last night, a hole in the earth opened up in the Roman Forum. Apparently, there is a hidden second layer beneath the ruined Temple of Janus."

"Okay," Teva said slowly, "but why are we going there?"

"The ruins of that temple may be able to empower an artefact of Janus, if we take it there."

Teva just nodded. Melissa knew how ridiculous she sounded, but she figured it was to her credit that she'd been able to take in the gobbledygook the two gods had been speaking.

Matt then spoke up, "So let's say that the beating you took in the Colosseum hasn't made you loopy. What artefact needs empowering?"

"This Janus Crystal," Apollo showed them.

"And what does it do?"

"Generates short-range portals."

"Right… and what happens at this Temple of Janus?"

"We open a portal to Afghanistan," Melissa chimed in, again feeling silly.

Matt paused in his effort to attach the silencer to his sniper.

"So," he continued, "we want to go to Afghanistan, why?"

"Because that is where I saw the entrance to the hidden Temple of Prometheus a couple of years ago," Melissa answered.

"You never mentioned a hidden temple when you were rescued," Teva interjected.

"I didn't really think about it at the time," Melissa shrugged.

"So, we are going to open a portal to the hidden Temple of Prometheus by magnifying the power of an artefact of Janus," Matt repeated, as if he was ticking items off from a mental checklist.

"Correct," Apollo said, after no one else spoke.

"Melissa, come on… we need to get out of this city. This isn't the time for games or indulging in fantasy," Teva pleaded.

"Look, guys. I don't know what to tell you. You're just going to have to trust me on this. I know that I have earned it from the both of you," Melissa said earnestly.

"What is in the Temple of Prometheus?" Matt asked, resuming the building of his sniper rifle.

"The flame he brought to humanity," Melissa answered.

"Ah yeah, you'll need to explain more."

"Do you know the story of Prometheus?" Apollo asked Matthew directly. "You should, all humans should. Of all the great tales, his is the most important."

"Give us the short version," Teva called from the driver's seat. "We are almost there. It looks like they cleared up the road from the crashes last night."

Apollo breathed deep and picked up the torch rolling beside Moros.

"Prometheus was a titan. He sided with the gods during the Titanomachy; the war between Zeus and his father, Cronus. It was long before my time, but Moros was around then."

Moros addressed the van, "Yes, it was devastating, the land was shattered."

"As you know, Zeus won and the gods reigned supreme. Prometheus and Zeus were great friends. The two of them saw the humans wandering the earth, and thought they could improve them."

"What, you mean like Neanderthals or something?" Matt asked.

"No, no. I mean you, like you are now, though lesser in your minds. Prometheus built his improved humans out of clay and

Athena breathed life into them on behalf of Zeus.

"These new humans were vastly superior. Physically, they were the same as you, but mentally, they had the brainpower of the gods. They saw the world in creative and new ways, and could communicate amongst each other with amazing depth and clarity."

"How long ago are talking here, 9000 years or so? When civilisation started?" Melissa asked. She wasn't well-versed in mythology, but her history was okay.

"Much before that," Moros said. "This would have been roughly 80000 years ago, give or take a few millennia."

Matt made a choking noise in his confusion. "What happened to these advanced people? Were they around for 70000 years while we hunted mammoths in the snow?"

"That is a different story. The people born of Prometheus built great cities and never ventured far from them. They were advanced and spectacular, yet their isolation and xenophobia put them on the path to decline. Regardless, Prometheus felt the plight of you Homo Sapiens, the natural people of the world. He watched as your kind attempted to spread out of northern Africa and were pushed back by your biological cousins. He saw your potential. All you needed was that same divine spark the people made from clay had."

Moros continued on from Apollo, "On Olympus, there was a well of holy fire. The flames contained the essence of the titans. The key to their DNA is a good way to understand it in a human context. It was won in the Titanomachy and Zeus forbade it to be interacted with. The flame was deadly to the gods. No matter how powerful he became, Zeus always feared his father and their kind. Prometheus chose to ignore Zeus' decree to leave the flame alone."

Apollo jumped back in, "To his personal detriment, but to humanity's great benefit."

Moros continued, "Your scientists now call it the 'cognitive revolution'. They put it down to a bizarre genetic mutation in your brains that suddenly boosted your intelligence and communication abilities."

"What it actually was," Apollo added, "was Prometheus bringing your kind the fire. He gave it to the tribes and unlocked their potential. The world was suddenly ready for the taking. The earlier advanced people congregated in large cities but never spread far. Your lot felt compelled to conquer the world. The people built from clay shunned you, so you set out on your own. Fearless little humans."

"Zeus didn't like this, I assume?" Teva asked from the front. The tone of his voice told Melissa that he wasn't taking any of this seriously.

"No," Moros answered. "Prometheus was chained to the side of a mountain, and a monstrous eagle ate his liver every day. It regrew itself at night, only to be torn out again. He spent tens of thousands of years suffering his punishment. It wasn't that long ago he was freed by the demi-god Heracles."

"Okay, good story," Matt said, inspecting his completed sniper rifle. "Why do we need this flame?"

"It contains divine essence. I can use it to restore my divinity."

"And you are?" Matt asked.

"The Greek God Apollo," he answered simply.

Matt turned to Melissa, "What have you gotten us into?"

"Something that is beyond my skills with paperwork," Melissa sighed.

Teva and Matt both shot uneasy glances at each other.

"One last question," Matt said, as the van pulled to a stop. "If this Prometheus was a Greek god, shouldn't his temple be in Greece?"

"No, Zeus would have obliterated it in his rage. The first natural humans Prometheus unlocked fully understood what he did for them. They made a deal with the advanced god-borne people to build a temple in Prometheus' honour, far from the prying eyes of Zeus. It makes sense it is where it is."

"Oh, glad that's all cleared up," Matt rolled his eyes.

"Hey, you asked," Melissa retorted.

The road that led towards the Colosseum, as it turned out, was still partially blocked off due to the events of the night before. Police were redirecting both foot and vehicle traffic, though Melissa could see that the crashed cars had been removed.

They parked on a side road, out of view from the public.

Melissa, at last, was able to properly prepare herself.

She kicked everyone out of the van while she changed into a black jumpsuit. Around her waist was a discreet belt, with only a holster for a pistol attached and a couple of pouches for spare magazines.

She laced up expensive all-purpose boots. She looked the part of an agent on a mission.

Melissa made sure she had a new earpiece in and that it was

working.

Teva loaded up a backpack with radios, spare ammunition, additional weapons, and some other pieces of tech that might have a use.

Matthew loaded his assembled sniper rifle into his blue duffel bag and slung it across his back, though the gun didn't fit in it.

When the three Australian operatives were ready, they set off towards the forum.

With the assistance of the grappling hook, and some additional bolt cutters, they were able to scramble their way back into the Foro Romano undetected.

The entire attraction had been closed down.

Melissa didn't notice any bio-hazard suits or tents, which meant the bodies of the slain demons hadn't yet been discovered.

She had to re-orient herself to retrace her steps from the previous night. A patch of blood on the grass gave her a much-needed clue as to the location of the Temple of Janus.

Soon enough, the group of five stood before the opening in the earth. It was roughly a metre squared.

The rotting stench of demons wafted out from within.

Teva wrinkled his nose in disgust.

"Somethings definitely dead down there," he said, turning away and taking a breath of fresh air.

"Four demons and two members of the Soncin crime family," Melissa informed him, before turning to Apollo. He was studying the ruins that sat above the Emperor's Portal.

There wasn't much of the structure left. Whatever had once stood in this spot was almost completely gone, aside from some white slabs in the grass and the crumbling bases of a couple of pillars.

"This seems right…" Apollo said. "I do recall a temple being here, quite a magnificent one. Its doors were always closed in times of peace and opened in times of war."

"So, this was Janus' temple?" Melissa asked, feeling a rush of adrenaline.

"Yes," Apollo confirmed. "I am certain of it. Inside, there was a statue of the god with two faces. Two-faced indeed if he helped the angels assault Olympus."

"If," Moros repeated. "We can't be certain. However…" she looked down at the hole, "If they built a secret portal to the Underworld here, after the fall of the Greek pantheon, it seems likely the God of Portals assisted them."

"We don't have to go down there, do we?" Teva asked.

"No," Moros replied. "I think the old site of Janus should be enough."

Melissa looked at the crystal in Apollo's hand. It still held its dull gleam, though it didn't appear any different. He handed it to Melissa.

"What do I do?" she asked.

"Simply visualise the Temple of Prometheus. If this works, using the crystal here should take us there. Once the image is clear in your head, throw the crystal to the ground."

Melissa rolled the crystal in her hand. She thought about Afghanistan. She saw the snowy barren landscape and the looming mountain that led into the extremist's base of operations. She remembered the smooth alien walls exposed by the exploding arsenal.

She threw the crystal to the ground.

Much like in the Vatican vaults, the air sucked into a single point. Then a jagged tear in reality manifested itself before them. Lightning sparked around its shifting borders.

Teva and Matt froze, their mouths agape.

"What the hell is that?" Matt yelped in alarm.

"Go now!" Apollo commanded, diving headfirst into it.

On the other side, Melissa could see the familiar bleak landscape she'd once traversed for three days.

Moros followed Apollo through the portal.

The sound of vehicles quickly appeared, and alongside them was the loud whir of a helicopter.

"There is every chance we could've been tracked from the Vatican," Teva grumbled.

"Let's not stay and find out," Mel said, throwing herself through the portal.

Matt hitched up his duffel bag and gave a small salute to Teva.

"Weird couple of days," he said, and he too moved through the breach.

With a shrug, Teva crossed the divide as well.

A sound like crashing thunder rang out, and the portal sealed itself behind him. Nothing was left behind but the swaying grass and the quiet ruins of the Roman Forum.

• • • • •

AS MELISSA STEPPED onto the rocky ground of the

Uruzgan province, she collapsed to her knees.

Visions swept through her mind. Visions of the place they'd just been. Something had triggered her prophetic sight. Except now, she saw the world in real-time. She watched Teva step through the portal from high above. Her ears were assaulted with the sound of spinning blades.

She realised she was looking down through the camera of an advanced micro-drone. The four-rotor remote-piloted device spun around, and its camera raised up. Melissa could see an Agusta A129A Mangusta Italian military helicopter approaching the Roman Forum. It was an impressive piece of equipment, with a 20mm Gatling gun fitted to its nose missile launchers. The helicopter banked left and moved away as a procession of troop carriers, including two armoured vehicles with 50-calibre machine guns rumbled down the roadway. When the convoy pulled to a stop it wasn't Italian soldiers that emerged, but heavily armed members of the Gladius Vaticanus.

Someone tried to shake Melissa free of her trance, but she resisted. She needed to see this.

She refocused.

The paramilitary soldiers quickly made it to the spot they'd just been. Some were carefully lowering themselves into the underground room that contained the portal to Hell.

Someone in fancy dress was approaching, flanked by guards.

No... it wasn't fancy dress. He was wearing cardinal's robes. It was Vasilije Markovic, the cardinal who'd spoken with her at the Vatican.

Melissa's vision shifted from the drone into the eyes of one of Cardinal Markovic's bodyguards.

She could hear everything that was being said.

"Well, where have they gone!" Markovic barked at one of his men.

"I don't know, sir, we are downloading the drone footage now."

"Sir!" one of the men called as he pulled himself up from the portal. "There is a hidden room down here. There are the bodies of both men and... monsters."

"Monsters?" Markovic frowned, shaking his head. "What do you mean, monsters?"

"There is a statue too, a ram's head with a five-pointed star carved into its temple."

Markovic looked puzzled. He seemed to recognise the symbology, but its meaning in this context escaped him.

The sky grew darker and a vicious wind whipped up.

Melissa felt a shiver run down her spine.

A deep threatening voice appeared on the air. Cardinal Markovic looked around, searching for its origin.

But no one around him was speaking, despite the dozens of soldiers.

To Melissa, it sounded as if the voice was coming from the earth itself. The words were distorted and difficult to make out. The menace though, that was unmistakable.

The sky turned blood red.

Lightning cracked and the wind howled.

Cardinal Markovic stood alone as the Roman Forum came crashing down around him. Huge chunks of stone went flying in the mighty wind.

The man looked utterly terrified.

Melissa wondered if she was seeing a vision within a vision. But that didn't seem correct. She now felt she was floating, like a disembodied pair of eyes, watching the cardinal turn frightfully.

There were whispers in the air. The words were foreign, but somehow Melissa knew they were saying dark and terrible things.

The ominous voice boomed out again. This time, its words were clear.

"Belial wanders the sands…"

The voice echoed through the air as thunder clapped in the sky.

"Find him Vasilije…"

"My Lord, it can't be you, can it?" Markovic asked nervously.

"I am the darkness that sits at the heart of the world. The fallen morning star…"

A shadow pooled on the ground in front of Cardinal Markovic.

Small plumes of grey smoke burst forth from it as it spread.

A towering shape rocketed out from the black pool. It was fifteen feet tall and had no discernable features, but its outline was humanoid with three monstrous heads.

Vasilije quickly fell to his knees and bowed before the great shadow.

Green fire raced across the grass, forming the shape of an upside-down crucifix.

"How can you speak with me so directly?" Markovic whispered.

"The walls have been weakened here. The barrier between

Hell and Earth is damaged. My influence can now seep into the mortal world…"

"You can cross through then, Lord Lucifer?"

"I cannot cross! Not until you complete your task," the voice boomed, sounding fierce against the torrent of wind.

"The Vatican has accepted the help of the Gladius Vaticanus. Michael understands that we have the same goal," Markovic said, still bowed before the creature of shadow.

"The Vatican and Michael will find the key. You will seize it when the time is right. The place of the god-king is MINE!"

Lightning struck the ground by Vasilije.

"Find Belial and capture Apollo. He carries the blood of Zeus in his veins! My power can open the portal here. Use it to follow them."

"Apollo…" Cardinal Markovic murmured. "What about the Australian girl who found the sword?"

"Golden Apollo, son of Zeus, has re-entered the world. He is mortal now. Get to him before he finds a way to rectify this."

The towering shadowy figure expanded. Melissa could see that a portal was opening inside it. A portal to them.

"Wake up!" she screamed to herself.

The shadow turned to face her.

She felt horror, despair and darkness well-up in her soul. An unending agony washed across her.

Then, she woke.

CHAPTER
TWENTY-SEVEN

BEFORE THE STORM

Melissa felt the hot breeze that swept across the Uruzgan province slap her in the face as she woke from her trance.

Both Matt and Teva were kneeling beside her. It looked like they'd been holding her upright.

"We have to go now," Melissa said, wiping away the drool that had puddled around the sides of her mouth.

"What did you see?" Moros asked sternly.

"The Gladius Vaticanus are coming. He is opening a portal for them now."

"Who is?"

"Lucifer."

"Lucifer? Was he actually there?" Apollo asked.

"No, it was like... a shadowy avatar. He said the barrier between Hell and Earth has been weakened. That was us, when I pulled you through, wasn't it?" Melissa asked him.

"Yes," Apollo answered, reaching a hand down for Melissa to grab. "The portal we created sealed up, but there is the possibility that the whole metaphysical structure was cracked, like splinters in glass. What else did he say?"

"He wanted the cardinal to find Belial. If he landed in Saudi Arabia, they won't be far from here."

"What else?"

"That the Vatican and Lucifer have the same goal. Also, they want you, Apollo. Something to do with Zeus... the blood of Zeus."

Melissa wiped the dust off her clothes.

"When you say Lucifer, you mean like the Devil, right?" Teva asked.

"Well, he is the principal deity of the Underworld, as he has been since the death of Hades. I wonder what this goal of his is?" Moros questioned. "Generally, the wills of Heaven and Hell don't align. I heard Lucifer never took his imprisonment in the Underworld well. When Tartarus finally released him, he wasn't the archangel he'd once been."

"You must tell me the story of Lucifer, Moros, for I do not know it," Apollo stated.

"I will be brief, for it seems time is not on our side," Moros began. "Lucifer was tricked by Persephone into being permanently stuck in the Underworld. But, when she realised his true power, she summoned Tartarus to swallow him. He was stuck in the darkness for years beyond counting, until Tartarus released him. He re-shaped the Underworld, which has been scorched beyond recognition by the Serpent of Heaven, into the realm of Hell. His relationship with his brothers has been rocky, to put it mildly."

"We will discuss this at length later," Apollo said.

Melissa looked at the mountain before them. It was made of brown rock and devoid of any vegetation. They'd landed right in front of the opening that she'd escaped from over two years earlier.

The place looked deserted. Pamphlets in Arabic and loose sheets of paper were scattered around the entrance of the tunnel. The lettering was faded, and the images were distorted from the sun.

The mountain hideout hadn't been used in a long time.

"The entrance to the temple isn't far down the tunnel," Melissa informed them as she gazed into the dark depths of the tunnel.

"It may look abandoned," Matt warned, "but if it connects to a larger underground cave system, this place could still be in use."

"I don't think that is our primary concern," Teva said, pointing towards the horizon.

A black cloud had emerged in the distance. The group could see the distant figures of vehicles bursting from it. The Gladius Vaticanus were here.

Fortunately, the portal looked quite far away. They had a little time.

"A difficult situation," Moros said.

Matt was looking at the mountain. Multiple rocks were jutting out from its face. It was very climbable.

He didn't need to be told what to do. He began his ascent.

Apollo looked at Melissa, "Guide me to the entrance."

Moros thrust the torch from Olympus into his waiting palm.

Melissa turned to Teva, "Good luck."

The two darted into the tunnel.

CHAPTER
TWENTY-EIGHT

ACTION HERO

Matt watched Teva unzip his backpack as he scaled the mountainside. It contained all kinds of gear, including weapons he'd obtained during their search for Melissa in Rome.

Moros reached inside and pulled out an automatic machine gun.

"Do you know how to use that?" Teva asked.

"I am capable," Moros responded, loading a magazine into the well.

"Aren't you a god?" Teva asked. "Why do you need a gun?"

"If I use my divine power, I will call down a foe much more powerful than the enemies approaching."

"Right…" Teva shrugged.

Moros ignored him and inspected her weapon with mild curiosity.

"We are exposed. We need a defensive position," Teva said as he considered their surroundings.

Moros looked into the tunnel entrance. There were several large boulders close to the mouth of the cave.

"We will make do with what we have. You take the boulder on the inside to the left; I'll take the one on the outside to the right."

Teva gulped. Matt understood why. It was shoddy cover at best.

The distant sound of spinning blades emerged as the Italian attack helicopter burst through the cloud and into Afghani airspace.

Matt reached a rocky precipice that connected to a small recess in the mountainside. He was mostly covered on all sides and had enough room to lie prone.

The Agusta A129A Mangusta attack helicopter roared ahead of the vehicle convoy; approaching fast.

This was going to be problematic. One missile could obliterate the cave's entrance. Neither he nor Teva had anything to deal with aircraft. They were meant to be spies, but now Matt felt like a soldier in an active warzone. He kind of liked it.

Matt breathed in deep and looked down the sights of his rifle.

The pilot was in range.

He squeezed the trigger.

A bullet flew from the barrel through the air towards the

helicopter. It embedded itself deep in the glass of the cockpit, causing a spider web of breaks to snake out. The helicopter banked hard to the right.

Matt fired again. This time his shot went wide. The helicopter disappeared behind the mountain.

The whirring of its blades didn't fade as it circled back around. It's 20mm Gatling gun opened fire on the cave entrance. Teva and Moros ducked for cover, though it was clear the pilots couldn't see anyone. They were just firing blind. Matt backed himself as far as he could into the little crevice he'd found.

He assessed his options. He could fire again at the cockpit. It may shatter the glass, but then it might not. He didn't want to risk exposing himself. If they found him, that Gatling gun would turn him into a bloody mess of bones and flesh.

He looked out at the convoy. They were still a few minutes away.

The helicopter was hovering very close and Matt's blue duffel bag was lying right next to him.

He thrust his hand inside his own bag, feeling his grappling hook. He found the hook's sling attachment, which he immediately lashed around his waist. He then clipped it to the back of the device.

He then fumbled for another object. He pulled what looked like an A5 sheet of paper with a raised metallic backing from the bag. Knowing he wouldn't have a free hand, he put its side in his mouth and held it with his teeth.

It was time for Matthew Pyne to be a hero. He was going to take down the helicopter.

He began crawling forward, waiting for the right moment when the pilots wouldn't see him.

The helicopter spun.

Matt stood and pointed the grappling hook at the helicopter's landing gear.

He fired. The four-pronged hook shot out and wrapped itself around the diagonal support beam of the landing gear, just above the wheel.

The pilots reacted immediately, swinging the helicopter around to face Matt. He hit the retract button on his hook. The sling dug into his sides as he was propelled through the air towards the aircraft.

Matt gripped the warm metal of the landing gear tight. He placed his other hand on the top of the wheel and pulled himself up.

The helicopter wobbled slightly under the shifting weight of the man now clinging to its side.

He could see the upper cockpit. The pilot was looking right at him.

Straining to hang on with one hand, he pulled the sheet of paper from his mouth and slammed it against the cockpit window. It stuck firmly.

The down-draught from the helicopter blades almost caused him to lose his balance, but he hung on by his fingertips. Fumbling for a discreet circular button on the paper's metallic backing, Matt gave it a satisfying push.

Matt lowered himself down as far as he could and waited out the three-second delay.

There was a small *bang* and a rain of glass shower over him.

The paper was experimental technology called a percussive sheet. It read the structural integrity of the object it was placed against, then used vibrations to shatter it — with no need for a loud explosion.

The helicopter spun wildly. Matt saw the brown earth quickly rotating below.

He drew his pistol and pulled himself up. With several daring shots, he fired directly into the control apparatus.

The electronics sparked and hissed.

The helicopter began descending.

Matt lowered himself to the wheel. He was hanging on entirely with his arms, and they were feeling the strain.

Risking death, he reached for his grappling hook. The ground was rushing closer and closer. The sling, with its elastic tether, was still snugly wrapped around Matt's waist. He needed to wait for the spinning helicopter to face the mountain, but it was moving too fast and his grip was loosening.

Matt chanced it, closing his eyes and firing his grappling hook. It connected with something on the mountainside. He hit the retract button and was pulled from the helicopter, narrowly missing its spinning blades.

In those glorious few seconds as Matt sailed through the air, he suddenly realised he hadn't thought this through. The grappling hook couldn't support his weight in motion as he descended. Matt was swinging downwards towards the rock frighteningly fast.

There was a crunch, then a crack, as Matt tumbled down

the hill and landed on a ledge. He spat blood from his mouth. Definitely an arm, a leg, and several ribs were broken.

He heard a massive crash as the helicopter came down before the entrance. The blades scraped against the ground and broke apart.

Moros and Teva dodged shrapnel as it flew towards the cave.

It was at that moment the convoy rolled in, skirting around the wreckage of the chopper.

Teva and Moros opened fire.

The soldiers of the Gladius Vaticanus scrambled out of their vehicles as the windows exploded into shards of glass. A few ran forward and ducked behind the crumpled helicopter.

Smoke grenades flew out, completely covering the two defenders' view of the Gladius soldiers.

A few soldiers ran through the wall of smoke, but were mowed down by Teva.

Matt, lying splayed out in a pool of blood above them, noticed something. A military plane was flying over the battlefield. It looked like there was a small black dot dropping from it towards them…. A figure was streaming towards the ground without a parachute.

It crashed into the dirt, landing on its feet and producing a colossal shockwave.

Belial, back in his human form, dressed in black military overalls, looked towards the cave entrance. Fire blazed in his eyes.

Moros moved out from her cover to meet this new threat head on.

Bullets flew at her from the Gladius Vaticanus. The mounted

machine guns opened fire in an orchestra of deafening blasts.

Moros waved her hand, and the cars exploded.

Despite being in great agony, Matt laughed. So, it was all real then... And it seemed this new threat was enough to make the librarian drop all pretense of being human.

Moros walked straight towards Belial.

He grinned wide, then started cackling, "Foolish move. They will be here soon, goddess."

"Then I will have to end you before they arrive," Moros responded. She punched the earth, and the convoy of troop carriers was tipped to the side. The Gladius Vaticanus scrambled to get out of the way of their falling cars.

Belial launched himself at Moros. The Goddess of Doom was now the guard to the Temple of Prometheus, and she would not see its entry breached lightly.

CHAPTER
TWENTY-NINE

THE FLAME OF PROMETHEUS

- SEPTEMBER 28 -
THE TEMPLE OF PROMETHEUS

Melissa and apollo sprinted the length of the tunnel. They passed the chamber where the cheaply-made archangel statue stood, paying it no heed.

The lights bolted to the ceiling were still on, although it seemed many of them had stopped working over the last couple of years.

Melissa also noticed a lot of spent shell casings on the ground. There had been a gunfight here. She imagined once the Australian Government reported this place to the US, they would've sent in soldiers to clear it out.

But no, that wasn't right. There was no way the US would leave an archaeological site, let alone one that was 75000 years old, alone in the desert.

She concluded that the Taliban must've cleared this area as they locked down the Uruzgan province.

It wasn't long before the pair reached the room that had, two years ago, held the Almalayikat Alsabea weapons cache. The same weapons cache that had saved Melissa's life.

The room was dark. All of the ceiling lights had been blown apart. Melissa knew the door was on the far wall, but couldn't see a thing.

She drew her pistol from its holster. Clipped to it was a light source. She flicked it on with her thumb and a surprisingly vast circle of light appeared on the rock wall. She moved it until she saw the shining silver. She found the door again, with its intricate detailing of Prometheus having his liver consumed by the eagle.

Apollo walked towards the door and touched the sculpted figure of the anguished titan.

"This is most certainly it," Apollo murmured. "Look at the construction, this is the work of the ancient humans."

"There," Melissa said, pointing her light at the empty clasp on the wall.

Apollo gently lowered the torch into place.

There was a soft metallic scraping sound, then a click. The door began sliding to the left. For the first time in tens of thousands of years, the temple was opening.

Melissa and Apollo stepped through the door onto a small silver ledge. Before them was a statue, an impossible statue. It was as tall as the Statue of Liberty and far more detailed. Before them, the Titan Prometheus stood, immortalised in grey stone.

Their ledge emerged at the statue's stomach. They were in a huge cylindrical room with polished silver walls all the way around. The giant sculpture dominated the vast area.

In one hand, the statue held the torch from Olympus, in which were expertly carved flames.

The vacant eyes of the statue gazed up at the stone fire.

It was reminiscent of the famous David by Michelangelo. Melissa could see the veins along his arms and the individually carved follicles of hair on its head. Around his waist was some kind of primitive cloth. The rest of him was bare.

Melissa had to take a moment to soak it in.

Apollo started moving down the stairs that descended to the right of the platform.

Unlike the cavern where the door had been revealed, it was bright inside the temple. Once her gaze had been removed from Prometheus, she noticed the balls of light zipping about the open spaces. They seemed to be chattering with one another.

"Primordial wisps," Apollo said.

"You've seen them before?" Melissa responded as she mustered her courage to take the leap down the first step. Each step was spaced roughly a metre lower than the one above it, leaving huge spaces to accidentally fall through.

"Actually no," Apollo admitted. "Heard about them, yes. They are ancient beyond ancient and of an unknown nature even to the gods. Why they are here, I can't tell you."

Melissa shrugged it off, she was starting to get a bit frustrated by all this godly nonsense.

She leapt, and landed uneasily.

Apollo, on the other hand, was sprinting down the steps ahead.

They both paused when they heard a crash echo in from outside. The fighting must've begun.

"Let us hurry," Apollo urged. Melissa could see the fire of determination burning in his eyes.

Several minutes of descent followed as Melissa and Apollo clambered down the needlessly tricky steps. They reached ground level, which appeared to cause the wisps to zoom about excitedly.

Melissa looked at Prometheus's expertly carved toes. Even they were magnificent.

Directly across from them was a door. It had a pattern etched onto it, depicting a tree with many branches, or a river that broke off into several streams. Melissa couldn't quite tell. She did admire the shining blue jewels that were built into the design though. They had an unworldly feel. She reached out and touched one. It was so smooth and surprisingly warm to the touch.

She jumped back as the door suddenly slid open.

Inside was a corridor that turned sharply to the right. The walls were high but didn't connect with the ceiling at all.

The roof was painted with an image of the cosmos. Stars and galaxies sat in place high above. In the middle of it all was a mountain top, which pierced through the back canvas. On the mountain's peak was a white city, floating among the heavenly bodies. There were dozens of buildings suspended in the air, all joined by white clouds.

"Olympus," Apollo said, pointing up. "As it appeared an age ago. Beauty beyond measure amongst the stars."

"This temple wasn't hastily constructed," Melissa said. "It is a work of art."

"I was thinking the same," Apollo replied. "Your kind loved Prometheus for his gift. But the ancient people also loved him and his brother, Epimetheus, for teaching them how to build wonders. I think they were happy to honour the titan alongside your people. It is a relic of an era humanity has forgotten."

Apollo looked to the wall at the side of the corridor. There was a series of lines carved into the silver.

"It's a maze," he deduced. "I didn't suspect that reaching the divine fire would be easy."

The maze on the wall was needlessly complex, and it faded halfway down. Visitors weren't given the complete path through.

"Use your sight," Apollo instructed Melissa. "Find the right path."

She nodded.

Melissa tried to activate her powers, but it wouldn't work. She and Apollo had no choice but to push forward through the maze, though she could feel the god's frustration with her.

The walls were sparkling silver and occasionally had images carved into their faces. Even to Apollo, some of the depictions of cities and forgotten places were foreign to him. He explained to Melissa that he was a relatively young god and hadn't been around when the ancient civilization flourished.

There was one carving he recognised beyond all doubt. The huge Temple to Poseidon gave away the image of Atlantis. Apollo paused to admire it for a second with Melissa, before rushing on.

They were moving blind. They came to dead ends several times.

Often, the pair would backtrack, only to end up at the same place.

The air was tense. Both Melissa and Apollo felt the pressure of time as distant booms echoed in from outside.

"Let's stop," Apollo sighed.

Melissa nodded. A thought occurred to her, "Can your sword cut through the silver? You got the through that thick door in the Vatican."

Apollo's eyes widened, then he thrust his sword at the nearest wall. The blade bounced off, not even leaving a scratch.

"You have to tap into your sight," Apollo urged. "You have the ability to. The power of prophecy is mysterious, but all Oracles of Delphi have the power to summon visions at will."

"But it's not working! And even when it does, I can't control what I see, sometimes it is completely abstract. I don't know the people or the places."

"Now that you know what you are and what you can do, you will slowly gain some control. It already seems that you don't just see forward, you can see events happening in real time right now, as you did with Lucifer opening the portal."

"Right," Melissa nodded. "You are the God of Prophecy, tell me again how to do it."

"Put your hand against the wall, close your eyes and breathe in deep. Clear your mind and let it come to you."

She did as instructed. She inhaled through her nose and exhaled slowly. She felt the cool metal on her palm.

Suddenly, her mind was running the length of the maze. She twisted left, then right, then straight. She passed a statue of a man and a woman with an open jar in front of them. She followed the walls further, taking turns and choosing the correct forks in the path. Every direction was seared into her brain.

She opened her eyes.

"Let's go," Melissa said.

The pair rushed through the maze, guided by an imprint that had been burned into Melissa's mind. It was easy now, too easy...

A strange booming sound carried into the temple from outside, though it wasn't from an explosion. It was both loud and quiet, and simultaneously serene and threatening.

"What the hell was that?" Melissa asked.

"A sound that heralds a foe we cannot face..." Apollo answered darkly.

Apollo gulped, then mumbled, "We are almost there."

The pair bounded through twists and turns. Melissa knew which path to take. Almost ten minutes passed as they ran at full speed through the puzzle.

The maze was enormous. The formidable painting of Olympus loomed over them the entire way.

Melissa thought she saw Apollo gazing up at it several times. She imagined he was comprehending what he'd lost.

At last, they burst out of the corridor into an enclosed archway. Before them was another silver door with blue jewels embedded into its surface.

Apollo pressed it, and it slid open.

A new expansive room opened before them. It was designed as a huge blue dome. The roof was painted to represent the sky. Soft white clouds were presented above. It was so realistic Melissa almost forgot she was inside an ancient structure.

The floor wasn't smooth. It was made of jagged yellow stones. Sharp points jutted out. Right in the middle of it all was an altar.

"We come to the punishment of Prometheus," Apollo informed Melissa. "I assume the maze represented humanity coming from the darkness into the light. Prometheus' gift. That is why half of that map was presented on the wall. Now, we must see his punishment for delivering the flame to Earth."

Melissa kind of understood the metaphor being presented, so nodded along.

They took off again, running and leaping over rocks towards the altar.

When they got there, the pair were presented with a large stone slab. Four individual sets of iron shackles were fastened to each corner.

Melissa scanned the circumference of the room. It didn't look like there was any kind of door present to move on further.

Apollo looked disappointed.

"Where do we go now?" Melissa asked.

"I will go no further," Apollo said. "I will take the place of Prometheus. You must retrieve the flame and bring it to me."

Melissa was taken aback, "What do you mean?"

"One cannot progress to the flame without undergoing Prometheus' punishment first."

Melissa looked toward the shackles and the slab.

"You mean…"

"Yes, you must bring the flame to me as fast as possible," Apollo said sternly.

"Don't be foolish Apollo. How do we know I can even interact with it? You need the flame."

"I cannot ask you to do this. You pulled me back into this world."

Melissa was resolute. She didn't know where her sudden resolve had come from, yet she knew that this was her path forward. Maybe it was her power as 'the Oracle of Delphi', or just the madness of the last few days taking its toll, but she knew she had to do this. The others were fighting outside, fighting for her. She couldn't live with herself if she let them do that without risking life and limb herself.

Melissa jumped onto the slab and lay flat on her back.

"Attach the shackles, Apollo," she commanded.

A job had to be done and she wasn't going to back away from it now.

Apollo didn't argue. Deep down, they both knew this was the way it had to be.

Melissa could see sadness wash over the god's face. Melissa wasn't sure what was going to happen once she was fastened to the slab, but she suspected it wasn't going to be pleasant.

The set-up of it all seemed sacrificial. She prayed Apollo wasn't going to have to stab her through the heart with his golden sword.

Apollo quickly closed the shackles around her wrists, then moved to her feet.

The metal was surprisingly cold against her skin. The chains were taught. Melissa couldn't move an inch.

Apollo stepped back, and as soon as he was away from the

slab, a piercing screech carried through the air.

The sound sent chills through Melissa's spine. It was a monstrous call.

A hole in the roof opened, and something came shooting out of it.

At first, it was just a dark shape catapulting through the air towards them. As it drew closer, Melissa could see wide wings against the blue backdrop. She suddenly knew what was coming.

A gigantic eagle, made of metal and gears landed on the stone slab. Its moving pieces clanked as they ground against each other. The machine was not elegantly designed. If anything, as it loomed above her, Melissa thought it looked very much like a prototype. Its wings were crafted in three segments. Its beak snapped open and closed on simple exposed levers. It looked razor sharp. Melissa noticed its hollow empty eyes, as its head turned side to side, observing her.

Melissa couldn't quite determine what the mechanical beast was made of. It looked bronze, and had a dull reflective gleam to it.

The mechanized eagle squeaked.

Melissa closed her eyes and braced.

Apollo stood resolute as the sharp beak of the eagle plunged into Melissa's side.

She screamed a horrifying scream as the flesh of her stomach was shredded. It was torn asunder in a torturous display. Blood poured from the gaping wound in waterfall onto the altar.

Melissa gasped, in complete shock. Her breathing became rapid and shallow.

The eagled reared up, then struck down again, tearing more of her insides open. Its head moved sharply back and forth as it dug through her.

The eagle retracted itself for a third time, then dived back in. Melissa's cries filled the air.

It was pain beyond recognition. It was immense. She was losing herself as the world darkened.

Blood started dripping from her mouth down her chin.

The eagle rose up, with Melissa's liver clasped firmly between its metallic jaws.

With another deafening screech, the eagle flapped its giant wings and took off.

Melissa exhaled sharply. Then, her body went still.

The entire slab shifted, revealing a hole in the floor beneath it.

"Hold on! Use your power and enter my mind, you will last longer!" Apollo commanded.

Melissa mumbled and her eyes flashed gold. She could now see through Apollo's eyes, though everything was foggy and dim.

The god jumped through the newly opened entryway. Apollo knew he had very little time, but he had one thing on his side. He was the God of Medicine and Healing. All Melissa had to do was hold on until his divinity was restored.

Apollo crashed into the room below.

It was dark, save for one thing.

Before him was a massive basin. It was a metre in diameter and completely white. A ring of gold ran along its top. At the front, carved in gold, was an image of Prometheus carrying a blazing torch.

Flickering inside the basin, floating in apparent mid-air, was the divine flame. The flame that had left Olympus 75000 years ago to inspire mankind.

It danced in the still air. Reds, oranges, greens and purples all blazed in and out of existence within the fire. The entire flame was translucent, almost completely see-through. It looked like fire from another world. In it was the very essence of the higher world, the world of the gods.

Apollo didn't think. He thrust his hand into the fire.

It didn't feel warm.

In fact, it didn't feel like anything.

The fire twirled around his fingers. It licked his hand and along his wrist.

Then, it exploded into an inferno.

The world shattered around Apollo.

He stood in a room of breaking mirrors, watching his human form fall into a million pieces.

He flashed back to the battle. He saw the Serpent of Heaven clamping its jaws around Demeter. He saw Michael impale him with his sword. The wound burned, and then he felt nothing.

Apollo's body turned golden.

The curse of the Michael Sword was broken.

It felt like the universe had awoken in the god's mind.

A cosmic river of energy flowed into him. He felt knowledge, felt prophecy, he could hear the music of nature in the air, the poem of life whirled around him. The Golden God had returned.

Apollo felt divine strength in his arms. He could see, hear and feel clearly again; reconnected to his domains.

The fire in the basin shrunk back down, and resumed dancing quietly in the dark.

Apollo jumped back through the entry way and flew toward Melissa.

She was lying cold and still. He placed his head to her heart. There was nothing to be heard.

He was the God of Healing, yet he could not bring life to those who had lost it, as it was a forbidden evil to perform such an act. Messing with life and death when it wasn't in a god's specific domain was a sacred rule that could never be broken.

Then, as if by a miracle, he heard a small thud. Melissa had held on; it was the last beat of her heart.

Apollo placed both his hands on Melissa's stomach. She was bathed in a warm orange light.

"Thank you, Oracle. Let your wounds be healed."

The horrendous wound on Melissa's side began sealing itself. Skin and sinew stretched over the gaping hole. The flesh snapped back together. The light rolled around her in coils.

Her eyes opened.

Melissa Pythia was back.

CHAPTER THIRTY

ARCHANGEL

Matt lay gasping on his rocky perch, coughing up blood. He squinted. Something else was now falling from the sky. A meteor seemed to be descending on the battlefield. The ball of fire raced toward the scorched earth where Moros and Belial battled.

With great difficulty, Matt rolled onto his side to look at the pair of supernatural monsters below. Belial wasn't holding back. The veins that lined his human face were throbbing as his eyes glowed red. The demonic man shot lightning bolts from his body as he struck at Moros with his sword of fire.

Moros unleashed her full power in a terrifying display. From her fingers, she summoned four coils of black energy that wrapped around Belial, binding him.

Moros's eyes went blank, and yellow light shined from them.

"I am the Goddess of DOOM and FATE," Moros boomed. "I SEE YOUR DESTINY."

Moros whipped Belial through the air to her left. Then, she flicked her hand the other way, causing Belial to be flung to the right.

The rocks splintered where the Knight of Hell made impact with the ground.

Belial's face was overcome with pure rage.

He exploded in a ball of fire, dissipating Moros's black energy.

Belial heaved his arms upwards and rocks encased Moros. Across them, demonic symbols began scrawling themselves into being. The symbols glowed red and began sucking the energy from Moros.

Moros tensed her entire body, and sent forth her own wave of power, exploding the prison she'd been set in and knocking Belial off his feet.

Moros flew forward, and manifested a writhing spear of black energy in her hand.

She aimed it right at Belial's demonic heart.

Strange red symbols glowed around the knight's wrist. He stood staunch as Moros flew toward him.

Thunder rumbled, and a colossal column of fire shot down from the sky. It engulfed the goddess.

Moros screamed out in frustration. She clasped her hands together. They crackled with black electricity and the hole in the sky above her sealed up.

Belial looked up, evidently disgruntled.

Then, a sound rang out. It was the call of a very loud horn. To Matt, it sounded like something from an ancient battlefield. Certainly, it seemed both Moros and Belial recognised it instantly.

Belial laughed and screamed at Moros, "That was the Horn of Heaven and it heralds a formidable warrior!"

"Michael is coming," Moros' voice said into Matt's head, as if he needed to know this information.

An eerie silence swept over the barren landscape. Everyone waited with baited breath. Matt saw Teva peek out from behind a rock riddled with bullet holes.

Just above ground level, the meteor stopped. The blue fire around it dispersed, and a man appeared.

Only he wasn't a man.

Six glorious white wings stretched wide from his back. In his right hand, he held a sword wreathed in translucent flame.

His face wasn't visible behind his golden helmet, carved to resemble the head of snarling lion. He was coated head to toe in shimmering body armour, with a blue cape flowing from his enormous white and gold shoulder guards to his pointed sabatons.

His white breast plate was lined with gold and on it were seven distinct angelic symbols, each carved in a different shining colour.

He looked magnificent.

Belial moved back into the crowd of Gladius Vaticanus soldiers who were huddled behind their overturned vehicles.

The newcomer snapped his fingers, and a serpent made

purely of light sprung from the earth and wrapped itself around Moros.

Even lying broken on the ledge, Matt could feel Michael's power.

It was impossible.

Unfathomable.

Bound by the serpent, Moros looked small and weak.

"Goddess of the old world," Michael began. "Why do you reveal yourself now?"

Moros looked at Michael and spoke calmly, "I am the Goddess of Doom and the Goddess of Fate. I see both of yours, archangel. What you fear will come to pass. You will fail, and your kingdom will come crumbling down."

"Many of your kind have made such a prediction, and all of you have fallen before my sword," Michael replied.

He didn't sound particularly menacing to Matt. If anything, the shining angel sounded perplexed as he spoke to Moros.

A panicked Gladius Vaticanus soldier fired on Michael.

As soon as he hit the trigger, he evaporated into floating specs of light. The rest of the Gladius Vaticanus moved further back.

"The heir of Zeus is reborn," Moros said as black energy swirled around her body. Her eyes went black. "He will rise higher than his father or grandfather could have ever imagined. Your doom has come."

Michael sheathed his sword and raised an arm. A glowing javelin of light manifested in his hand. He aimed it at Moros.

"I bid you, RISE GOLDEN APOLLO!" Moros shouted.

Storm clouds appeared above the battlefield.

Michael launched the javelin at her. It sparked with lightning as it soared through the air.

Thunder rumbled above.

From the cave's entrance, the shining form a golden man flew at impossible speed into the path of the lance.

With his golden sword in hand, Apollo sent it careening away.

Around him, the aura of the divine fire flared.

The Golden God had returned to the world.

CHAPTER THIRTY-ONE

RISE GOLDEN APOLLO

Not only was Apollo back in spectacular divine form, he was also empowered. The divine flame had supercharged him. Even Moros couldn't have predicted such a result. Certainly, she expected the flame to restore his godhood, but this level of empowerment was unprecedented.

The serpent of light, that had been wrapped around Moros, unbound itself and struck out at Apollo.

With a swift slash, Apollo cut through the creature's neck. It exploded into particles of light, which drifted away in the wind.

The soldiers of the Gladius Vaticanus looked at Apollo in awe. He was swimming in precious metal come to life. The aura of the divine fire consumed him. Flames of purple, green and red licked and danced around his body.

"I have beaten you once, Apollo. I will beat you again," Michael warned.

"You had an army and a dragon last time. Now, I see you standing alone," Apollo replied, his voice booming.

"On my word, angels in their thousands will descend on this place. Each one more powerful than the gods of old," Michael paused. "However, they are not necessary. I am the earth and the sky. I am the sword of heaven, and I will smite you alone. Such is my duty after you escaped last time."

"I think the last seventeen hundred years have gone to your head," Apollo sneered. He raised his sword. "Besides, I hear the humans are turning away from your kind. You must be getting weaker and weaker."

"Wait, Michael came alone?" Moros thought. That was a very foolish mistake on his part.

Belial was barking orders at his soldiers to advance into the tunnel, but none dared cross paths with the celestial beings who blocked the way.

"Where did you go?" Michael suddenly demanded of Apollo. "I stabbed you; it was done. Then, you vanished out of time, space and all knowledge."

"For all your power, knowledge eludes you," Apollo replied.

"Like the humans I must learn, Apollo. I have never begrudged this fact. Assumptions and the perceived inherent right to rule were the way of the old order, the order we vanquished. Your return now means nothing, you are but the dying gasp of the way things were."

"As your cursed blade could not strike me down then, your words now cannot prevent the return of the gods and the undoing of Heaven."

"How did you live that strike? That blade was designed by our prisoner, the master blacksmith, to be infallible. I saw no lie in his eyes when he admitted the Michael Sword could not be overcome, yet you did it, Apollo. How?"

"You underestimate the gods," Apollo answered simply. "There is more to us than the simple accumulation of power. Our natures were determined by Chaos himself. We are not like you angels."

"Perhaps Hecate will answer what you will not, when she has rotted for long enough in the Citadel of Heaven," Michael stated.

Lightning started striking the ground around them. There was no rain, but a wild wind howled across the empty land. Small pebbles began floating upwards, defying gravity.

There was a feeling of raw power in the air.

The new god Michael, and the old god Apollo, floated for a long moment; just watching each other.

"I must admit I was surprised when Hecate revealed herself. She caused trouble for generations untold, teaching humans her magic. We had the Church hunt her followers down, as we had the Church exterminate all relics of the old ways. It never ended the appearance of her witches across the world. She was crafty and knew how to evade our watching eyes. I knew something major must've happened for her to finally appear in the open after all these years," Michael said.

"Hecate prophesied that my return would be the moment the

tide turns against you," Apollo responded.

"We will let our swords determine the destiny of our kinds. The stroke of my blade will quell the rising tide and settle the angry seas," Michael said as he readied himself.

Like two comets of light colliding, Apollo and Michael flew toward one another at the speed of sound. Their swords collided, and a shockwave rippled out, upturning the soil.

With every clash of their weapons, additional bolts of lightning sparked out and flew into the crowd of soldiers.

Some vehicles were tossed away, others exploded on impact.

The prayer-fueled archangel and the divine flame-boosted god were testing each other's limits.

Their swords collided. They held them together, equal in their struggle of wills.

Moros reacted to the realization that Michael had come alone. She wanted to help Apollo, but knew that wasn't her place in this story. Michael was well beyond her power, and while Apollo was boosted by the divine flame it seemed he could match the angel. It wouldn't last long though. Apollo had to win quickly, and in that regard, she was no more than a hindrance.

However, she could do something about Belial.

The fallen angel was nothing more than a monster. A monster in the service of the Underworld, for whatever purpose Lucifer had in mind.

Moros became invisible and moved into the group of soldiers, searching for the Knight of Hell. She couldn't find Belial among them, even though he'd been there just a moment ago.

Michael sheathed his sword and threw his arms backwards.

The clouds above rumbled.

Three enormous tornados of blue fire erupted from the sky and burst down onto the battlefield. The soldiers of the Gladius Vaticanus were incinerated as the swirling super-heated flames passed across them.

Moros shielded herself with energy and watched as a waterfall of fire fell around her.

She noticed that Teva had quickly begun climbing the rocks to reach Matt, who was gasping and wheezing, unable to move.

"Apollo!" Teva shouted. "Help Matt!"

Apollo flicked his eyes towards the limp figure of Matthew. He pointed a finger at him and the ASIS agent became wrapped in orange light.

The god then tilted his head to the left, right as a heavenly javelin narrowly missed his face and embedded itself in the mountain.

Apollo burst forward with a shockwave.

Teva stumbled towards Matt.

"You alright, mate?"

"Yeah," Matt smiled weakly. "I think all of my broken bones just healed themselves…"

Teva helped him up.

"Nice job with the helicopter."

"Cheers, bro," Matt responded. "What do we do now?"

"Let's get away from the tornados of fire, for a start. Melissa is still inside; she may need our help."

"Melissa," Moros thought. *"Belial has gone for Melissa."*

CHAPTER THIRTY-TWO

REVELATIONS

Melissa was still running back through the maze. After Apollo had healed her, he'd taken off.

"*It must be nice to be able to fly,*" she thought.

She kept rubbing the side of her stomach up and down. The wound was completely gone, but the pain lingered. She'd been literally torn open. It seemed Apollo could heal well enough, but he couldn't remove the trauma her body had felt.

Melissa retraced her steps through the maze.

Her black and blue eyes, and significant cut on her right cheek, were emblematic of the couple of days she'd had. She'd really been put through the ringer on this one. And it wasn't over yet.

As she ran, she grew weary. She wanted to rest, but she could hear the echoes of battle outside.

Melissa came to the base of the giant statue of Prometheus and began her climb back up the stairs. She had to leap to get up each one. It was tiring and dangerous work.

At last, she came to the entryway, half-way up the statue, and exited the temple buried in the mountain.

The dark room of the old weapons cache was now bright. Some of the chattering wisps had escaped through the open door and were now frolicking about the rocky cavernous room.

Their soft light illuminated everything, including someone who was standing there waiting for her to emerge.

Melissa was once again confronted with the snarling face of Belial. She backed herself against the wall as the Knight of Hell stalked forward, licking his lips.

"No magic staff this time, girly," he cruelly laughed.

His human form was melting away again. The red-skinned horned demon with a serpent's tail now stood before her.

Even against impossible odds, she wasn't going down without a fight.

She leapt at Belial with a flying kick, though her foot passed straight through his body.

Suddenly, the room filled with a half-dozen copies of the demon.

He was creating illusions to toy with her.

"Playing with mortals is such fun," he said casually. "I get such a KICK out of it."

He threw one of his goat's feet at Melissa's head.

"No more pain today," Melissa thought, as she nimbly rolled out

of the way.

Melissa drew her gun and fired two shots at Belial. The bullets passed straight through him. Another illusion.

"Focus!" Melissa said to herself. Her irises turned gold. The illusions disappeared, and she could see the real fallen angel.

She fired at him. The bullets clanged off his skin.

"Your little bullets can't hurt me!" Belial hissed.

Melissa then remembered something Apollo had said to her, back in the ruins of the Roman Forum. He'd said her gaze can humble the divine… She again turned her golden eyes on Belial and focused her power.

She fired another bullet, and this time Belial flinched when it hit him.

"What magic is this?" he screamed.

"The magic of the Oracle of Delphi," Melissa grinned. For the first time, Melissa was embracing her destiny.

"Your little bullets are nothing more than stinging bees! They will not hurt me!" Belial raged.

"I bet this one will," a male voice called.

It was Matt! He had his sniper rifle aimed right at the monster's head.

He fired.

The bullet impacted with Belial's skull, blasting it open. He held his hand to the wound and screamed a terrifying scream.

Melissa rushed forward and pressed her gun into his stomach. She fired a series of quick shots at point blank range, causing Belial to double back in pain.

Teva ran up and punched him in the face, then immediately

hit him with a spinning kick, though narrowly avoided a bite from the snapping green tail.

"How are you mortals hurting me?" Belial spat in confused anger.

"The vision of a prophet is a powerful thing," a new voice called. "The truth is a great equalizer, and she sees your truth, angel."

Moros had entered the room. She shot black lightning at Belial, and he fell into a squirming heap.

"I have some questions to ask this creature," the goddess stated. "When we have our answers, we will help Apollo."

Moros grabbed the fallen angel by the throat with black energy radiating from her hands. Belial's skin sizzled in her grip.

"What does Lucifer want?" she asked plainly.

Belial struggled as Moros zapped him with her power. His entire body went rigid, then relaxed.

"Don't make me ask again, monster from Hell. I am the Goddess of Fate, and my domain compels you to answer!"

"Lucifer wants the same thing as Michael," Belial choked.

"What?"

"Eternity as a god-king," Belial wheezed.

"Explain," Moros commanded, her eyes glowing.

"There is an empty space in the world, one left by your leader, Zeus. Both Michael and Lucifer wish to assume the place of Zeus in the cosmos."

Moros released her grip so Belial could breathe a little easier.

"Why?" she demanded.

Melissa couldn't help but notice that Moros looked extremely confused by this revelation.

"As you know, a god who rules other gods has power untold. The very fabric of reality bends to their will. Even the might of the archangels now, with the faith of billions of humans, could not rival Zeus at his peak, with dozens and dozens of gods, each being worshipped by humans, bowing to him."

"So what?" Moros said. "Michael has power beyond measure already."

"He fears losing it!" Belial cried, attempting to wriggle free.

Melissa thought back to the six devices she'd seen in the Vatican archive, the ones used to steal defeated god's power.

"He used that device to absorb Hades' power. Hades was one of the most powerful of us, I thought he could never drop below the level of Hades now," Moros said.

"In the right circumstances, even you could challenge Hades. The gods of old were not that powerful considering the world of today. Back in the Battle of the Underworld, Michael as he was then rivalled Hades!"

"So, it was a poor back-up plan then?" Moros asked.

"Their conquest of the world made a lot of enemies. If the Palestinian religions fail, that back-up will be all the archangels have. There are surviving gods out there. When the reign of Christianity ends, they will hunt Michael and the others like they are animals!" Belial explained.

"Michael is worried Hades' power isn't enough then, he wishes to gain even more..." Moros said.

"Yes, the empty position of Zeus calls to him. All of that power, just waiting for Michael to take it. Neither of us wants that," Belial said, choking as Moros tightened her grip.

"How do you know about this 'power of Zeus'? I have never heard of such a thing. We don't even know what happened to him. Something very bizarre and specific must've occurred for Zeus to leave behind a secret horde of his power that could be consumed by another," Moros said, though it sounded more like she was thinking aloud.

She threw Belial to the ground.

"So, both Michael and Lucifer are aiming to mantle Zeus? In essence, they wish to become him, to assume his old position? Is this right?"

"Yes," Belial spat as he lay on his side.

"Michael sees it as a way to legitimize his power and make it eternal. Why does Lucifer want to do it?"

"Michael and Lucifer see humans very differently. Lucifer is like your kind. He sees the humans as nothing more than tools to be used. He would subjugate them to build the empire of Heaven."

"Empire of Heaven?" Moros laughed. "Lucifer is bound to Hell eternally."

"If he can take that kingly power, he thinks the curse of Persephone will be undone. His power will eclipse any curse," Belial muttered.

"So that is the truth of it. Lucifer seeks a way to be free. This is an unpleasant fate for the world, should Lucifer's rage be felt outside of Hell. The last seventeen hundred years have twisted and distorted him into some kind of monster."

"You don't know what it was like to be trapped by Tartarus.

Hell became a place for the damned. A place of suffering alone. Through that suffering, Lucifer will rise."

Moros contemplated this for a moment.

She spoke slowly, piecing the puzzle together in her mind. "Two brothers, both with the same goal. I'm guessing you have uncovered a ritual... a ritual that requires certain steps and objects to fulfill..."

"Yes. Difficult things to obtain are needed. This information is all new, found in dark and terrible writings."

"Tell me what you know so far of this ritual, Belial," Moros demanded of the squirming demon.

"You need a direct link to Zeus' power to assume his position. That we know for sure, though much is still unclear. Some legacy of his that still lingers in the mortal world... We need his blood and we need an artefact that he is known for. Michael and Lucifer's goals align for now, as they both agree that this power is a good insurance policy for one of them to have."

"Where would you find a link to Zeus' power now? He is nothing but a myth to modern humans, and even back in the ancient world he was never really one to lay down curses," Moros wondered.

Belial rose to his feet, "That is the question, isn't it? For now, we collect what we can in relation to the old world, in the hope that something will manifest itself."

"Thank you for the information, Belial," Moros said. "I would kill you, but fate tells me you still have a part to play in all of this. So, enjoy your time in Hell."

Belial laughed, "If you do not kill me, I will kill you."

"I don't think your master believes that to be the case," Moros grinned, looking at the ground around Belial.

Black smoke was rising.

"What, no, Lucifer!" Belial yelled.

The black smoke, the same that had allowed the convoy to cross from Rome, swallowed the Knight of Hell entirely.

The cavern was still.

Lucifer had pulled his soldier back into Hell.

The Archangel Michael still needed to be removed from the equation.

"Go to Apollo. Use your vision," Moros nodded at Mel.

CHAPTER THIRTY-THREE

THE DOOM OF A STAR

Michael paused and Apollo knew why. For the briefest moment, they'd both felt Lucifer's power in the mortal world.

The fighting recommenced with greater ferocity. The mystery of Lucifer could be solved after there was a victor. Huge craters appeared in the ground as Apollo and Michael soared through the air. Both had sheathed their swords and had resorted to punching each other as hard as they could. Michael's white armour was cracking with each impact.

"Explain this new power of yours!" he commanded. "Have you assumed your father's position?"

Apollo noted the concern in the archangel's voice.

The Golden God smiled as he flew backwards. He summoned his silver bow and began launching arrows, wreathed in divine fire, at Michael.

Of course he had not assumed Zeus' position, and he was curious as to why Michael would ask such a bizarre question.

Michael's armour finally gave way on impact with the arrows. The archangel threw his helmet to the ground and looked directly at Apollo with his shining eyes.

Apollo noticed Melissa, Teva and Matt come running from the tunnel, each of them with an assortment of new weapons. Matt had a large cylindrical rocket launcher on his shoulder.

Melissa called up to Apollo, yelling, "You know that weird papier-mâché archangel in the prayer room that we ran past? Turns out it had a bunch of guns hidden inside it!"

Apollo frowned. Though powerful, mortal weapons were useless against Michael. Unless... unless Melissa could tap into her vision and use her powers on the archangel! Such was the power of the Oracle of Delphi to humble the divine in her gaze!

Teva loaded a rocket into the back of Matt's launcher.

Melissa looked at Michael with her golden eyes.

Matt fired. The rocket whizzed towards Michael. He ignored it, clearly expecting it to do nothing. The rocket exploded, knocking Michael backward. He looked utterly bewildered.

Apollo laughed. His oracle would be useful as a minor distraction, but he needed Moros' help to actually win.

"How are you doing this?" Teva asked Melissa down below. "It's like when you look at these monsters with your golden eyes they get weakened somehow. I doubt an angel should be affected by an exploding missile…"

"I don't know," she said, firing her own rocket at Michael. This time, he swerved to avoid it, only to be crash tackled midair by Apollo. They both fell into a crater with a boom.

Michael was now frustrated, his teeth bared and his eyes full of rage. It had been a long time since the archangel had been challenged, and it seemed that he didn't enjoy it.

Apollo pointed his sword at the archangel, attempting to plunge it into Michael's stomach, but the angel rolled out of the way, blocking the strike.

"Why did you want my sword?" Apollo demanded.

With a twist and thrust, Michael pushed Apollo's sword away.

"I don't want your sword! I want you; you fool! You are a son of Zeus, you carry his ichor in your veins!"

Apollo shot a fireball at Michael, but the archangel absorbed it.

"What does Zeus have to do with any of this? He was gone long before you marched on Olympus!" Apollo spat, flaring up his aura of flame.

"There is a slumbering threat in this world. Even now its influence is spreading into the roots of the Earth. I need the power of Zeus to fight it, or everything could be undone!"

"Zeus is gone," Apollo frowned. "As is his power."

"No, Zeus disappeared at the height of his strength. He left a hole in the universe! One that can be filled by those who are willing!"

The two divine beings continued to parry each other's attacks.

"You would mantle Zeus? Become him? How? How do you even know this?"

Michael answered through gritted teeth, "If I find a direct link to his power, I can use it to assume his position as it was an age ago. I have heard whispers in my dreams of something coming from the darkness... something I must face. You will not stand in my way, Apollo."

"This is a fairytale!" Apollo shouted.

"No, the humans found the path recently. Dark writings revealed that Zeus was pulled from this universe, leaving behind all that pooled power. I know what is needed to claim it!"

The two continued fighting, as the ground disintegrated around them.

Apollo could feel the fire of Prometheus dimming within him. Soon, he would be an ant under Michael's shoe. He had to act now, and fortunately, through the corner of his eyes, he saw that Moros had reappeared.

"I cannot kill you, archangel. You may have raw strength on your side, but you are a fool to underestimate the power of the gods! When next we meet, the tables will have turned," Apollo stated.

Michael barely paid him any attention as he worked to shield himself from the annoying barrage of gunfire coming from the humans below. It wasn't hurting Michael, but it was proving to be an annoyance.

Apollo concentrated his power and an orb of fire swirled around the archangel. By the time the Michael comprehended what was happening, he was completely encased in the roaring sun Apollo had generated.

"Moros!" Apollo called.

Moros soared through the air towards him. She saw the newly born star glowing brighter with Michael inside.

"The old Sun God," she smiled.

The Goddess of Doom raised her hands, and black energy wrapped itself around the sun.

"Show us the doom of a star!" Apollo yelled.

Moros' energy was increasing the density of the star rapidly. It started to collapse in on itself, with Michael still inside. Within moments, the star was gone, and a spinning singularity hung in the air.

Melissa's hair whipped towards it. Apollo saw her being swept off her feet. Both Teva and Matt collapsed to the ground, clinging to whatever they could as the black hole started sucking rocks and stones towards it.

Even the destroyed cars started shifting.

Apollo didn't seem to be able to resist the pull of the star. He knew it was only Moros that could. She floated over to it, and pressed her palm against the void.

It disappeared in a flash.

Everything went quiet. The tornados disappeared and the storm clouds faded.

They'd won.

They'd created a small star, collapsed it and imprisoned Michael inside.

"How exactly does a black hole stop a god?" Teva asked.

"Black holes, much like gods, don't follow the rules of your world. They exist in a higher plane. For now, that will be a useful prison for Michael. It will take some time for him to break free of it."

"Where did it go?" Melissa asked.

"I sent it far off into space," Moros answered promptly.

"So, you can just make black holes?" Melissa asked Apollo.

"No, I can make a temporary sun," Apollo said, looking weary. "Black holes are the ultimate representation of doom. Not just for life, but for all things in the universe. Moros has a unique control over them."

"But I saw one of the Knights of Hell generate a black hole in the Vatican vault," Melissa said, exasperated at the vague rules of the gods.

"A unique power, I am sure," Moros said. "A small one like that will burn itself out quickly. To capture a being such as Michael, a very powerful one had to be generated. I'm guessing it could only be achieved with a Sun God and Doom God together. We will see how long it holds him."

Apollo scanned the sky, looking for signs of more angels descending. He felt the flame of Prometheus finally die inside him. At least his divinity was restored.

"Can you zap us out of here, before more of them come?" Matt asked.

"As of this moment I dare not use my power," Apollo said. "Michael paid for his hubris by coming alone. He probably had a point to prove. Now that the divine flame has dimmed, I do not wish to challenge another angel, should they notice that Michael's power is now absent."

"What do we do now?" Melissa asked, wiping the sweat from her brow.

"We know what they want," Moros said. "Zeus left a hole in the universe and they want to fill it. To do that, they basically need to become him. And to do that, they need a direct connection to his power, plus some other pieces."

"What will you do, Moros?" Apollo asked.

"This development troubles me, so I will uncover all I can. We are behind in this game. I will return to Rome; I expect there will be a job opening at the Vatican library very soon. Now that I know what we are looking for, I can begin searching for something Zeus left behind."

"What do we do?" Melissa asked.

"We need to beat them," Apollo said. "Find what they are looking for first."

"Aren't you the God of Knowledge? Shouldn't you know what we need to find?" Matt interjected.

"It doesn't quite work like that, knowledge is a kind of vague godly domain, as usually knowledge is gained through learning. Admittedly, when I need a snapshot of the world, I have access to it, but specifics often elude me."

Teva, also looking a little worse for wear, walked in to join the conversation.

He turned to Melissa, "What do we report about this mission?"

Just then, Melissa's mobile phone rang. She extracted it from her pocket.

"Hello," Melissa said.

"Hello, Agent Pythia, this is Brett Sayer, of the Australian Supernatural Taskforce," the voice on the other end said. "As I understand it, you are currently working on a case in Australia with Liam Sager?"

"That is correct," Melissa said. "Although I was pulled off it recently and sent to Rome."

"That is why I am calling," Brett Sayer said. "Perhaps you could do me a favour?"

CHAPTER THIRTY-FOUR

THE WAY FORWARD

- SEPTEMBER 28 -
AFGHANISTAN

After a brief conversation with the boss of the secretive government agency, Melissa turned back to the group. "I have been directed to the Greek island of Corfu before I resume my mission in Australia."

Teva and Matt both looked at her with questions burning in their eyes.

"Greece is the place for me to go as well. As such I will join you," Apollo said.

Melissa nodded, then added, "Give your sword to Matt and Teva. They will need it for this mission to not have been a total disaster, and you will hardly be inconspicuous carrying that around."

Apollo paused, then reluctantly agreed. He handed the heavy golden sword to Matthew.

Matt studied the sword and asked, "Can someone fill us in on the greater mission here? I don't really understand what Zeus has to do with it..."

Apollo looked to Moros, then addressed the group. "A couple hundred years before the Battle of the Underworld, my father disappeared. He didn't fade, as gods can choose to do, nor did he die. We searched for a time, but then stopped... it was odd. Like, a cloud drifted over the minds of the Olympians, causing them not to care."

"As we have just learned," Moros started, "apparently both the angels and forces of Hell have discovered that whatever happened to Zeus caused all the divine power flowing up to him just to pool in the universe around his empty position. Unbeknownst to any of us, all these long years there has been a pocket of unimaginable power sitting there for the taking."

"Michael said 'dark writings' led them to this discovery, whatever that means..." Apollo muttered.

"They need a direct link to Zeus' power, it seems," Moros stated.

"And me, they need the blood of Zeus. Or ichor, if you want to be more accurate," Apollo added.

"This mystery will take some time to solve. My guess is the spell required to assume the position of a missing god will be complex. I will begin searching for answers at once. You two will come back to Rome with me," Moros said, turning to Matt and Teva. "With the Gladius Vaticanus gone, only Belial and Michael know the location of this temple. Hopefully, we can keep it hidden from world governments until its secrets have been unearthed. I will bury the door behind rock, as it was for a long time."

"Take the sword to Rome and wrap up our mission for ASIO as if we were never in Afghanistan. I will work out how to inform ASIO and ASIS about the truth of all this when we have to, though I am now thinking I should funnel this all through the AST first..." Melissa trailed off, lost in thought. This was a complex issue.

"We do have good cover," Teva shrugged. "If we are very lucky, the open fighting between the Gladius Vaticanus and the Soncins in central Rome could cover our tracks completely."

Moros turned and strode into the tunnel.

"Be quick, and move the rocks by hand. We do not know how long we have before Heaven realizes Michael is no longer here," Apollo called to her.

"How do we get back to Rome?" Matt finally asked.

Apollo walked over to one of the flipped-over troop carriers, and with a single finger, lifted it up and put it back on its wheels.

"We will find an airport, and get a plane," Melissa said.

"This is going to be fun..." Matt rolled his eyes.

"We all know what to do, so when Moros returns, we should get going," Melissa suggested.

"You can't possibly think it is going to be *that* easy?" Matt asked Melissa incredulously.

"Who is going to clean up this mess?" Teva asked, preventing an argument breaking out between Matt and Melissa.

"Luckily, we are in Afghanistan, a country where destroyed

military vehicles aren't out of place," Melissa said.

"Right, so the five of us are going to smuggle ourselves out of Afghanistan into Rome. Moros will go to the Vatican. Teva and I will render our mission complete as you and Apollo head off to Greece, is that right?" Matt confirmed.

Melissa nodded.

When Moros returned from sealing the entrance to the temple of Prometheus, they all piled into the troop carrier.

It roared to life, and just like that, they zoomed off.

Getting out of Afghanistan was going to be a hell of mission on its own, without considering the true scope of the journey ahead.

Now, this small group of Australian operatives and their divine companions were headed onwards to Greece, Rome, and most importantly, to find the connection to Zeus the great powers of the world were seeking.

Where they would find it, none knew.

But they did have weapons on their side. Sitting in the front seats were Golden Apollo, the son of the God-King Zeus and his prophet, Melissa Pythia, the reincarnated Oracle of Delphi.

Sitting in the back, Moros mused over her domains of doom and fate.

It seemed destiny was rapidly approaching.

The Earth was turning, heading for a new age, and she knew, for better or worse, Melissa Pythia had a significant role to play in the events to come.

Epilogue

THE GREATER MISSION

Melissa felt the warm sand between her toes. It was a beautiful day on the Greek island of Corfu. For the first time in ages, after the struggle of covertly smuggling themselves out of Afghanistan and back into Italy, she had a chance to relax.

She privately hoped she'd come across some more of those Janus Crystals, they were exceedingly useful. The knowledge that using them in the Foro Romano could open a portal to anywhere in the world was also a nice secret she intended on keeping and using when it was most advantageous.

People had been giving her funny looks since arriving on Corfu, mostly due to the prominent black eyes and glaring cut on her face, but she didn't care.

Melissa had deliberately avoided work since arriving in Greece. She'd swum in the ocean this morning and felt the salt-water cleanse her skin. A well-earned break was needed, and she was only here to do some snooping around before flying home. It wasn't anything like the job in Rome.

All in all, the mission to recover the golden sword had gone well. For once, Matt would be dealing with the bulk of the paperwork back in Australia while she relaxed.

She didn't feel guilty as the rest had been hard won.

Melissa had been hit in the face, fought a battle against fallen angels, been slashed by a magically summoned knife, and had her liver torn out by a steam-punk eagle. It was a lot to go through in a couple of days

Her travelling companion, the God Apollo, a divine being hiding in the form of a human, had been pleasant. He'd been excited to return to Greece, and was hoping to find some evidence that his sister, Artemis, had survived the angels' attempted genocide of the old gods.

He was careful to remain hidden, and suppressed his divine power entirely. He was just a tall, blonde-haired blue-eyed man. One that got a lot of attention from young women as they passed by. He seemed to return their affections equally, proving that some of the myths about the Greek gods were very true.

Just up from the beach was an old blue restaurant with white window frames. It had a large patio covered with plastic tables and chairs. Melissa had wanted somewhere to go on the island that was a bit more secluded, but as she watched the white yachts bob up and down on the waves just off shore, she realised that this area wasn't secluded at all. It was just avoided by the locals because of the amount of young people that came through on youth adventure trips. She was only 28, and realistically could be one of them.

Melissa yawned, embracing the Greek sun. At last, she felt the urge to investigate.

"Better do some work," she said grumpily, getting up. She was starting to feel a bit burnt, and had quickly developed a tan.

One of the reasons Melissa had picked this beach, other than the assumption of privacy, was that this was one of the locations reportedly visited by a young Australian man in July.

It was a place that needed investigating.

Melissa got up and shook off her towel. From her hand bag, she drew a scrunched up long green summer dress and pulled it over herself. She tried to flatten the wrinkles with her palm, to no success.

Her enthusiasm to ask questions of the restaurant owners was low, but it had to be done.

Earlier in the year, in August, there had been a brutal massacre in the city of Cairns, in north-eastern Australia. Due to the strange circumstances, and abundant clear evidence that something paranormal had taken place, the Australian Supernatural Taskforce had been called in to investigate.

Melissa was in their deployable pool of operatives. It was actually the case that she'd been working on before her arrival in Rome. The sudden reappearance of the golden sword had been a more pressing issue, and she was withdrawn.

However, as her phone call with Brett Sayer had indicated, the main suspect in the massacre had been in Europe. More specifically, strange stories about him had emerged from this exact spot in Corfu.

Melissa was here to chase up what leads she could.

She walked into the restaurant and was welcomed by an old man missing several teeth. He absent-mindedly stroked his silver beard.

"Excuse me, sir?" Melissa said, pulling the owner aside. "I was just curious, a couple of months ago you had a man in a tour group stay here? Apparently, he had blood all over his leg?"

The man gave Melissa a suspicious look.

"Are you police?" he asked immediately.

"No," Melissa answered truthfully.

"I will tell you what I told all the different police. I don't know him. We have hundreds of young people come here, get drunk, go into town, we don't know about the death."

"What death?" Melissa asked, her ears perking up.

"Oh, you know the one," the owner said, visibly annoyed. "Achilles Aetos. He was found naked in a field just down the road from here."

Melissa just shook her head.

"Well, the police heard about the man with the blood, who slept here the same night Achilles died. But the autopsy showed that he died of natural causes, no injuries."

"Who was this Achilles?" Melissa asked.

"Local business man. Very wealthy. Had a small private zoo in his estate, as well as a large collection of ancient treasures.

Dealt with some shady people…" The owner twisted his head to make sure no one else was listening, then whispered. "Including the Soncin crime family."

The Soncin crime family, the same ones who'd recovered the sword, only dealt in high end artefacts. This Achilles Aetos must've been a serious collector.

"What did he get from the Soncins?" Melissa asked.

The owner's annoyance was dissipating the more he engaged in this juicy local gossip.

"Well, his zoo got a new addition, a wolf cub. The last of a very rare breed. Rumour said he almost went broke buying it. The same night he died; the wolf cub was also butchered."

"Did the police have any leads?"

The silver-bearded man leaned in close to Melissa and said, "The Wolf of the Vatican was on Corfu that night."

"The Vatican is involved? Who is this Wolf of the Vatican?"

The owner rushed over behind the bar and promptly came back, holding a picture. It was of the head of a thin man with horrific scars stretching across his face. His eyes looked dangerous.

"He is an assassin, owned by the Vatican. He was on Corfu that day! He came to this bar."

Melissa frowned. "How do you know he is a Vatican assassin?"

The old man just winked and said, "I have my sources."

This was most certainly of interest to Melissa. There was no way this didn't relate to her case in Australia. Now, it seemed that the Soncin crime family and the Vatican were involved in some way too.

"I don't think it had anything to do with the tourist. Many

stray dogs about in the area. He probably just got a bite on the leg. Achilles Aetos was killed by the Wolf of the Vatican! I know it. Why else would he be here?"

"One more question," Melissa asked, "Back to the Australian tourist, where did he go that night?"

The old man answered, "A local nightclub, called the Chariot of the Sun God. Its only just down the road, you can't miss it."

Just then, the tall figure of Apollo walked up. He'd been sitting by himself eating lunch while Melissa lounged about on the beach.

"Who is talking about sun gods?" he asked.

Melissa instinctively rubbed the back of her hand. The strange rune that Hecate had burned into her skin was now almost invisible, even in the presence of the now fully divine Apollo. Melissa was privately glad that it hadn't been a permanent gift.

"I must go," the owner said, unnerved by the interruption from this stranger. He shuffled off to serve some customers waiting at the bar. Melissa watched as he pulled a bottle of what looked like homemade alcohol from behind the counter.

"So, a man died near here. A man who'd just bought a rare wolf. According to the intel file we received, a young Australian man showed up here that night, with one leg covered in blood. He was also rambling about monsters in the moonlight. Then, a month later, a monster shows up in northern Australia..."

Melissa paused as she put all the pieces together.

"I think it was here on Corfu that *he* was bitten by a werewolf. I think whoever killed Achilles Aetos and his puppy have now followed *him* to Australia. I assume if this Wolf of the Vatican was in Vatican City when we were, we would've encountered him."

"A werewolf? One of those creatures descended from Lycaon?" Apollo asked.

"Well, like a half-man, half-dog kind of thing."

Apollo nodded. "We had them in Greece a long time ago. They sprang out from Arcadia like a plague."

"I think we should head to this nightclub down the road. I'd like to ask some questions as to what happened there."

· · · · ·

MELISSA AND APOLLO arrived at the nightclub strip of a nearby town after a short drive along a bumpy road. She imagined that under the bright lights of the neon signs, the area looked beautiful. Under the midday sun, the area looked grimy and unkempt. The road was littered with plastic cups and smashed bottles. Fast food wrappers drifted along in the breeze. There were definite vomit stains on the pavement.

Their destination however, the Chariot of the Sun God, looked spectacular. It was clearly modelled in the image of ancient Greek buildings. Its entry was marked with four enormous white pillars that held up a balcony on the second level.

The front door was locked.

Apollo looked at the building curiously.

"This was built in my honour," he said. "This bar is like a modern temple to me. It is good to see the people remember the old gods."

"People know the name Apollo, I'm not sure it is in your honour. People know of the Greek gods, but they aren't worshipped anymore," Melissa explained, before knocking loudly on the door.

They waited for a few minutes. Apollo continued marveling at the exterior design of the bar.

The door opened, and a man poked his head through the gap.

"Who is it?" he asked. He twisted his gaze from Melissa to Apollo.

The man looked odd. He was older, with slicked-back grey hair and two distinctly different coloured eyes. One was blue and the other yellow.

His mouth dropped open when he saw Apollo.

Apollo turned to look at the man and paused.

"Brother?" he said.

"Apollo, you are alive? How can this be?"

The barman swung the door open and rushed out to embrace Apollo.

The two looked like old friends who hadn't seen each other in a long time.

"Come inside, quickly!" the barman said excitedly.

He ushered the pair in a shut the door quickly.

The room was expansive, with a circular bar right in the middle. It was empty, save for the three of them.

"You two know each other, then?" Melissa asked.

"Dear prophet," Apollo started, turning to Melissa, "this is my half-brother, the God of Speed and Cunning. Melissa, meet Hermes."

Melissa looked at the barman sceptically.

She turned to Apollo, "Another god? Really?"

"Humans these days," Hermes laughed. "No respect."

"I know, I have seen it for myself. But, I have also seen them display great courage and sacrifice in my short time here, too." He looked at Melissa proudly.

"Where have you been all these years?" Hermes asked Apollo eagerly.

"I was sent out of time to heal from a grievous wound inflicted by the Archangel Michael."

"Ah, and I see the Oracle of Delphi reincarnated to greet your return. I thought that had happened, I felt it in the air a few decades ago. The smallest spark of Apollo re-entering the world," Hermes glanced towards Melissa.

"She pulled me from the fires of Hell," Apollo said. "And what of you, brother?"

"Word never spread that you'd fallen in battle. But you were gone. I thought perhaps you'd fought and died alone, or chosen to fade. I wasn't on Olympus when it fell, but I went into hiding, as the other survivors did. I watched as mighty Rome crumbled and the world entered a dark age," Hermes answered.

"So, you have been in hiding this whole time, posing as a human business man?" Apollo asked, almost sounding disappointed in his brother.

"It has been seventeen hundred years, Apollo, I have been many things. The war against the angels has been fought on many fronts. I now see why Hecate gave me that task."

"What task?" Apollo asked.

"Hundreds of years ago, Hecate gave me the Helm of Darkness. At the time, I wandered the world in the guise of a poet named Virgil. She asked me, when I was next in Hell, to seek a magically hidden cave that held a wound in time. She told me to leave the Helm by the wound. As I had occasion to go into Hell, I did as she asked, but never knew why."

"It was that Helm that allowed me to escape," Apollo bowed. "I thank you, brother."

Melissa interjected, wanting to get the conversation back on track, "So, on the night an Australian man came here, there was a Greek god, a Vatican assassin, and potentially the Soncin crime family active?"

Hermes looked at her curiously, "What information do you seek?"

"A man in Australia, who we believe is afflicted by the werewolf curse, is being hunted by another afflicted by the same curse... it seems," Melissa said lamely.

"Oh yes, makes sense. Achilles Aetos purchased what I believe is the last remaining canine descendant of Lycaon. Isn't it amazing how that line survived for so long? It carried Zeus' original curse. Achilles Aetos was bitten and received the closest to a pure strain of Lycaon's curse as you can get."

"You helped him, didn't you?" Apollo asked.

"Of course," Hermes replied.

"And let me guess, you didn't inform him that he'd become a ferocious monster on the full moon?"

"Of course not," Hermes said, equally as brightly. "I was curious. Naturally, the Vatican had their own pet monster hunting the wolf pups. Werewolves are uniquely attuned to finding their own kind. They found Achilles, and they found the pup, and put them both out of their misery."

"But not before this Achilles passed on the curse..." Melissa deduced.

"Well, he was only a werewolf for a few hours, and most don't survive an encounter with one. I assume the Vatican were onto him right away. Only a very lucky man would've survived if they met Achilles out in the fields."

Hermes paused, as if something had suddenly occurred to him.

"Someone was very lucky that night..." he said slowly. "A young man came to the bar. He was lost with life. I blessed him with a little bit of luck for his night out."

Hermes clapped his hands to the sides of his head.

"Oh! And then that man encountered Achilles in the field, and he survived because of my blessing! Let me guess? You have a new werewolf in Australia, a very pure one?"

"Yes," Melissa said, "it is very wolfish. Big and black with orange eyes. I've seen it."

"Isn't that fun?" Hermes smiled. "Zeus' power lives on in the world. It was Zeus who created the werewolf curse you know?"

"Wait..." Melissa gasped, "if the werewolf curse was created by Zeus. Would it be a direct link to his power?"

Apollo's eyes lit up.

"Hermes," Apollo said excitedly, "are you saying there is a semi-pure version of the Lycaon curse left in this world?"

"Yes. The Vatican werewolf is too distant to really be

considered Zeus' curse proper, it has been passed down too many times and mutated too much. Barely any of the original power remains. But this new one would be quite close to the source."

"He is somewhere in Australia right now!" Melissa exclaimed. "If the Vatican work that out, and pass it onto the angels, then won't those archangels come for him? They need him to assume Zeus' position!"

"The Vatican mustn't have realised yet. Not many people know that the original werewolf curse came from Zeus. We must find the boy before the Vatican, or the Knights of Hell do. What is his name?"

"Joshua Dare," Melissa said. "The key to unlocking Zeus' lost power is in a man named Joshua Dare."

THE OLD WORLD SAGA SO FAR...

BOOK ONE: IN THE SHADOW OF MONSTROUS THINGS

A European holiday takes a sinister turn when Joshua Dare encounters a werewolf. Feeling its bite, Josh escapes, but soon realises that he is now inflicted with an ancient curse. Having to learn how to manage his full moon affliction, Josh is thrust into a world of secret organisations, government operatives and mysterious strangers hunting him. Josh has entered a larger story of gods and monsters, and this is just the beginning...

NOVELLA ONE: THE WENDIGO INCIDENT

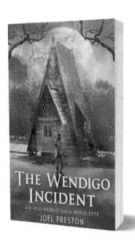

Something has angered a supernatural terror in the forests of Minnesota, and the US Government needs help dealing with it. Fortunately, rumours have reached them that the Australians have captured a werewolf. Sometimes to kill a monster, you need a monster of your own. Now, Joshua Dare is off to the USA to assist in bringing down one of Native American folklore's greatest monsters - the wendigo. Other sinister things seem to be happening in that forest too....

BOOK THREE: IN THE SHADOW OF THE OLD WORLD

Fearing an information leak and seeking to bolster their alliance with The Old World, the Australian Government has moved Josh Dare to Japan. He is soon tracked down by malevolent supernatural forces who want to exploit his curse. He is the best link to the empty position of Zeus, the vanished god-king. Now, a small team of Australian and US operatives need to work with the gods of old to fulfill an ancient ritual and stop that power falling into the wrong hands.

NOVELLA TWO: EARTH'S MIGHTIEST WARRIOR

Long ago lived a warrior renowned as the greatest to ever live. Sigurd of the Volsung line has had his story told through the ages, though not all of it. It was thought his tale ended with his death, but then came the war of gods and angels. Now, Sigurd survives as a rat and a champion in Lucifer's new Hell. The tale of Earth's mightiest warrior is only half told. The new legend of Sigurd takes him across the fiery planes of the Underworld, with beings far beyond Norse myth, on his greatest adventure yet.

BOOK FOUR: FALL SILVER ARTEMIS

Danni Quinn has completed her training and is on her first mission. The goal: finding an artefact of the lost God Zeus. Danni and her boss, the reincarnated Oracle of Delphi, Melissa Pythia, set out to find the Goddess Artemis. Travelling across the scorched plains of Hell they meet the long dead hero, Sigurd the Volsung, who agrees to aide them on their quest. Danni's team heads down a path towards sunken cities and alien horrors. With the help of her former flame, Joshua Dare, and the rest of the AST, Danni will risk everything to complete her mission…

NOVELLA THREE: STRANGE LIGHTS IN A DARK WORLD

Randall Dare thought he was solving a complex equation. Little did he know that the act of writing some numbers on blackboard would catapult him across dimensions to a strange realm known as the Dark World.

Now, as he works to find a way home, he must face off against the monstrous octopus-headed aliens, cosmic gods and the mysterious creatures that call the bizarre planet home. And time is ticking, as Randall is carrying a warning that needs to reach the team back on Earth. Something dreadful has woken up, and his new allies can help to stop it...

ACKNOWLEDGEMENTS

Hello reader and welcome the section where I once again get to thank all of the wonderful people who have helped to bring this novel to life!

Firstly, I have to start with everyone who gave me feedback on the second edition of Rise Golden Apollo. Writing novels continues to be a journey of learning, and in some cases (like this one), that learning needs to be retroactively applied. I'm going to thank all the contributors to this book's creation, including the usual suspects.

Talha Kun, the artist who drew all of the illustrations you found in the visual guide did a wonderful job. I asked for simple sketches to bring the characters from myth to life and Talha went above and beyond. Make sure you check out Talha's online profiles if you would look to order work to be drawn for yourself!

I also need to thank Simon Abbott and The Wicked Goblin in Cairns for so enthusiastically stocking my books and getting the word out. It can be tough for self-published authors so people like you are worth your weight in gold.

My ever-helpful editors, Elizabeth King and Alexandra Marshall did a wonderful job again. One day I will learn to write with fewer mistakes...

Countless others assisted with proof-reads, significant among them Teva and Michael. You guys are legends and my gratitude can't be expressed enough.

Warren of Warrendesign once again did a stellar job on the cover. I'm sure you'll be seeing more of his work soon...

Lastly, thanks to everyone who went on this epic adventure through mythology. The Old World Saga is drawing closer to an end now, and I promise it will be epic!

Cheers, Joel!